Call Me Cupid

FIONA HARPER
NINA HARRINGTON
HEIDI RICE

MILLS & BOON

First Published in Great Britain 2018
by Mills & Boon, an imprint of HarperCollins*Publishers*
1 London Bridge Street, London, SE1 9GF

CALL ME CUPID © 2018 Harlequin Books S. A.

The Guy To Be Seen With © Fiona Harper 2013
The First Crush Is the Deepest © Nina Harrington 2013
Too Close for Comfort © Heidi Rice 2013

ISBN: 978-0-263-26617-7

05-0218

MIX
Paper from
responsible sources
FSC® C007454

This book is produced from independently certified FSC™ paper to ensure responsible forest management.

For more information visit: www.harpercollins.co.uk/green

Printed and bound in Spain
by CPI, Barcelona

THE GUY TO BE SEEN WITH

FIONA HARPER

For Nikki—we made a great team!
And for Andy, my own triffid-loving Indiana Jones.

CHAPTER ONE

DANIEL ALWAYS GRUMBLED that his mobile phone rang at the most inconvenient of moments, and it didn't disappoint him now. Just as he was lifting a delicate Venus flytrap out of its pot, his hands full of roots and compost, his trouser pocket buzzed. Since he refused to assign fancy ringtones to everyone in his contact list the double ring of an old-fashioned phone told him precisely nothing about the caller's identity.

Once upon a time, he'd have ignored it—his hands being full of an uprooted *Dionaea muscipula* and all—but these days he could never quite push the thought from his mind that it might be his younger sister, telling him she was ill again. Or worse, a stranger telling him she'd collapsed and was in Accident and Emergency, and casually requesting he pick her kids up from pre-school.

Reluctantly, he shook the earth off his right hand, cupped the clump of roots and foliage in his left and fumbled in the thigh pocket of his cargo trousers for his phone. He balanced the handset on his shoulder and squeezed his cheek onto it to keep it in place as he attempted to brush more of the compost that caked his fingers off on the back of his trousers.

'Yup.'

The phone started to slide and he quickly grabbed for it with his still-dirty hand.

'Daniel Bradford?' a deep yet annoyingly upbeat male voice asked.

'Yup,' he repeated, more focused on trying to replace the prize specimen in its pot with the use of only one hand. It wasn't going well. He wasn't planning on dividing this one for propagation yet but it was threatening to do just that.

'Well, Daniel, this is Doug Harley and you're live on Radio EROS, London's most romantic radio station!'

Daniel stood up straight, then twisted round, scanning the tropical nursery at London's famous Kew Gardens, expecting to see a group of snickering underlings hiding behind a palm in an adjacent room of the sprawling greenhouse. This had to be a prank, right? And, if there was one advantage of working in a place where ninety per cent of the buildings were made of glass, it was that there was nowhere to hide. He'd find them and make their lives hell for this.

But all he could see was a lone horticultural student, wheeling a trolley of seedlings past the door, plugged into his music and oblivious to the world. The rest of the multi-roomed greenhouse was unusually quiet.

'Daniel?' the silky smooth voice crooned in his ear.

He pulled the phone away from his head and stared at the display, seriously considering just hanging up. He didn't have time for this.

'What do you want?' he barked at the man as he put the phone back up to his ear. 'I'm busy.'

There was an equally smooth—and equally irritating— chuckle on the other end of the line. 'Not too busy for this, Daniel. I promise you.'

He clenched his jaw. The over-familiar manner in which the DJ kept inserting his name into every sentence was getting on his nerves.

'Convince me,' he said.

The chuckle again. As if the man was the insider to some joke that Daniel didn't know about. His eyes narrowed.

'I'm sure you know what day it is today, Daniel?'

Confusion wrinkled his brow further. It was Tuesday. So what?

Oh.

He swore inside his head, remembering the collection of red and pink envelopes that had been sitting on his desk when he'd arrived for work this morning. He'd shaken his head, pushed them to one side unopened and had done his best to forget about them. Not just any Tuesday, but one slap-bang in the middle of February.

'Or what year it is…' the voice added.

Daniel let out a huff. He'd been right all along. A half-baked radio contest run by some sappy station he'd never heard of. He was pretty sure he didn't want whatever prize this idiot was offering. Seriously, couldn't they come up with a better question than what year it was? Even his four-year-old nephew could answer that one. He was just about to tell Mr Silky Smooth that when he was interrupted.

'Of course, leap years have their perks,' the man said, and a rumble of perfectly pitched deep laughter followed. 'We know it's a couple of weeks until the twenty-ninth, but we've got a Valentine's surprise for you, Daniel. There's a young lady who'd like to ask you something.'

Daniel looked down at the plant in his hand. Even in its current uprooted state, a fly was attracted to the sweet nectar oozing from the glands in its trap. It darted around, weaving in and out of the leaves, looking for somewhere to land.

'Dan?' This voice was soft and feminine. One he recognised instantly.

He froze. His brain told him what was coming, but he refused to believe it.

'Georgia?'

That hadn't come out right. He'd sounded grumpy and defensive, not pleasantly surprised, at hearing his girlfriend's voice. He tried again. 'What are you doing?'

Nope. That hadn't been any better.

He heard her swallow in a great gulp of air. 'Daniel…I know you've had a tough time recently, and I've been happy to be there for you…but things are looking up now and I really believe we could be good together.'

Daniel's mouth moved but no words—not even any sounds—came out.

He wanted to close his eyes, as if doing so could block out the sound of her voice, but he was transfixed by the sight of the fly settling on the fleshy pad of one of the plant's open traps. He shook his head, warning the insect off.

Fly away. Escape while you still can.

'So, what I'm doing, Daniel…' She paused, gave a little nervous laugh. 'What I'm saying is…is that I'd like you to marry me.'

In one swift, smooth motion the flytrap closed over the fly. Not so much a snapping as an elegant but relentless squeezing. Daniel could hear the creature's frantic buzzing, see it struggling in the trap as the teeth-like cilia closed tighter and tighter over its head.

Don't. Struggling only makes it worse.

A terrible silence settled around him. All sound disappeared. Even the visitors to the botanical gardens, who could often still be heard from the private nurseries, had hushed. It seemed the whole of London was holding its breath, waiting for his answer.

'Is this a joke, George?' he croaked, a horrible pleading tone in his voice.

This wasn't the Georgia he knew. The nice, uncomplicated, undemanding woman he'd been seeing for almost a year. His Georgia knew he didn't have the emotional space for a proper relationship right now, let alone a marriage. His Georgia understood that and accepted that. So who was this, borrowing her voice and asking him out-of-the-blue questions—on the *radio*, for heaven's sake? Not even person to person, face to face.

Who proposed in public, anyway? It should be done privately and quietly. Preferably to someone other than him.

He squeezed his teeth together to stop himself from demanding an explanation, right here, right now. He was suddenly furious with her for springing this on him, for changing the rules and moving the goalposts of their relationship while he hadn't been looking. This wasn't what they were about and she knew that.

At least, he'd *thought* she'd known that.

Silky Smooth chuckled again. 'Well, Georgia, you seem to have rendered the poor man speechless! What do you say, Daniel? Are you going to put this gorgeous girl out of her misery or what?'

That doused his billowing temper quick smart.

What *was* he going to say?

He could imagine Georgia sitting there at the radio station, a fixed smile on her face and fear in her eyes, bravely trying to pretend it was all right, when really her heart was pounding and her eyes filling.

It wasn't that Georgia wasn't a lovely woman. She was determined and intelligent and sensible. Any man would be lucky to have her. He should *want* to say yes.

But he didn't.

He really didn't.

He wasn't ever going to go down that road again, no matter how lovely the woman in question.

There was a crackle on the line and noise started filtering through again—the hiss of the automatic misting system in the nursery next door, the squeak of a door farther down the corridor, a plane flying low overhead on its way to Heathrow. And Daniel was suddenly very aware that more than a hundred thousand pairs of ears might be listening to this conversation, of just how public and complete his girlfriend's humiliation would be if he gave her the wrong answer.

Unfortunately, where he and Georgia were concerned, the wrong answer was the right answer.

He didn't love her. He wasn't sure he ever would, and she deserved better than that. Gently, he balanced his phone on his shoulder again and carefully put the now-satisfied Venus flytrap plant back down in its pot.

He should have known their relationship wouldn't stay in wonderful, comfortable stasis they'd created. In this world, things moved on, grew, or they decayed.

He'd first met Georgia when Kelly had been halfway through her chemo. She'd been easy to be around. She'd helped him forget that his little sister might not see another Christmas, to forget that his rat of a brother-in-law had run off with his personal trainer and left his shell-shocked wife to deal with a cancer diagnosis—and two under-fives—all on her own. Without Georgia, he'd have hunted Tim down and fed him, bit by bit, to the largest and ugliest *Nepenthes* in his collection.

Daniel shook his head. The Venus flytap was completely closed now; he couldn't even see the squirming fly inside.

He should have known that, eventually, Georgia would get ideas. The awful situation they were in now was as much his fault as it was hers. She wasn't really asking anything horrendous of him, was she? But she was asking for something he wasn't capable of. Not any more. And he'd been very clear about that.

'I'm sorry…' he said, more for not paying attention to what had been growing right under his nose than for what he was about to say. 'We weren't heading for marriage, I thought you knew that…That's what made our thing so perfect…'

Our thing… Subtle, Daniel.

He could hear her breathing on the other end of the line, and he wished he could see her face to face, explain, without listening ears hanging on every syllable.

'It's okay,' she said, and he could hear the artificial brightness in her tone, could almost see the sheen in her eyes. He felt as if he'd been kicked in the chest by a horse.

He shook his head. No, it wasn't okay. He was hurting her horribly, but that didn't mean he could say yes and condemn them to a lie that would ultimately make them both unhappy. He had to do what was best for Georgia, for both of them. He had to set her free for someone who could give her what she wanted.

'I can't, Georgia. You know why I can't say yes.'

There was a moment of ghastly silence and then the DJ began talking again, laughing nervously, trying to smooth things over. Daniel didn't hear any of his words. He didn't even notice when music started to play in his ear.

He felt like a worm.

No, worse than that, because worms were useful, at least, and they didn't harm anything.

He picked up the unearthed flytrap, plastic pot and all, and flung it against the wall of the carnivorous plants nursery. It hit the glass with a resounding bang that echoed over half the gardens. The cracked pot fell away, and the frail plant followed, landing with an almost soundless thump on the floor. Compost that had smeared against the glass began to crumble away and rain down on top of it.

That was when the disadvantages of working in a greenhouse made themselves apparent. Half a dozen curious pairs of eyes stared at him from various parts of the nursery. They must have thought the Head of Tropical Plants had lost his mind.

Or worse. They might have been listening to the radio.

Daniel closed his eyes, ran his hand through his hair, then swore loudly when he realised his fingers had still been covered in peat and perlite.

He opened his lids to find no one had moved. He glared at each and every pair of staring eyes in turn. 'What?' he yelled and, as one mass, the underlings scurried away back into their holes.

All he wanted was for this awful, consumer-fuelled excuse of a day to be over, so he could get back to normal, live his life without anyone listening to what he was saying or spying on what he was doing.

God, he hated Valentine's Day.

Daniel froze as he was crouched down, his hand on the papery flute of a *Sarracenia*. Sunlight streamed through the glass roof, warming his back, and around him visitors milled, casually inspecting the exotic plants of the Princess of Wales Conservatory, one of Kew's modern glasshouses. All in all, it seemed like a normal March day.

Except that, as he worked, the fine hairs on his arms and the back of his neck lifted.

He stood up and glanced around. He was in a vast greenhouse with ten climate-controlled zones, so it would be stupid not to expect people to see him, but it was more than that. It felt as if someone was *watching* him.

Georgia's flopped Valentine's proposal had produced a flurry of unexpected media attention. More than once in the last month he'd found himself staring at the business end of a paparazzo's lens as he was trying to work. But that hadn't been the only unwanted side-effect of publicly humiliating his ex-girlfriend. Now there seemed to be eyes on him everywhere, watching him, judging him.

Until his sister's illness had forced him to come back to England, he'd loved his job working from Kew's base in Madagascar. He'd loved being a seed hunter—searching out rare plants to collect their treasure, tracking down nearly extinct species. But this bizarre media interest made him feel much more like the prey than a hunter, and he didn't like that one bit. No, not a role reversal he was comfortable with.

He finished checking the fine white and green patterned

flutes of the pitcher plant and pushed open the door of the small Temperate Carnivorous Plants area and entered the much larger Wet Tropics zone. Here the heat-and-moisture-loving tropical varieties grew, including a large draping display of green and warm purple hanging pitchers. He worked methodically through the twisting tendrils, looking for dried out pitchers that needed to be dead-headed, checking for disease and parasites.

That was when he heard them.

'Do *you* think he looks like Harrison Ford?' a feminine voice said in a not-so-quiet whisper. 'I'm not sure. He's more like that one from the spy series on BBC.'

Daniel froze and imagined a horrible, jungle-related death for the reporter who'd jokingly compared him to the film legend. While the journalist had obviously been quite pleased with his 'Indiana Jones with secateurs' crack, Daniel hadn't heard the end of it from his mates.

'Not sure,' a second voice said thoughtfully, and just as loudly. 'But he's definitely got that brooding, intelligent-but-dangerous thing going on. Have you seen those arm muscles…?'

There was a muffled snort from the first speaker. '*Arms?* I was too busy checking out his nice, tight little—'

Right. That was it.

He was fed up of being treated like a piece of meat, something to be stalked and discussed and ogled. Perhaps he should just jump up on one of the earthy beds and sit there with the plants, because as far as he could see he'd stopped being one of the staff and had morphed into a prime attraction.

When would this end? It was bad enough that the London press had picked up on his and Georgia's story and run with it like a greyhound on amphetamines. They'd been the subject of countless column inches, magazine features and chat show discussions—not that either of them had fuelled it in any way by agreeing to speak or be interviewed. It seemed the whole of the city had been split down the middle, divided into two camps, one supporting him and one supporting her.

But the whole situation had a nasty little side effect, too.

He'd now become The One That Got Away. An irresistible label to the female population of London, it seemed, because en masse they'd decided it was an open season. Every day for the first couple of weeks after the proposal they'd appeared in ones and twos like this, coming to the gardens specifically to track him down. But it had been quiet for almost a week, and he'd finally hoped it was all petering out. No such luck.

Not that a bit—or even a lot—of female interest bothered him in the slightest. He was as open to it as the next guy. But this was different. They didn't know when to stop. They acted as if they hadn't heard the proposal on the radio, as if they didn't know he wasn't in the market for love, let alone marriage. The whole thing was just stupid. And very irritating.

He was dragged back into the present by a heartfelt sigh behind him. They'd moved closer.

'Shall I go and ask him for his autograph,' one said.

That was it. Hunter or not, Daniel was out of there. He turned and walked briskly down the path, down the steps to the aquatic exhibit half hidden under a man-made 'hill' in the centre of the conservatory, and ducked through a short tunnel to come out on the other side of the zone. He then climbed the path that led him to the upper levels on top of the hill, then doubled back through the ferns and down some more stairs.

He knew this labyrinthine glasshouse like the back of his hand and it wasn't more than a minute before he was crouching down and peering at the two women from a vantage point inside the orchid display. He could have left and gone back to the propagation greenhouses, he supposed, but he liked the idea of turning the tables, of watching *them* hunt fruitlessly for him, before disappearing for good. It would restore his sense of balance, of control.

Now he could see them, his eyes popped. They were over

seventy, for goodness' sake! All sensible shoes and nylon trousers. He could see them looking around, having a minor disagreement about which way they should go to pick up his trail.

He almost chuckled to himself. Almost.

At least, he might have done if those hairs on the back of his neck hadn't prickled again.

Seriously? Another one?

He was tempted to turn round and let loose, but he knew he had a bit of a temper, and having a supposedly 'dangerous' edge didn't mean he was allowed to attack paying visitors then use them for lovely, nutritious compost for his favourite plants. There were laws against that kind of thing. Unfortunately.

He was just going to have to bite his tongue and leave. However, if this Valentine's fuelled media circus didn't end soon, he'd be stuck in an office or a greenhouse, not able to go about his job as he pleased, and he'd hate that. It had been hard enough to leave the field and take this post in the first place; he'd only done it because Kelly had needed him to come home and help look after her and the boys.

'Why, if it isn't Indiana himself!' a husky female voice drawled. 'Although I was led to believe you'd swapped the whip for a pair of secateurs these days.'

Daniel swivelled around, still crouching. The first thing he saw was a pair of hot-pink kitten heels with polka dot bows on the front. Definitely not a pensioner, this one. His gaze was inevitably drawn up to a pair of slender ankles and then to shapely calves. For a moment, he forgot all thoughts of running.

Then there was the black pencil skirt. Tight round a pair of generous hips, hugging the thighs... He swallowed.

'So where are they?' she asked.

That was when he realised he was still half squatting. He

looked up, past the form-fitting pink blouse to the face on top of it. Red lips. That was what he saw first. Vibrant red lips.

Who'd cut the water supply off from his throat? He swallowed again. 'What?'

Stand up. You're kneeling at her feet, looking like a drooling Neanderthal.

Thankfully, his brain cooperated this time, sending the message to his legs to straighten, and he stood. Finally, he was looking down at her instead of up. Only, it didn't help much. From down below the view of her impressive cleavage hadn't been so obvious. Now his brain was too busy working his eyeballs to do the talking thing.

'The secateurs,' she said with a slight twitch of one expertly plucked brow. 'Are they in your pocket?'

Daniel nodded dumbly and pulled them out. She was blonde. Marilyn Monroe blonde. With shoulder length waves that curled around her face.

'Shame,' the lips said. 'And there was I hoping you were just pleased to see me.'

His mouth hung open a little. Brain still struggling. Much to his disgust, he managed a faint grunt.

'Sorry…couldn't resist,' she said, and offered her slim hand. 'Don't you just love Mae West?'

Daniel stared at the hand for a second or so, at the long red fingernails that matched her lips, then a movement at chest level distracted him. A staff pass on a lanyard was around her neck but, due to the impressive cleavage it was hanging just below, it was twirling gently in some unseen breeze, the photo and name obscured.

She frowned slightly. 'Not a Mae fan, then.'

He nodded, but he wasn't sure if he was agreeing or disagreeing.

'Chloe Michaels,' she said, grabbing his hand and shaking it firmly. 'Orchid specialist and new girl at Kew.'

'Daniel Bradford,' he said, shaking back vigorously. Maybe

a little too vigorously. He let go, but then he didn't seem to know what to do with his hand. He stuffed it back in his pocket.

'I know,' she said, and a wry smile curved those red lips. 'You've read the papers…'

She gave a little shrug. 'Well, a girl would have to be dead to not have seen something of your recent press coverage. However, I knew who you were before that. I've got one of your books at home.'

Air emptied from his lungs and he felt his torso relax. Plants and horticulture. Finally, he'd come across a woman who could talk sense. 'Nice to meet you,' he said. And he genuinely meant it.

She just nodded and the smile grew brighter. 'The guys in the tropical nursery said I'd find you here, and I just thought I'd come and introduce myself,' she said, turning to leave.

Daniel had just started to feel somewhere close to normal again, but her exit gave him another view he hadn't quite been ready for… The way that pencil skirt tightened round her backside was positively sinful.

She looked over her shoulder before she exited the temperate orchid display through the opposite door. Daniel snapped his gaze upwards. She hadn't caught him checking her out, had she? That was a schoolboy error.

'By the way,' she said, nodding in his direction, 'incoming at eleven o'clock.'

He hadn't the faintest idea what she meant, but it wasn't until she'd disappeared into the next zone that he even started to try and work it out.

A bang on the glass above him made him jump. He pivoted round and looked up to find his two pursuers in the fern enclosure at the top of the stairs, faces pressed up against the glass, grinning like mad.

Oh, heck.

One of them spotted the door further along the wall. Her eyes lit up and she started waving a pen and a notepad at him.

Daniel did what any sensible man in his position would have done.

He ran.

CHAPTER TWO

A SKIRT THIS tight and heels this high did not help with an elegant exit, Chloe thought as she kept her back straight and cemented her gaze on the door. She'd thought she'd need the extra confidence her favourite pair of shoes gave her this morning but, when they were teamed with the skirt, every step was barely more than a hobble, and it took a torturously long time until she was out of the orchid display area and amidst the agaves and cacti of the adjoining section.

She paused for a heartbeat as the glass door swung shut behind her, then blinked a few times and carried on walking.

He hadn't recognised her.

She'd been prepared to go in smiling, laugh that embarrassing incident in their past off and put it down to not being able to hold her liquor. In short, she'd planned to be every bit as sophisticated as her wardrobe suggested she could be.

But she hadn't needed to.

She pressed a palm against her sternum. Her heart was fluttering like a hummingbird.

That was good, wasn't it? That he hadn't connected Chloe Michaels the horticultural student with Chloe Michaels, new Head Orchid Keeper. They could just start afresh, behave like mature adults.

Inwardly, Chloe winced as she continued walking along the metal-grilled flooring, past an array of spiky plants from across the globe.

Okay, last time they'd met, Daniel Bradford hadn't had any problems behaving maturely and appropriately. Any *mis*behaving had been purely down to her. Her cheeks flushed at the memory, even all these years later.

She was being stupid. He must have taught loads of courses over the years, met hundreds of awestruck students. Why would he remember one frizzy-haired mouse who'd hidden her ample curves in men's T-shirts and baggy trousers? He wouldn't. It made sense he hadn't even remembered her name.

Or her face.

That, too, made sense. She looked very different now.

This Cinderella hadn't needed a fairy godmother to give her a makeover; she'd done it herself the summer she'd left horticultural college. No pumpkins, no fairy dust. Just the horrified look on Prince Charming's face had been enough to shove her in the right direction. The Mouse was long gone; long live the new Chloe Michaels. And she'd been doing a very good job of reigning supreme for almost a decade.

Only…

A little part of her—a previously undiscovered masochistic part of her—had obviously been hoping he *would* remember, because now disappointment was sucking her insides flat like a deflated balloon. She sighed. She never had had any sense where the gorgeous Daniel Bradford had been concerned. But show her a human being with a double X chromosome who did.

It was something to do with those long legs, that lean physique, those pale green, almost glacial eyes. Add a hint of rawness to the package, the sense that he'd just barely made it back from the last expedition into a dark and remote jungle, and it tended to do strange things to a girl's head.

Maybe that could explain the way she'd acted back there, the things she'd said…

Mae West? What had she been thinking?

While she knew the 'new and improved' Chloe had easy

self-assurance, there was confidence and there was sheer recklessness. She'd intended to be calm and professional. She certainly hadn't intended to tease him... *flirt* with him.

However, a little voice in her head had been pushing her, feeding her lines, especially when his eyeballs had all but popped out of his head when he'd been trying to read her spinning name tag. There had been something so satisfying about seeing him that close to drooling that she just hadn't been able to stop herself.

It wouldn't happen again, though. Couldn't.

But Chloe's lips curved as she pushed the main door of the conservatory open and walked out into the spring sunshine. She wiped the smile off her face—literally—with a manicured hand and shook her head.

It didn't matter just how much saliva had pooled in the bottom of Daniel Bradford's mouth when he'd looked at her, because she was never, ever going down that road again. And it didn't matter just how ferocious the monster crush she'd had on him ten years ago had been, because there was one thing she was certain of...

She'd shoot herself before she got within kissing distance of him ever again.

Daniel hung from a spot halfway up the climbing wall at his local sports centre and peered down at the top of his friend's helmet. 'Hurry up, Al,' he called out. 'You're out of shape. Must have spent too much time lolling on a sun lounger while you were on holiday.'

Alan eventually caught up. He wasn't looking as chirpy as normal.

'What's up with you?' he said, still panting. 'You were up this wall like the hounds of hell were on your tail, and you only climb like that when trouble's brewing—usually woman trouble.'

Daniel shrugged and pulled a face. 'Of a sort.'

Alan grinned at him hopefully.

'Georgia came by the gardens today.'

Alan stopped grinning and said a word Daniel thought most appropriate. 'What did she want? She didn't rush tearfully into your arms and beg for a second chance, did she?'

Daniel shook his head. 'No, thank goodness.'

He realised how insensitive that sounded, but Alan understood. He was a guy.

Daniel shifted his hand grip. 'It's over,' he said. 'Maybe it never should have started.'

Alan shrugged. 'I thought you had a good thing going there. All the perks and none of the drama.'

That was what Daniel had thought too, when he'd thought about it at all. That also sounded insensitive, he realised. But he and Georgia had been friends, her work at Kew's millennium seed bank throwing them together occasionally, and somewhere along the line friendship had slipped into something more. At the time he'd hardly noticed it happening.

Normally, he was much more focused about his love life. He'd spot a woman that appealed to him, pick her out from the pack, and then he'd go about pursuing her, changing her mind… Because, if there was one contrary thing about him, it was that he liked the ones that were hard work, took a little chasing. It made the whole thing so much more fun.

But Kelly had been ill, vomiting half the day, and Daniel—apart from being scared out of his wits for his sister—had been thrown in the deep end of caring for two small boys. He supposed all his 'chasing' energy had been tied up elsewhere, and maybe that was why he'd slid into his easy relationship with Georgia.

He'd thought she'd wanted that too. Something with no complications, no dramas. Definitely no wedding rings.

He should have known. If a relationship lasted more than six months, that diamond encrusted time bomb was always there, ticking away in the background. And Daniel knew just how deep that glittery shrapnel could embed itself.

He started climbing again. 'That's not all, though,' he said, glancing at Alan, who was now keeping pace. 'She told me the radio station is holding her to the contract she signed with them.'

Alan looked shocked. 'What? How can they do that? There's no wedding to cover. You said *no*.'

Daniel nodded. 'That's what I said. But, for some unknown reason, she feels the need to reinvent herself, and they're going to follow her around all year while she does it. The *Year of Georgia,* they're calling it.' As if he didn't feel enough of a heel already.

Alan's gift for expletives made itself known again.

But it wasn't really the extra media coverage that warranted such a well-timed word. It was a horrible feeling that, by saying no to Georgia, he'd somehow broken her and now she thought she needed to fix herself.

He scrubbed a hand over his face. This was the very reason he chose women carefully, avoided commitment. He wasn't looking for love and marriage. It was like his pitcher plants— a sticky, sweet-scented trap. Thankfully, unlike a mindless fly, Daniel had a well-developed urge for self-preservation and he usually prided himself on not falling for the lie and getting stuck.

Until Georgia, of course. A mistake he wouldn't make again.

Damn her for seeming so self-sufficient and sensible when underneath she'd been horribly vulnerable. Damn himself for being too caught up in other things to see the truth.

'This thing's never going to end, is it?' he asked Alan as he started off towards the top of the wall with renewed vigour.

Alan shook his head, more in disbelief than in judgement. 'Look on the bright side,' he said as he scrambled to keep up. 'Most men I know would give their right arm to be where you are right now—women flinging themselves at you on a daily basis. It's like shooting fish in a barrel...'

Daniel frowned as he swung a foot into place and pushed himself up over an overhang. He didn't want to shoot fish in a barrel. That was the point!

He didn't want wide-eyed adoration from a woman; she was likely to start wanting more than he was prepared to give. No, he liked to meet a woman on equal terms, play the game, have fun while it lasted and move on.

'Most men you know are bloody idiots, then,' he shouted back at Alan. 'There's interested and then there's desperate and clingy. I know which I prefer.' And then he shot away from his friend and headed for the top of the wall.

As he climbed the burning in his fingertips, in his shoulders and arms, soothed him. He forgot all about radio stations and marriage proposals and bloody Valentine's Day. Instead, he concentrated on the physical sensations of foot meeting wall, fingers grasping hand hold, and after a while a different set of images—a much more appealing set of images—flitted through his brain.

A flash of a hot-pink shoe. The curve of that tight black skirt as it had gone in and out. The glint of the sun on pale blonde hair as it slanted through the conservatory roof. The wry and sexy curve of a pair of crimson lips as she teased him.

That staff pass, twirling gently underneath...

Daniel realised he'd run out of wall. He blinked and looked down. Alan was still struggling with that last overhang.

Hardly surprising his mind had turned to Chloe Michaels. He'd been thinking about that day in the Princess of Wales Conservatory a lot recently. Unfortunately, memories were all he had at the moment, because he'd hardly seen her at all lately. She was like the disappearing woman, always leaving a place just as he arrived.

'Mate,' Alan said, panting. 'If you don't sort out this

woman trouble, you're going to finish me off. You've got to let the whole Georgia thing go.'

Daniel nodded. Yes. Georgia. That was the only woman trouble he had at the moment. The only woman trouble he *should* have at the moment.

But that pair of crimson lips was laughing at him, breathing gently in his ear…

He shook his head. *Bad idea, Daniel. Trap that thought and put it on hold.*

He'd just jumped from the frying pan of one relationship— very publicly—and he wasn't planning on landing in another romantic fire right now. He needed to sit back and take stock, give himself some breathing room. He shouldn't be thinking of starting something new, no matter how prettily those little flames danced and invited him in.

He craned his neck to look at the ceiling. It was far too close to his head. He could do with at least another fifty feet of wall to conquer, something to help him shed this restless energy.

'Women are the last thing on my mind at the moment,' he told Alan. 'It's this wall that's the problem. I've climbed it so many times it's easy.'

Alan just grunted.

With one final look at the ceiling, Daniel started to rappel back down towards the floor. His friend followed suit, matching his pace. 'I need some real rocks to climb. A proper mountain,' Daniel added. 'That's all.'

Twenty minutes later, round the corner in The Railway pub near Kew Gardens station, Alan plopped a full pint glass in front of Daniel at the bar. 'You miss it, don't you?' his friend said. 'Being out in the field?'

Daniel stared at the tiny bubbles swirling and popping on the surface of his beer. His jaw jutted forwards. 'I do,' he replied. Not just the rocks, but the rain on his skin and the wind in his face. The feeling that he was totally free.

'I'm grateful to you for letting me know when this job opened up,' he said. 'But it's just maternity cover, remember? I'll stick it out until your old boss is back. Kelly will be feeling better by then.'

He'd suggested his sister move into his house in Chiswick when she'd split up with her husband; he'd been happy to have someone watching over it when he'd been overseas. Before Madagascar, he'd worked at different bases all over South East Asia, collecting seeds, helping various universities and botanical gardens set up their own seed banks, searching for species that had yet to be named and catalogued.

But then the news had come about Kelly's diagnosis, and he'd come home and moved in himself. There was no way Kelly could have managed through her surgery and chemotherapy without him.

The Head of Tropical Plants job had come up shortly afterwards and he'd jumped at it. The perfect solution while he stayed in London and helped his sister with her two rowdy boys, and while he enjoyed the chance to work closely with his favourite plants, to see if he couldn't produce and name a new variation or two, it had just confirmed to him that Alan was right. This wasn't what he wanted long-term.

'It's been over a year now,' Alan said, 'and Kelly's looking pretty fine to me.'

While Alan's face had been suspiciously blank, there had been a glint of something in his eyes that Daniel didn't like. Instantly, he was on his feet. Much as he liked his college friend, he knew what Alan was like with women. 'Don't you even dare think about my sister that way,' he said. 'She's off-limits.'

Alan held his hands up, palms outwards. 'Whoa there, mate.'

Daniel sat down again. 'Sorry,' he mumbled. Maybe Alan was right about him being on edge about something. He knew he had a bit of a short fuse, but even the *hint* of a spark was setting him off these days. 'She's been through a lot, Al. The last thing she needs right now is more complications.'

'Gee, thanks,' Alan said, his tone full of mock offence. 'That's a very nice way to refer to your oldest mate—a *complication*.'

Daniel's mouth twitched, despite himself. 'You know what I mean.'

Alan just grinned at him. 'Are you sure there's not woman trouble somewhere on the horizon? Other than your over-enthusiastic ex, that is?'

He shook his head. 'No, nothing like that.'

However, an image flashed across his brain: a saucy smile playing on bright red lips, the little wiggle in her hips as she'd walked away...

Alan downed a fair amount of his pint and put his glass back down on the bar. 'In that case, I'd say you really need to get back out to the wilds of God-knows-where again soon.'

Daniel didn't answer. He knew what he wanted, what he ached for, but as *fine* as Kelly looked these days she still tired very easily, and with two small boys to run around after that happened on a fairly regular basis. He reckoned he was here for another six months at the very least.

'I will,' he replied. 'When I can. Besides...I'm trying to write a second book.'

The one he'd been planning for years and finally had time to concentrate on.

His friend just snorted. 'Leave the book for when you're old and grey. In the meantime, you should do something more than rock climbing to blow off steam.' He took another sip of his beer. 'How about deer stalking? One of my father's old friends has invited us on a weekend at his Scottish castle. I can cadge you an invite.'

Daniel shook his head. Holed up in a draughty old castle with some big city businessmen for the weekend? He'd rather let the deer go free and shoot himself. 'Not my kind of thing,' he said firmly.

'Rubbish,' Alan replied. 'We're hunters, you and I. Oh, not in the traditional sense—but you're always after that rare bit of green stuff no one else can locate. It's buried deep in our genetic code, the desire to track and conquer…'

Daniel didn't add that the tendency to become long-winded after only half a pint was also hardwired into Alan's DNA. The best thing to do when his friend got like this was to nod and sip his beer in silence, which was exactly what he did.

Alan made a large gesture with his free hand. 'Men like us, we need the thrill of the chase!'

Daniel gave him a sideways look. 'And when exactly do you hunt?'

Alan blinked. 'I fish,' he said, quite seriously. 'But what I mean is that sitting in that nursery, with all those captive specimens neatly laid out in rows, must be driving you crazy.'

Maybe it was. Because how else could he explain falling into a comfortable relationship with Georgia, of not ending it when he should have? When had he ever been the one to take the path of least resistance? All this tame London living must be lulling him into a coma.

'Don't you worry about me,' he told Alan as he drained the last of his beer. 'I might not be up for tramping through damp heather after a bit of venison, but I'll find something to keep me from going stir crazy. Anyway, there's more than one way of hunting—the plants I work with have taught me that much.'

'Bloody triffids,' Alan said, waving his hand at the barmaid to order another beer. Alan wasn't a fan. He preferred trees. Palms, mostly.

But Daniel could have told him that the majority of insectivorous plants had no moving parts at all. Perhaps, instead of taking his frustration at the currently slow pace of his life out on innocent climbing walls, he should follow their example: be patient, keep still and see what life brought his way.

And since, at the moment, life had brought him a nice cold beer, that was what he intended to concentrate on. He took another gulp and let the cool liquid run down the back of his throat.

'Holy Moly,' Alan suddenly said, swivelling his head towards the door. He slapped Daniel on the side of his arm to get his attention, and Daniel's nice cold beer sloshed down his front. It seemed that what life gave with one hand it took with the other.

He swatted at the wet patch on his shirt, then looked past Alan to see what all the fuss was about.

Holy Moly was about right.

Chloe Michaels, the disappearing woman, had reappeared in time for after-work drinks with one of the other women from work—Emma, who was passionate about bamboo and eccentric as they came.

Surprisingly, Chloe doing casual work clothes was every bit as mouth-drying as Chloe Michaels doing smart ones. Those skinny black jeans worked on curves like that—boy, they really did. The ankle-high lace-up boots should have made him think of functional things, like mud and wheelbarrows, but the criss-cross laces brought corsets to mind instead. And then there was the softly clinging grey longsleeved T-shirt and the leather jacket over the top...

Leather. In his present state of mind that was a very dangerous word.

An itch started, right deep inside him. He suddenly knew that he didn't want to sit back and be patient, see what opportunities life brought his way. He'd spent too long running from the chaos in his life at the moment, letting circumstances chase him. Looking at Chloe Michaels as she glanced round the pub for a seat, her skin fresh, her lips glossy and pink, he knew what he wanted to do.

Alan was right. It was hard-wired into his Y chromosome. He wanted to hunt.

Chloe's heart had stuttered when she'd walked in the door of The Railway. Damn. She should have known it was a stupid idea to go somewhere so close to the gardens. Because there, not more than fifteen feet away, was Daniel Bradford—or Drop-Dead Daniel, as some of the social media sites were now calling him—hunched over a beer. And he was looking every bit as gorgeous as his new nickname suggested.

Nope, she told herself. *You're finished with that crush.* It'd breathed its last breath ten years ago, and she wasn't planning on resurrecting it. Still, there wasn't any harm in hedging her bets and just keeping out of his way to make sure. She tugged at Emma's sleeve, about to suggest they try the wine bar farther down the smart little parade of shops and cafés, but Daniel chose that moment to turn round.

Their gazes locked, and the heat filling his eyes short-circuited her vocal cords.

It also made her very angry.

His timing really sucked, didn't it? Because if he'd looked at her like that a decade ago she wouldn't be in this mess right now. She might have been in a whole different kind of mess, but at least she wouldn't have been humiliated beyond belief.

'Hi, Daniel!' Now Emma was waving and making her way over to him. Great.

Chloe's plan had been going so well. She'd been effortlessly avoiding Mr *Drop Dead*, but maybe she should have guessed it had all been too easy, that she would have to put her resolve to the test at some point. So she tipped her chin up, smiled and followed Emma towards the bar.

It was at that point she realised Daniel was with someone—a good-looking blond—so she transferred her gaze to him, offered him her smile instead. The grin he returned said he wasn't ungrateful for it.

A dark thundercloud passed across Daniel's expression and settled there. The skin on the backs of Chloe's knees started to tingle and the smile on her face set. She didn't let it drop, though. No need to panic. A quick chat with the two men and she and Emma would be on their way.

She nodded at him. 'Hey there, Indiana.'

A flash of lightning left that thundercloud and zapped her right between the eyebrows.

She left Emma to gush at Daniel while she turned her attention back to the blond. 'Who's your friend?' she asked, slightly disappointed that there was not even a hint of a tickle at the backs of her knees as she met his appreciative gaze, even though this man was every bit as good-looking as his friend.

'You two know each other?' the blond asked incredulously. 'How come you've never introduced us before?' He held out his hand. 'Alan Harrison,' he said, enfolding Chloe's hand in his own, before turning back to Daniel. 'And you call yourself a mate.'

'You've only just got back from Greece,' Daniel muttered. 'She started while you were away.'

Chloe attempted to release her hand, but it seemed Alan wasn't quite ready to let go of it yet. She smiled coolly. 'I'm new at the botanical gardens.'

Alan's eyes widened. 'You're another plant nerd, like us? I'd never have guessed.'

She flinched inwardly at his words, but her smile grew ever brighter on the surface. 'Guilty as charged.' Really guilty. So she'd got a good haircut, learned how to apply liquid eyeliner… Deep inside she was still as much of a plant nerd as she'd ever been.

Alan rested an elbow on the bar and casually looked her up

and down. 'You really don't look like one,' he said, a slightly wolfish glimmer creeping into his eyes.

Chloe kept her smile fixed. 'Haven't you heard?' She nodded in Daniel's direction. 'Thanks to your pal there, *plant nerd* is the new *sexy*.'

'Oh, it really is,' Emma said in a breathy rush, looking at Daniel.

Chloe pressed her lips together to stop herself from laughing. Daniel's expression had darkened further, but there was a hint of panic at the backs of his eyes, one she recognised from the day she'd met him hiding from his silver-haired fan club.

But then Daniel looked back at her, and that glint of something changed and warmed. Suddenly, she was the one panicking inside.

She didn't want him to look at her like that, as if he'd like to…

She wasn't going to finish that thought. It was far too X-rated. And far too dangerous.

'What can we get you two ladies to drink?' Alan asked.

Chloe tried to speak, tried to tell him that it was okay, that she and Emma were just going to find a quiet table in the corner and chat about bamboo, but nothing came out. Not quickly enough, anyway.

'Gin and tonic, please,' Emma said loudly.

Chloe didn't have much of a choice now. It would look really rude if she refused. Still, Emma had to be away in half an hour. How bad could it be? She was going to have to work alongside Daniel occasionally. Maybe this would be good practice.

But she made the mistake of catching his eye as she cleared her throat and said, 'White wine would be lovely.' The tingling was back behind her knees, threatening to send rogue messages to her muscles stop keeping her upright and just… *melt*.

Thankfully, a group of people sitting at a table near them

got up to leave. Alan stopped leaning on the bar and motioned in its direction. 'Shall we?' He walked over to the table, pulling out a chair for Emma first. Chloe decided she liked him a lot better for that.

She decided it was safer to sit on the same side of the rectangular table as Emma. Alan quickly bagged the seat opposite, which left Daniel no choice but to subject himself to Emma's adoring gaze.

Chloe chuckled to herself while simultaneously breathing a sigh of relief. Emma was doing a very nice job of deflecting the attention from her. She could definitely handle a quick drink with these two men if her colleague kept this up.

In fact, Emma kept Daniel so completely monopolised with her barrage of questions about a new subspecies of bamboo he'd encountered in his previous job that Chloe was free to sit back, sip her wine and listen to a long story Alan was telling about his trip to Corfu.

Every so often she'd glance across at Daniel. He seemed quite happy to answer Emma's queries, but when the other woman smiled and fiddled with her hair his expression remained neutral. When Emma leaned forward across the table, he leaned back. Chloe's amusement at Daniel's expense waned.

She knew what that was like. Knew *just* what it was like. To want him so badly that you threw everything you had into getting him, letting your mouth run away with you, letting your body language go into overdrive. Emma seemed oblivious, though. She just kept ploughing on.

There was no doubt that she was attractive for her age, but as she talked Chloe just itched to suggest a girls' night in so she could apply serum and a pair of straighteners to that hair. She took a sip of her wine. There were products on the market these days to combat that amount of frizz. If anyone should know, it was Chloe...

Her insides chilled.

There but for the grace of God...

She had not so much a flashback as a flash forward—to who she might have been, had she not subjected herself to that post-graduation makeover.

Stop, she wanted to tell Emma. *Don't do it. He'll push you away, make you feel small and insignificant, not good enough for him.*

She and Emma had chatted enough for her to know that the older woman was unhappily single. Chloe didn't want her to go home that evening after her failed play for Daniel, look in the mirror and decide that if life handed out report cards, the overwhelming verdict would be *could do better.*

Should do better. Must do better.

Chloe knew how much that smarted.

She placed a hand on Emma's arm, grasping at something she'd told her earlier. 'Didn't you say you needed to be out of here at seven-thirty?' she said. 'It's almost that now.'

Well, seventeen minutes past, but who was counting?

Emma paused her interrogation and looked at her watch. 'Oh, cripes! Yes, I almost completely forgot! And I booked this adult education course months ago—the waiting list was huge.' She dragged her eyes from Daniel and sighed. 'I'll have to hear all about Mount Kinabalu another time,' she said, a hint of trailing hopefulness in her voice.

Chloe stood up. 'Come on,' she told Emma, glancing through the vast window that looked over the empty platform. 'The next train is due in a couple of minutes. I'll wait with you.'

'You can't go yet,' Alan said, leaning past her to place a couple of full glasses on the table. 'I got you another wine.' Chloe hadn't even realised he'd left to go to the bar.

Emma glanced between Chloe and Alan and a little smile curved her lips. Chloe started to shake her head. No, she wasn't interested in Alan, and she didn't want Emma's attempt at 'subtle' matchmaking to make him think otherwise.

Unfortunately, despite her love of bamboo, it turned out that Emma wasn't very good with sticks—because she'd obviously got the wrong end of this one.

'No, you stay,' her colleague said, grinning at Alan. 'There's no need for you to miss out because of me.'

'Uh—' Chloe didn't get any further with that sentence, because Emma had scooped up her bag and her coat and was heading for the exit.

Alan pressed a full glass of wine into Chloe's hand before calling after the disappearing Emma. '*Another* evening class?' he shouted. 'What is it this time?' then he took another sip of his drink.

Emma stopped and turned in the middle of the room. Chloe could only half see her it was so crowded. 'Pole dancing,' she called back cheerily, and suddenly the whole pub was very quiet. Apart from the sound of Alan softly choking on his beer, of course.

CHAPTER THREE

CHLOE LOOKED AT an equally flabbergasted Daniel and they both burst out laughing. Whether it was at Emma's parting shot or Alan's beer-fuelled snorting from the other side of the table, neither of them really knew. But the urge to giggle subsided quickly when she found herself staring across the table at Daniel Bradford. He wasn't finding the whole thing funny any more, either.

She tugged at the collar of her leather jacket with a finger. Hot. That was what she was finding the whole thing now. Her feet were tingling and her cheeks felt flushed and a delicious warmth was spreading deep inside. And it had nothing to do with the therapeutic effects of having a good laugh.

She swallowed.

Unfortunately, it had everything to do with the not-so-therapeutic effects of staring deep into Daniel Bradford's eyes and wondering what it would be like to kiss him.

She closed her eyes as she took her next sip of wine, breaking the connection.

Nope. Been there, done that, survived the train wreck. Just.

Alan, who had obviously now recovered from his coughing fit, came and sat in the seat beside her and draped a well-toned arm across the back of her chair. 'You're not joining her?'

Chloe had to admire the ego that allowed him to bounce back from having lager spurt out of his nose then continue to flirt as if nothing had happened. She shook her head and nudged her chair further away while pretending she was reaching for her handbag.

'Don't tell me...' Alan said, leaning forward slightly '...you're already proficient?'

This time it was Daniel's turn to choke on his beer.

Too smooth for his own good, Chloe thought as she blinked and looked back at Alan. Still, it didn't worry her. She could handle him. One of the key pieces of reasoning behind the 'new and improved' Chloe was that she'd decided she'd much rather be the kind of woman men ran after than the kind they ran away from. In the intervening decade she'd learned a thing or two about over-enthusiastic suitors—and the disposal thereof.

She just smiled mysteriously and looked away. 'I doubt you'll ever find out.' No point telling him the only poles she was really proficient with were the little green canes she used to support her orchids.

This was her cue to exit. She half stood up and looked at both men in turn. 'Thanks for the drinks, guys, but I really must be going.'

'Must you?' Alan said, half rising from his seat and sporting what he probably considered was his most appealing smile. Chloe glanced over at Daniel. Once again, her blood danced along in her veins to the beat of bongo drums.

Yep. She really *must* go—before things got totally out of hand.

But then a few things happened in tandem, and she never really got her suitably cool and aloof goodbye out of her mouth. Alan's phone rang and he jumped up, pulled it out of his back trouser pocket and answered it. However, it seemed that Daniel thought Alan was making an ill-advised lunge for her, because he shot to his feet too, eyes flaming, and knocked the table in the process. Chloe's half-finished wine landed in her lap and the glass rolled onto the floor with an almighty crash.

And then Chloe was also on her feet and wine was running down her T-shirt and trousers. Even her boots were wet. She'd be smelling like the back room of an off-licence on the walk home. Most attractive.

Once again, the whole pub had fallen quiet to watch the show. They were certainly getting their money's worth tonight. She pushed past Alan—who was very gallantly continuing his phone conversation—shot a desperate look at Daniel and headed for the door.

From the way her audience's eyes kept switching from her to something behind her, she could tell she was being pursued. She really didn't know what would be worse: to turn round and discover it was Alan, or to turn round and discover it was Daniel, so she just kept weaving through the narrow tables until she could push her way through the crowd to reach the door.

Once outside, she breathed in a mouthful of cold March air and set off down the street. She lived within walking distance, anyway, and hopefully she'd dry off a little on the way home.

Unfortunately, she wasn't the only one hurrying down the street back towards the gardens. Her pursuer obviously wasn't giving up. She decided to play ignorant. Perhaps, if she pretended she didn't know someone was following her, they might just give up and go away.

It didn't work. And with every step Chloe's blood pressure rose until she thought her curls would stand on end. Eventually, she stopped and spun round so fast her pursuer almost crashed into her.

She was inches from a broad chest. 'What?' she asked it hoarsely.

The chest moved up and down and she could hear him breathing. She must have been walking a lot faster than she'd thought. He didn't say anything, though, so she tilted her eyeballs upwards until she could see that it was Daniel Bradford staring back down at her.

He held up one of the little bar towels that all good pubs had stocked away somewhere. 'You had wine on your jacket,' he said gruffly.

'Oh.' She stared at him.

He was still holding up the towel. She was still not taking it.

Slowly, and with surprising gentleness, he took the towel and dabbed at the drips on her left arm, which had now run from biceps to wrist. When he picked up her hand to clean up her cuff, she stopped breathing. From the eerie silence in the dark street, she realised he had too. Simultaneously, they both stopped looking at her sleeve and looked at each other.

Go on, an evil little voice on her shoulder whispered. *Pucker up and launch yourself at him again. It might work this time.*

No!

No. She'd seen the way he'd looked at Emma that evening. How could she be thinking of taking it one step further? Did she have a strange psychotic illness no one had ever diagnosed? *Bradforditis.* One look at the man and she was all sorts of crazy.

She wriggled her hand out of his grasp, almost whimpering as the pads of his fingers brushed the soft underside of her wrist, and stepped away.

'Thank you,' she said, folding her arms across her chest as best she could. With the engineering marvel of a bra she was wearing, it wasn't easy. 'This is my favourite jacket.'

Daniel stepped forward. 'Look…about Alan…'

She raised a hand, held him at bay. 'No need. I'm quite used to taking care of myself. He didn't offend me.'

'When you ran out—'

She shook her head, cutting him off. Why *had* she run out? 'I just…decided I'd rather clean up without an audience,' she said. 'Any more drama from our table and someone would have stood up in the corner and started selling ice creams.'

And then Daniel Bradford spoiled all her attempts at backing off and being sophisticated by crinkling up his pale green eyes and smiling at her.

Ping!

Yep. She was pretty sure another thread of her sanity had just snapped.

'*Do* you fancy an ice cream?' he said softly, still smiling.

Chloe let her arms drop by her sides. 'You know what?' she said. 'I really do.'

'Come on.' He led her a few shops down to the little express supermarket that was still open. Once inside he strode over to the tiny freezer containing ice creams and slid the lid open. 'Take your pick.'

She chose a decadent one: two layers of chocolate with caramel trapped between. Daniel grabbed something plainer. And once he'd paid they walked out of the shop, quickly rid the ice creams of their wrappers and walked down the street in silence, only the cracking of thin chocolate and the slurping of ice cream could be heard.

'Thank you,' she said, when they reached the end of the short parade of shops and stopped by an old horse trough, now filled with daffodils. 'For the ice cream and the mop up job.'

He shrugged. 'No problem.'

He was staring at her lips again. Chloe's heart began to pound, but Daniel lifted a finger to the edge of his own mouth, not hers. 'You've got a bit of…'

Pulse still thudding in her ears, she shot out her tongue and captured a bit of stray caramel that had stuck to the corner of her lip. Daniel Bradford seemed to be very interested in the process. In fact, he seemed to be leaning in closer to get a better look.

Run.

Don't think about it, just run.

Ah. That must be the angel sitting on the opposite shoulder from the other little voice. About time it showed up and offered some sensible advice.

He cleared his throat, looked down intently at her. 'I know this is a bit back to front, that we've just had what could be considered dessert…'

She licked her lips again. More out of nervousness than because of stray caramel.

'But why don't we round it all up by having a starter and a main course somewhere else?' He smiled again, and Chloe discovered the caramel had travelled to her knees.

Oh, it was so tempting…

This was what she'd fantasised about, aged nineteen, on many a night in her student digs—Daniel Bradford, looking at her this way, asking her in that deep, earthy voice of his if they could go somewhere alone together.

She shook her head, and just that motion helped the next words out. 'I'm not sure that's a good idea…We're colleagues. People will talk…and I want to get on at Kew because of what I can do,' she said quietly, 'not because people think I'm sleeping with the boss.'

His lips curved into the sexiest of smiles, telling her that he had an answer for that one. 'There's no rule against it,' he said. 'And we don't have to broadcast it. It'll be our secret.'

She shook her head. 'With the attention you're generating right now that's nigh on impossible.'

She was a genius for coming up with that one! It was perfect.

He nodded, pressed his lips together in grim acceptance. 'I can understand that. My life is a bit of a circus at present. But maybe later, when all the fuss has died down?'

Chloe knew she must be earning brownie points with someone somewhere, because she found the strength to shake her head again, her curls gently moving side to side.

'Sorry, Indiana. Thank you, though… It was very sweet of you to ask.'

And then she turned and walked away, leaving him staring after her.

It should have felt like a victory.

Daniel marched the half mile from the Princess of Wales conservatory to the tropical nurseries in record time the following morning. He wasn't in a good mood.

He passed The Orangery restaurant and headed up the main path towards the kids' play area, then slipped through an iron gate next to the café and left the public area of the gardens behind in favour of the relative sanctuary of the propagation and research greenhouses.

A soursop tree was due to arrive this morning, part of a trade with the botanical gardens in St Lucia, and Daniel wanted to see the specimen for himself. Alan was standing back and supervising while a couple of horticultural students moved the waxy-leafed tree with its spiky fruit from a trolley onto the floor. He turned round when he heard Daniel approaching.

'You okay?' he said.

Daniel gave him a weary, having-one-heck-of-a-day nod. 'Yup.'

A couple of people had asked him exactly the same thing this morning. Why did they keep doing that? It was most strange.

Alan issued a couple of final instructions to the students before shooing them away. When the two lads were gone and the sliding door of the nursery was closed, he turned to look at his boss.

'There's something you need to see.' He gave Daniel a hooded look and pulled his smartphone from his back pocket. 'I thought you needed to know before it goes viral.'

He punched a couple of buttons then twisted the phone round to show Daniel the screen. Daniel swore loudly and fluently, then snatched the phone from Alan's hand. Unfortunately, seeing it up close and staring hard at it didn't make the Internet news headline go away.

Valentine's man finally trapped? it screamed, and underneath it was a picture of him and Chloe, obviously taken the night before, although he'd had no idea anyone had been walking past with a mobile phone to capture the moment. It must have been when he'd been wiping the wine off Chloe's jacket, a very innocent pastime, he'd have thought, but this photo showed him holding her wrist and they were staring at each other, lost to everyone else. Chloe's lips were parted and he was leaning in slightly, making it look as if he were about to kiss her.

Daniel closed his eyes and handed the phone back to his friend before opening them again.

'This isn't what it looks like,' he said.

Alan just shrugged. 'I knew the minute she walked in the door that you were toast. Can't blame a guy for trying, though.'

Well, at least Alan was being philosophical about it. 'Who's seen this?'

Alan pressed his lips together and shook his head. 'Not sure. The girls in the café had been cooing over it for half an hour when I stumbled upon them.'

Just when he thought his crazy life was getting back to normal.

'So...what's the story with Miss Fancy Knickers?' Alan said, smiling a little.

Daniel forgot to look cross. 'Who?' he asked, genuinely confused.

'That's the nickname some of the students coined for Miss Orchid House.' He held up his hands. 'It's not that I don't appreciate the view, but those shoes and skirts she wears some days are hardly practical wear for a job like ours, even if she is just messing around with flowers instead of digging beds.' He leaned forward and lowered his voice. 'So...*are* they?'

Daniel's voice was low and warning. 'Are they what?'

Alan's smile upgraded itself into a lascivious grin. 'Fancy.'

'Not you too!' Daniel turned and pulled the sliding door open. 'I believe the official phrase is: *No comment*,' he said just before he slammed it closed again.

He strode away. A couple of the nursery team ducked for cover. Just as well, really. They'd obviously worked out that he was liable to assign the grottiest jobs to anyone who got in his way when he was feeling like this. And, with having to watch Kelly struggling through her chemo for months on end, there had been plenty of days when he'd been in a mood like this.

Fancy knickers. Humph.

No chance of him finding that out at present. He'd barely touched her, let alone got on first name terms with her underwear. And just thinking about said underwear was making it very difficult to calm down.

And it would have to be 'no comment' if anyone else asked him about Chloe, because he wasn't about to tell anyone he'd asked her out and she'd turned him down. That would be too humiliating.

Like what you did to Georgia.

No. That wasn't the same. Georgia had gone live on air and made the choice to publicise her ill-advised proposal. That hadn't been his fault at all. He'd asked Chloe out in private, just the two of them. Or so he'd thought.

Still, if he was feeling a fraction of the mortification Georgia had felt on Valentine's Day, it was no wonder it had taken her a month before she'd been able to face him in person. That must have been the pits.

Oh, heck.

Georgia.

He had a pretty good idea she hadn't seen this yet, and when she did she was going to kill him. He'd been able to tell from her expression yesterday that she was still feeling raw, even if she agreed that ending it had been the best thing for both of them.

To Georgia it would look as if he'd taken her visit yesterday to go out and bed the nearest available hottie. It didn't help to know he'd been on that train of thought himself last night, hardly stopping to think how it might look to anyone else. And Georgia had always had a bit of a thing about women like Chloe...

Oh, bloody hell. *Chloe.*

When Georgia was finished with him, Chloe would bring him back to life and make him suffer a second time. What a mess.

He yanked the greenhouse door open and strode out into the fresh air. There was only one thing to do: he had to talk to both of them before they found out about it from anyone else.

The morning had been a hectic one and Chloe decided to go and sit on a bench to eat her lunch. While it was cold enough to still need her coat, it was the best kind of day March could deliver, and she was determined to mop up as much sun as she could.

She'd always wanted to work at Kew, ever since she'd trained here. It was the most amazing place in the world as far as she was concerned. And who wanted to hide away in an office or a staff tearoom when there were acres of beautiful gardens on their doorstep?

An empty bench was waiting for her just away from one of the main paths. She made her way to it and sat down, trying to let the tranquillity seep into her, but she hardly took in the carpet of lilac-blue crocuses or the swathes of daffodils covering some of the sloping banks, because her mind was too busy living the events of the night before.

Half of her was screaming at the other half for having walked away from Daniel, and the other half congratulated itself on being safe and sensible. While the two continued to have a tug of war inside her skull, she closed her eyes and let her head slip back, enjoying the sun on her face.

She wasn't sure how long she stayed like that, but the snap of a twig nearby disturbed her. She sat up quickly and opened her eyes. Her heart had started to pump a little faster when she'd heard that noise and now she knew why. Indiana Jones, minus his secateurs, had come to pay her a visit.

She snapped the lid back on her salad and looked him evenly in the eye. That was the sort of thing New Chloe did. That girl wasn't scared of anything.

However, for the first time in years she was aware of another presence at the fringes of her consciousness. Deep down inside, another Chloe—the naive frizzy mouse—was huddled in a corner, twitching.

No, she thought. *That sad, geeky girl is dead. Something far better has risen from her ashes.* She clamped down hard on the ghostly presence. That was all it was. A memory. An echo.

'Don't suppose you have another ice cream on you?' she asked, closing her eyes again briefly. 'It's more the weather for it today.'

He shook his head and silently pulled a smartphone with a large screen from his pocket. 'I'm sorry,' he said as he handed it to her. 'This isn't anywhere near as nice as ice cream.'

Chloe scrolled through the whole blog entry carefully, reading every word. It was the picture that did the most damage, though. In the grainy photograph she was looking up at Daniel as he leant towards her, her eyes wide, her lips... waiting.

She handed the phone back to him without saying anything, not wanting to see it any more. She must have made a face, because he shook his head and then said, 'You've every right to be upset.'

It wasn't that. She wasn't upset that people thought she was romantically involved with Daniel Bradford. It might make her life at Kew a little more complicated, sure, but it was hardly anything to get her knickers in a twist about. No, what she was really worried about was that photograph.

'How many people have seen this?' she asked, looking straight ahead, eyes fixed on the Georgian orangery that now served as the gardens' main restaurant.

She heard the fragments of pine cones and twigs beneath his feet crunch as he shifted his weight. 'There's no way of knowing, but I think we have to assume *everyone*.'

Chloe nodded. Okay. She could cope with this. People might see the picture, but they wouldn't recognise it, wouldn't know what it meant.

She turned her head to look at him, made her cheek muscles tighten to pull the corners of her lips upwards. Then she shifted along the bench and made room for him. He blinked, confusion etched into his features, and sat down.

He was probably expecting a scene. Lots of women did scenes. Luckily for him, New Chloe had banished them from her life. She only did confident and breezy and unfazed.

'So…what do we do now?' she asked, leaning back and feigning a relaxed posture.

He stared intently at her for a moment. 'That's up to you,' he said. 'I could contact the blog, make a statement…'

Chloe thought for a moment. 'No…I don't think it's worth it.'

Unfortunately, the old adage was true: pictures did speak louder than words, and that one of her and Daniel was gabbling uncontrollably, contradicting any carefully worded denial they could come up with. There was no point.

'Are you sure?' The closed, slightly guarded look he'd been giving her softened. Chloe nodded brightly. She didn't want his concern, didn't want to see any more flashes of that warm, more caring side she'd just glimpsed of Daniel Bradford. Things were hard enough as it was.

She stood up and walked a little bit before turning back

to face him. 'It'd be like shouting into the wind. People will think what they want to think, no matter what we say.'

Daniel scowled. 'We can't just sit back and do nothing.'

She shook her head. 'I didn't say we should do nothing. I just said we shouldn't bother contacting the press to deny it. We don't have to go on the offensive to beat this thing.'

He looked at her as if she were speaking a foreign language. To Daniel Bradford, she probably was. She smiled. Properly this time.

She walked over to him, slid the phone from his hand without touching his fingers and showed him the picture. 'It's not as if we're in a full lip-lock,' she said, ignoring the shiver that ran up her spine at the thought. 'It's innocent enough. I think we should just ignore it, go on as normal. People will soon realise there's nothing in it.'

Daniel took the phone back from her, and this time their fingers did touch. And the way his eyes lit up, she guessed it wasn't entirely an accident. She pulled her hand away and stuffed it in her coat pocket, where it continued to tingle.

'No comment?'

'No comment,' she agreed. 'Perfect. That's exactly what people say in circumstances like this.'

Daniel stood up. 'You're saying you just want to ride whatever comes, ignore it?'

She nodded again. She was good at ignoring things.

Daniel shook his head as he put the phone back in his pocket.

'You haven't given an interview since Valentine's Day, have you?' she asked.

'No…' He looked away and then back at her. He was still frowning, but now she could tell he was turning her idea over instead of just resisting it. 'I suppose you're right. Starting a dialogue may just increase the frenzy.'

Chloe walked forward, sat down on the bench and picked

up her salad box again. 'Great. All sorted,' she said, unclipping the lid.

Daniel stared at her, brow still furrowed. He seemed on the verge of saying something, but he finally said, 'I'd better go and give Alan back his phone.'

She smiled back and waved her fork slightly before popping a cherry tomato in her mouth and swallowing it almost whole. 'Well, if Alan is as addicted to his smartphone as I am to mine, you'd better hurry. He may already be having withdrawal symptoms.'

Daniel gave a wry smile and stared at the phone, as if he couldn't quite believe in the seductive pull in that little bit of technology. 'I appreciate you being understanding about this,' he said as he put it back in his pocket.

'No problem,' she said, managing to sound fairly normal, although she was fairly sure that tomato had lodged itself somewhere in her throat. 'And if Alan is shaking and sweating when you get back to him, I recommend an early lunch break. Half an hour of Vengeful Ducks should get him back on track.'

'Let me thank you somehow,' Daniel said, lowering his voice, and an irresistible little glimmer of naughtiness twitched his mouth into an off-centre smile. 'How about dinner?'

Chloe blinked slowly and licked her lips. 'I thought we talked about this last night,' she said, looking at her salad and using her fork to tease a bit of carrot.

When she looked back up at Daniel he was still smiling at her. It took all she had not to fling her salad to one side and have him for lunch instead.

'Can't blame a guy for trying,' he said, then nodded and headed back towards the nurseries.

When he was out of earshot Chloe let go of her intercostal muscles and allowed the coughing fit she'd been holding back to take over. Eventually, the tomato made its way down the right hole.

She put her salad box down on the bench beside her, put her elbows on her knees and rested her face in her hands. She really didn't want to go back to who she'd been when she'd first met Daniel. That Chloe had been a nice enough girl, the class swot, always excelling at everything. She hadn't cared that she hadn't followed the latest fashion trends or had only a passing acquaintance with the opposite sex. Because that Chloe had known that everything came easy to her, that she'd hardly ever had to try to be good at anything.

And then Daniel Bradford had walked into her life and had shown her exactly where she'd been lacking.

She hadn't realised she wasn't any good at being a girl until he'd come along. And that was a pretty important thing when you were one.

For a girl who'd never failed at anything, crashing and burning so spectacularly in the male-female stakes had come not just as a shock, but a reality slap. That was what the grown-up world was all about. And nice-but-geeky Chloe just hadn't been cutting it.

She couldn't have that.

Right from an early age her parents had pushed their rather precocious only child to excel, to be the best at everything she did. So how had she failed at something so basic, something that was supposed to come naturally?

She drew in a breath and sat up. It didn't matter any more. She'd fixed it. Now being not just a girl, but a woman, was something Chloe Michaels got top marks in, so she really shouldn't worry.

A wisp of breeze curled itself around her, lifted a strand of hair and pushed it across her face. She brushed it aside. There was no point in dwelling on the past—she had a problem in the present that needed fixing.

Unfortunately, the root was the same: Daniel.

What was she going to do about him, about this stupid article?

Ignore it, she told herself firmly. *That's what you've got to do. Ignore the stupid blog. Ignore the way Indiana there makes your skin tighten and your pulse zing. Most of all, ignore that horrible photograph.*

A cold feeling spiked through Chloe and she masked it by sitting up and spearing another vegetable, chewing it quickly then swallowing it fast.

Yes, ignore the fact that, despite the trademark blonde curls and the red lips, she hadn't recognised herself in that photo. Not the version of herself she was today, anyway.

Because, in the grainy greyness of that mobile phone picture, it hadn't been 'new and improved' Chloe staring up at Daniel all wide-eyed and breathy; it had been the Mouse.

CHAPTER FOUR

DANIEL CAUGHT A flash of colour out of the corner of his eye as he flicked a paintbrush full of pollen over a plant he was trying to propagate. Instinctively, he swung round to find it again.

Just a brightly coloured plastic bag one of the staff had walked past the door of his nursery with. Not a pink shoe, or an emerald blouse or even a pair of smiling ruby lips.

He stood up and scrubbed a hand over his face.

He was losing it, wasn't he?

Just a hint of colour, which he now seemed to associate with Chloe, because everyone else here wore variations of brown and green and navy blue, or a scent like her perfume—an easy mistake to make in a greenhouse full of flowers—and he'd react. He'd seek first and think later, making him just like the insects who were lured by the smell and hue of the plant he was tending. They couldn't help it.

He couldn't help it.

Another dash of soft pink at the edge of his peripheral vision. He turned immediately, then swore.

This time it was Chloe, popping her head in the door of one of the other rooms and asking one of the horticultural students something. She was wearing a top that clung in all the right places. She smiled at the two young men, was charming and poised. Just as she was with him. No difference.

No difference at all.

It was driving him mad.

He'd tried everything, every trick up his sleeve—every look, every line—and she was still completely unaffected.

He bowed his head and turned his attention back to the bulbous *Nepenthes hamata* he was working on. Most people thought of plants as pretty things, but this specimen was dark and fierce-looking. He thought it was beautiful, but with vicious-looking black teeth round the opening of the pitcher it resembled something out of a science-fiction movie more than a bloom fit for a bridal bouquet.

He was trying to cross it with another species that was a deep purply-black. If he succeeded, he'd have a plant that would give even Sigourney Weaver nightmares.

He glanced up again, but realised he was subconsciously searching for soft pink, and made himself focus on the plant instead.

Not her. This plant wouldn't scare her. In fact, nothing seemed to rattle her, and he both admired and resented that ability. Chloe Michaels was like her own unique subspecies of womankind. Bred to resist him.

And, with all the lurid rumours flying round about them, her apathy just rubbed salt into the wound. Maybe it was just stubbornness on his part, an unwillingness to admit defeat?

A fly buzzed round the *Nepenthes,* alighting on the slippery edge of the plant's mouth and climbing inside. Daniel knew that was the last he'd see of it. The waxy interior would prevent any escape.

He studied the plant once again. So beautiful, but so deadly, luring most unwitting insects in with the promise of sweetness but the reality of slow drowning and digestion.

He heard heels on the concrete floor, sensed a patch of pink walk past his nursery door, but, despite the urge to turn, he kept his eyes trained on the shiny black teeth at the gaping mouth of the pitcher.

Maybe he would do well to learn a lesson from that fly.

* * *

Emma slid into the empty chair next to Chloe in the Orangery restaurant. It was a bright May afternoon, temperatures approaching those of high summer.

'So…' Emma said, leaning in close and lowering her voice. 'How are things going between you and the gorgeous Daniel?'

Chloe stopped chewing. If she had to say the equivalent of *no comment* just one more time she thought she'd scream. Even if it had been her clever idea.

'There's nothing to tell,' she said, after swallowing her mouthful.

Emma just grinned at her. When the rumours about her and Daniel had first surfaced Emma had given her a wide berth, but now she'd decided to buddy up with Chloe and live vicariously through her colleague's fictitious love life.

'I know that's the *official* line,' Emma said, her eyes gleaming over the top of her soup bowl, 'but everybody knows there's more to it than that. Come on…just one juicy detail…*please*?'

Chloe's eyebrows raised. 'Everybody? Still?'

'Pretty much,' Emma said as she slurped butternut squash soup off her spoon.

Chloe stared at her sandwich in dismay. She'd hardly seen Daniel in the last few weeks, let alone spoken to him. This 'deny everything' tactic had given her the perfect excuse to keep her distance.

'I don't know how you're managing to be so discreet,' Emma added between mouthfuls, so enthusiastic she dribbled a big glob of orange soup down her front. 'If I owned a man like that, I wouldn't be able to keep my hands off him—at home *or* at work.'

Chloe closed her eyes. It didn't matter what they did, did it? They were damned if they did and damned if they didn't. Keeping their distance, only nodding at each other in hallways when they passed, was just as much a confirmation of a steamy relationship as if they'd stripped naked and done it in the middle of the Palm House.

But it had worked. Media attention on Daniel and his ex had lulled. Thanks to that blog article, Daniel wasn't The One Who Got Away any more; he was The One Who'd Been Snared. Nowhere near as appealing. The women of London were moving on to pastures new.

'How's the pole dancing going?' she asked Emma, and thankfully her friend took the bait.

'The course finished and I've switched to belly dancing. You should try it!'

And as Emma gushed on about her new hobby an idea solidified in Chloe's head.

She would go and talk to Daniel, suggest they end this *no comment* nonsense. She felt as if invisible ropes, projected by other people's minds, were tying the pair of them together, each day becoming tighter and tighter, and it was making her itchy. It was time to break free.

And, thankfully, since Alan had also mentioned that the carnivorous plant display in the Princess of Wales Conservatory was being updated today, she knew just where to find him.

When Chloe entered the Wet Tropics zone of the Princess of Wales Conservatory she almost bumped into a woman in a raincoat standing at the slope that led down to the lily-pad pool.

'Sorry,' she said, but the woman didn't hear her. She was too busy staring at something on the other side of the pond. Chloe followed her gaze and quickly worked out why. Not bothering to wait for a ladder or any other suitable piece of equipment, Daniel had climbed outside the railing of the stepped walkway that led from the pond's edge over the water to the upper level. His attempts to hook a recently planted basket of trailing pitchers from a chain suspended from the ceiling were drawing quite a crowd.

Chloe folded her arms and enjoyed the view. She knew he relished finding plants in inaccessible places, particularly mountainsides, and he seemed totally at home hanging off the walkway, his feet pressing down onto the edge of the concrete path and the taut muscles of his outstretched left arm gripping onto the railing. His T-shirt stretched tight across his back and when he leaned a little bit further, exposing a band of tanned skin between hem and belt, there was a collective female sigh from the crowd of onlookers.

Chloe almost joined in herself. This was what had attracted her to him in the first place as an impressionable young student. Not just the good looks, but his passion for his area of study, the way he flung himself wholeheartedly into everything.

She frowned. While present-day Daniel obviously still liked a physical challenge, if she compared him to the Daniel she'd crushed over in her student days she realised there were subtle differences too. A decade ago he'd smiled more, laughed more. Present-day Daniel seemed more tense, more self-contained. Less…happy.

The woman next to her made a funny noise. Chloe turned to look at her. 'Are you okay?'

'Oh, yes,' the woman replied emphatically, her eyes still fixed on Daniel. 'Just getting up my nerve.'

Chloe stared at her for a second and began to walk quickly towards the crowd by the pool. A strange tickling under her skin told her she needed to get to him, and she needed to get to him fast. As she neared the pool he disappointed the sighing onlookers by finishing his task and hopping back over the railing to stand on the walkway. The round of applause he received took him completely by surprise.

She was just trying to fight the tide of the dispersing crowd when the woman she'd bumped into earlier dashed past her and ran up the ramp towards Daniel. He was facing the other direction but he must have heard her approach, because when she was within a few feet of him he turned round.

The woman skidded to a halt, fiddled with the buttons of her raincoat, then ripped the flaps open.

Chloe pushed her way through the onlookers and ran up the ramp behind her. Even from that vantage point she could see there was way too much bare skin under that coat. Daniel just stared at the woman, eyes on stalks. And not in a good way.

Everything stopped. The only thing moving was Chloe and the only noise was the overhead misters, hissing their displeasure. Exactly why she was racing to Daniel's side she wasn't sure; she just knew she had to do something.

When she reached the woman, she noted—thank goodness—that it wasn't as bad as she'd first feared. At least she was wearing a set of sexy black lingerie…and a message, written on what looked like permanent marker on her torso.

I do, Daniel, it read. *Do you?*

He just stared at the writing, a look of frozen horror on his face.

Chloe stared too, unable to work out just what kind of desperation drove a woman to do something like that, but then her gaze drifted from midriff to face. What she saw there was possibly even more shocking.

Not just desperation but longing.

The same kind of longing she'd seen in the mirror all those years ago when she'd first met Daniel. The agitation she'd felt while she'd been pushing her way through the crowd quickly turned to sympathy.

'I…I…' Daniel managed to stutter, and suddenly Chloe knew exactly what she had to do.

She hitched the fallen raincoat from round the woman's elbows and draped it across her shoulders, then she went to stand beside Daniel. After taking a deep breath, she slid her fingers into his.

He did a good job of hiding his flinch of surprise, and a second later his larger, stronger hand closed firmly around hers.

The woman's slightly glazed expression melted into one of horror. 'You're…you're the girl in the picture,' she said, her voice high and wavering, 'on that website…'

Chloe nodded and moved close to Daniel, pressing herself into his side. 'Yes,' she said. 'Sorry.'

The woman nodded and clutched the coat around herself. 'Oh, God,' she muttered. 'I feel so stupid.'

Chloe stepped forward, but it seemed Daniel was reluctant to let go of her hand. He still hadn't moved and his jaw was set in a hard line. She shot him a *work with me* look and he unclenched his hand enough to let her wiggle her fingers free.

She put her arm around the woman and led her further along the walkway, high above the Wet Tropics zone and through a glass door into another section, away from the staring crowd.

'I'm so sorry,' the woman said. 'I saw that picture of you two online, but there'd never been anything more. I didn't realise you two… I thought he was available.'

'It's okay,' Chloe said softly. 'I understand. He…he has this weird effect on people. On women.'

He certainly had a weird effect on Chloe.

Tears slid from between the woman's lashes. She nodded and looked at the floor. 'He just looked like…seemed to be…I don't know…the kind of man who'd really know how to look after a woman.' Her head jerked up. 'Is he?' she asked, slightly desperately, her fierce gaze demanding Chloe made eye contact.

Chloe didn't know what to say to that. She hardly knew Daniel, not really. And the truth was she'd been on the receiving end of one of the most humiliating and mortifying moments of her life at his hand. She certainly hadn't felt very special or looked after at that moment.

But this woman didn't need to hear that, and there was something in the tone of her question that begged for something positive to cling to from this whole sorry experience.

Chloe spotted a couple of the Kew constabulary slowly making their way towards them. She didn't know what experiences this woman had had with the opposite sex to get herself in this state, but they couldn't have been good ones. Maybe she just needed to know that all men weren't rats, that there were some good ones out there.

She thought about the way Daniel tended his plants, how gentle and patient he could be. Now, if he could bring some of that into his personal life, he really would be a catch. It wasn't too much of a stretch to give the right answer. She met the woman's gaze.

'Yes, he is,' she said quietly. And as the two constables reached them she reached down and squeezed the woman's hand.

'I think she might just need a strong cup of tea and a sympathetic ear,' she told the constables. 'No harm done.'

The female officer of the pair smiled and nodded, and Chloe let out a breath. She really hoped the poor woman would get the help she needed.

As for Chloe? Well, maybe she was in need of a little help herself.

No harm done. Really?

She wasn't so sure about that.

Because she knew that by her actions a few moments ago she'd announced to the onlookers, including Kew staff, and maybe even to the whole world—via the considerate people who'd silently recorded the whole episode on their smartphones—that she and Daniel Bradford were a couple.

The crowd, who were far too nosey to disperse, watched along with Daniel as Chloe re-entered the Wet Tropics zone and walked back towards him. Her chin was high and her make-up perfect. She looked so in control, so assured…

So different from that crazy woman in the raincoat.

The contrast soothed his soul.

At least, it did until she was right in front of him. Just as she reached him he saw a flicker of something else behind the perfection, something in her eyes as she looked up at him—uncertainty, blended with a pinch of nerves.

That shook him.

For weeks now she'd had him convinced that she was impervious, iron-clad. Chloe Michaels was merely a delectable package he was itching to unwrap. A prize to be won. So it was a shock to be reminded that she was a real woman, one maybe, that still had all the idiosyncrasies and puzzling insecurities they seemed to be preprogrammed with.

But then the *something* he'd seen was gone, and she was back to normal—all gloss and glamour. All colour and scent. He breathed out, relieved that she'd tucked whatever it was he'd seen away, out of reach, and he didn't need to worry about it any more.

He didn't say anything to her, just closed the distance between them, caught her hand in his, then led her out of the Princess of Wales Conservatory.

Once outside they kept walking, still joined, far away from the glasshouse, up the Broadwalk and on. They stopped briefly by the lake in front of the vast Palm House.

'We need to talk,' he said, 'about what just happened back there.'

She nodded.

'Somewhere private,' he added.

They turned their heads in unison and looked at the Victorian marvel of curved white iron and thin panes of glass not more than a hundred feet away. Although it was one of the prime visitor spots at Kew, and unlikely to be empty, it was filled with drooping plants and massive leaves. Daniel knew there were plenty of places to hide if one knew where to go.

Once inside, he ignored the 'No Entry' sign at the bottom of one of the ornate spiral staircases that led from the floor of the Palm House to the gallery that ringed the dome. 'They've just finished trimming the giant bamboo,' he explained, 'so we should be the only ones up here for now.'

Chloe nodded and let him pull her up the stairs, unable to say anything sensible. She'd been fine while the whole drama had been unfolding back in the Princess of Wales Conservatory, cool as the proverbial cucumber, but now, as the damp heat of the tropical greenhouse seeped beneath her clothes and moistened her skin, she couldn't stop thinking about the woman in the raincoat.

The way the crowd had looked at her, with a mixture of curiosity and disgust… The poor woman had seemed so lost and desperate. How had she not known that what she was about to do would be a horrible mistake?

The heels of Chloe's boots clanged on the scrollwork metal steps and she shifted her weight so she was treading on the balls of her feet. She felt as if she'd left her stomach on the iron-grated floor below them. The air grew hotter and wetter, making it hard to gulp it in as she climbed.

Ten years ago, was that how Daniel had seen her? Had he felt that same mix of revulsion and pity? She shivered at the thought.

They'd reached the top of the curling staircase and she paused, taking in a steadying breath before following Daniel down the narrow gallery until they were almost completely hidden from view by a giant palm and a bushy cannonball tree.

Daniel turned and looked at her.

Yes, this was the expression she wanted to see on his face. Not a hint of revulsion. Slighty perplexed, if anything, because he'd lost that perpetual frown and his expression was the most open she'd ever seen it.

'Thank you for what you did back there. I had no idea how to handle that gracefully. After Georgia…I just didn't want to say the wrong thing.'

Chloe couldn't help but smile, just a little. Hanging off bridges and scaling mountains were what Daniel Bradford was graceful at. The interpersonal stuff, not so much.

He shook his head. 'This whole thing, ever since that stupid radio show, has been crazy.'

'I'm hoping today's particular manifestation was a one-off,' Chloe said, feeling less scorn for the woman than was coming out in her voice. For some reason, she didn't want Daniel to know that she'd identified with the poor soul at all.

He shook his head, looked away for a second, and the tug on her hand as his weight shifted reminded her he hadn't let go of it. She should step back, make it look natural, but she should break contact.

She should. But she didn't.

'I don't know how I'm going to take nine more months of this.'

'Nine months?' She wrinkled her brow. 'I didn't realise there was a set timescale for Valentine's-related insanity. Or an expiry date.'

One corner of his mouth twisted. 'No, it's not that. I'm getting out of here—going on the expedition with the South Asia team. Early next spring I'll be back in Borneo and all this so-called civilisation will only be a distant nightmare.'

Nine months? Chloe didn't like the way her chest squeezed at that thought.

'It'll die down,' she said.

He frowned. 'That's what I thought at first but, if anything, it's getting worse.'

'I heard your ex on the radio yesterday,' she said, 'doing her monthly spot about her bounce-back year.'

Daniel looked thunderous. 'I can't really hold it against her—the radio station is making her do it—but it's the broadcasting equivalent of a full moon. Brings out all the crazies…' His expression softened. 'You helped, though. That woman backed off when she thought we were together.'

Chloe nodded. 'I guess the cat's out of the bag—even if it was an illusory bag and an illusory cat. *No comment* isn't going to cut it now.'

He gave her an uneven smile. 'If today was anything to go by, *No comment* wasn't cutting it anyway.'

There was that.

She sighed and gently slid her hand out of his. He didn't stop her. Then she turned and rested her forearms on the gallery rail and stared out over the Palm House, even though, because of the secluded spot they'd chosen, much of what she could see was the dark waxy leaves of the bushy tree in front of her. It was so hot up here. Her jumper was starting to cling and her fringe was growing damp against her forehead.

'So what do you want to do about it?' he asked, then leant on the rail beside her, mirroring her pose.

For a long time neither of them said anything but, eventually, a seed of an idea dropped into Chloe's brain from somewhere, floating on the wind. A few minutes later it had grown into a little green shoot of a plan, new and fresh and unexpected. She didn't want to see any more women suffering the way that lady had today. And she didn't think Daniel deserved the embarrassment, either.

She pushed her weight back onto her feet and straightened. 'Let's make it work for us,' she said.

He turned to look at her, clearly unconvinced that was possible. 'How?'

She took a deep breath. Her heart began to pump faster. *This must be what it feels like for them*, she thought, *for the guys, when they're gathering up the courage to ask a girl out*.

But this wasn't like that. Not really. Because she wasn't

really asking him out; she certainly wouldn't risk being refused by Daniel a second time.

So she swallowed her nerves down, then looked him in the eye. 'I have a proposal for you.'

CHAPTER FIVE

ALARM FILLED DANIEL'S eyes. Chloe could practically hear the word *proposal* ringing round his head. He was feeling panicked? Good. At least that meant they were on even ground now.

'Not that kind of proposal,' she added wearily.

Daniel folded his arms across his chest and leaned back on the opposite railing, close to the curved glass of the Palm House's roof. 'What do you mean, then?'

Chloe swallowed. 'Have dinner with me,' she said, her heart pumping. 'Or something else. Once a month—just before Georgia does her latest radio segment. Just like today, it might keep the crazies at bay.'

He blinked slowly. 'You said you didn't think it was a good idea to go out with me.'

She nodded. 'I'm not suggesting we date, just that once in a while we let ourselves be seen together in public, let everyone join the dots. It won't be our fault if they draw entirely the wrong picture.'

'And at work?'

'We do what we've been doing. Keep it cool and professional. People will think that we're trying to be discreet.'

He stared at her for the longest time. Chloe held her breath and refused to fidget. No way was she going to let him see how nervous she felt. She was very glad she let go of his hands now, because her palms were sweating.

It's not real. You're not asking him out on a real date...

'Why are you doing this for me?' he asked warily.

She shook her head. She didn't know, really. It was stupid. Crazy.

You do know, a little voice inside her head whispered. *You want an excuse to spend time alone with Drop-Dead Daniel, so you can make believe, torment yourself...*

No. That wasn't it. She couldn't *let* that be it.

'Someone told me about your sister,' she finally said. That was true. 'Let's just say I thought you could do with a break.' That was also true. It just hadn't been in her head when she'd put her proposition to Daniel.

His lips pressed together. 'I don't need your pity,' he said coldly, and he pushed himself up from the railing and walked off down the gallery.

Chloe let out a huff of frustration and then trotted after him. Damn male pride...

'It's not pity,' she said crossly as she closed in on him. 'It's a friend helping a friend. That's all.'

He stopped, pivoted around to face her. 'Friends? That's all?'

She nodded, not trusting her mouth to toe the party line.

He looked beyond her, up to the vast curving glass and ironwork ceiling. Despite his knee-jerk temper, he seemed to be chewing it over.

'I do confess I'm not being completely altruistic,' she added, finally finding something sensible to say, something much more slick and smooth and *Chloe* to say. The sort of thing he'd come to expect from her—ambivalent, flirty, slightly mocking. 'After all, you'll be paying for dinner.' And then she smiled brightly at him, just to prove there was nothing to worry about, that he needn't be scared of her getting the wrong idea and joining the ranks of his stalkers.

Amusement warmed his previously stony expression. 'Oh, I am, am I?'

She nodded again. This time because her mouth wasn't working, not because she was scared it was about to take off on its own.

There was something about his manner that completely changed. One moment he had been closed off, cold, almost backing away from her. But now there was fire in his eyes and even though she'd swear he hadn't moved he seemed to be getting closer.

Suddenly her cheeks felt very hot. She looked up at him, almost leaning over her.

'D-Daniel? What are you doing?'

'If it's my money we're going to be spending, my life we're going to be messing around with, then I get to say what goes.'

Her chin bobbed up and down. She got that. Daniel had been completely blindsided by the morning's events. He felt out of control. This request was just about reclaiming lost ground, that was all. She could let him have that much.

But then Daniel stepped towards her, pressing his body up against hers, pinning her between him and the wooden rail at her waist. His hands clutched the rail either side of her, his strong, taut arms preventing escape, and Chloe realised just how *off* her calculation of the situation had been.

It wasn't lost ground he was about to claim, but her.

He paused for a moment, just as his lips were millimetres from her. Her pulse lurched and her breath came in uneven bursts.

And then he was kissing her, expertly wiping any protest away with his firm lips. Chloe clung to his shirt for support. The difference in their height meant she felt she was arching back over the railing, feeling as if she'd fall at any moment.

But even that fear was quickly erased by the sensations erupting through her body. Sweet heaven, this was better even than she'd imagined it would be. He knew just when to take, just when to tease… Just how to leave her breathless and dizzy, even without the use of his hands, which were still making sure she stayed right where he wanted her.

If Chloe had been able to string a coherent sentence together, she'd have been able to tell him it wasn't necessary. As much as her brain was screaming for her to run, her body had been waiting too long for this. It was going to enjoy it while it lasted.

And enjoy it she did. Pretty soon her hands were unclenching from Daniel's T-shirt, exploring his rather fine chest, reaching up to pull him closer so she could really lose herself in him. Suddenly, she was claiming him back. And, damn, if that didn't just turn him on more. He moved his hands to her waist and for a second she thought he was going to lift her up and sit her on the rail. She grabbed him tighter, hoping he'd remember where they were, just how far she could fall if he lost concentration and let go.

She could feel him starting to lift her, his hands tightening around her ribs. She stiffened, and her eyes flew open, just in time to see him cock an eyelid. He pulled away, a decidedly wicked smile on his face, looking far more pleased with himself than a man had a right to after just such a stunt.

Even though she was pressing into him rather than leaning back over the railing, she still clutched onto him. At least she did until another noise filtered through her consciousness. She turned her head, slightly dazed, to find a small group of people on the ground staring up at them. Some of them were wearing the distinctive blue polo shirts with Kew's embroidered logo.

Drat. She'd forgotten they'd moved out of the cover of their secluded little corner.

Smiling nervously, she lifted her hand and gave them a little wave. They responded with a round of applause and a couple of wolf whistles.

She turned back to Daniel, keeping her eyes on his chest,

and carefully smoothed his T-shirt flat with her palms before gathering the courage to look up at him.

'I thought the plan was to keep it discreet,' she said shakily.

Daniel's grin became even broader. Damn the man for enjoying this!

'Plans change,' he said, not in the least bit repentant. And then he stepped away and made tracks to the spiral staircase, whistling as he went.

Chloe walked forwards and rested her forehead against the misty glass on the other side of the gallery. Not only had she *not* kept her distance from Daniel Bradford, but she'd actually proposed spending more time with him. Alone. In what messed up universe did that idea make sense?

She pressed her fingertips to her lips. She'd never had much self-control where Daniel had been concerned, and now look where it had got her. She'd made herself a trap, and she had no idea how she was going to climb out of it.

He found her in the orchid nursery the next morning, working on a plant she'd been growing from a seed that had lost its label during a collections trip. They needed to confirm what species it was, but until the plant flowered it was impossible to know. This one was stubbornly refusing. But Chloe knew all about being stubborn, didn't she?

The slight hesitation in her movement told him she'd heard him coming, but she carried on with her work. Not ignoring him, just finishing what she was doing. Indifferent, almost.

When she was ready she put the pot down and cocked an eyebrow. 'Well, if it isn't Indiana. Here to pound your chest?'

Daniel grinned at her. The way he was feeling this morning, a little chest pounding wouldn't be amiss. 'Don't know what you mean.'

'That's what that kiss was about, right? Putting on a good show, some macho attempt to mark me as yours?' She shook her head. 'All those jungle plants you work with must have activated your dormant monkey brain.'

Ouch. He was used to her being witty; he just hadn't realised she could be so cutting with it. But he liked *cutting*. It was way better than polite and impervious.

'Pretty much,' he said, looking her up and down. Today she was the smartest and slickest he'd ever seen. The pencil skirt had made a reappearance, along with a dark pink top and the trademark red lips.

He was lying, though. He hadn't had a plan. Not of any shape or any kind. He'd kissed her because he'd wanted to, because she'd been driving him crazy for weeks and he hadn't been able *not* to.

Since Valentine's Day he'd been at the mercy of the situation not of his making and he hated that. And, while Chloe's idea had merit, it felt an awful lot like being rescued. He hated that more. If anyone was going to be doing the rescuing it was going to be him.

So when the urge to kiss her had hit, he'd gone with it, had taken back control in one swift and delicious move. He wasn't prepared to regret it. Not after the way she'd responded to him. That had been no play-acting for the audience below. She'd been right there with him, dragging him deeper.

Indifferent? Yeah, right.

Chloe Michaels might do a good job of painting it that way on the surface, but underneath she was as hungry for him as he was for her. She just didn't want to admit it. Daniel didn't really care why. Not now he knew it was *game on* again— and that he'd had the first victory.

'Well, I'm glad that you got whatever it was out of your system,' she said starchily and turned her attention back to her orchid.

He moved a little closer. 'No action replays?'

She pursed her lips and scowled at him. 'I know the London press thinks you're God's gift, Indiana, but I think it's gone to your head. You're starting to believe your own hype.'

Daniel just chuckled. He so wasn't. But Chloe was acting as if he were as sexually neutral as that plant she was tending. He had a point to prove.

'Fine,' she said. 'If you don't like my idea, we'll scrap the whole thing. Good luck with the next raincoat flasher, though.'

'I didn't say I was backing out.'

Far from it.

'Well, then. We keep it on my terms,' she said. 'Strictly platonic. No more stunts like the one in the Palm House yesterday.'

'What if *you* cave and end up kissing *me* senseless?'

She made a scoffing noise. 'Not going to happen.'

He shrugged. 'Whatever you say. But if you give me the signals, I'm not going to ignore them.'

She let out a dry laugh. 'You are so big-headed! And so wrong.'

He so wasn't. But this was what he'd been waiting for from her. This was all part of the fun, the push and pull of the chase, letting her think she was in charge, when actually he was reeling her in bit by bit. She'd change her tune soon enough.

'How about that little Italian restaurant for our next outing?' he said.

Chloe's expression reminded him of how his grandmother used to look at him over the top of her glasses. Even that made him want to whistle again. Oh, he was going to have so much fun with her. She was going to be worth every bit of this torturous wait.

Because he'd realised what he'd told Alan at the pub was true. There was more than one way to hunt. Chloe obviously didn't respond to the more direct approach—that only sent her running—so he was going to have to be more clever, more subtle. Just like his plants, he was going to make himself so irresistible to her that *she* wouldn't be able to help herself.

He thought of the species of *Sarracenia* whose tall pitchers contained narcotic liquor, drugging the insects it captured so they didn't even consider escaping. Chloe would be like one of those happy little flies when he'd finished with her.

'No Italian,' she said. 'I don't think the grapevine needs any more convincing at present. Yesterday did the trick quite nicely.' She picked up the pot and examined the moisture level. 'When's Georgia's next on-air segment?'

'I think it's the first Tuesday of the month,' he said.

She put the pot down again. 'Well, call me in June, then.'

Daniel grinned at her attempt to dismiss him. He'd go, but only because it was part of a bigger plan. He couldn't help letting her know that, though. He walked over to her, leaned in close and opened his mouth to whisper in her ear. She snapped the small green cane she was holding in half and every muscle in her body went taut.

So *not* indifferent.

'Till June,' he whispered, letting his breath warm the sensitive parts of the ear lobe, and he actually saw the moment she suppressed a shiver.

Two more dates and he'd have her eating out of his hand.

As May bled into June Chloe got more and more agitated. Stupid, stupid idea. What had she been thinking?

Well, obviously, she hadn't.

She'd resorted to her old way of doing things, reacting on impulse rather than taking a measured decision. It was just that kind of behaviour that had got her into trouble with Daniel Bradford all those years ago, the sort of thing New Chloe didn't do.

Thankfully, however stupid her plan was, however self-destructive, it actually looked as if it was working. There had been no more 'raincoat' incidents, and Daniel had reported a drop in interested female visitors. The plan had its down-side too, though. After being so excited to get her dream job as Kew's Head Orchid Keeper, Chloe now found her working days tense and stressful. She went home every evening with a headache.

It wasn't that Daniel had repeated the kiss in the Palm House. He'd kept his distance, just as they planned. Physically. That didn't mean he'd left her alone.

When they passed each other at work—which was often—he'd give her a smile he reserved just for her. Warm, intense... inviting. Just the sort of special smile lovers shared. It was messing with her head, big time. And he knew it.

Then, in early June, just as she'd suggested, Daniel's phone call came. He wanted to come and pick her up at home, but she made an excuse about having to work late, so he came and collected her from her nursery at the allotted time instead.

They walked through the gardens together to the staff car park. Plenty of people noticed their exit. Chloe could almost hear the whispers as they passed, see the nods and winks behind their backs. It was almost a relief to slide into the passenger seat of his car and shut the world out again. Or it would have been, if the clunk of the door hadn't created another little universe. A universe where the atmosphere became so hot the atoms danced and shimmered. A universe where she and Daniel were the only occupants. She faced forward and stared blindly at the windscreen. 'Where are we going?'

He just put the car into gear and pulled away. 'Somewhere lively,' he said, and Chloe's insides unclenched a little.

That was just what she needed. Somewhere busy, bustling with people. Somewhere she wouldn't be left alone with him.

The car joined the rush-hour traffic through Kew and on into Chiswick. Chloe's mood brightened further. There were some lovely restaurants here. She scanned the high street as they drove down it, wondering which one he'd picked.

Thai? French? Lebanese?

But when they turned into a side street he didn't park, even though there were plenty of spaces. Instead he kept driving, turning this way and that until he stopped in a residential street. They were outside a smart brick house with a large bay window and a glossy black front door. He turned the engine off and got out, opened the door for her. Chloe stayed in her seat, clutching her handbag.

'We're here?' she asked. 'Where are we?'

Daniel did a little bow. 'My house.'

She swallowed. 'I thought you said we were going somewhere lively.'

Daniel just smiled. 'You haven't been inside yet.'

Run, something inside her shouted. *Get out of the car and run.*

It was probably her common sense making a last-ditch attempt to save her. She let it scream its frustration then sprint down the road without her.

He held out his hand and she took it, let him help her from the car. Then he ushered her up the garden path and she stood aside while he produced his keys from his pocket and opened the front door.

The minute he'd stepped into the hallway he was practically bowled over by two running bundles of energy. Chloe blinked. It took her a second to work out they were two small boys, one a slightly smaller version of the other, both with Daniel's grey-green eyes.

He had…? They were…?

But then they both started shouting, 'Uncle Dan! Uncle Dan!' and the penny dropped. But the minute that puzzle had been solved another one elbowed its way in. This was where Daniel took girls on a *date*?

He turned and gave her a rueful smile, a small boy hanging off each arm, and led the way down the hall and into a kitchen-diner in the back of the house, with a lounge area under a conservatory at the far end. A tall, slender woman was stirring something on the hob. Same dark hair with a bit of a kink, same pale eyes. That had to be his sister.

'Boys,' she said, 'try not to pull your uncle's arms off.' Then she looked up and smiled at Chloe. 'Hi.'

'Hi,' Chloe said.

'Welcome to the madhouse,' she said. 'I'm Kelly.' She indicated each of the boys in turn with her wooden spoon. 'That's Cal… That's Ben. Say hello to Uncle Dan's friend, boys.'

But the boys were too busy wrestling their uncle to the ground. For two people so small, they really knew what they were doing, Chloe thought, as Daniel's knees buckled and he was felled with a thud.

'They'll calm down in a minute,' Kelly said. 'They do that every night when he comes in.' She sighed. 'Their father took a hike a couple of years ago and the lack of male influence makes them a little full on when they get the chance to do some "boy bonding".'

Chloe's eyebrows rose. 'Beating each other half to death is *boy bonding*?'

Kelly grinned as she added some chopped tomatoes to the pan. 'You don't have brothers, do you?'

Chloe shook her head. Just her. And her doting, but rather hard to impress parents. It took a lot to carry the weight of all that parental expectation on one pair of shoulders. She'd often wished she'd had a sibling or two to share the load. 'Why can't they just paint each other's nails and snivel their way through a good film, like normal people do?'

Kelly laughed. 'Wow, it's good to have a bit of sanity around here. I thought I was in danger of drowning in all the testosterone. This house has been a bit lacking in female company since Georgia—' She bit her lip. 'Sorry.'

Chloe held up her hands. 'No, it's okay. Me and Daniel, we're just…'

Friends sounded so lame. *In cahoots* too much like a cheesy thriller. She settled for the safest option.

'...colleagues.'

Kelly scrubbed the pan with the wooden spoon. Chloe thought she could see a bit of burnt onion refusing to behave. 'Yep,' she said, giving the mixture a vigorous stir that made Chloe realise that Daniel wasn't the only one in the family who liked to get physical, 'and I'm just Gordon Ramsay.'

Chloe didn't say much after that. From the past couple of months at work, she knew it was no good to convince her otherwise. And it was an easy enough assumption to make. Why would Daniel be bringing her home otherwise?

The ruckus from the lounge end of the room was getting rather loud. Kelly handed the saucepan to Chloe and went to intervene.

'Boys!' she yelled. 'Pyjamas! Now!'

Instantly, the knot of testosterone on the floor disentangled itself. Then, one by one, they headed towards the stairs, pouts pushing their bottom lips forward. Daniel brought up the rear, copying their expression, which only made them giggle again. The whole scene would have descended back into chaos if Kelly hadn't given her big brother a clip round the ear.

The boys bounced in the doorway. 'We want Uncle Dan to read us a story,' they yelled repeatedly.

Uncle Dan looked up at Chloe, who was still holding the saucepan, and gave her an apologetic look. 'Do you mind?'

She shook her head. She'd been trying to keep her distance from him for weeks now. Why would she mind if he volunteered to do just that?

Kelly came and took the saucepan from her. Just as well Chloe had heard the thunder of little—and big—feet on the stairs, because Kelly's verdict on her own cooking was not for children's ears. 'I always was crap at cooking,' she explained. 'Dan said I should just get some posh stuff to reheat from the supermarket, but I had to decide to go all cordon bleu, didn't I?' She tipped the contents of the saucepan into the bin and banged it back down on the hob. Chloe quickly leaned forward and turned the gas off before another catastrophe occurred.

Kelly rummaged in a drawer and produced a fan of takeaway leaflets. 'Curry, curry, Chinese or curry,' she said brightly.

Chloe looked at the other ingredients lined up on the counter. Bacon, garlic, chilli flakes... 'Amatriciana sauce, right?'

Kelly nodded, looking at Chloe as if she were the bearer of ancient and hallowed wisdom.

'It'd be a shame to waste all that lovely fresh pasta,' Chloe said. 'Have you got another onion and more tomatoes? I'm sure I could help...if you wouldn't mind?'

Kelly looked as if she was going to prostrate herself at Chloe's feet. She grabbed Chloe's hand. 'Please marry him,' she said, and then she added, 'As you can see, my tact is as well developed as my culinary skills. Blame it on having two thickheaded brothers. Blunt and direct was what was required round our house when we were growing up. Never quite learned how to switch it off.'

Chloe grinned at her. She couldn't help liking Kelly. Her say-whatever-fell-into-her-head approach was rather refreshing. There must be something lovely about going through life like that, not having to worry about saying the wrong thing or accidentally showing a part of yourself you'd rather other people didn't know about.

'I take it there is wine somewhere in this kitchen?' she asked.

'Do you need it for the sauce?'

'No,' said Chloe, smiling. 'I need it in a glass. Now where are those tomatoes?'

Kelly provided both wine and tomatoes. 'Forget marrying Dan,' she said as she watched Chloe sweat some finely diced onion. 'Move in and adopt *me*.'

Chloe chuckled, and they continued to chat as she made

headway in making the pasta sauce. Kelly was more a hindrance than a help, though, and Chloe quickly suggested she put her feet up, saying that looking after pre-schoolers must be very tiring.

She nodded in the direction of the ceiling as Kelly collected her wine glass and flopped on the sofa. 'He's great with the boys.'

'He is that.' Kelly looked up, a soft smile on her face. 'He'll make a really good dad some—' She froze, scratched her nose and looked away. 'Forget I said that.'

Inside Chloe was frowning, but on the outside she batted Kelly's stray comment away and smiled cheerfully back, mentally searching for something to say that would dispel the odd, slightly sad atmosphere that had settled on the other woman.

'Well, there is one thing I can guarantee,' Chloe said jokingly as she added some garlic to the pan. 'It's that I won't ever be marrying your brother.'

CHAPTER SIX

DANIEL PAUSED ON the stairs as he heard Chloe's voice and smiled.

No marrying him. Ever. That was practically a guarantee.

He bounced back into the kitchen to find Chloe standing at the stove and Kelly lounging on the sofa sipping Merlot. What was wrong with that picture?

'I invited you for dinner,' he told Chloe, 'not the other way round.'

Chloe shrugged. 'I like cooking, and your sister…'

'Your sister burnt the crap out of the first attempt,' Kelly said helpfully. 'I've been banished to the sofa. She won't even let me help.'

Daniel gave his sister a very *brotherly* kind of look. 'And I can see it's just eating you up inside.'

Kelly held up her wine glass and toasted him with it before downing the remainder in one gulp. He shook his head and turned his attention to his guest.

'That smells amazing,' he said. 'You must be pretty good at this.'

She bowed her head and looked at the wooden spoon as she stirred the sauce. 'I like picking up new skills, perfecting them.'

Daniel smiled to himself as he and Kelly laid the table. His plan was working. He could tell from the way Chloe hummed to herself as she put the finishing touches to the pasta sauce that she was starting to relax. Just what he wanted.

He didn't want a date with starchy, let's-pretend-we're-being-discreet-at-work Chloe. He wanted a date with the Chloe who'd been within a hair's breadth of ripping his T-shirt off on the balcony of the Palm House. There was a girl who knew how to have fun.

He'd been given the job of cooking the pasta and she started teasing him when she realised it was overcooked and sticking to the bottom of the pan.

'Honestly,' she said, snatching it from him. 'The pair of you are as bad as each other. I don't know how those two poor children haven't starved to death.'

'I have extensive skills with a can opener and advanced microwave training,' he told her, quite seriously.

Kelly, who was now sitting at the table, glass of wine in hand, also piped up. 'And I make a mean chicken nuggets and oven chips.'

Chloe just shook her head.

'I'll bet you know how to make fancy pastry and everything,' Kelly said mournfully as they dished up.

Chloe tried to act nonchalant, but he could see just a hint of self-satisfaction in her reply. 'I've done a cookery course or two,' she said quietly.

His sister slumped on the table. 'Ugh. I hate women like you,' she said dramatically, but the delivery just made Chloe laugh.

Daniel decided he was a genius. Kelly was probably his best weapon this evening. Chloe liked her, despite the fact that, beside his immaculately dressed and perfectly contained date, his sister seemed a little too loud and uncensored. It was like putting an elegant pink orchid and a dandelion in the same pot together: it shouldn't work. But the two women were getting on like a house on fire and he wasn't going to do anything to upset that.

Chloe *was* like one of her orchids, he decided as they chatted over the simple dinner. Beautiful. Poised. Aloof. Just like the graceful flowers she tended, she was almost too perfect to be true.

After dinner he moved to phase two of the plan. Kelly loaded the dishwasher, batting Chloe's efforts to help away and telling her she'd better leave it to the expert. Daniel made the coffee. Fresh not instant. One thing in the kitchen he could do really well. Then Kelly put her coat on and picked up her handbag.

Chloe's easy demeanour slipped a little. 'You're going?'

Kelly nodded. 'Big brother here promised he'd babysit tonight. He owes me.' She gave Daniel a knowing look. 'First night out with the girls in weeks,' she said, then she blew them both a kiss and hurried out of the front door before anyone could stop her.

Daniel brought Chloe a coffee and sat down at the table with her. He glanced at the comfy sofa in the conservatory, with ample room for two. That would have been his preferred location, but he sensed he needed to tread carefully now his secret weapon was off to the wine bar to drink cocktails with her girlfriends.

'For a long time Kelly wouldn't go anywhere,' he told Chloe. 'Too tired. Too self-conscious about her hair. It was very patchy when it first grew back.'

A look of pain crossed Chloe's features and she absentmindedly fiddled with the end of a loose ringlet. 'How awful for her. Girls need their hair.'

He nodded, understanding that now. Personally, he wouldn't have cared if his hair was down to his knees or in a marine buzz cut, but the wallop Kelly had given him when he'd suggested, very practically, that she should just borrow his clippers and even it all out had let him know just how differently men and women saw this issue.

He and Chloe chatted about easy things. Safe things. Work.

Plants. Mutual acquaintances. When she drained her cup, Daniel stood up and reached for the wine bottle. 'Another glass?'

She looked at him thoughtfully, and then she said, 'Just half. It was rather drinkable.'

He got fresh glasses from the cupboard as, thanks to Kelly's post-dinner clearing frenzy, the previous ones were already sloshing around in the dishwasher. But instead of joining her at the table he walked over and placed her glass on the table beside the sofa and then sprawled at the other end.

Chloe looked at him for a second and then stood up and came to join him, sitting neatly and very upright in the opposite corner. 'No funny business,' she said, and sipped her wine. 'You promised.'

He just smiled at her. 'I don't think I actually promised, but I did say that it would be up to you to make the first move.'

Chloe's shoulders relaxed a little, but her expression remained pinched. 'As nice as dinner was, I don't see how hiding away in your house is going to help us.'

'Ah,' he said. 'Well, it came about partly because I'd forgotten I'd told Kelly I'd babysit...' He frowned. 'In fact, sometimes I think she just pulls that one when she wants a night out, because I don't remember the original request at all.'

Chloe chuckled, and he knew he was taking the right approach. 'But then I realised it could help.'

Her eyebrows lifted.

'Kelly works in the admin office,' he told her.

'Oh, I didn't know that.'

'News that you've been round for dinner will be all around Kew—and I mean the district, not just the gardens—by noon tomorrow.

'The opening came up a couple of months ago. I saw the notice and suggested she apply. She needed something part-time—something that would fit around the boys and would help build confidence. And, as she told me quite pointedly, to stop her going insane after what seemed like months of being stuck indoors.'

Chloe had been clutching her wine glass against her chest and now she lowered it as she stared out of the windows at the darkening sky. 'She's very brave, isn't she?'

Daniel stopped looking at Chloe, stopped gauging every action and reaction, and joined her in staring out of the window. 'She says she's had to be. Wasn't her choice.'

He knew all about that. Knew all about surviving, not because he was strong and courageous, but because he was still alive and breathing, had found himself trudging onward with no choice about where to put his foot next. Sometimes survival wasn't a choice but a sentence.

But he didn't want to think about those dark days in his life. He wanted fun. He wanted to remember the joy in living.

A waft of Chloe's floral perfume hit him, dragging him back into the present, filling his nostrils and making his pulse kick. He turned to look at her. *This* was what was important. Now. This night, this woman. What he wanted right now was Chloe Michaels.

He caught her gaze, leaned in closer...

But she wasn't going to let him off the hook that easily. 'I haven't got any brothers or sisters,' she said, just the faintest twinge of envy in her voice.

Her parents must have thought they'd won the lottery, then, Daniel thought as he let his eyes rove over her once again. She was beautiful, confident, clever. She'd been their only chance and they'd lucked out. While other people...

Sometimes their only chance was wiped out before it had hardly begun.

He looked away and downed a huge mouthful of wine.

No. He'd shut that door. Done his grieving. He really wasn't going to think about it tonight. That would really be a buzz kill. He needed to get control of himself, of his thoughts.

But Chloe made it very difficult. He'd start on the track of conversation that seemed totally innocent, trying to get her to let down those polished walls a little more, and somehow he'd end up telling her things he didn't normally reveal to anybody—like the fact he had a touch of dyslexia, leading to stories about ridiculous errors with Latin plant names during his student days, something that only another horticulturist would truly appreciate. Or how he'd once accidentally leaned against a macaw palm during an expedition and had been picking its thorny black spines out of his backside for a week.

Talking to her was easy. As it had been with Georgia.

A chill rippled through him.

No. Chloe was nothing like his ex. He needed to remember that. This one was smart and savvy and she knew the game. Georgia…hadn't. But then he hadn't been playing games with Georgia. As cruel as it sounded, he'd just been passing time. And so had Georgia, she'd just tried to tell herself there was more to it.

But what was he doing thinking about his *almost* fiancée? He was losing focus. He'd invited Chloe here tonight with one thing in mind: to move forwards in his plan, and while she was relaxed and smiling he should press on.

He put his wine glass down and went to fetch the bottle from the kitchen counter. He filled his glass first then reclaimed his spot on the sofa, a little closer to Chloe this time, and he leaned across to top her up. She trailed off, losing the thread of what she was talking about, and her eyes widened as the wine filled her glass.

He placed the empty bottle on the table behind her head, but didn't move back. Their faces were only a couple of inches apart now. Unconsciously, she moistened her lips with her tongue, still staring at him.

He let go of the bottle and placed his hand on her shoulder, curling his fingers round her nape. She shivered slightly as his thumb brushed her neck and her gaze dropped to his lips. His core temperature rose.

He slid the glass from her fingers and put it next to the empty bottle. She let him.

He didn't lean in and close the distance, though. Even though the air seemed to shimmer and thud between them. He'd told her the next move would be hers and he was going to stand by his word.

Okay, he hadn't left it completely up to her. He'd made a hundred little moves to manoeuvre her to this point, but the final leap would be all hers. There'd be no backing out then. No more running away and pretending she wasn't interested.

He heard, and felt, the shaky in-breath that parted her lips, watched her eyelids start to slide closed. He closed his eyes too, not wanting to distract himself in the sweet surrender he knew was coming…

There was a crash from the other side of the room, followed by a rhythmic thudding.

'Uncle Daniel!'

He opened his eyes to find Cal standing almost as close to him as he was to Chloe, looking between the two of them with open curiosity.

Chloe pressed herself backwards into the corner of the sofa and looked away.

'There's a crocodile under my bed,' Cal said, quite matter-of-factly. 'He wants to eat my toes.'

'Cal…' Daniel warned, his voice a little sharper than he'd intended it to be.

'He says he's going to gobble me up, bit by bit.' Cal blinked, the picture of childish innocence. Had Kelly put him up to this?

Daniel was still so close to Chloe that he could feel her chest shaking as she tried to suppress a laugh.

Unfortunately, he wasn't finding this the least bit funny. He'd had his own plans for this evening. Maybe of a similar pattern—starting with the toes, and working his way up, bit by bit…

Just that thought alone made him ache.

Reluctantly, he got up off the sofa and took Cal back upstairs. A complete search—involving torches—was made of the under bed area, and it was only when Daniel had tucked the duvet in round his nephew and read him yet another story that Cal consented to lie down and close his eyes.

When he got back downstairs Chloe wasn't on the sofa where he'd left her, but in the hallway, putting on her coat.

'Thanks for a lovely evening,' she said. The dazzling smile she wore informed him that whatever barriers he'd managed to coax down in the last half-hour had sprung up again while he'd been hunting for Cal's crocodile.

Damn.

He couldn't wait another month to try again. It would seem like an eternity.

'Are you sure you don't want another glass of wine?'

Chloe shook her head and her curls bounced. 'I think I've had enough.' The seriousness that crept into her eyes told him she wasn't just talking about the Merlot. But he wasn't quite ready to let her go that easily.

'Think how much it would help our case if Kelly could tell everybody that you'd stayed for breakfast?'

Chloe sighed. 'Daniel... That's not the deal, and you know it.'

Damn again. So close.

'Maybe,' he said, smiling slowly. 'But optimism is one of my most appealing traits.'

At least she laughed. 'Of course it is,' she said and patted him on the arm as if he were an elderly aunt. Ouch.

He wanted to ask her to stay, to give him another chance, but it sounded suspiciously like begging inside his head, and he didn't do begging. Persuading, yes. Pursuing, definitely. But never begging.

The muffled hoot of a car horn outside took him by surprise.

'That's my cab,' she said.

Her cab.

She'd called a cab?

Suddenly Daniel didn't feel as firmly in control as he had been before. He liked the chase, but this quarry was intent on running him in new and unexpected directions. He couldn't quite decide whether he loved it or hated it.

'Night, Daniel,' she murmured, and then, without a flicker of hesitation or nerves, she leaned in close and pressed her lips gently to his cheek.

And then she was gone into the balmy night air, her little handbag swinging off her fingers.

Daniel shut the door when the cab drove away and gave out a loud growl of frustration.

'Uncle Daniel!' The terrified shriek came from Cal's room, and a few seconds later he was standing at the top of the stairs. 'The crocodile's back!' he said between sobs. 'And he's really, really angry.'

Daniel rubbed a hand through his hair and tramped up the stairs, scooping up the small, snivelling boy when he got to the top.

'Don't want to sleep in my room,' Cal hiccupped as Daniel headed across the landing. 'Can't I sleep with you?'

Daniel looked at the clock. Not even nine-thirty. When he'd dreamed of an early night, snuggling up with a warm body in his bed this evening, this was *not* what he'd had in mind.

He took his nephew into his darkened bedroom, making sure the landing light was on and the door wide, and he climbed on top of the covers while Cal slid underneath. It wasn't ten minutes before he could hear small-boy snoring and the rhythmic smack of Cal's lips against his stubby thumb.

Daniel lay there a little longer, just to make sure he didn't wake his nephew when he carried him back to bed. He couldn't be cross, not really. Both boys had been very clingy since their dad had left and Kelly had slipped into the habit of letting them sneak into her bed if they woke in the night.

As he lay there he stared at the wedge of orange light the street lamp had painted on his ceiling and let out a heavy breath. Chloe Michaels was a mystery to him. One minute she was all wide-eyed and trembling at his proximity, the next she was cool and detached and contained.

As much as he hated all those silly women turning up since George's proposal, at least they proved something—that he wasn't totally repellent. Quite the opposite. So why could Chloe resist him so easily? What made her so different? He just had to find out.

Thank goodness for small boys with crocodiles under their beds.

Chloe repeated the phrase to herself a hundred times as she got ready for work the next day.

Normally, she brushed her teeth on automatic, mind drifting, but this morning she watched herself in the mirror, her face free of make-up and her hair hidden beneath a twisted towel. She looked quite different from the woman who'd walked in the door last night.

She'd thought the Mouse was long gone, buried beneath years of being so cool and confident that play-acting had become reality. But she was still there. As Chloe brushed her teeth she occasionally caught a glimpse of her—something about a tightness in her jaw, a flicker of hesitancy in those eyes.

Chloe—the real Chloe—was glad she'd been handed an excuse to leave Daniel the night before. But the Mouse, stupid thing, was feeling all fluttery and excited about the way he'd looked at her, obvious desire in his eyes.

He wasn't looking at you, Chloe told the Mouse in the mirror. *He was looking at me. He likes me.*

The Mouse got all defiant then, asking her why, if Drop-

Dead Daniel liked her, she wasn't doing anything about it. It was safe, after all, if the Mouse was really still safely under lock and key.

Why are you so scared...?

Chloe spat out her toothpaste and rinsed her mouth, and then she met her own eyes in the mirror again.

I'm not scared. It's just a bad idea.

Because...?

We are colleagues. We're... I just...

She pulled the towel from her head and released the damp curls darkened by the recent washing.

Okay, she admitted it. She was worried. Not scared, just a little concerned.

Because, as drop dead as he was, there was something about Daniel Bradford that burrowed beneath her armour.

Maybe it was because she'd liked him before New Chloe had taken form, because she had the oddest feeling he was the one person who had the power to crack her open and release the Mouse. Already the damn creature had come scratching around, making her say stupid things, do stupid things—like not breezily and smoothly disentangling herself when he first pressed his lips to hers in the Palm House. Like saying yes to that second glass of wine instead of going home.

She sighed. The Mouse wanted to relive that memory for a while, but Chloe shut it down swiftly.

No. It couldn't happen. She wouldn't let it. Because she couldn't go back to being that pathetic person. It would be too sad.

So she faced herself down in the mirror again, applied camouflage in the form of foundation and concealer, obliterated the creature with a wave of a magic mascara wand and her favourite tube of Valentine Rose lipstick. And when she was finished, she slid her feet into the highest, most impractical shoes she owned and made the journey to work.

CHAPTER SEVEN

CHLOE FOUND DANIEL waiting for her outside the tropical plant nurseries after work. A large wicker picnic basket was swinging from his hand. She stared at it, already guessing where they were going for their July date. Just as well she'd changed into something casual and summery.

'I hope you like live music,' he said.

She nodded and smiled, determined not to show she was nervous at the prospect of another evening in his company.

While all months at Kew had their own special appeal, July was bold and bright and showy. Everywhere flowers bloomed, filling the gardens with a stunning palette of colours and a cocktail of scents. They walked the half-mile to their destination: past the Palm House, through the Mediterranean garden with its temple, and on to the largest of Kew's glasshouses, the Temperate House.

Each year Kew hosted a week-long music festival, erecting a stage in front of the three-sectioned greenhouse. As dusk fell the Temperate House became the backdrop for the performance, and coloured lights inside would bathe the trees emerald and turquoise and magenta, and bands would play into the night as the audience picnicked on the lawn in front.

The music selection was different each night. There was classical. There was jazz. There were top-name chart acts and old-timers touring on a second wind of fame. Tonight,

Kat de Souza, one of the rising stars of the UK music industry, was playing.

Chloe had asked Emma if she wanted to come, but she'd cried off, saying some hot young guy had turned up at her belly-dancing class a couple of weeks ago and she didn't want to miss one in case he came back. So, secretly, Chloe was very pleased Daniel had chosen this for their July 'date'.

He led her to a reserved section of lawn near the stage, pulled a thick woollen blanket from the top of the basket and spread it on the ground. Chloe sat down as elegantly as she could in her knee-length summer dress, crossing one leg over the other. He wrestled with something in the picnic basket behind her and then there was the distinctive breathy pop of a champagne bottle being opened. Seconds later he passed a slim flute to her.

'Thank you,' she said and took a sip. 'This is lovely, if a bit…well…public.'

He sat down beside her and lounged back, stretching his long legs out and resting on one elbow. 'You complained our last date wasn't public enough.'

'I did not complain. I merely commented,' she said in her smoothest voice.

Daniel chuckled. 'Believe me, after living with my sister for the last year and a half, I am well aware that in the female species those terms are practically interchangeable.'

'Rubbish,' Chloe said, but her lips curled at the edges.

He just raised his eyebrows and did a pretty passable impression of Kelly. 'Daniel, there are muddy boots in the hallway… Daniel, there's some weird compost—like rotting muesli—in the bathroom sink…'

Chloe couldn't help but laugh. She liked this side of Daniel. When she'd first come back to Kew she'd thought him more buttoned-down than before. But he seemed much more like his old self now. Maybe it had just been a result of all the stressful press attention in those early months.

He unpacked the picnic—one of Kew's gourmet affairs that he must have pre-ordered when he'd booked the tickets. Just as well, given Daniel's culinary skills. There were appetisers and Greek salad, poached salmon and strawberries and cream. Chloe helped herself to a miniature tartlet. It was heavenly.

The last month had gone seamlessly. The Mouse had been banished and she and Daniel were executing their plan perfectly. They'd reached a silent understanding after their last date. As a result, it wasn't awkward when they bumped into each other at work any more. He often dropped by her nursery when he was passing, occasionally bringing her a cup of her favourite coffee from the nearby café. They were friends. And if people saw their easy banter and read more into it, then she let them.

The first act came on as the sun fell low in the sky and music permeated the balmy evening air. Chloe leaned back on her hands and felt all the tension melt from her shoulders.

They were good. A lively little swing band that had the audience's toes tapping and heads nodding. She and Daniel worked their way through the picnic and a little more of the champagne. He was attentive, giving her the lion's share of the strawberries, offering to top up her glass if it got too low, and they chatted easily as the band played and twilight fell.

And he was being the perfect gentleman, which made things so much easier.

Chloe sighed with contentment. So she didn't want to get romantically entangled with Daniel. It wasn't a crime to spend time with a man who enjoyed being with her. And he *did* enjoy being with her. She could tell that from every look, every scrap of body language.

She should have paid attention to the wave of warmth that flooded her torso at that thought, but she didn't. She was too busy stripping the ghosts of the past of all their power.

Before, she'd just been a faceless girl to him. One of the

many anonymous bodies in a packed lecture hall. He hadn't known her when he'd pushed her away, told her to get a grip on herself. But now…

Now Daniel did know her, and he liked what he saw. It changed everything.

So when the breeze picked up and Chloe gave a little shiver, causing Daniel to shift closer so she could rest against his shoulder if she wanted to, she didn't wriggle away. And when the swing band finished their set and everyone got up to dance for their final number, she let him pull her to her feet.

The music was so loud that he had to lean in very close to talk into her ear. His breath was warm on her neck. 'You're good at this,' he said, after she spun out and then back in again. 'You've got the moves right down.'

Chloe showed off by doing a tuck and spin. 'I had a few lessons,' she said, a little smugly.

Daniel looked suitably impressed. He twirled her out again perfectly, but when she came back he was closer and she all but crashed into him. Her palm splayed across his chest was the only thing that stopped the entire length of their torsos touching.

'You're a woman of many talents,' he said, sliding his hands round her waist. 'Are you this good at everything you do?'

'I make sure I am,' she replied. She'd meant it quite innocently, but the husky tone to her voice added a whole extra layer of meaning.

Daniel's eyebrows rose in reply and his smile widened. Then he pulled her closer so her temple was pressed against his cheek. 'I'll bet you are,' he whispered into her ear, and Chloe started to shake deep down inside.

The song came to an end and people started clapping. Chloe and Daniel didn't move. An invisible force field had glued them together, even when the applause faded and people started sitting back down to continue eating and drinking in the break before the next artist. The slap of the double bass was still pounding in Chloe's ears, even though the band had left the stage minutes ago.

There was no comfortable, easy conversation now. They'd gone beyond words, the delicious little undercurrent zapping between them was doing all the talking.

Would it really be so bad?

To give in to this tugging deep down inside, the one that was drawing her to Daniel? They were both single, both grown-ups. Wasn't this what she'd wanted—longed for—for years? She couldn't quite remember why she was so set on denying herself now.

While she was still contemplating this, the stage darkened and the crowd hushed in anticipation. Reluctantly, they pulled apart and sat down as Kat de Souza walked onto the stage, her feet bare, in tight fitting jeans, a simple sleeveless black T-shirt and a multitude of necklaces and bangles. When she reached the centre she sat down on a stool. Everyone went quiet. Chloe could even imagine the trees in the arboretum leaning just a little bit closer to listen.

Kat's first song was one of her early hits. Chloe found herself mouthing the words and swaying slightly, knees bent, feet together, body hugged against her knees. She was completely lost in the moment until she heard a deep, rich voice beside her, humming. She turned to find Daniel singing.

She leaned closer so he could hear her without her shouting. 'You know every note.'

He gave a rueful smile. 'Kelly mainlined this album for about three months. I could probably recite the lyrics in my sleep, if I really wanted to. It's not really my kind of stuff, but it grew on me.'

'Let me guess,' Chloe said. 'You're more of a rock guy?'

He smiled at her in a way that made her insides avalanche. She turned to face the stage again and carried on singing silently, feeling a wee bit oxygen starved.

The song was a bewitching one of love and passion and regret, and the magic it wove throughout the crowd deepened the spell working on Chloe. The sky grew dark, the rainbow lights in the Temperate House glowed and the champagne danced in her veins. Daniel shuffled in behind her and she sank back into him, while she kept her eyes on the young woman on the stage.

Every part of her that touched him was fizzing with electricity, and she didn't want it to stop. And that only meant one thing.

Dared she really do this? Was she really that brave?

Daniel moved so he could talk into her ear. 'Your lips are moving, but you're not making any sound.'

She twisted towards him and found his face breathtakingly close. 'How do you know? I was facing away from you and it's too loud to hear me even if I was.'

His arm snaked around her and he flattened his palm against her lower ribs. And then he just looked at her. Looked into her eyes. Looked at her lips. 'I can't feel any vibrations in your torso,' he said quietly.

He couldn't? Chloe sure as hell could.

But he was right—she hadn't been singing.

'Singing is the one thing I've never been any good at, no matter how hard I tried.' And, boy, had she tried. Two years of private singing lessons hadn't been able to get a good note out of her.

Strangely, this made Daniel smile.

'What?' she said, knowing her cheeks were colouring further.

'It's nice to know you've got a few imperfections like the rest of us.'

He'd meant it as a compliment, but Chloe couldn't help the instinctive bristling at his words. A spike of something cold went through her. She was an attractive, confident, sexy woman now. It had been a long time since her parents' suffocating ambition for her had weighed on her heavily. She knew she didn't have to be brilliant at everything, but it was hard to let go of the little inner push that told her to try harder, be better. And she was feeling a little of that pressure tonight.

New Chloe had been her most important self-improvement package to date. What was the point in excelling at Italian cooking or swing dancing or Spanish guitar if you failed at the most important thing—being a woman? Deep down inside, even if she hadn't admitted it to herself, her decade-long quest had been to turn herself into the kind of woman Daniel Bradford wouldn't turn down. And tonight, if she was brave enough, she could have her answer. One way or another.

Oh, the thought scared her so. She went to turn her head away, catch her breath for a moment, but he caught it with his hand, hooking his fingers round the curve of her neck, letting his thumb trail her cheek. 'Don't.'

She held her breath.

This was it, wasn't it? She could reach for what she wanted—what she'd always wanted—or she could shrink back like a coward.

She took in every feature of his face, lingering over the line of his jaw, the not quite straight nose, the tiny scar she'd never noticed before almost completely hidden by his left eyebrow.

And he held still and let her, meeting her gaze. Not flinching, as she might well have done.

This wasn't the same as that awful night in the pub car park ten years ago. How could it be? He'd been giving her the signals for months. He wasn't going to push her away, this time. He wasn't going to run.

She swallowed and dropped her gaze to his lips, knew the exact moment he did the same.

Stop, a voice inside her head said. *You've been here before. You remember how it ends.* But even this voice sounded half-hearted and unconvincing.

Keeping her eyes fixed on the firm curve of his lower lip, she leant forward to taste it.

Daniel stayed completely still at first, letting her discover the hint of strawberries still lingering on his mouth. She took her time, exploring fully—the little dents at the corners of his lips, the fullness of the bottom one, the sculptured curve of the top.

And then something seemed to snap inside him and he hauled her onto his lap and took over. If Chloe had thought that sweet, slow exploration had been worth a decade of waiting, Daniel's fully-loaded response was more than she ever could have imagined. It swept conscious thought and common sense completely from her brain.

Daniel's head was spinning. Kissing Chloe was every bit as good as he remembered. Possibly better. Because this time she wasn't blindsided, taken by surprise. This time he'd let her come to him, let her take charge.

Why, for heaven's sake, had he never used this approach before? He'd still been hunting, but it hadn't been a crashing-through-the-forest kind of hunting; it had been patient and stealthy, all about the wait rather than the pursuit, and the prolonged anticipation had only made the final moment so much sweeter. Instead of feeling as if he'd worn her down, broken something inside her to let him in, he felt alive because she was blooming right there in his arms.

When they pulled away from each other, her eyes stayed closed, a delicious little smile on her lips. Daniel was very tempted just to lean in close and taste them again, but he wanted her to open her eyes and look at him.

She was a contradiction, this Chloe Michaels. He'd expected her to be as slick and expert with her lips as she was in everything else. She was, but not in the way he'd anticipated. There'd been a rawness, a sweetness, an exuberance to her response that had caught him totally by surprise.

Her lids parted and she held his gaze.

It was there. What he'd been waiting to see, even though he couldn't quite put a name to it.

Once wasn't enough. Not nearly enough. But he had to keep reminding himself he was sitting on a lawn with a couple of thousand other people, and that it might not be the greatest idea to keep going right now. He knew where he wanted to spend the night, and it wasn't in a police cell.

As good as the music was, it was torture to wait for Kat to finish her set. He kept in contact with Chloe any way he could. He wrapped himself around her, linking his arms in front, pressing butterfly kisses into her neck and hearing the low noises of appreciation deep in her throat as she closed her eyes and tilted her head to give him better access.

Eventually, the last chord was played, the applause welled and faded, and the stage lights dimmed. People around them began to move. Daniel reluctantly peeled himself away from Chloe and stood up.

'I'll be back in a second,' he told her and disappeared off to a marquee to dispose of the now-empty picnic basket and supplies.

When he returned, he saw her long before he cleared the rest of the crowd. She was the only thing in focus as he made his way towards her, the soft smile on her lips, the way her eyes took on extra sparkle when she looked at him… It was making his blood simmer.

He had to kiss her again when he reached her, couldn't help himself, couldn't get close enough.

'This time I'm taking you home,' he said, stepping away and turning in the direction of the car park.

She tugged him back and delayed him with another swift kiss. 'Not that way,' she murmured huskily. 'We can walk through the gardens and leave through the gate near the river. I only live a few minutes from there.'

Daniel thought of the modern apartment blocks on the

other side of the river. Dark wood, white stucco and steel. They suited her perfectly. Stylish, modern, free from any clutter and complications.

They walked through the gardens in silence. Every now and then they paused to kiss—one moment with her pressed up against the rough bark of a tree, the next in the middle of a lonely path, beautiful vistas spreading out unseen around them in every direction. Each meeting of their bodies and lips grew more heated, more frantic. Daniel realised he needed to slow this down a little or he'd explode before they even reached the boundary of the park. As wonderful as making love to Chloe on the soft dark grass would be, if Security caught them they'd both be out of a job in the morning.

Finally they reached Brentford Gate and walked through the car park and along the tow path. The lights in the apartment blocks glinted temptingly across the water and he willed himself to last until they got there. However, it was only a few steps before Chloe stopped and turned.

'Here we are,' she said.

Daniel frowned and looked around. There were no houses here, just trees. Not even a path or a gate to a back garden, as there were farther up the tow path.

'No…this way,' she said softly and tugged at his hand. He turned one-eighty, but all he could see past the row of houseboats was the river, glinting gold and silver from the moon and the streetlights on the far bank.

Houseboats…

He stopped looking at the water and turned his attention back to Chloe. 'Here?'

'Come aboard,' she said, pulling his hand and heading down a narrow gangplank to a double-storey boat with a flat roof, decorated with enamel buckets full of summer flowers.

He was a little confused at first. This really wasn't the sort of place he'd pictured her living in. It was charming enough, but it wasn't slick and luxurious like Chloe herself.

However, he quickly decided he didn't really care where she lived. That she was actively dragging him inside was the important thing, surely?

He followed her down into the cabin, and the interior was as much of a surprise as the outside. Half of the top deck was a living-dining-kitchen area with vast square windows one end that led onto a railed deck.

No clean lines and minimalist furniture here. It was a riot of colour and texture. Two purple velvet sofas that didn't match, embroidered and bejewelled cushions in pinks, reds and oranges. Bookcases lined one wall, full of not only gardening books and paperbacks, but all other kinds of ornaments. And, of course, there were orchids. Various common varieties, but also some spectacular rarer ones too.

Chloe walked over to the kitchen and kicked off her shoes. 'I'm afraid my drinks selection is rather sparse,' she confessed. 'Unless you're really gasping for mineral water, it's just white wine.'

He nodded. 'That'll do fine.'

He knew he should sound more enthused, but he couldn't quite stop looking around Chloe's living room. It wasn't just that every corner held something that drew the eye, but that he felt something about it was significant. Something he was missing.

He walked over to the kitchen and took a glass she offered. Without her shoes on she was just that little bit shorter, which, for some strange reason, also made her seem younger.

'I didn't picture you living on a houseboat,' he told her.

She smiled at him. 'I always wanted to, ever since I was a student here and used to walk past them on my journey from Kew Bridge station. When I got the chance to rent one, I jumped at it.'

He took a sip of his wine. 'Of course, I forgot you said you trained here. When was that? Our paths might have crossed.

I've been doing specialist lectures here for what…maybe eight or nine years?'

Chloe suddenly found something very urgent to do in the fridge. She opened the door, blocking his view of her, and rummaged around inside.

Daniel smiled to himself. Possibly not. He'd certainly have remembered seeing someone like Chloe amongst the muddy hordes of horticultural students. She stood out in a crowd, wasn't like the rest. That was what he liked about her.

Anyway, he was much more interested in the here and now. Chloe was still leaning into the large retro-style fridge and he walked up behind her and slid his hands around her waist. Whatever she'd been looking for in there obviously hadn't been very important, because she stood up, let the fridge door bang closed and turned to face him, her face serious, her pupils wide.

He dipped his head low and kissed her. Softly, slowly. This had been a long time coming and he didn't want to rush things. Strangely, it seemed as if he were kissing her for the first time. Maybe it was this place—or this slightly shy and nervous Chloe—that made him feel as if this were all fresh and new.

Whatever it was, he decided both of them were wearing far too many clothes, even though, including lingerie, Chloe must have only had three garments on. Heat flooded through him. He didn't care which one went first—each presented an interesting option—but something needed to go, and it needed to go now.

He'd never been one for noting clothes designers, but he blessed the man, because it had almost certainly been a man, who'd decided to put a long row of little hooks and eyes down the front of Chloe's tight-bodiced floral dress. His fingers fairly itched at the thought of starting at the top and working his way down.

Maybe he was wrong about three garments. Maybe a little

exploration in that department would yield even richer results. He'd been kissing her neck, hands roving her back, and now he moved on to either side of her waist, then he picked up and deposited her on the kitchen counter. She ran her hands up his chest and into his hair, pulling him back to kiss her on the mouth, pulling him closer and hooking her lower calves around his thighs to keep him there.

In Daniel's experience, some women let a man take charge completely when it came to the physical stuff but he much preferred it if there was equality, give and take, when they got to this moment. So he liked the fact that Chloe not only responded to him but spurred him on, took him in new and unexpected directions.

Even better, he could tell by the way she threw her head back and closed her eyes, the little noises she made in the back of her throat, the unchoreographed motions of her hands, that none of this was rehearsed moves or seductive tricks. She was totally lost in the moment, and this response that had his clothes feeling three sizes too small was just pure Chloe.

He pulled away from kissing her to focus his eyes on the top of her dress. The hooks were tiny. He could've undone them by touch alone, but he wanted to see her, every perfect inch, when he reached low enough to uncover what was underneath.

Chloe was kissing his face, and when she felt the pads of his thumbs graze the upper curve of her breasts as he reached for the first hook she made a sharp intake of breath and held it. Her legs hugged him tighter, pulling him as close as he could possibly get still clothed.

Daniel suddenly questioned the hook-by-hook approach. What idiot made something so small and fiddly? He was really tempted to just start ripping.

Chloe fidgeted again, but this time she placed her hands lightly on his chest. 'Daniel…' she whispered.

He leant in and began to tease her ear lobe with his tongue. 'Uh-huh?'

There was a little bit of a push behind those palms now. He drew back, confused. Were they both not on the same track? Had he read her wrong somehow?

But the pink flush creeping up her creamy skin from breasts to face told him he'd been reading the situation just right. 'Are you okay?' he asked softly.

'Oh, yes,' she said, nodding emphatically. 'More than okay.'

Daniel smiled. Not just because she was as into this as he was, but because he'd never seen this flustered, slightly dishevelled side to Chloe before, and he kind of liked it. Somehow it made her seem all the more human. Which translated into making her seem all the more touchable. His gaze drifted back to the single opened hook at the centre of her breasts.

'I just need to…' Chloe shakily pushed her hair back off her face and released her legs from around his. 'There's just something I need to do…I'll be right back.'

'Promise?' he said, feeling a lot more desperate than he actually sounded.

She smiled sweetly at him, and pressed a kiss against his lips. 'Promise,' she murmured as she pulled away.

She jumped down from the counter and picked up her shoes. 'I won't be long.'

He wandered over to the bookcase. His eyes instantly found a spine that was so familiar he couldn't help but prise it from its position. She turned as she reached the door and saw what he was doing.

She smiled saucily. 'Isn't that a little vain? Picking your own book out from the bookshelf?' Forgetting her urgent errand, she walked over to him. '*The Secrets of Mount Kinabalu* by Daniel Bedford,' she read from the cover. 'I got this as a student. Your description of the orchids is what fired my interest in them.'

He shook his head, both frowning and smiling at the same time. 'I can't believe you've got this,' he said. 'And it looks as if it's been read a hundred times.'

Chloe stiffened slightly but then she smiled her cat-like smile again. 'I lent it out to other people in my year. It was kind of a favourite.'

'That's a lot of people with a burning interest in carnivorous plants and other rare species,' he said.

Chloe just laughed, reached out and turned the book over, where there was a horrible picture of him in khaki clothes and a wide-brimmed hat. 'I think this is what some of them had the burning interest in,' she said. 'This is where the whole Indiana Jones thing started, wasn't it?'

He nodded grimly. He hadn't made the connection before, but he supposed it was. 'Some fool publicist's idea. I've always hated the stupid picture.'

'I'll bet you sold a load more books because of it, though. Didn't I hear talk of a TV series once?'

Daniel snorted. 'I knocked that one on the head pretty fast.'

She took the book from him and leafed through it, smiling as if she was remembering happy memories. She stopped at a colourful plate of a particularly rare slipper orchid. 'Did you really take this picture? See it yourself?'

He gave her a one-sided smile and nodded.

'I wish I could,' she said wistfully. 'I can't think of anything more beautiful.'

He reached for her face, brushed a golden tendril away from her cheek and slid his fingers into her hair before pulling her closer for a soft, sweet kiss. 'I've seen it for myself,' he whispered, 'but, believe me, it's nothing compared to what's in front of me right now.'

Chloe caught him by surprise. She threw her arms around his neck, gave him a hot, drawn-out kiss, promising all sorts of things that got him very excited indeed. And it hadn't even been a line. He really did think she was more stunning than the speckles and stripes of the elusive flower.

When she finally pulled away, she rested her forehead against his and breathed out hard.

'Didn't you say you…had something to do?' he said hoarsely.

She nodded wordlessly and he let his arms drop.

As much as he didn't want to let her go, he didn't want to interrupt things later on. Daniel didn't want to be distracted by anything next time he had Chloe in his arms. Not for hours and hours and hours.

CHAPTER EIGHT

CHLOE RAN QUICKLY and lightly down the narrow hallway that led to her bedroom. Once inside she pulled the duvet straight and plumped a pillow, then turned her attention to the other item that needed to be dealt with: the graduation photo sitting on her bedside table.

Ugh. Frizzy hair and badly applied eyeshadow.

She only displayed it in the privacy of her bedroom because she was really, really proud of her qualifications, even if the tight smiles of her parents standing behind her reminded her how they'd have preferred for her to go to a big-hitting university and get a 'proper' degree.

She couldn't risk just putting it face down, so she pulled the underwear drawer of her dressing table open and stuffed the frame under the tangle of straps and things. But the sight of some of her better underwear sitting in the top of the drawer made her stop and think.

She hadn't been planning on anyone seeing her underwear when she'd got dressed this morning. It was nude-coloured and functional. Nice enough, just not pretty like those were.

And you're planning on someone seeing your underwear now?

Chloe thought for a moment.

Hell, yeah.

The problem was that her current bra was strapless and her dress had spaghetti straps. It would be weird if she changed into her eye-wateringly expensive silk and lace set and went out there with hot-pink straps showing. Not very subtle.

Forget subtle. Ditch the dress and go back out there in just the pink satin with the creamy lace trim.

Chloe let out a gasp. She couldn't, could she? She'd never been quite that bold before—at least, not on a first night together. It wasn't her.

Or was it?

The Chloe she'd invented for herself to grow into would do it. She was sassy and worldly-wise and confident. Maybe she never had before, but that was because she liked a man to do all the running, to *prove* he was interested. And, deep down, if she admitted it to herself, she liked it that way because then it was him not her who had to endure that horrible feeling of free fall once he'd made the first move and was waiting to see if she'd accept or reject him.

But this time it was different. The way Daniel had been looking at her…touching her… Well, she was pretty sure he wasn't going to try and fend her off this time.

Maybe she needed to do this. Not to get him to prove anything, but to prove something to herself.

Quickly, before she could talk herself out of it, she stripped off her underwear and reached for the pink silk. Once it was on, she turned to inspect herself in the mirror.

There were a few lumps and bumps she wished weren't there. After prodding her stomach, which jiggled a little, she looked longingly at the functional bra and knickers and sundress on the floor. There was something about walking out there as she was now that made her feel very…naked.

She looked herself in the eye and pulled herself up straight, sucked things in a little. That was what New Chloe would do. So she had a few curves, but Daniel didn't seem to mind, and she wasn't that blobby little nineteen-year-old any more. New Chloe knew she worked out, that she was toned. New Chloe knew she looked good.

She bent down, picked up her discarded clothes and threw them in the wardrobe. A pair of hot-pink heels winked at her from inside and she quickly reached for them and slid them on her feet. Then, without looking back, she strutted down the corridor back to the living room, reminding herself to breathe.

Since Daniel had picked up a framed photo of her on holiday last year, she took the opportunity of reaching for the dimmer switch and taking the lighting down to a more *intimate* level as she entered the room.

The change in brightness made him look up and round to where she was standing.

He dropped the frame.

It bounced on the floor but didn't break.

The look on his face right then was all Chloe needed to wipe all those years of insecurity away. Never had she felt so feminine, so beautiful…so wanted.

She could pull this off, she really could. New Chloe had been a project that had worked from the outside in, but she had the feeling that after tonight that version of herself would no longer be a work in progress. One night with Daniel Bradford would banish the Mouse for ever and cement New Chloe into place. The transformation would be complete.

Since Daniel didn't seem capable of movement at the moment, let alone speech, she walked slowly towards him, crouched to pick up the picture—aware that the angle of her knees and the high heels were doing amazing things for her legs—and handed it back to him and nodded towards the bookcase. He replaced it without taking his eyes off her.

And then, taking advantage of his paralysed state, which only gave her some kind of weird exultant power, she gave him a gentle shove and he sat down suddenly on the sofa. She had one knee on the sofa beside his leg, preparing to slide onto his lap, when he shifted slightly and reached beneath him. He pulled out the book—his book—that she'd thrown there earlier. Knowing they were definitely not going to be doing any reading in the next few hours, Chloe took it from his fingers and tossed it onto the adjacent sofa cushion.

As she did so a slip of coloured paper dislodged itself from the pages and fluttered to land on Daniel's lap. He picked it up and stared at it. Chloe took the opportunity to place her other knee on the sofa and sank down until soft, rounded bottom met hard thighs. She attempted to pluck the paper from his hands, but he wouldn't let go.

'What's this?' he asked, obviously having recovered the use of his tongue. Chloe wasn't very happy about that. For the money she'd paid for this bra and the way it made her boobs look he should have been drooling, his tongue thick in his mouth, for at least another half-hour.

He frowned. 'Who...? Why have you got this?'

It was then she realised it was a photograph.

'That's me,' he said, sounding slightly dazed, 'in the middle.'

Chloe's stomach rocketed down so hard she reckoned it had gone through the hull of her houseboat and was now wedged in the mud at the bottom of the river.

She'd forgotten all about that photo, tucked lovingly in the back of her favourite book, the one she'd never, *ever* lent to anyone else. A snap someone had taken on the last day of Daniel's tropical plants course of a bunch of students and their much-admired lecturer.

'Oh, that,' she said blithely, trying once again to dislodge it from his fingers without seeming as if she was desperate. 'That's from my college days.'

'You attended my course?' he asked, still looking at the photo and not the pink lingerie. That was starting to annoy Chloe.

She let out a huff of air. 'I told you I was a student at Kew,' she said.

Finally, he made eye contact. He still wasn't letting go of the photo, though. 'Why didn't you say anything?'

Chloe swallowed. What was she going to tell him? That she was the girl who'd humiliated herself in front of him? No way. 'When we first met it was obvious you didn't remember me—why would you?—so I decided not to bring it up. I didn't want to make you feel awkward.'

Hah! Biggest fib ever. It had been nothing to do with not wanting *Daniel* to feel awkward.

He frowned and looked back at the photograph. 'I do remember a few of these people,' he said slowly, his eyes flitting between one face and the next.

Chloe decided drastic measures were needed. In a few seconds he'd realise *she* was in that photo. And while he hadn't put two and two together yet, that didn't mean he wouldn't if he stared at it long enough.

She peeled his fingers from the photograph, let it flutter to the floor and placed his hands high on her waist, just on her lower ribs, and then she leaned forward and delivered the kiss of her life.

Thankfully, after a few seconds, she felt him relax, felt his jaw soften as he kissed her back. She let him set the pace, take control, knowing that was what he needed at that moment to keep his mind occupied. Within sixty seconds she wasn't thinking about anything but his lips and the lazy circles his thumbs were making on her torso, travelling slowly upward. If he didn't get to that pink silk soon she was going to explode.

Just as he'd pulled her closer, as his thumb had grazed the underside of her breast and Chloe had let out a low moan, his hands slowed down. And then they stopped. She tried to keep on kissing him but eventually his lips stopped too. He pulled away.

Chloe's heart raced, and not from the recent thumb activity. This time her pulse was struggling to push frozen blood through her veins.

He leaned past her to reach for the photograph at his feet, and Chloe slowly climbed off his lap. He picked it up and looked first at the photo and back at her, then he studied the photo again.

When he spoke his words were measured and cool. 'Where are you in this photograph?'

Chloe shook her head, lips moving, not able to produce any sound.

Daniel's brows lowered. 'Don't lie to me,' he said. 'Don't tell me you're not in here.'

A tiny noise escaped her mouth. The kind of weak croak any self-respecting frog would be ashamed of.

The urge to curl up and hide was irresistible. She knelt on the other side of the sofa and buried her face in her hands, hiding her exposed flesh as much as possible.

Daniel leapt to his feet. 'All the time it was you and you never told me! What is this? Some kind of sick joke? You're…you're just like the rest of them…just another obsessive woman.'

The tears began to stream down Chloe's face. She wiped the first wave away and looked at him, still trying to curl into the sofa and disappear. 'That's not true! I made it quite clear from the beginning I didn't want to get involved, but you just kept wearing me down…'

He let out a harsh, dry laugh. The look on his face was pure revulsion. 'That was all part of the plan, wasn't it? And I fell for it—hook, line and sinker. That idea to "help" me out with those fake dates…' He shook his head, as if he was hardly able to believe the thoughts running through his head. 'God, I was suckered right in, wasn't I?'

Anger was taking over now, and Chloe let it. It was a much better sensation than cold humiliation. She stood up and folded her arms tightly across her chest. 'There was no plan! You're being paranoid.' She walked right up to him. He backed away.

That hurt.

'Admit it!' she yelled. 'You did all the chasing. You wouldn't leave me alone. That wasn't a trick. You *wanted* me!'

His expression set like stone. 'I wanted *her*,' he said softly, almost too reasonably. 'The woman I thought you were. Not—' he gestured towards the photo still in his right hand '—this.'

Chloe's ribs tightened so hard that she couldn't open her mouth to breathe.

'I would never want *this*,' he said, glaring at the photo and then transferring that scalding gaze to her. 'Not the sort of person who lies and manipulates, who can't just come out and tell the truth. I can't believe you strung me along for so long,' he said, shaking his head. 'You played me for a right fool. But, you know what? I'm not the fool here—you are.'

He looked her up and down one last time before snarling his last judgement. 'You're pathetic.'

And then he turned and strode out of the door.

Daniel's team kept out of his way the following day. Every time he entered a room in the tropical plant nursery it wouldn't exactly empty immediately, but after about ten minutes of concentrated work he'd look up to find himself totally alone. He was so angry he couldn't see straight.

Much more so than when Georgia had made her stupid proposal. He understood now that his ex's actions had been a combination of a ticking biological clock mixed with a healthy dose of panic. It had been a daft reflex action, and he could forgive her for that.

But Chloe...

Chloe had lied.

He'd thought he'd been so clever, carefully reeling her in, when all along it had been the other way around. She wasn't an orchid at all. She was a sneaky, twisting, climbing weed.

There was a cracking sound and he realised he'd been gripping a square plastic pot a little too tightly. That was the third one today. For punishment he threw it across the nursery.

There was a flash of movement near the door, and he turned to find Alan standing there, waving a blue and white checked tea towel above his head.

'What are you doing?' Daniel barked.

Alan stopped waving and let his arm drop to his side. 'It was the closest I could find to a white flag,' he muttered.

'Don't be ridiculous!' Daniel said. He hadn't been that bad, had he?

'I have staff volunteering for manure duty,' Alan said, 'just so they can get out of here for the afternoon. What the hell is wrong with you?'

Daniel just gave him a thunderous look.

Alan nodded knowingly. 'Ah, woman trouble.' He put the tea towel down on the bench near the door and walked over to Daniel. 'What's Fancy Knickers done now?'

'Shut up, Alan,' Daniel said.

He didn't want to think about Chloe. Especially not combined with the phrase Fancy Knickers. He'd been having rogue flashbacks enough as it was, and he didn't want to prompt any more.

Too late.

An image of her leaning over him as he sat on the sofa, a pale thigh either side of his jeans, and the ringside view of just what a good bra could do for a cleavage assaulted him.

He batted the image away, attempting to replace it with the tacky-leaved *Drosera* on the bench in front of him. It wasn't much competition, really. His mind started to slide in the wrong direction once again.

He made himself focus on the plant. *Remember*, he told himself, *they're both the same really—covered in sweetness that promises heaven but is really a fatal trap.* One he'd only just survived before. Nothing on earth would tempt him to go back there again.

'Have you seen her today?' he asked Alan. Daniel hadn't. Which meant she'd had the good sense to keep out of his way.

Alan shook his head. 'She didn't come in this morning.'

That just stoked Daniel's anger further. Not just a liar but a coward, too.

'What did she do, mate?' Alan asked. 'It has to be pretty monumental to get you in this state.'

'She… She…'

What *had* she done?

His brain flooded with images from the night before: Chloe, sweet and sexy, half naked and responsive beneath his hands… Her easy smile and that killer body… That darn tiny hook at the top of her dress.

He opened his mouth and then shut it again. Telling Alan she'd invited him back to her place, stripped down to the most eye-popping lingerie he'd ever seen and then had tried to seduce him just didn't sound very awful. Alan definitely wouldn't understand.

In fact, at the mercy of the movie reel of memories inside his own head, Daniel was finding it harder to understand it himself.

But then another image in his brain came sharply into focus—the photograph that had been hidden in the book— and suddenly his anger came flooding back.

She'd promised him one thing and then had delivered him something else entirely.

Promised you?

Yes. Promised him. With every wiggle of her hips, with every cool and casual comment, every retreat when he'd advanced. She'd made him believe they were the same, that they wanted the same thing. And it hadn't been true at all.

He could have slept with her anyway, but that wasn't his style, and he knew it would have been a mistake. Those tendrils, like jungle creepers, would have started to wind around him, to suffocate him.

'It's complicated,' he told Alan. 'You know women.'

Alan nodded sagely.

'I'll be fine in a while,' Daniel told him. 'I just need to let off some steam first.'

Alan chuckled. 'The rate you're going, we can just turn the misters and the heating off and let you regulate the nursery single-handed.'

Daniel let out a reluctant laugh.

Alan walked back over to the door. 'That's the problem with women. We want to chase them, but we then have to deal with them when we catch them.'

You did all the chasing...

Chloe's words from the evening before echoed round his head. He had chased her. He'd chased hard. The fact she was right only made him more angry.

But that had been part of his downfall. He'd been so busy trying to break down her barriers that he hadn't realised he hadn't been tending his own.

He picked up the *Drosera* and inspected it closely. Tiny black flies decorated its sticky leaves.

Stupid man, he told himself. *Because you thought she was safe, that she didn't want diamonds and confetti and wedding rings, you let yourself like her.* Because he had genuinely liked being with her. It hadn't all been about getting her into bed.

He hadn't wanted her to be one of those clingy, silly women who just threw themselves at him. He'd wanted to spend time with her, have a wild and crazy affair that lasted as long as it lasted. And who wouldn't? Because, despite how she'd acted in the past, the Chloe Michaels of today was clever and funny and sexy, and she'd reminded him of who he'd used to be before...

A chill settled over him. Maybe that was why. Maybe, even though he hadn't realised it, because she was from that time in his life when he was really happy, he'd recognised that on some subconscious level, been drawn to it.

Which meant he had to stay away from her now. He didn't want any memories of that time. Because remembering the good years meant remembering what came after. And it had taken him too long travelling the world, seeking adventure to make him forget.

He was good at forgetting. At blocking out.

And now he had one more thing to block out from his life—Chloe Michaels.

Chloe was very glad that the day after her sickie was a Saturday and she wasn't due to go in to work. She did better than the previous day, where she'd mostly sat in the cramped space between her bed and her chest of drawers, her back to the wall, and cried. She made it out of her bedroom and into the living room. Not for long, though. Every stick of furniture in her room seemed to have some link with Thursday night.

The problem with living so close to the botanical gardens was that she was scared to go outside in case she met someone from work. In the end, she resorted to desperate measures and rang her parents to say she was coming home for the weekend for a surprise visit.

Mum and Dad were just as they always were. They looked after her, they fed her cups of tea and shortcake—which was all lovely—but then there were the dinner-table conversations. How pleased they were that she was working somewhere as prestigious as Kew, even if was just looking after one tiny section. Never mind. In a few years she could go for promotion and really do something.

Chloe wanted to tell them she was doing something, that she loved her job and didn't yearn for corporate headship, or knighthood—or sainthood—whatever it was they wanted for her, but she didn't have the energy. Besides, if they kept on about her professional life they wouldn't ask about her personal life.

It had started a couple of years ago. First the veiled questions, but they'd grown less and less subtle. Had she met anyone nice? Was anyone serious about her? Of course, she'd always looked better with longer hair so maybe she should grow it out, and she'd do well not to forget that it was all downhill after thirty and they really wanted some grandchildren while her eggs were still good.

They meant well, they really did.

But Chloe didn't need a reminder that her personal life was going down the toilet. At least, if her parents kept on about work, she'd avoid having to tell them it had been her who'd pulled the chain.

But Monday would not be put off for ever.

She woke before dawn and stared at her ceiling, listening to the planes coming in to land at Heathrow, her stomach churning. She really didn't want to go in. She couldn't face it, couldn't face seeing him, especially after what he'd said to her.

You're pathetic.

Those words had lodged in her chest like an arrow's shaft and would not be shaken loose.

She *was* pathetic. What serious, grown-up horticulturist fantasised about taking a taxi to the airport, buying a one-way ticket and just getting on a plane? Any plane. As long as it took her thousands of miles away.

Five months. That was all she'd had in her dream job before it had turned into a nightmare.

Even though it was not yet six, Chloe dragged herself out of bed and made herself get dressed. Lying there feeling sorry for herself was not going to help. She needed to get ready, get some serious armour in place if she was going to survive today, both physical and emotional. If there was one thing she was not going to give up it was her job. Daniel Bradford would just have to deal with that.

She'd chosen her usual confidence-boosting uniform of pink blouse and black skirt, but when she opened her wardrobe to look for matching shoes she realised they were still under her bed where she'd kicked them off after Daniel had left. She staggered back from the open wardrobe and her bottom met the end of the bed with a bump. For a few seconds, she stared straight ahead, but then she reached underneath the bed and her fingers closed around the hard and spiky heel of a pink stiletto. She pulled it out and stared at it.

She didn't ever want to wear those shoes again. She certainly didn't want to wear them today. Daniel would just think she was sending him some creepy, stalker-type message or something. The man was paranoid.

And vain. And arrogant.

And so gorgeous she couldn't think straight.

How—after all he'd said to her, after how he'd made her feel—could she still be attracted to him? Daniel Bradford was right. She *was* pathetic. She needed to get herself a life, and she needed to do it fast.

Which, unfortunately, meant she really was going to have to get up off her backside and go to work today. Because work was all she had left at the moment.

She threw the pink heel into the back of her wardrobe, plucked its twin from under the bed and did the same, then pulled out some less spectacular black shoes with a lower heel. They were comfortable, though, she thought as she slid her feet into them, which would be good, because she'd bet those shoes were the only thing that was going to be comfortable about her working day today.

CHAPTER NINE

CHLOE WALKED INTO the tropical nurseries with her head held high and went straight to her section, looking neither to the left nor the right. She didn't care where Daniel was. If she ran into him, she ran into him. But she wasn't going to give the other staff a show by confronting him. She knew what they called her behind her back, but today she was going to be *Classy Knickers* instead of *Fancy Knickers*.

She reached her section and began checking out the various orchids she was propagating. Still that one *Paphiopedilum* she'd grown from an unidentified seed refused to flower, no matter what she did. She'd noticed from the package that it had come from Georgia Stone at the Millennium Seed Bank. Daniel's ex.

Perhaps it was absorbing all her pent up guilt at wanting him after he'd ditched the other woman so publicly. Georgia needn't worry, though. Now Chloe was part of the same exclusive club. As humiliating as being turned down live on air must have been, at least she hadn't been wearing just her underwear. Underwear supposedly guaranteed to provoke an entirely different reaction in the male of the species.

Chloe shook her head and tried to banish those thoughts by searching for tips on the Internet and emailing other enthusiasts, but she couldn't lose herself in her work as she normally did. Every sense—especially her hearing—was on full alert. In the backstage area of her brain she was straining to hear his deep, rich voice. And whatever it was that was working overtime just didn't seem to have an off switch.

In the end she gave up trying. Every sound had her jumping out of her skin. As much as she told herself she didn't care if she saw him, she really did. She was just dreading seeing that same look of disgust in his eyes, telling her she was pointless and pathetic.

She decided to get some fresh air, go down to the Princess of Wales Conservatory and check on her orchids. There was something soothing about the two rooms filled with logs and ferns and perfect flowers. She and Daniel had discussed doing a joint display around the little boggy pool in the Temperate Orchid section—long-fluted pitcher plants mixed with delicate woodland orchids—but that obviously wasn't going to happen now, so she might as well head down there and get some new ideas.

Walking back through the network of nurseries to the entrance was skin-crawlingly embarrassing. Not many people had seen her arrive, but now word must have gone round because they were certainly watching her leave. Every time she passed a door the noise level dropped as those inside stopped what they were doing.

It only made her tip her chin higher, straighten her spine further.

They'd be calling her *Iron Knickers* by the end of the day, because she'd be blasted if she'd let any of them see her crumble. It had been bad enough to have Daniel witness her steady disintegration. She didn't need their pity. Didn't want it.

The short walk to the conservatory was like an oasis in a desert of stress. Though there were a handful of Kew employees around, they were rolling wheelbarrows or chopping down trees. None of them stopped and stared. The gossip obviously hadn't reached the tree gang or the bedding crew yet, but it would.

She'd walked via the quieter paths to the south entrance

of the glasshouse, and then she zigzagged down its angular paths, keeping to the side routes as much as possible. She was within feet of one of the orchid enclosures when she saw a figure she recognised coming from the offices hidden under the earth and foliage.

Emma. But instead of saying something totally inappropriate, the other woman merely laid a sympathetic hand on her arm. 'How are you doing?'

The contact seemed to burn like acid. Chloe had a sudden and horrifying flashback to the day the woman in the raincoat had pounced on Daniel. They were standing in almost exactly the same spot where she'd rubbed the woman's arm and spoke comforting words. Never in a million years had Chloe expected to be on the receiving end of the same pitying looks.

Poor Chloe. Just another one of Drop-Dead Daniel's corpses...

She stiffened under Emma's touch. 'Okay.'

The other woman studied her face. 'Really?'

Chloe's stomach dropped like a plummeting lift and she nodded dumbly. 'I don't really want to talk about it,' she said scratchily.

Emma just nodded sympathetically and returned to her work. None of the usual platitudes, but that wasn't really Emma. Nothing about the healing properties of time, or alternative fishing locations. Nothing about Chloe being too good for him anyway.

Because everyone knew that wasn't true.

Especially Daniel.

She walked stiffly to the plate glass door that led to the orchid enclosure, relishing the climate-controlled cool air on her skin after the humidity of the Wet Tropics zone. Once there she stared into one of the display cases—rarer specimens protected by a wall of glass—and exhaled.

She'd been so stupid, hadn't she?

For a decade she'd been turning herself into a turbo-charged, bionic version of herself, determined to never be the sort of woman a man like Daniel could ever reject, and it hadn't worked.

He'd run from the frizzy-haired mouse.

He'd also run from New Chloe. Twice as fast.

She didn't know what to do now, didn't know who to be. Her best just hadn't been good enough, not by a long shot, and she didn't have the energy to build better and higher. Not yet.

She turned around, pressed her back against the glass and let her knees buckle under her until she was crouching on the floor. The display across the enclosure was beautiful, rocks and logs, dripping with colourful blooms. It was like salve to her jagged emotions.

Perhaps she would just be the girl who loved orchids for a while, the girl who loved their fragile and ostentatious beauty, because, at the moment, it was the only thing she thought she was good at.

Chloe stood nervously outside Daniel's smart black door and looked for somewhere to place the gift bag in her hands so she could disappear back into the twilight. Somewhere Kelly would see it if she opened the door or came back home, but not somewhere inviting enough that someone on the street might see it and pinch it.

There was a small alcove on one side of the small tiled porch, offering some cover from anyone walking along the pavement. She was just reaching over to place the bag on the floor next to some empty milk bottles when the door opened—just a notch. Chloe froze.

She looked up to find Cal blinking at her. She pressed a finger to her lips, began to back away, but he suddenly threw his head back and yelled, 'There's someone at the door,' in the full-volumed way only a four-year-old could.

Chloe barely had time to back away before the door was yanked wide and she was staring at a broad, T-shirted chest.

Oh, poop.

She hadn't seen him much since that night on her boat. A glimpse of him here and there over the last week, always glaring at her, as if she had no right to be in *his* nursery, be one of *his* staff. It had got right on her nerves.

And then everything had gone quiet. People at work had seemed to relax a little, had stopped scanning the corridors when either she or Daniel was around, waiting for the other one to appear. When she'd told Emma, the other woman explained that Daniel had asked for emergency leave— something to do with his sister.

That news had made Chloe go cold all over. That could only mean one thing: Daniel was required to look after the boys because something had happened to Kelly. After his sister's recent health scares, she didn't even dare imagine what. It was too awful.

She and Daniel might not be getting along at the moment— she guffawed mentally at the understatement—but she liked Kelly, had admired how strong she seemed after all she'd been through. So she'd gone out and bought some pampering things, just some nice body lotion and some bath soak. The plan had been to pop it on the doorstep and sneak away before anyone spotted her.

The plan had obviously been flawed.

He folded his arms across his chest. 'What in hell's name are you doing here?' he said in a low, menacing whisper.

'I… Ah…'

Body not working. Brain not working. Lips definitely not working. She was going for the full house here.

Instead she dived for the bag, meaning to just take it and flee, but unfortunately Daniel lunged for it at the same time and their skulls produced a beautiful clear cracking sound as they made contact. Chloe staggered back, clutching her crown. Daniel, however, must have had an iron-capped skull, because he didn't seem to be in quite as much pain, although the swear word he uttered was very colourful.

Then a little voice from behind his knees repeated it beautifully, with the same intonation and gusto.

'Cal,' he said, and she could hear the strain that told her he was hanging onto his last thread of patience, 'just go back inside and see what Ben is up to, will you?'

'Okay, Uncle Daniel,' the voice said chirpily, and then Chloe could hear him skipping off down the hall, testing his new word out all the way.

Still holding her head, she straightened and came eye to eye with a rather angry Daniel Bradford. Good. She was angry too.

Angry at being made to feel like a pariah in her workplace. Angry that every time he'd set eyes on her since that night he'd looked as if he'd like to set fire to her with his glare. Angry that he hadn't let her explain, and that she'd known instinctively that he wouldn't have listened.

'I asked you a question,' he growled.

Chloe smoothed her T-shirt down with her free hand. 'I was just dropping these off for—'

He made a dismissive gesture towards the bag in her hand but, unfortunately, the edge of his hand caught it and the bottles went flying. His first reaction was shock, but then his expression hardened again. 'I don't want anything you've got to give me.'

Unfortunately, since Chloe had bought Kelly some rather nice lotions, the bottles were glass not plastic. One bounced on the small lawn, but the other one hit the path and smashed.

'Now look what you've done!' she shouted.

She knew it was pointless, but she reached out to pick up the bits from amidst the fragrant, snowy white lotion now oozing into the dirt. She couldn't leave it there. One of the boys might tread on it.

'You really are unhinged, aren't you?' a superior voice said from above her. 'I had no idea how bad it was.'

'Listen, you egotistical jerk—ow!' Chloe flinched away as her fingertip met glass. Instinctively, she stuck her finger in her mouth but instantly spat it out again. That lotion definitely did not taste as good as it smelled.

He let out a frustrated sigh. 'I'm sorry you've hurt yourself, but this can't continue…I don't need any of your gifts. And I don't want you hanging around outside my house.'

Chloe's lips twitched, then a high-pitched laugh burst out of her mouth. And once she'd started she couldn't stop. She clamped her good hand over her mouth to muffle the noise. This man was priceless! He actually thought she was *stalking* him? Just how vain could a man get?

She looked up at him, the look of twisted confusion on his features at her sudden outburst, and that just made her laugh all the harder.

When she could finally manage a sentence in one go, she said, 'This wasn't for you, Daniel. It was for Kelly.'

The look of astonishment on his face was almost worth the pain in her finger.

'For Kelly…' he repeated slowly.

'Yes,' said Chloe, feeling her hilarity subside and her temper rise again. 'You know—tall, dark-haired female who lives with you and shares a gene pool, God help her.'

'Why…?' he said. 'Why are you bringing presents for Kelly? It's not her birthday.'

A week ago, if she'd seen Daniel Bradford rendered defenceless by confusion like this, she'd have thought it was sweet. Now Chloe just revelled in it. He was so full of himself, thought he knew who she was and what she was capable of, did he?

'I heard you'd had to take leave because of Kelly,' she said. 'I thought she might be…well, you know, that she might have found out…' She shoved the undamaged bottle in Daniel's direction. 'Look, I just thought she might need some girly pampering to cheer her up, okay? It's hardly a crime.'

His mouth worked. 'But I thought...'

'Yes, I know what you thought,' she said. 'And, believe me, I've got much better things to do with my time than stalk you. You made it abundantly clear you're not interested.'

Daniel's gaze drifted to her finger. The blob of lotion on her hand was now looking like raspberry-ripple ice cream, with a swirl of red amongst the thick white. 'You'd better come inside.'

Chloe shook her head. 'Not likely. I'm not giving you any more ammunition than I have already. Next thing I know you'll have the police down here.'

'Don't be idiotic,' he said, regaining some of his usual charm.

Chloe started to laugh again, a dry, airless sound. 'You've destroyed your sister's gift and accused me of stalking you, and *I'm* the one who's idiotic?'

He folded his arms again. 'Well, after the other night...'

'For goodness' sake! All I did was get a little friendly with a man I *thought* was interested. And now I'm a stalker? Haven't you ever made a pass at the wrong person before? It didn't make you an evil monster, did it?'

His mouth moved, but Chloe was very satisfied to discover that he had no words to rebut her valid argument. It just spurred her on.

'And, up until that moment, I didn't hear you complaining one bit. Quite the reverse.'

He glared down at her. 'Are you quite finished?'

Chloe sucked in air through her nostrils and let it out through her mouth. 'Actually, I think I am.' And she was feeling much better now.

Daniel was staring at her finger again. It was starting to drip.

'I really think you'd better come inside,' he said.

Looking at her finger, Chloe did too. 'Okay. But as long as you understand that it's only for medical attention and you will in no way be applying for a restraining order if I step foot over that threshold for a few minutes.'

His eyes narrowed. 'Done.'

So Chloe gathered up her courage, and her pride, and followed him inside.

Daniel fetched the first-aid kit from the kitchen cupboard and placed it on the kitchen table, thereby avoiding any need for physical contact. Whose benefit that was for, he wasn't sure. Despite Chloe's recent behaviour, his brain had not got the message through to his libido that she was better left alone. What business did she have looking so soft and approachable, even when she was staring up at him defiantly and telling him just how badly he'd got it wrong?

'There are plasters and disinfectant in there,' he said.

Chloe gave him a withering look. 'I haven't lost my IQ in the last week, you know,' she said. 'I have a fairly good grasp on the contents of a first-aid kit.'

Daniel squeezed his teeth together and said nothing.

Chloe ran her finger under the tap, attempting to clean the thick lotion away so she could see the damage. 'It's not very deep,' she said, moving it back and forth under the stream of water, 'just bleeding impressively. A plaster should do it.'

Daniel handed her a clean towel. She took it without looking at him. As she dried her finger she shook her head gently.

'We spent a lot of time together over the last couple of months, but you don't know me at all.'

'That's hardly surprising, since you were pretending to be something you're not.'

Much to his surprise, Chloe laughed softly. 'No, I wasn't. I just didn't look like the silly nineteen-year-old you remembered, but I'm still the same person on the inside. You didn't look deep enough—now or then—to see the truth.'

She dabbed her finger with the towel, decorating it with tiny red smears. 'You were just fixated on the outside package. You didn't care what was underneath. And you're *still* fixated on the outside package. All you can see now is one of those silly women who follow you around, and I'm not one of them, either.'

A look of relief washed over her face as she said that last sentence. She inhaled and the hint of a smile played on her lips.

Daniel frowned. He didn't want to think about whether she was right about that. Anyway, she hadn't acted perfectly in the situation, either. 'You should have been upfront and honest with me, right from the start. It would have stopped me—'

She laughed. 'What? Making a fool of yourself? Welcome to the club, Daniel.'

He supposed she had him there. However stupid he must have felt knowing he hadn't realised who she was, she must have felt ten times as bad when he'd stormed off her boat the previous week.

'Why hide it?' he asked. 'If you were okay with it?'

She checked her finger and clamped the towel back around it. 'I didn't.' She looked down at the red-flecked towel, and then she met his eyes. 'At least, I didn't plan to. That first day when I came to find you, I was making a pre-emptive strike. I'd planned to 'fess up and make light of it, let you know I'd grown up and moved on... But you didn't remember me. As far as I knew, you didn't remember that night either.'

'So you lied.'

Chloe shook her head and sighed. 'Oh, how wonderful it must be to live in that perfect black-and-white world of yours. I didn't lie, I just decided not to dredge it up if you'd forgotten the whole thing. How would you have reacted if I'd said: "Hi, Daniel! Remember that tubby student who launched herself at you a few years back? That was me! Aren't you thrilled?"'

Okay, he kind of saw her point.

She pulled the towel away from her hand and inspected the cut. It wasn't oozing any more, so, forgetting about the *not touching* thing, Daniel reached for a plaster, unpeeled its wrapper and stuck it over the cut, winding the ends firmly round her finger.

Chloe didn't say anything while he did this, but when he stepped away again she said, 'I just thought the past could stay in the past, where it belonged—neither of us are the same people we were back then—and that we could work together as sensible adults. That was my plan, and I stuck to it. It was you who tipped everything on its head!'

Daniel straightened and stared at her. 'Me?'

That twinkle of humour that he now recognised as a precursor to one of Chloe's stinging truths appeared in her eyes. 'Yes, *you*, Indiana. Who was it who decided to kiss me in the Palm House, to flirt with me continually? Who was it that was trying to woo me?'

'I did not *woo*,' he said, slightly affronted. That term made him think of lovesick idiots who couldn't help themselves.

'Yes, you certainly did woo. What was that picnic about, then? Or the cosy dinner with your family to get me to let my guard down…?' She saw the expression on his face and carried on vindicated. 'Oh, yes, I'm wise to the way you operate now, and you can't chalk all that up as my desperate behaviour. I didn't engineer any of those things, you did. You know what…?'

He wasn't really sure he did want to know, but she was on a roll now.

'In fact,' she said, 'if I was a man and you were a woman, you'd be the stalker and I'd be the stud. How fair is that?'

Not fair at all. But Daniel wasn't going to tell her that. Not when he was remembering just how much he had *wooed*. Just how much he hadn't been able to help himself, how desperate he'd been to make her his. In the physical sense, of course. It had nothing to do with her bright personality and quick humour, the way he felt lighter—freer—when he was with her.

Chloe inspected her finger and seemed pleased with it. She zipped the little green first-aid kit back up and put it on the table with a slight lift of one eyebrow. Copying him. Mocking him.

'I'm not obsessed with you,' she said. 'And rest assured I will not attempt to seduce you ever again.'

Why did his body tighten in response to her words, rather than back away?

'I think it's a good idea if we just steer clear of each other from now on,' she added.

'Okay.' Daniel nodded, but he didn't really like that idea for some reason. There'd been a great deal of satisfaction in striding round the tropical plant nursery like a bear with a sore head, feeling the injured party. It had blocked out all those niggling little regrets he'd had about that night: how he'd spoken to her. Even worse, how he wished he'd stayed...

'Let's just be calm and professional. That way everyone at work can go back to minding their own business again—no drama to see—and we can get on with our jobs and our lives.'

'Okay...'

Her brow wrinkled, and Daniel couldn't help remember how, when she'd been sitting on his lap, all but naked, she'd made the same face as his lips trailed down her neck and across her shoulder, how it had seemed she'd been lost in concentrating on every touch and taste.

'It sounds as if there's a *but* in there somewhere.'

'No,' he said, mildly confused with all the conflicting messages his body and brain were sending him. One was saying run; one was telling him to make her make that slightly pained look of pleasure again. 'It's just that I'm not used to—'

'Women being so reasonable around you?' she interjected saucily. 'Using their silly heads instead of being ramped up on their hormones and acting desperate?'

She waited for him to answer, but he didn't want to give her the satisfaction.

'I know you've had to put up with some weird behaviour since Valentine's Day,' she said, her demeanour softening slightly, 'but, honestly, you need to get over yourself. Not every woman you meet wants to marry you, Daniel. But, one day, somebody might, and if you don't calm down you're going to scare her off.'

He shook his head. 'I'm never getting married,' he said emphatically. Maybe too emphatically, because Chloe suddenly looked at him with a mixture of realisation and pity. He hated the pity the most. But he needn't have worried. It quickly clouded over with a darker emotion.

'Then you're a coward as well as a bighead,' she said.

Ouch.

'What is the big, bad, adventuring Daniel Bradford scared of?'

'Nothing,' he said blandly.

She backed away towards the door. 'Now who's the liar?' she said softly. 'Okay, I got it wrong—I made a move on the wrong person—but at least I had the guts to try. I made myself vulnerable, took a chance. I'll never find the right man for me if I don't.'

He must have had horror written all over his face at her words, because he saw her read him, saw her muscles tighten and her jaw clench.

'Yes, I want to get married…some day,' she said, lifting her chin. 'What's so wrong with that? Millions of people do every year. But you…' The look she gave him made his insides wither. It reminded him of another look, another woman, another barrage of accusations he hadn't been able to defend himself against. Rather than crumble under the weight of them, Daniel fired up his temper to match hers.

'You,' she continued, her voice shaking slightly, 'you're too scared to even try. A wedding ring won't melt your finger like acid, you know! One conquest after the next… Is that really what you want? Does that really make you happy?'

No! he wanted to yell at her.

So he did.

'No, but I've been down the other path and I'm not going back there!'

There was a flicker of hesitation in her self-righteous expression and it fuelled him further. He couldn't let her be right about everything, couldn't let her make him seem shallow and pathetic.

'What do you mean?' she asked, 'What "other path"?'

He marched over to her, stared her down, let her know he wasn't scared of her and her words. He'd lived through far worse. 'I mean,' he said, his voice low and silky, 'that I once had a wife and a son. I did the whole marriage thing, the whole 'til-death-do-us-part thing and it didn't work out so well.'

When he mentioned the word *death* her lashes blinked rapidly and she swallowed. 'She died?' she asked, barely more than whispering.

'No,' Daniel said, turning away, hardly able to look at Chloe again. He hated the fact that a tiny voice had piped up inside his head, telling him it might have been better that way. 'No, it was until "death do us part" but it wasn't hers.' His voice dried and he had to swallow to get it back. 'My son. Cot death. Six months old.'

He turned back to Chloe. He'd thought he'd feel vindicated, but the look of complete shock on her face actually made him feel a little queasy. He could tell she was searching for words. There weren't any. He knew that for a fact.

'Something as fragile as a marriage can't handle that,' he said. 'I wasn't even there…I was off in some jungle, being the big explorer.'

He let out a huff of dry laughter.

'She never forgave me, you know. It killed everything we

had. So, no, I don't want to get married again. Excuse me for that.'

Chloe's eyes filled with tears. She swallowed them down, stepped forward and reached for him. 'Oh, Daniel...I'm so sorry.'

He shook his head, backed away until his backside met the counter. He didn't want her pity. 'Thank you for Kelly's present,' he said calmly. 'She's fine, by the way. A last-minute opportunity to go on a training course that she couldn't pass up. Nothing to worry about.' He looked at the paper bag with its drooping string handles, still where he'd left it in the centre of the kitchen table. 'If you'll tell me where you got it, I'll replace the broken one.'

She shook her head.

So she didn't want to owe him anything now, not even that. Maybe it was for the best.

'Daniel...'

He turned to stare out of the window, down the garden. 'You're right,' he said. 'Let's just steer clear of each other. Calm and professional.'

For a long time she didn't move; he could hear her breathing softly, a slight catch in the rhythm now and then. He screwed up his face, desperately trying to hold onto the churning chaos inside that he'd called up with his admission. Eventually, he heard the rustle of the paper bag as she lifted it off the table, her heels on the tiled hallway, the soft thud of the front door being closed gently.

And then Daniel let go of the breath he'd been holding and did something he hadn't done in years. He cried.

CHAPTER TEN

AND THAT WAS what Daniel and Chloe did for the next few months, through the bright days of August, the balmy warmth of an Indian Summer and into the rusts and golds of October. They steered clear of each other. Not too much, of course, because that would have created even more tension and gossip, but they were cordial and professional and those around them eventually lost interest.

Chloe also discovered a pleasing side effect of being Daniel's supposed ex—her nickname died out, and some of the female staff who'd previously kept their distance made an effort to befriend her, asked her out after work sometimes. It seemed everyone had a story to tell about a failed crush on Daniel Bradford. She and Georgia weren't the only members of that club. But with her credentials, Chloe thought she should be president. Or possibly queen…

But maybe it also had something to do with the fact that, as the trees lost their leaves, Chloe also shed some of her less practical work clothes. She swapped skirts for trousers, left the uncomfortable shoes for the weekends. One morning she'd just found herself staring in the mirror, red lipstick in hand. What was the point now? Who was she trying to impress?

Not Daniel, even though he was constantly in her thoughts. She couldn't stop thinking about what he'd told her. No wonder he avoided anything approaching intimacy. No wonder a woman who looked as if she might cling on and never let go was a threat. She understood it all now. And she ached for him because, while she understood it, she knew he was closing every open door around himself, and one day he'd wake up old and lonely. It was a sad future for a man who was so energetic and fearless in other areas of his life, a man who had such passion.

One morning Chloe checked her email before starting work and found a message from Kew's PR team. She'd been summoned to a meeting regarding the upcoming orchid festival. Every February, when the grounds outside were still grey and brown, when only the tips of the first crocuses were pushing through the grass, the Princess of Wales Conservatory became a riot of colour and beauty. Chloe had been looking forward to it all year; it would be her chance to really shine, show her superiors what she could do. And she desperately needed something in her life to go right at the moment.

At the appointed hour, she made her way to the PR offices and knocked on Sarah Milton's door. When she entered the office, however, she got a surprise. She wasn't the only one who'd been summoned. Daniel was also there, sitting in one of the chairs opposite Sarah's desk.

Chloe shook Sarah's hand, smiling, and then did the same to Daniel, figuring it would look odd if she treated him differently. It had been the first time they'd really touched since that awful night on her houseboat, and she'd hoped that all residual attraction would have faded by now.

She couldn't have been more wrong.

Instead, her skin leapt to life, tingling all the way up her arm. As if her nerve-endings had been lying dormant, waiting for something to wake them up. Waiting for *him* to wake them up.

She sat down in the remaining vacant chair and folded her hands in her lap.

Sarah, an elegant woman in her late forties, smiled at both of them and leaned forward on her desk, lacing her fingers together. 'I heard the two of you had plans for a combined display in the Princess of Wales,' she said, raising her eyebrows slightly.

She and Daniel looked at each other, then back at Sarah. 'Yes, but we kind of…put it on hold,' Chloe said.

The minuscule nod of Sarah's head said she knew that—and exactly why.

'We'd like you to resurrect the idea for this year's orchid festival in February,' she said. 'We're thinking of calling the festival something like "Beauty and the Beast" or "Savage Beauty". It'll be great for PR to do something a little different this year.'

Chloe sneaked a look at Daniel. His expression told her just how enthused he was by that idea.

'The last thing I need is more media attention,' he said.

Sarah just smiled at him, a long, thin, lizard's smile. 'Well, it's not really about you, is it, Daniel? It's supposed to be about the plants.'

Daniel just glared back at her.

Chloe found she just couldn't sit there and say nothing. 'I know it *should* be about the plants, but we all know the media will get any story they can out of it, the juicier the better. You have to admit that Daniel will be a target.'

Now Daniel was glaring at her instead. Great.

Sarah, however, wasn't fazed. 'We're going to run the festival for a week, with an auction for some of the display pieces on the last day to raise money for the Kew foundation,' she said. 'So book the fourteenth off in your diaries.'

'The *fourteenth*?' she and Daniel said in unison.

Daniel shook his head. 'But that's exactly one year on from—'

'Look, there's going to be media interest anyway,' Sarah said quickly. 'We might as well do it on our terms. What do you think?'

Chloe exhaled. What did she think about it? She loved the

idea, knowing that the orchids and pitcher plants would look amazing together, but it would mean working with Daniel. She tipped her head a little and looked across at him again. His expression was unreadable, features set like stone. But saying no to the powers that be on her very first festival would not go down well. She'd waited years for this job, and she didn't want to jeopardise her future here by being labelled as difficult.

'I think we can make it work,' she said, knowing that Daniel had just transferred his caustic gaze from Sarah to her once again. She turned and met him head-on. 'There's no reason we can't work calmly together.'

'I'm glad to hear it,' Sarah said, looking a little smug. 'Daniel?'

Chloe leaned forward a little, towards Daniel. He watched her, but didn't move back. 'She's right, you know. About the media. At least this way you can talk about the plants, get some good media coverage for the gardens... Do a good enough job of it and no one is going to have time to ask you about your love life.'

At least, that was what Chloe was hoping. Especially as she'd been the one blip on his radar all year—as far as she knew.

Something in his eyes changed. 'Okay,' he said, looking back at Sarah.

'Great,' Sarah said, reaching for her mouse and giving her computer screen a glance. They were effectively dismissed. 'I'll leave you two to work out some more details, then we'll catch up again in a couple of weeks to see how things are coming along.'

Daniel worked his way through the Orangery restaurant to a table in the corner. Chloe was already there, head bent over a notepad. She couldn't possibly have heard him through the dull hum of afternoon tea, but she lifted her head and looked at him while he was still ten feet away.

'Hi,' she said.

He nodded in return.

Her voice had been calm and even, her expression neutral, but he sensed she was more nervous than she was letting on.

It was strange. It was as if Chloe were a two-way mirror and, for a long time, all he'd been able to see was what she reflected back to him on the surface. But someone had now switched a switch somewhere or turned a light on, and suddenly he could see everything she'd been hiding behind. Was it just that he hadn't been looking properly before? Could he have seen this all along if only he'd tried?

She wore dark jeans, boots and a sweatshirt. Her hair was still curled as usual, but she hardly looked as if she had any make-up on at all. She looked fresh and young, an odd mix of the woman he'd pursued so relentlessly and the student who'd got her timing wrong. How he hadn't recognised her the instant he'd seen her again, he didn't know.

He sat down. 'Do you want another drink?'

She shook her head, even though her cup was nearly empty. 'No, I'm fine.'

'So…Beauty and the Beast…' He shrugged. 'I reckon we all know who's who in that scenario.'

Her lips flattened and her brows lowered. 'We've managed just fine for months without any name-calling—'

He shook his head, leaned forward a little. 'I didn't mean *you* were the Beast,' he said. 'I thought it was obvious I was talking about me…that you were the…' He trailed off and didn't finish his sentence. Coward.

'Oh,' she said, and the resulting confusion on her face made her look younger still, very much like the girl he remembered. 'That's very… Thank you.'

She stared down at her notebook for a second.

'You're not…flirting…with me, are you? Because I don't think that's a good idea.'

He hadn't meant to, but then he hadn't meant to say anything like that at all. It had just popped out. 'No,' he said. 'It was just my backhanded way of saying I didn't handle things very well back in the summer.' He shrugged. 'You've met my sister, so you know subtlety is not a strong family trait.'

That earned him the beginnings of a smile. He could live with that.

What surprised him was the tug inside telling him it wasn't enough, that he wanted to see her eyes light up and her lips stretch the way he had done before, back when things had been easy between them, back when she'd still been a potential *something* to him.

He decided to ignore it and gestured towards the sketch pad. 'You have some ideas?'

She nodded, but didn't flap it over to show him. Not yet. It took her a couple of seconds before she worked up the nerve. And he didn't blame her. He'd been a complete pig to her, belittled everything she was. He didn't have to lie, though, when he saw her sketches and notes; she had some really good ideas. Chloe was much more imaginative than he'd realised.

Oh, you realised. When her hands were on your chest and her teeth were nipping your neck, you knew just how creative she had the potential to be.

Daniel wiped that thought away. He shouldn't think about her that way any more.

Okay, he was in trouble already, because he couldn't seem to *stop* thinking about her that way nowadays. But he needed to try. If he didn't, he'd be facing a sexual harassment suit. No way was Chloe Michaels ever going to let him within touching distance of her ever again. And he was supposed to be pleased about that.

He pulled the tatty piece of paper out of his jeans pocket. It was stained and crumpled, even though he'd only scratched his ideas on it about an hour ago, nothing as neat as Chloe's little black book with the elastic strap and colour-coded markers.

For the next half-hour they talked designs and specimens, discussed how to use different areas of the vast Wet Tropics zone of the Princess of Wales Conservatory. It was usual to have a large display by the lily-pad pool, but Chloe had ideas about how to use some of the smaller nooks and crannies of the area too. Together they worked on an idea of contrasting the ugliest and most vicious-looking plants in the collection with the most fragile and colourful orchids. She wanted hanging displays and islands in the ponds, great towers of orchids in spiralling colours. It was going to look stunning.

Eventually, she closed her notebook and looked around. While they'd been talking a couple of the other nursery staff had wandered over to see what they were planning, but she'd always found a way to lean over her notebook or distract them from its contents. 'I want this to be a surprise,' she said. 'I know we'll need a huge team of helpers closer to the date, but for now I'd like to keep this just between ourselves.'

He couldn't help smiling a little. 'Need to know basis only. Got it. Anyone finds out too much and we *deal* with them.'

Her lips twitched. 'Exactly. There's some rather hungry piranhas in the aquatic display. I'm sure they'd appreciate the nutritional supplement.' And then she grew more serious again. 'I don't want you to take this the wrong way, Daniel, but... Do you think we could meet somewhere less...public... next time?'

'I'm not taking it the wrong way,' he said. How could he? For the last three months she'd been true to her word. She hadn't so much as looked at him with a flicker of interest. There'd been no text messages, no voicemails, no scented envelopes in the post. All completely what he'd asked for. So he shouldn't really mind, should he?

She'd moved on. Got over him. So maybe she was right:

maybe he was big-headed, because he wasn't liking the fact it had been so easy for her. The fact that she'd dealt with the whole situation with poise and dignity—much more than he had—only made him admire her more.

But there was where the problem lay: usually, when he *admired* a woman, he let her know, he pursued her. He didn't quite know what to do with all these new, noble feelings he was having for Chloe that meant it wasn't going to end with a good night in bed. It was most unsettling.

'Okay,' he said. 'How about meeting at my house next Thursday?'

She opened her mouth and he could tell she was about to knock him back.

'I'll ask Kelly to hang around,' he added, knowing they'd struck up a friendship of late. 'She usually has some pithy opinions on my great plans.'

Chloe relaxed a little and nodded. 'Okay.'

'Okay.'

A cute little line appeared between her brows. 'We can do this, can't we? We can act like professionals and make this thing a success. Because I really want this thing to be a success.'

He nodded. 'Sure.'

But as she walked away he drew in a deep breath and held it. He made himself turn to the wall and look at the white-painted plaster rather than at her rather fine retreating backside in its denim covering.

See? He could do it. He was practically being a saint.

Okay. Well, he was going to try his best. That was all anyone could ask.

Chloe closed her notebook, leaned back in one of Daniel's dining-room chairs and sighed. 'Finally, I think we have a handle on this thing,' she said, and then she smiled, just a little. 'You know this is going to be the best festival yet, don't you?'

Daniel grinned at her. Chloe smiled more than just a little.

She lifted her tote bag off the floor and placed her notebook inside before pushing her chair back, getting ready to stand up. 'Wait?' he asked softly.

She dropped back down onto the chair.

'Before you go,' he said, 'I'd like to talk to you about some things…clear the air.'

The air was clear as far as Chloe was concerned. Okay, maybe not totally clear; Daniel's pheromones seemed to be particularly strong this evening. But if they were talking about their relationship—or non-relationship—she was fine.

'It's okay. Really,' she said, flicking a loose ringlet out of her eyes with a nod of her head.

'No, it isn't. I want to—need to—apologise for the things I said that night.'

Chloe blinked and her lids stayed shut a fraction too long. When she looked back at him, he was waiting, eyes intense, face serious. But there was an honesty, an openness, about him that she'd never seen before.

But it wasn't like those heated looks from the early days of their relationship. No, it was much more dangerous. This was the kind of look that made a woman ache for a man, somewhere deep, deep down inside, and Chloe was already too bruised in that place. She was also too weak to resist if he kept it up.

'I'm sorry I called you pathetic,' he said, his voice rough. 'I don't think you're pathetic at all. Far from it.'

She nodded. Her heart rate tripled.

'And you were right. I overreacted…'

Chloe licked her lips and twitched her shoulders in the slightest of shrugs. 'Maybe just a little,' she said dryly.

'What happened that night…'

She sat up straighter. 'I really don't want to rehash what went on at my houseboat—for all sorts of reasons.'

He looked down, then back up at her. 'No, I didn't mean

that night. I meant the other one—back when you were a student.'

Chloe said something most unladylike. The only effect it had on Daniel was to make him laugh.

'Seriously, nothing to explain,' she said. 'I got a little tipsy, you offered to walk me outside for some fresh air and then I made a total and complete fool of myself by trying to kiss you. Believe me, after all these years it's crystal clear.'

She couldn't quite believe she'd said that, put it all so bluntly. And to Daniel, of all people. Why hadn't a large pit opened up in his kitchen floor and swallowed her whole?

'You were a student,' he said. 'It would have been completely unethical, even if I'd wanted to.'

Chloe swallowed hard and nodded. Yes, she'd known that. Hadn't stopped her doing it anyway. She'd never, ever drunk cheap cider again after that night. She tried to smile, but it felt more as if she was wincing. 'It's okay. You don't have to say that. I know you wouldn't have wanted to.' She broke eye contact with Daniel and looked away.

He was silent for a few seconds. 'I *shouldn't* have wanted to.'

She whipped her head round to stare at him. Why was he teasing her like that? He was supposed to be apologising, she thought, not making it worse.

'Daniel, so far you've been brutally honest about that… incident. You don't have to lie now. You didn't remember me at all.'

'I didn't make the connection,' he replied. 'And the details are still a little fuzzy, but I do remember an eager girl who always sat at the front for every lecture, who asked pertinent questions, who showed all the other students up with her passion and enthusiasm.'

Passion and enthusiasm? Was that another way of saying *huge crush on the teacher*? She folded her arms on the table in front of her and propped herself up with them. 'That girl was a joke.'

'No… She was sweet and young and had one too many,' he said. 'What student hasn't? But I should have handled that night better too.' He paused and frowned slightly. 'I probably would have, if it had just been any old sloppy drunken kiss.'

The look in his pale eyes made her hold her breath.

'You know we have great chemistry,' he said, his voice deepening. 'It was there then.'

Chloe shook her head slightly. That couldn't be. Yes, there had been fireworks and tingling and melting into a puddle at his feet, but that had been all her. It hadn't been him. He'd pushed her away, body rigid, eyes full of shock, eyes full of…

She looked back at him and he held her gaze.

Eyes full of surprise, with wide pupils—just as they were now—not pinpricks of disgust.

Oh.

She swallowed. That didn't change anything. He'd still done the right thing. If he hadn't he'd have lost his job and her reputation would have been even worse than it had been. At least no one had seen that drunken pass in the car park. At least they'd only teased her about her obvious crush.

She found she couldn't speak above a whisper. 'I don't know how that helps anything, but thank you for being honest with me.'

He exhaled. 'I don't know how it helps, either. I hadn't quite planned on saying it. But maybe it needed to be said.'

Chloe nodded. She wasn't sure if she agreed. It was hard to feel that distance between them now. She needed that distance. Because she had her own apology to give, her own admission to make.

But at that moment Kelly appeared in the doorway. 'Uncle Daniel's presence is required. Apparently, Mummy cannot read *The Gruffalo* with all the right voices.'

Chloe stared at the table top. See? That was why she

needed distance. Because Daniel Bradford was the kind of man who did voices at story time. She hadn't known that about him. But there was a lot she hadn't known about him.

Daniel gave a weary shrug—one Chloe didn't buy in the slightest—and headed upstairs. Kelly went to one of the kitchen cabinets, pulled out some wine glasses, filled them with Chardonnay from the fridge and plopped one down in front of Chloe.

'Really, I shouldn't…'

Kelly just nudged the glass closer.

Chloe picked it up and took a tiny sip. She'd accused Daniel of only seeing what he'd wanted to see in her. Hadn't she been just as bad? Even though it had been ten years on, he hadn't lost that fantasy edge for her. He'd been that two-dimensional object of a crush, the unattainable alpha man, and she hadn't looked any deeper than he had. She'd been too busy caught up in the fact that the unattainable had suddenly become attainable.

Chloe took a bigger sip.

But now she was seeing the man inside. Not a fantasy. Not a dream. Just a wounded man who was trying to deal with the bullets life had shot through his heart. And, damn, if that didn't mean she was starting to fall for him.

She took a whacking great gulp of wine.

'How's things?' Kelly said, eyeing her up and down.

Chloe slumped forward and let her forehead hit the table. 'That good, huh?'

Her brow squeaked against the varnished wood as she nodded. Kelly just went and got the bottle out of the fridge and placed it on the table between them.

'What's my brother done now?' she asked.

Chloe sat up and shook her head, pursing her lips. Where on earth should she start?

'He likes you, you know.'

Chloe didn't say anything. That was what she was afraid

of. It was much easier when he was hating her, pitying her. There was no chance of hoping then. She decided to take another tack.

'He told me about his wife and son,' she said quietly.

Kelly nodded and took a long swig of her wine. 'Pretty much destroyed him,' she said. 'He loved that boy so much…'

She trailed off and her focus became distant. It was a while before she could speak again. It was a while before Chloe was ready for her to.

'And he worshipped Paula. But they couldn't put what they'd had back together after Joshua died. She retreated into a world of bitterness and guilt and he didn't know how to follow.' Kelly looked at Chloe. 'She hated him for that.'

She reached over and covered Chloe's hand with hers. 'He's just really scared, you know? It's not that he doesn't know how to love, but that when he does it's so full-on…' She shook her head. 'He can't stand the thought of loving and losing again, so he just doesn't let himself care. Be patient with him.'

Chloe wanted to pull her hand away, but she thought it might offend her friend. 'Oh, I'm not sure if…' If what? If she wanted him to care? She wanted it so badly it hurt. Didn't mean it was going to happen.

'Is that what happened with Georgia?' she asked.

Kelly frowned and stared into her glass of wine for a moment. 'Maybe. I don't know. On paper they should have been perfect for each other. I really love Georgia, really hoped she'd be able to get him to unlock, but for a long time they just drifted along and then I think she pushed him too hard, too fast.'

Chloe nodded, and then she asked the question she really didn't want the answer to. 'Do you think he'll ever be ready?'

Kelly stared at her, a pained expression on her face. 'I don't know…I want him to be, and I thought he was getting better, but me being ill brought it all up again. He seemed to shut down further. I think I scared the hell out of him.'

Chloe smiled softly. 'He loves you. Anyone can see that.'

One corner of Kelly's mouth curled. 'Well, I am pretty lovable.'

There was a noise on the stairs—Daniel's heavy tread— and Chloe gathered the rest of her belongings together and put them in her bag. She stood up and smiled first at Kelly and then at Daniel as he entered the room.

'I'd better be going,' she said. 'It's been a long day.'

Before she had any more wine. Before she let it encourage her to do something stupid—like believing she could mend Daniel Bradford if she wanted to badly enough.

CHAPTER ELEVEN

IT WAS A BRIGHT, crisp Saturday afternoon. Chloe and Daniel met in her living room, more out of choice than necessity. It was Ben's third birthday and Daniel's house was undergoing a mutiny at the hands of a gang of knee-high pirates.

It felt like returning to the scene of a crime, even though it was her own space. She'd managed to block the memories out while she'd been on her own, but when Daniel rapped on the big glass door at the end of her living room, it all came flooding back. Thank goodness for the steely winter light seeping into every corner, making everything seem bleak and grey. She didn't think she could have stood it if it had been like that night—humid and warm and intimate.

They sat at her dining table, Chloe filling in the huge master plan she'd sketched out while Daniel pointed and made suggestions.

'I've had an idea for that arch we're going to have over the pool,' she told him. 'I know we said colourful, but I wondered if, rather than an explosion of shades, we did something more structured?'

Daniel stopped scribbling on a scrap of paper in his scratchy handwriting. 'Like?'

'I'm thinking the arch could be a spectrum of colours, like a rainbow.'

Daniel screwed up his face. 'Stripes? I don't think we've got enough room.'

She shook her head gently. 'No…not so literal. I was thinking more of a gradual colour change, starting with reds and oranges at one end of the arch and subtly merging all the way through the different shades until we get to purples and violets at the other.' She pulled her notebook out and showed him a sketch she'd done the night before. 'Like this…with ferns and pitchers and palm leaves all interspersed throughout.' And she made a few deft pencil lines on the drawing to show him what she meant.

He picked the pad up and stared at it, and then he looked at her.

It was that expression again. The one that made her want to throw 'calm and professional' out of the window and drown it in the river. She pushed her chair back and headed for her kitchenette.

'I want a coffee. Do you want a coffee?' And then she busied herself filling the kettle so she didn't have to wait for his answer.

She heard him cross the carpet to meet her, but she kept on fussing with sugar pots and instant coffee jars all the same.

'Chloe?' His voice was soft as velvet.

'I'll be right with you in a minute,' she said brightly, and noticed her hand was shaking as she tried to pour boiling water into the mugs.

Daniel came up behind her, took the kettle out of her hand and placed it back on its base. Then he put a hand on each shoulder and turned her to face him. 'I think the arch idea is very much like the woman who created it.'

Chloe swallowed. Naive? Out of step? Been there, done that before?

He smiled a little as he read the emotions flitting over her face. 'I think it's inspired,' he said. 'Complicated. Unique.'

Oh, hell, thought Chloe.

Then he leaned towards her and brushed his lips against

hers. She froze for a moment, before kissing him back then pulling away. 'This isn't a good idea.'

'Why not?'

She stepped away and folded her arms across her middle to keep them from doing anything stupid. 'Because, one day, I will want a husband and a family and you don't want those things.'

'One day isn't today, Chloe. Can't we just have now? You know this is more than just a fling.'

She did know. She just wasn't sure what to do with that knowledge.

'Maybe I'll want those things too,' he said. 'One day.'

One day... He'd spoken so softly, but he still hadn't been able to hide his tension as he'd said those words, as if he secretly preferred it was the kind of tomorrow that was always one day out of reach.

She looked at him. Maybe wasn't good enough. She couldn't live with *maybe* from Daniel. He'd rejected her twice already and she wasn't prepared to risk it again.

The last time they'd been in this room had been bad enough, but really he'd just been rejecting New Chloe. Fake Chloe, as she'd now started to refer to her alter ego. The shell she'd built to protect herself from the likes of Daniel Bradford.

He'd actually done her a favour. While it hadn't felt good, that shell had needed to be broken. It had become so thick that she was isolating herself from everyone behind a wall of supposed perfection. New Chloe had deserved to be smashed to smithereens.

However, what had emerged in her place wasn't the Mouse. It was someone new. A Chloe cocktail—a mix of the best of both with a little something extra thrown in for good measure. This fledgling Chloe had some of the confidence and maturity of the new, tempered with the approachableness and warmth of the old. A little of her impulsiveness too—

but not so much to make her want to press the self-destruct button again.

But this new creature was delicate. Only just formed, with skin like paper. Daniel wasn't ready for this Chloe. And she couldn't wait another ten years for him to be ready. She needed to get on with her life, start living it for herself instead of what everyone else expected for her.

'I can't get involved with you, Daniel. I like you too much.'

He looked at her as if she'd lost her senses. 'What kind of bizarre female logic is that?'

Chloe's expression hardened. 'The kind that's going to save us both a whole lot of grief.'

'You're wrong,' he said. 'I'm not that same man who ran a mile from an unexpected proposal last year. I've changed. Come out with me on a proper date.' He gave her that smile he knew she couldn't resist, the rotter. 'We never did try that Italian...'

She walked out of the double doors that led out onto a small deck with a table and chairs and a variety of terracotta planters filled with ivy and heather and miniature evergreens. Daniel followed her. She leaned on the rail and looked over the greyish-green glossy water that glinted in the winter sun.

'We've been on this merry-go-round before. It's not the dates—or the lack of them—that's the problem.' She twisted her head to look at him. 'We just always seem to do it for the wrong reason, and I'm not sure this time's any different.'

'Don't say that.' He stepped in close behind her, folded his arms around her front and buried his face in the hollow of her neck. It was all Chloe could do not to melt against him.

'I can't be your experiment,' she told him in a whisper, 'to see if you're ready for more than a fling.'

'Why not? Isn't life about taking chances, exploring new possibilities? Think of the plants we work with. We wouldn't even know of their existence if everyone decided to stay home and never go into unexplored territory.'

She slid out of his grasp and walked to the opposite corner of the deck. 'But some risks are too costly. I know you know what I'm talking about.'

The smile slid from his face.

'There are places inside us that can hurt so badly that we never want to go back there,' she said, knowing he understood every syllable, that his mind had wandered to his devastated marriage and the little boy he'd never got to watch grow up. 'And you're not the only one who has them.'

His gaze grew intense.

She inhaled and let the air out slowly, gathering her courage. 'Last time we were together here—'

'I explained about that…apologised…'

She nodded. She knew he had, but he needed to understand.

'What you said hurt,' she replied firmly, catching his eye and keeping his focus locked on her. 'But, really, it wasn't anything more than wounded pride. You didn't even know me then, not really, because I was being so good at being Miss Fancy Knickers—yes, I know what they used to call me—that I didn't even know myself.'

She let out a little laugh that died quickly.

'This is it, now…' She held her arms out wide. 'This is me. It's different. I *feel* different. And you know who Chloe is now. Not a geeky student with a crush. Not a vamp with perfect nail polish. Just a girl who likes orchids and happens to possess a killer shoe collection.'

'Of course it's different. That's why it could work this time.'

Could. That sounded an awful lot like *maybe* to her.

'Call me a coward, but I can't take that chance. If you did it again—if you pushed me away one more time—it'd kill me.'

'But I won't!'

'You're saying you won't ever push me away? I thought you didn't *do* for ever any more.'

Daniel stuttered, and she knew he'd just reacted to her words without thinking them through.

'We both know you're not in the market for that. If it's not going to end in wedding rings and honeymoons then, one day, someone will leave, and I have the feeling it would be you.'

'Why? Why would it be me?'

He just kept coming, didn't he? Batting away her arguments one by one, because that was his way: he set his mind to a goal and he pursued it relentlessly, no matter what. But he'd set his heart on the wrong goal this time. She wasn't something to be won; she was something to be treasured. Kept. And he just couldn't promise her that. So she stepped forward, looked him straight in the eye and said the one thing she knew would scare him away for good.

'Because I'm falling in love with you,' she said simply, and watched the colour drain from his face as her words hit home. She'd known it would happen, but it hadn't made it any easier to watch.

'I…I…'

'Please!' She held up a palm. 'Don't try to say it back. You'd be insulting both of us.'

He closed his mouth and it became a grim line.

She walked back into the living room. 'You can go now.'

'Chloe…'

'I know you want to,' she said. 'I can see it in your eyes.'

He didn't deny it, damn him. He didn't deny it.

She pulled herself up straight, put her best professional face on. 'No need for any more meetings. Next week we'll be revealing the plans to our team and starting work. We've done as much as we can do, you and I. "Calm and professional"— that was what we said, didn't we?' She stopped and looked at her shoes. 'Maybe we should have just stuck to that.'

And then she turned and walked back indoors, because she couldn't watch him leave. Not one more time.

* * *

Daniel hated himself for walking away from Chloe's house-boat. But he'd had that sudden reality check that only one fly in ten got when it was hovering above one of his plants. The future promised to be bright and sweet and full of everything he secretly wanted, but he knew that once he gave into that feeling, once he climbed down inside it and let go, there would be no going back, even if he realised it had been a terrible mistake.

He tried to make up for it in little ways over the following weeks. One morning he brought her a cup of her favourite coffee and put it in her nursery just minutes before she arrived for work. Another day he left a copy of an article he'd seen in a magazine that she'd find interesting. Chloe didn't say anything about it at all. In fact, she seemed to have gone back to being that strange robot she'd been after that unfortunate night in the summer. But she seemed to manage to smile and laugh and talk with the other staff as they prepared for the Beauty and the Beast Festival.

He knew he couldn't give her what she really wanted, but that didn't mean they couldn't be friends, right? He missed her. Missed hearing her laugh, or seeing her deep in conversation about something she was excited about, her hands moving rapidly as she spoke with both body and voice.

They had to work together for the next couple of weeks and he'd much prefer they left it on a good footing. Then he could leave on the expedition to Borneo knowing he'd done as much as he could, and he'd be free, no longer weighed down by the guilt that had been steadily solidifying in him since he'd seen that hurt look in her eyes.

So, at the end of the working day, as everyone was packing up, preparing to go home, he made his way to her part of the nursery.

'Hi,' he said as he walked in the door.

She looked up from what she was doing. 'Hi.' And then she just stared at him.

He held out a square object wrapped in a supermarket carrier bag. A peace offering. Not one for gift-wrapping, was Daniel.

Her features pinched together, but she took it from him. The rustling of the thin plastic seemed unnaturally loud in the deserted greenhouse. She pulled the square object out and looked at it. For a long time she was very still, and then, just moving her eyes and leaving her head bowed, she looked at him. 'What is this?'

'It's a print of the slipper orchid from my book. I thought you'd like it.'

She stared back at the picture. What? Was it out of focus? Had he put it in backwards?

'Is there something wrong?' he asked, not liking the frown that was bunching up her forehead.

She took a step forward. 'Yes, there is. I want you to stop being nice to me.'

'I beg your pardon?'

'It's just making it all that much harder,' she said.

'I was just trying to…I don't know…apologise.'

'What for?' She folded her arms across her chest. 'For not being in love with me? As much as I love a good moccachino or a pretty picture, even I don't think they're quite going to cover that one.'

When she put it like that, maybe…

'I wasn't trying to upset you,' he said. 'But I leave on the fifteenth of next month. I just didn't want things to be weird between us up until then.'

The frown melted and her features sagged. 'The fifteenth? That's the day after the festival.'

'I know.'

She nodded, looked away. 'Okay. Maybe that's a good thing.' The way her jaw was clamped together made him believe otherwise. She met his gaze again. 'So we just have to last another three weeks and then you'll be gone.'

Last another three weeks? That sounded very ominous. Very final.

'I'm not going for good,' he reminded her.

'For long enough, though,' she replied. 'Almost two months.'

He nodded, and he realised that the thought of the trip no longer filled him with the same restless energy that he'd experienced when he'd set it all up. Somehow, it felt like running away, even though it seemed Chloe was quite keen for him to put on his shoes and sprint.

He hadn't wanted it to end like this. Awkward. Sad.

'Is bringing you a coffee now and then really that bad?' he asked.

'Yes,' she said and her eyes began to shimmer.

He walked towards her but she held up a hand. 'Don't… Please…'

'But—'

She shook her head and suddenly that shimmer in her eyes turned to anger.

'I know you're not meaning to, but you're just playing games with me. It's the whole "want what you can't have" thing. You can't help yourself.'

That wasn't it at all. He opened his mouth to tell her as much, but she cut in before the words had left his mouth.

'It's got to stop, Daniel! You're not being fair. Please…' That little waver in her voice, right there, got him right down in his gut. Her lip wobbled and the next word was barely a whisper. '*Please*, just leave me alone.'

And then she turned and walked out of the door, leaving the framed print on the bench.

When Daniel got home he found his sister waiting for him. She met him at the kitchen door with a bottle of chilled champagne in her hand.

He really didn't feel like celebrating. 'What's this in aid of?' he asked her.

Kelly nodded to an open manila envelope on the kitchen table. 'Papers arrived. As of today, I am officially divorced.' She waved the bottle at him. 'But I didn't want to drink this on my own, because that would just be…you know…sad.' And then she grinned at him, just to prove how elated she was.

Daniel walked over to her, took the bottle out of her hand, placed it on the table and pulled her into a fierce hug.

After a moment, she pushed herself away, exhaling hard. 'Just don't be too nice to me, okay?'

Daniel threw his hands in the air in mock surrender. What was wrong with the womankind today? Seriously?

He opened the champagne while Kelly got two flutes from the cupboard and when their glasses were filled they both went to sit on the sofa at the end of the conservatory.

'So, how does it feel to be finally free?' he asked, slightly elated himself that her rat of an ex-husband was out of his life also. Kelly had moaned long and hard about the process of eradicating that scum from her life.

'Bloody terrible,' she said and downed almost the whole glass in one go.

'But—'

'Oh, I don't want him back,' she added quickly. 'But it's hard, you know.' She glanced at the kitchen ceiling, which also happened to be the underside of Cal's bedroom. 'Hard on the boys and hard to feel so…alone.'

He nodded. He'd felt that way once, but then he'd become so used to it he hadn't been able to remember a time when it was easier not to be that way. And now? Now he just wanted…

Chloe.

He wanted to be with Chloe.

But she didn't want to be with him—and he had to admit she might have some very good reasons for that. He sighed.

Kelly slugged back the last of her champagne. 'Oh, and I ought to tell you that I think the boys and I should move out when you get back from the jungle. Late April, maybe.'

He sat up, almost snorted bubbles out of his left nostril. 'What?' he half said, half coughed.

Kelly gave him a rueful smile. 'It's not that the boys and I don't love living here,' she said, 'but it's time I stood on my own two feet, faced the world.'

'Kells, you don't have to! Think of the money…!'

She laid a firm hand on his arm. 'I know. But I need to do this. For me.'

He shrugged. Kelly had made up her mind. And when a Bradford made up their mind there was no budging them.

'Then I'll help any way I can,' he said.

That was when his sister burst into tears.

She crawled up to him, buried her head in his shoulder and sobbed until there was no more moisture left in her body, it seemed. Daniel didn't quite know what to do. If she were a plant he'd stand her in a bucket of water to rehydrate her, but if there was one thing he'd learnt this year it was that people were a heck of a lot more complicated than plants.

She peeled herself from him, blew her nose and went to refill her glass from the bottle on the table. As she crossed the room she fixed him with those beady eyes of hers.

'So…' she said as she sat down '…we know all about me, but what's got *you* looking as joyful as a turkey at Christmas?'

He aimed for humour and ended up with *disgruntled*. 'Chloe thinks I'm stalking her.'

Kelly threw back her head and laughed. When she'd finished wiping a fresh batch of tears from her eyes she said, 'Thanks, I needed that.'

'Your sympathy is duly noted and appreciated.'

Kelly just grinned at him. 'Why does she think that?'

'It's stupid,' he said, and he was just about to tell her how stupid when he could hear his own voice in his head, laying out his case. But instead he started to think about all those women who'd turned up at Kew just to see him. Had they not been able to think about anything else for more than five minutes at a time? Had they had the same urge to get as close to him as possible, for as long as they could? Was this what obsession felt like?

Oh, hell. It was, wasn't it?

Maybe he needed psychiatric help.

'Oh, I've been saying that for years,' his sister said over the top of her champagne glass.

Daniel glared at her. Had he actually said that out loud? Things were worse than he thought.

And then she reached over and ruffled his hair. 'It needs a cut,' she said as she put her glass down and stood up. 'And I need some shut-eye.'

She walked over to the table, retrieved the bottle and topped his glass up. 'And, for what it's worth, I don't think you're crazy. In fact, this is the most sensible I've seen you in years.'

She dumped her empty glass in the dishwasher. 'If you like, Dr Kelly will give you her diagnosis.'

Daniel made a face that said she'd better not try, but as Kelly walked across the room and kissed him on the cheek she whispered in his ear, 'I'd say the problem is this—you've got it bad.'

CHAPTER TWELVE

'DANIEL?' IT WAS Kelly's voice on the other end of the line, but not her usual sarcastic drawl. His little sister sounded really panicked.

It was the first day of the orchid festival, and Daniel and Chloe and the whole team had arrived early and were working hard to make all the finishing touches before the grand opening later that morning. The Princess of Wales Conservatory was looking amazing, dripping with colour and unusual displays. Next to the other-worldly shapes of some of the pitchers and other carnivores, the orchids only seemed more delicate and fragile.

Daniel ducked into the Temperate Carnivores section, letting the door close behind him, cutting off the noise of the work party. 'What is it?'

'It's Ben,' she whimpered. 'He fell off the climbing frame at pre-school and cracked his head.' There was a pause while she took a great, snuffling breath. 'We're in the hospital. He's unconscious, Dan.'

Daniel didn't waste any time joining his sister in panicking. He got the name of the A&E department they were in, explained the situation to the nearest person with a Kew T-shirt and sprinted off in the direction of the staff car park. Within fifteen minutes he was at the hospital, haranguing the young guy on Reception into telling him where his sister and nephew were.

He found Kelly, sitting quietly and composed in a cubicle, with her son drowsy on the trolley beside her. Her body was rigid, her knees clamped together and her knuckles white as she gripped onto herself for comfort.

'He came round,' she said in a tight voice. 'The doctor says that's a good sign, but they did scans and they want to keep him in for observation.'

Daniel just walked over to his sister and pulled her up out of the chair and into his arms. He was angry. Really angry. Angry this had happened to Ben. Angry Kelly had to face something like this all on her own. Angry at Ben's father… just *because*. And he decided he'd like to stay angry, because angry was a lot better than *scared witless*.

'You're cutting off my air supply,' Kelly said hoarsely and poked him in the ribs.

'Sorry,' he said, standing her back from him and holding her at arm's length, his hands on her shoulders. He looked her up and down. 'Are you okay?'

'I am now,' she said, and he saw a hint of the old Kelly in her thin smile. She was a fighter, his sister. The strongest person he knew.

He walked over to Ben's trolley. The little boy's eyelids were fluttering and he hauled them open. 'Uncle Daniel,' he said, and his chubby fingers made a grasping motion. Daniel stuck his index finger in Ben's palm, as he had done when Ben had been a baby, and the boy grabbed onto it tightly. His lids drifted closed.

He couldn't go anywhere now without disturbing his nephew. A throb of panic set itself inside Daniel's temple. He wasn't sure if he could do this. Even though he hadn't been there when Joshua had—

He couldn't finish that thought.

Even though he hadn't been there, something about seeing this tiny body curled up on the pristine white of a hospital sheet was bringing all those feelings flooding back. He glanced at the gap in the cubicle curtain. The urge to dart through it was overpowering, but with Ben holding tightly onto his finger he was trapped.

He looked at Ben, his almost-translucent lids closed and his mouth relaxed into an 'o' shape, and something inside Daniel's chest cramped. Since Kelly had moved in, he'd really let himself get attached to his nephews. He wanted to scold himself for being reckless, but how could he? That was what families were supposed to do—care about each other. That was what people were supposed to do in general.

But if Daniel tried to count on one hand the number of people that he'd truly let himself care about since the end of his marriage, he realised he still had a couple of fingers left. Even Kelly and the boys had to worm their way in slowly. What kind of brother did that make him?

What kind of man did that make him?

Kelly came to stand by the trolley and rhythmically smoothed her son's hair from his forehead, then she reached out and circled Daniel's other thumb with her smaller hand, mirroring her son's gesture, and the three of them stayed like that in silence for a moment, joined like a circle.

'This,' he said croakily, 'is why I can't do it again.'

She nodded and a tear dripped from the corner of one eye. She couldn't wipe it away without breaking contact, so she let it run down her cheek, the overhang of her jaw and onto her neck.

'I get that, Dan,' she said softly—far too softly for his ballsy little sister. 'But tell me this: would you rather have had those six months with Joshua or would you rather that he hadn't existed at all?'

Daniel flinched at the mention of his son's name. He realised he hadn't said it out loud for years. It was just as well it wasn't him hooked up to one of those heart monitors, because the little cubicle would've been filled with the sound of a galloping electronic horse.

Thankfully, he was rescued from answering Kelly's question by the arrival of a doctor. He prised his finger from Ben's hand, shot a quick look at Kelly, then went to wait outside while the doctor delivered her news.

Kelly opened her mouth and reached a hand in his direction, and he knew she was going to say it was fine for him to stay, but he needed to get out of there. If it was going to be bad news, he didn't know if he could take it.

Inside, deep down in his core, he was shaking and cold. And as he searched for a free plastic chair to perch on his conscience began to nibble away at him too, adding a dash of nausea to the already uncomfortable internal cocktail.

He glanced at Ben's pale blue cubicle curtain, knowing that inside Kelly was probably feeling worse than he was, that he'd left her there alone to deal with whatever was coming.

He'd told himself that he was brave because he liked climbing high walls and tramped through rain forests and knew how to deal with leeches and ticks, but this was where it counted. Here. In this drab city hospital. This was where he would prove he was a man or not.

Brave? Don't make him laugh.

So Daniel paused for a moment, rubbed his face with both hands, then he marched back over to the curtain, pulled it aside and went to join his sister.

That evening, after Ben had been discharged from the hospital, the doctors assuring his mother he'd be fine, Daniel travelled halfway across London to go climbing. Even though this centre had a wall thirty feet taller than the one at his local climbing place, it still wasn't high enough.

Never mind, a sarcastic little voice in his head said. *You'll be in reach of a real mountain in a week's time. You'll be happy then.*

He grabbed for another handhold, pulled himself up and searched for the next place to put his foot. Maybe this wall wasn't tall enough, but he could climb it more than once, couldn't he?

But now there was a second voice inside his head. Most annoyingly, it belonged to his sister. And he realised he'd been doing a pretty good job of ignoring it since the night they'd toasted her divorce papers.

He decided he was under the wrong bit of the overhang to make his way past it, so he backtracked a bit and chose another route. As he groped sideways for a handhold he noticed a lean, dark-haired guy about his own age looking at him, studying him.

Daniel scowled at him briefly before continuing his climb. What was his problem?

As he climbed he considered the question Kelly had posed to him in the hospital. Would he, given the chance, erase his wife and son from his life completely, make it as if they had never existed? Would he choose freedom over pain?

He cracked the door of his memory open and saw Josh's gummy smile, how his face had lit up every time Daniel had come home from work. He remembered how his son had smelled after a bath, and how, as a newborn, he'd clung monkey-like to his shoulder as Daniel had paced and sung to him in the small hours of the night.

Would he want to erase those memories if he could? Maybe he would. He'd tried his hardest to pretend they weren't there for so long.

But when he tried to stuff the images he'd let loose away, they refused to go. Instead, they settled themselves into a corner of his consciousness, and when he let his mind wander in that direction he found, not necessarily joy, but warmth. Comfort. Not the screaming six-headed black dragon he'd expected to find. It seemed odd he'd run from them for so long.

Daniel stopped where he was on the wall, arrested by that thought. A couple of other climbers had to work their way round him while he hung there.

Running.

Not like a hunter chasing something, but like something being hunted. Had he really, all these years, had it all back to front?

And running from what? What was it that terrified him? He took a deep breath and mentally turned round to face it.

Love.

That was what it was. In any shape or any form. He'd even run from his family until circumstances had caused him to let Kelly and her boys into his life. But that was understandable, because love wasn't a pretty thing full of hearts and flowers and rose petals. No, love *was* the six-headed monster, viciously devouring everything in its path, mincing it up and spitting it out to bleed.

He almost closed his eyes to block out the image, but then those memories that had been sitting quietly in the corner tapped him on the shoulder. They replayed themselves for him, and then they introduced him to a few more.

Daniel hauled in a shuddering breath.

Just like plants, human beings needed certain things to thrive. Oh, it would be so easy if those things were just light and water and good manure. So easy. But, no, humans needed more complicated things. Things like closeness and connection. Otherwise they could be healthy specimens on the outside, but they'd be dried up and withered inside. Human beings needed love.

He started climbing again, more slowly this time. He'd always be hunted by it until the last of his days. And he was so tired of running. He didn't want to do it any more. It didn't bring peace. It didn't bring safety. All it brought was the promise that the next day would be another sprint. And the next. And the next...

And, really, there was no point in him running anyway. He was already in that trap, with no escape. Just like the fly that stupidly buzzed and exhausted itself trying to get out of the pitcher he was exhausting himself for nothing.

There was no point in struggling. It only made things worse.

He thought about Kelly, how she'd smoothed Ben's hair in the hospital, a look of fierce determination on her face. She didn't run. She chose to stay and fight, no matter what. Over the last couple of years she'd shown a strength and courage that put him to shame.

And that knowledge stirred something inside him.

They were made of the same stuff, him and Kelly. And, maybe, just maybe, if she could do this, so could he.

Oh, how Chloe hated Valentine's Day.

It seemed the whole twenty-four hours had decided to gang up and make a mockery of her. Not only was it the last day of the orchid festival—the one packed with all the PR events, meaning she was forced to stay close to Daniel—but in the back of her head was a clock, counting down to the following morning, when he would leave.

It was torture.

If only…a little part of her kept saying. If only he was ready… If only he felt the same way about you that you feel about him…

A camera flash went off, hitting the back of her eyeballs with searing force. She blinked and tried to maintain the smile the PR woman had insisted they paste on, all the while trying to ignore the prickling of her skin because he was near.

She was worrying herself. Mainly because she was having recurrent fantasies where she invited him back to her houseboat for one last hot night before he disappeared from her life. Possibly for good.

It was a bad, bad idea.

Because she'd fallen in love with him anyway. And, if she felt as if something were ripping her insides out piece by piece now, what would it be like if she truly removed every last barrier and gave herself completely to him? She had to hang onto something, some piece of herself she wouldn't lose. And, while she mourned Daniel's inability to let himself love anything or anyone, she totally, totally understood it. If only she could achieve that nirvana of numbness herself.

She was standing beside him at the edge of the lily pad pool, in front of the brightly coloured rainbow of flowers she'd designed, but shortly everyone would move along to the Nash Conservatory, another of Kew's old glasshouses, where the auction itself would be held.

'That's all for now,' the photographer yelled as she checked her display, and Chloe started to leave. She saw Daniel move towards her, but after a second of eye contact that made her almost dizzy holding everything she was feeling back, she looked away, allowed herself to be bustled along to the next event. As much as she didn't want to see him go, she was pretty sure she would fall apart completely if she had to talk to him.

As she'd said—torture.

The rest of the afternoon went in a bit of a blur. Before she knew it the sun was low in the sky, painting gold squares through the windows onto the wall of the Nash Conservatory, and she was sitting on a low platform near the auctioneer's lectern with a few other select members of the team, ready to give a brief description of each specimen on sale that night. At least Daniel was at the other end of the row, giving her a vague chance of breathing.

However, the fact she knew he was looking at her, even though she refused to meet his gaze, was counteracting that completely.

The place was packed. Full of orchid and carnivorous plant enthusiasts as well as fervent Kew supporters, the general public and quite a few reporters and TV cameras. More than once she saw them zoom in on Daniel, who was looking wonderfully gruff and brooding with his arms crossed over his front as he slouched in his chair.

She closed her eyes and sent up a silent prayer.

Please...please, let her get through this without making a total fool of herself. That was all she asked.

Daniel was definitely *not* in the mood to smile for the cameras, even if the Channel Six woman batted her lashes at him so hard she started a typhoon. All day long he'd been trying to talk to Chloe, and all day long he'd failed. Partly because of the flurry of activity it took to pull an event like this together, but partly because he sensed she was keeping her distance. It was driving him bananas.

He needed to talk to her—face to face, one to one—and now it looked as if he might be robbed of that chance entirely he wasn't inclined to look very happy. And Daniel was not good at pretending to be happy when he wasn't.

He saw a camera pointed in his direction, a zoom lens being focused, and he just scowled harder. He had things he needed to discuss with Chloe—plans—and it couldn't wait until tomorrow. In just over twelve hours he'd be at the airport.

The auctioneer banged his gavel and Daniel jumped. One of Chloe's lots was up first. She walked past him and a waft of her perfume hit his nostrils. She began to talk about the Miltonia hybrid in her husky voice and he felt as if he wanted to climb out of his skin. He'd wanted to hear that voice all afternoon, but not giving facts and growing instructions; he wanted to hear her saying his name.

It seemed as if a thousand lots passed before his eyes, as if they'd sold off the entire contents of all the glasshouses and the arboretum, but really the whole auction must have lasted less than two hours.

Even then there was no let-up. The PR team wouldn't set them free, insisting on more photos and, to top it all, a live

TV interview for the evening news. The team was directed back onto the stage in front of some of the larger orchid displays that had been transported from the Princess of Wales Conservatory to be used as a backdrop.

Someone from the news crew rearranged the interviewees and he ended up standing next to Chloe. He caught her eye and she held his gaze for just a moment, but it was long enough. Long enough to know she was finding this just as unbearable as he was. He'd find a way to talk to her somehow, he would. They just needed to get through this interview first.

The reporter turned to the camera, smiled, and started her spiel. 'This is Melissa Morgan for Channel Six news, live at Kew Gardens after their very successful tropical plant auction, which has raised thousands of pounds to go towards their conservation work all over the world...'

Daniel tuned her out. He only tuned back in again when he heard her mention first Chloe's name then his own as she introduced them as team leaders for the festival. She looked at Daniel and pointed the microphone too close to his face.

'As Head of Tropical Plants here at Kew, do you feel the festival has been a success?'

'Yes,' he said, then closed his mouth and folded his arms.

She opened her mouth to ask him a question, but he must have been looking particularly uncooperative because at the last moment she swung the microphone in Chloe's direction instead and asked her about the design of the display and what her favourite orchid was.

He snorted gently to himself. It figured. Who'd talk to the Beast when Beauty was at hand?

He could tell Chloe was nervous, however, from the slight waver in her first words, but she was warm and articulate, and he knew the viewing public would be transfixed, just as he was. They would love her.

Just as he did.

But that reporter didn't miss a trick. Too late he saw her

notice the way he was looking at Chloe. Too late he looked away, crumpling his features back into his earlier scowl.

The reporter let Chloe finish her sentence and then she turned back to Daniel. He didn't miss the slight arch of one eyebrow as she fired off her next question. Guess it hadn't been such a good idea to tick her off.

'This isn't your first Valentine's Day in the spotlight, is it, Daniel?'

If she thought she was getting even one word out of him now she was sadly mistaken. He merely blinked at her, raised his eyebrows in return.

Her eyes narrowed. 'And how is it one year on after your Leap Year proposal?' Her gaze flicked across to Chloe and then back to him. 'Is there any special woman in your life you'd like to give a Valentine's message to?'

Beside him, Chloe stiffened. He saw her glance at the exit.

'I don't think that's any of your business,' he said firmly.

Miss Morgan didn't like that any better than the monosyllable he'd offered her earlier. She narrowed her eyes and turned the microphone back in Chloe's direction.

'And how about you, Chloe? I saw a very interesting picture of you on the Internet a couple of months ago…' She gave Daniel a sideways glance. 'What was it like to finally hook The One That Got Away? Did you decide to throw him back?'

Chloe's mouth moved and she flushed deep pink. He could see the panic in her eyes, knew she was hating every second of this public interrogation.

'You know what?' he said suddenly. 'I would like to answer your question. Maybe it's time I set the record straight, then people might actually get on with their own lives instead of poking their noses into mine.'

'Daniel…' Chloe whispered beside him. 'You don't have to.'

Yes, he did. It was his fault Chloe had been put on the spot like this, and maybe it was time to stop running from this and face it head-on. Maybe it was time to face a lot of things head-on.

'I said no when my girlfriend proposed to me last year,' he began, 'and I don't regret it. What's more, after the success of the Year of Georgia on Radio EROS—' he watched in satisfaction as the reporter frowned at the mention of a rival media company '—I think it's obvious that she's doing much better without me than she was with me. And I can't blame her. I wasn't ready for love or marriage or anything like that then.'

A glint appeared in Melissa Morgan's eyes. He knew what that was—killer instinct. She knew she had a story here and she was going to hunt it down. Luckily for her, Daniel had decided he was going to hand it to her on a plate.

'And you're ready now?' she asked smoothly.

He'd spent weeks trying to let Chloe know how he felt. Unfortunately for him, he hadn't quite realised what those feelings were until it was too late. No wonder she didn't trust him, didn't believe in him. Every time she'd put herself on the line for him, he'd pulled back. Well, now it was his turn, and he wasn't going to run away from it.

He let the scowl melt from his features, looked the reporter in the eye and began to talk. 'Turning Georgia down was the best thing I ever did—for me and for her. Without that, I wouldn't have had the spotlight turned on me, and, in turn, I wouldn't have had to take a good, hard look at myself.'

Beside him, Chloe started to fidget. He stopped looking at the reporter and looked at her instead. She met his gaze, and he could see hope and fear and sadness and discomfort warring behind her eyes. 'This year I met someone,' he said softly.

Morgan nudged the microphone closer and he resisted the urge to bat it away. She needed to hear this. Everyone needed to hear this, especially Chloe.

'I met a woman,' he continued. 'An amazing, brave woman, who showed me what it really meant to be fearless, who showed me what courage—what dignity—looked like…and I fell completely and hopelessly in love with her.'

Chloe's eyes began to shimmer. She shook her head gently, her hand pressed against her breastbone.

'Yes,' he said, starting to smile, willing her to join him. 'I love you, Chloe.'

And then he shoved the microphone out of the way, stepped forward and kissed her. The room, which had descended into a thick silence as soon as he'd begun to talk, suddenly erupted into cheers and applause. There was a gentle tapping on his shoulder, but he ignored it, because Chloe was kissing him back, kissing him so softly and sweetly that he finally had no doubt that she felt the same way.

But the tapping continued and he dragged himself away from Chloe's lips. 'What?' he said gruffly. 'Can't you see I'm busy?'

That earned him a laugh. Even Chloe chuckled. He was funny. Who knew?

Melissa Morgan was grinning at him, but her grin had an edge of something else in it too. 'I can see that,' she said, laughing softly, but Daniel was close enough to see the calculating glint in her eye. 'But I thought I might repeat my earlier question…'

She looked between Chloe and Daniel, blinked slowly, and then positioned the microphone in Daniel's direction. 'So…*is* there a Valentine's message you'd like to deliver?'

The meaning behind her words hit him like a lightning bolt. He knew what she was asking, what she was pushing for…the Valentine's story to top all other Valentine's stories this year. And he also knew it was the one way he could convince Chloe he was serious about this, serious about her…

He made a nod so minuscule that only the reporter saw it. One corner of her mouth hiked up in a knowing smile, and she stepped back a little, still holding the microphone out.

Daniel swallowed. Nerves hit him in a wave of nausea,

but he knew he had to do this, knew now that he wanted it more than anything. Maybe that was why he'd been running so hard in the other direction all year.

It was now or never. The six-headed monster needed to be slain once and for all, and hadn't he always said he was the hunter, not the prey?

He took Chloe's fingers, lifted them in his own and covered them with his other hand, then he slid one foot back and let both knees bend, one up in front of the other. The crowd around them gasped.

He looked into Chloe's face and realised he couldn't tell what she was thinking. A moment ago, she'd been smiling blissfully, but now her features had frozen and she was blinking rapidly.

He took a deep breath. 'I love you,' he said again, and saw her nod, just slightly, and he knew she believed him. That made the next bit a little easier. 'I know I'm the biggest idiot in the universe…' he saw a glimmer of something in her eyes that just might have been humour and that spurred him on '…and I don't deserve another chance, but I can't go without proving how serious I am.' He took in a deep breath. 'Chloe Michaels, will you marry me?'

Chloe stared at Daniel. She thought her heart might have stopped beating. Her brain had certainly stopped working. She could feel her pulse throbbing in the hand he was holding. It rushed and pumped, filling the silence, filling every part of her.

She couldn't doubt the sincerity in his eyes. He'd meant what he'd said, yet…

Yet…

A couple of weeks ago he hadn't even been able to say how he felt about her. She knew he had baggage. *Lots* of baggage. Was this really the right time? And, if he hadn't been going overseas tomorrow, if he hadn't been pushed into it by that witch of a TV reporter, would he have asked her today? Would he have asked her at all?

The room had been perfectly still for far too many seconds, but that immaculate silence now broke. People began to move. Somebody coughed. She glanced over her shoulder at the gathered crowd. Every single face was turned towards her. Every pair of eyes was heavy on her.

She looked back at Daniel.

She wanted to believe him, really wanted to…but he'd backed off too many times before. When would be the next time? At the altar? She couldn't let it go that far. She had to be certain.

She opened her mouth, and Daniel pulled her hand towards his lips and then he closed his eyes and kissed it tenderly. A tear slipped down Chloe's cheek.

All of her. He'd said he'd loved all of her.

And heaven knew he'd seen the worst of her—the bits no one else had a clue existed.

He opened his eyes and looked at her again. The proof of his feelings was there for anyone to see. Intensity, yes, but softness too, and a tenderness she'd never seen before.

Chloe swallowed. She knew.

She knew what her answer had to be.

She moistened her lips with the tip of her tongue, and every single backside in that room shifted forward on its seat. She looked into Daniel's eyes, let him know how real her love was for him before she formed the words with her mouth.

Her voice rang out clear, even though she was sure it was going to catch on the barbs in her throat. 'I'm sorry,' she said, shaking her head. 'No. I can't marry you, Daniel.'

The room around them went wild.

CHAPTER THIRTEEN

CHLOE SHIVERED AS she stood on Daniel's porch. At this time of year, dawn was still an hour or so away. Was it too early to knock? She had no idea what time Kelly and the boys got up and she didn't want to disturb them. But she also didn't know what time Daniel's flight was—apart from this morning— and she had to see him before he left.

She checked her watch again. Five fifty-six. She watched the second hand sweep round. When it hit twelve again she screwed up her face, grabbed for the door knocker and rapped twice. It sounded like gunshots in the silent street.

For the longest time there was no light, no movement at all, but then she saw a patch of dull orange through the obscured glass of the Victorian door. And then she heard thudding on the stairs. Moments later the door opened and she was face to face with a crumpled-looking Kelly, a fluffy pink dressing gown clutched around her and held tight with the hand that wasn't on the door. When she saw Chloe her expression changed from one of sleepy befuddlement to something entirely less welcoming.

'For heaven's sake, Chloe! Have you gone *completely* insane?'

Chloe wet her lips with her tongue. She considered nodding, but instead she said, 'Can I see him?' Her breath came out in shaky white puffs on the predawn air.

Kelly's brow lowered further. 'Too late. He's already gone.'

Chloe hadn't been prepared for the cold stab to her stomach at that news. 'No...' she murmured, feeling a violent stinging in the bridge of her nose.

Kelly stared at her, and then she said, 'Oh, for crying out loud! Come in. I need to talk to you.'

She hesitated for a second, but she followed Kelly into the house, down the hall and through to the kitchen. When they reached the dining area, Kelly turned round and surveyed her with steely eyes. Chloe knew that expression. It was the one Daniel wore when he was a hair's breadth from losing his temper.

'Do you know...?' she asked, with a quiver in her voice, her pitch rising. 'Do you know what it took for him to ask you that—in front of all those people?'

She nodded dumbly.

'Then why, for God's sake, didn't you say yes?' Kelly shouted, then remembered the two sleeping boys upstairs and curtailed her volume.

'I...I...'

Kelly's eyes narrowed. 'Yeah, I got that much on the evening news last night.'

Chloe's head swam and she had to close her eyes to regain her balance. The evening news.

And Kelly had seen it?

'I'm so sorry,' she mumbled, and met Kelly's fiery gaze.

'And then you just left him to sit it out here, waiting for his plane, didn't even explain... Didn't even *talk* to him afterwards!'

'I couldn't!' Chloe replied. 'They—the PR team—they whisked us off in opposite directions. I tried to get to him, but everything was going wild... There were microphones and reporters everywhere.' She shook her head. 'Even if I could have got to him, he wouldn't have wanted it aired for the whole nation to see! I decided I would wait a bit…talk to him once the fuss died down…'

Kelly's expression softened a little. 'So why didn't you?'

'He wouldn't answer his phone. I thought maybe—' a small hiccupping sob caught her by surprise '—maybe he just needed some space…'

And then a big fat tear rolled down her cheek.

Kelly puffed out a breath. 'Sounds about right. You know Daniel… He doesn't do *crushed*, he does *angry* instead.'

Chloe nodded. 'That's what I thought. But I couldn't let him go without talking to him.' Oh, help. Here came the tears again, and this time they'd brought reinforcements.

Kelly pulled out a dining chair and motioned for Chloe to sit, then she did the same. 'Why did you say no?' she asked, her features drooping. 'You love him, don't you?'

Chloe hiccupped again and nodded vehemently. 'We've hardly even talked for weeks…'

'Because you asked him to leave you alone,' Kelly interjected, far too reasonably.

Oh, crap. She had, hadn't she?

'I wasn't sure…I'm still not sure…if he just said it as a knee-jerk thing, if that reporter kind of pushed him into it… If it's me he really wants,' she added, with a desperate look at Kelly, 'or if it's just the prize of getting me to say yes.' She swallowed. 'You know what he's like…'

'Yes, I do,' she said firmly. 'I know that he was broken inside until he met you, Chloe. I know he struggled to let himself care about anyone or anything.' Her expression grew grave. 'You've broken his heart, you know. He meant it. Every stupid word.'

Chloe felt a shiver start deep in her belly and work its way up through her body, through her shoulders and out of her mouth on a breath. 'I know,' she whispered. 'But meaning it and following through with it are two very different things. What if he changed his mind?' He had before. Twice. 'I couldn't live with it if he did it again,' she added, almost to herself.

Kelly shook her head. 'He's not like that,' she said, her eyes glistening a little. 'Believe me, if anyone knows about guys who run hot and cold, it's me. But Daniel… It takes him a bit of time to get there, but when he's in, he's all in.'

Something warm blossomed within Chloe, even as her stomach swirled with ice.

'Oh, Kelly… What have I done?' she whispered, and then louder, 'What time's his flight?'

Kelly was on her feet so fast her chair almost toppled backwards. 'He only left ten minutes before you knocked on the door. You could catch him with a fast enough driver.' But then she pressed her lips together and shook her head again. 'I don't know how you're going to get him to listen to you, though. The kind of foul mood he was in this morning won't lift for at least another week. The idiot will probably fly the plane himself to avoid talking to you at the moment.'

'Oh.' Chloe felt dizzy. There were too many things to think about. 'I don't have a car.'

'I do,' Kelly said, and then she ran to the bottom of the stairs and yelled, 'Boys! Get your coats and shoes on! We're going on an adventure.' Moments later a pair of dark heads appeared in the kitchen doorway.

'Cool!' Cal said, putting his wellington boots on the wrong feet. Ben didn't say anything—he was too busy watching his brother and copying everything he did. Including the wellies.

'Can we really get there in time?' Chloe asked breathlessly.

'I can outgun any cabby in London,' Kelly replied, 'but that still doesn't mean he's going to listen to you.'

For a moment her brain froze, too terrified by Kelly's words to think of any way round it, but then she said, 'I can think of one way to get his undivided attention for at least a couple of seconds. But I need to borrow some lipstick—the brightest and reddest you've got.'

Kelly looked her up and down. It was true that Chloe was not looking her best. She was wearing leggings with a ratty old pullover and her long red coat slung over the top. 'Honey,' Kelly said, 'you can borrow whatever you want. But I think you're going to need a hell of a lot more than lipstick.'

Daniel stared at Alan's back as they queued to go through airport security. He shuffled forward, passport in hand, handing it over when required and receiving it back without even noticing if it had been a man or a woman who'd inspected it. All he could think about was the journey ahead of him. Almost twenty-four hours on two planes. That was a long time to sit and think.

And, to be honest, the *sitting* part didn't worry him so much.

'Daniel!'

The shout came from behind him. Instantly, his skin puckered into goosebumps. He turned on autopilot, even as his brain was screaming at him to keep walking forward.

He wasn't ready for this.

Wasn't ready to talk to her, wasn't ready to see her.

But he was…seeing her. Just the other side of the passport check desks, behind a clump of queueing travellers. She wore a look of ragged desperation, her forehead bunched, her eyes pleading. Even with her hair a total uncombed mess she was still the most beautiful thing he'd ever seen. His rib muscles spasmed, squeezing his chest cavity.

He held her gaze for a second, then turned away.

He knew she was soft-hearted under all that gloss, that she wanted to explain—or, even worse, apologise—but he just wasn't ready.

He was one of those flies, caught in a pitcher, who'd

worked it out and had given up struggling. Only one thing left to do now… Drown in that clear, sticky fluid while slowly being digested alive. None of that lovely drugging, narcotic syrup for him, though. He would feel every second of it. So, no, he couldn't look at her again. Not because he hated her, not because he didn't love her. Quite the reverse.

There was some kind of commotion going on behind him. He ignored it at first, but then he heard her again. 'Daniel Bradford, don't you dare run!'

He froze.

'I love you!' She yelled it so loud that everyone in the security queue stopped and he smacked into Alan's back.

'Flipping hell,' Alan said, turning round, his eyes going wide.

Daniel couldn't resist any longer. He spun round to find Chloe balanced on top of a trolley piled with cases, elevating her above the crowd. Where she'd hijacked it from, he had no idea.

Her gaze connected with his and locked. Not so much desperation in those eyes now as determination. Without looking away, she fumbled with the tie on her coat. Then she pulled both the edges wide, her chin tilted up.

Daniel's heart stopped. Now she had his full and undivided attention.

'Flipping hell,' Alan mumbled again.

There wasn't much under that coat. But not fancy knickers. Plain, functional underwear. Didn't matter to him. She was still spectacular. But it was the bit *between* bra and pants that really caught his attention. Scrawled there in bright red… something…were some words.

I do! it read above her belly button in large block capitals, and beneath, *Do you?*

All this happened in a matter of seconds. When she'd seen he'd read and understood, the coat closed again and she knotted the tie firmly round her waist. Just as well, really. Already he could see a couple of security guards looking her way, trying to work out what all the fuss was about.

With no more distractions, his gaze was drawn back to her face. He could see it all there now—the pain, the embarrassment of what she'd just done, the apology he wouldn't have listened to any other way and, most importantly, the truth. The love.

I do.

Do you...?

He looked over his shoulder at Alan, standing behind him open-mouthed, and then back to Chloe.

He *so* did.

And then he was shoving his way past the half dozen people who'd piled through the passport check after him. Alan reached out and grabbed his sleeve.

'Hey! Where are you going? You just can't—'

Daniel wrenched his arm free and looked his colleague in the face. 'There'll be another plane tomorrow,' he said, 'but there won't be another woman like this one. Not for me.'

The two of them stared at each other, then Alan shrugged. 'Fair enough.'

When he turned again the crowd had melted away. People were standing back and grinning expectantly, leaving a clear path between him and the woman in the red coat—off the trolley now—hands clasped together and a million questions in her eyes.

And, off to the side, with his nephews, was his sister. Yup. He should have guessed she'd had something to do with this.

But he didn't care about the whys and wherefores now; he just ran to Chloe, scooped her up so her feet left the floor and delivered the kiss he'd been holding back for far too long. From the response she gave him, he'd guess she had one of her own to let loose.

'I'm sorry…so sorry…' she mumbled between kisses.

He pulled back, caught her face between his palms and waited for her to open her eyes. Her lids fluttered open. She focused on him and swallowed.

'You took me by surprise,' she said softly, her eyes glistening. 'I *do* love you. I do want to be with you. It was just a lot to take in unexpectedly. I panicked…'

Daniel leaned in and kissed her, communicating his understanding the best way he knew how. Softly. Tenderly. Skin upon skin. After all, there had been more times when she'd been the brave one, had hung everything she felt on the line, and he'd been the one to back away.

There was a not-so-subtle cough beside him, disguising the phrase *Get a room!* in his sister's dulcet tones. He smiled against Chloe's lips then broke contact. Her eyes were closed and she looked blissfully happy, totally lost. Good. So was he.

But then her lids snapped open and she looked at the departures board, panic written all over her features. 'Oh, Daniel! Your plane…'

He shook his head. 'It can leave without me. Borneo can wait another twenty-four hours.'

She clung onto him, buried her face in his shoulder. 'I'm going to miss you so much.'

'Come with me,' he whispered into her ear.

She pulled away and stared at him. 'I can't! My job—'

He silenced her with a quick, hot kiss. 'I started badgering the powers that be about the sudden need for an orchid expert on the team. Seven hundred species on that mountain alone…'

Chloe shook her head, her eyes full of disbelief. 'You didn't!'

He grinned at her. 'I did. And they said yes. It was supposed to be a surprise. I was going to tell you last night, but things didn't exactly go according to plan.'

She blinked at him, as if she couldn't quite make sense of what he was saying.

'If you want, you can join us next week,' he added.

That was when Chloe launched herself at him and kissed him until he couldn't remember if he was here because he was supposed to be getting on a plane or whether he'd just come off one.

'Oh, for goodness' sake,' a grumpy-voiced Kelly said somewhere to his left. 'At this rate we're never going to make it out of the airport.'

'Up there!'

Chloe pushed the damp hair back out of her eyes and looked where Daniel was pointing. The sun filtered through the canopy above their heads in shafts, dappling the rainforest floor with gold, lighting up the backs of leaves and adding yet more shades of green into the endless forest.

'Where?' She couldn't see anything.

Daniel came in close behind her. Much closer than a colleague on a seed-collecting expedition should. Thankfully, he was much more than that. No ring as yet—no time to shop—but she didn't care about that. And this, what he was giving her now, was so much more than metal and stones. That could come later.

She followed the line of his finger to a fallen log, its bark almost completely obscured by the ferns and mosses and creepers that clung to it.

'Oh!'

She saw it—the distinctive yellow and brown stripes of the rare slipper orchid. Her heart lurched. She wanted to go and see it up close, but first there was something she wanted to do even more. She turned towards him, sliding round under his outstretched arm, and pressed a kiss to his chin as she wound her arms around his neck.

'I was pretty clever proposing to you,' she said. 'Not many women get to marry a man who makes their long-cherished dreams come true.'

Daniel went still and stared down at her. There was a definite hint of challenge in his eyes. 'That's not quite right, is it?' he replied, slipping his arms under hers around her torso. '*I* proposed to you.'

She nodded, and one eyebrow lifted a little. 'Yes, you did, but—'

'I asked first,' he interjected. 'You wouldn't have pulled that stunt if it hadn't been for me.'

She licked her lips and looked sideways before returning her gaze to him. 'Yes,' she said, 'but mine's the one that stuck.'

He opened his mouth to argue, but she stalled him with a kiss. 'Shut up,' she said. 'We've got an orchid to catalogue.'

And after that, they had the rest of their lives to argue that one out.

* * * * *

THE FIRST CRUSH
IS THE DEEPEST

NINA HARRINGTON

CHAPTER ONE

AMBER DUBOIS CLOSED her eyes and tried to stay calm. 'Yes, Heath,' she replied. 'Of course I am taking care of myself. No, I am not staying out too long this evening. That's right, a couple of hours at most.'

The limo slowed and she squinted out at the impressive stone pillars of the swish London private members club. 'Ah. I think we have arrived. Time for you to get back to your office. Don't you have a company to sort out? Bye, Heath. Love you. Bye.'

She sighed out loud then quickly stowed her phone in a tiny designer shoulder bag. Heath meant well but in his eyes she was still the teenage unwanted stepsister who he had been told to look after and had never quite learnt to let go. But he cared and she knew that she could rely on him for anything. And that meant a lot when you were at a low point in your life.

Like now.

Amber looked up through the drizzle and was just about to tell the limo driver that she had changed her mind when a plump blonde in a purple bandage dress two sizes too small for her burst out of the club and almost dragged Amber out of the rain and into the foyer.

She looked a little like the mousey-haired girl who had lorded over everyone from the posh girls' table at high school.

Right now Amber watched Miss Snooty 'my dad's a

banker' rear back in horror when she realised that the star of the ten-year school reunion alumni had a plaster cast over her right wrist, but recovered enough to bend forward and air kiss her on both cheeks with a loud *mmwwahh*.

'Amber. Darling. How lovely to see you again. We are so pleased that you could make our little get-together—especially when you lead such an exciting life these days. Do come inside. We want to know everything!'

Amber was practically propelled across the lovely marble floor, which was tricky to do in platform designer slingbacks. She had barely caught her breath when a hand at her back pushed her forwards into a huge room. The walls were covered with cream brocade, broken up by floor to ceiling mirrors, and huge gilded chandeliers hung from the ceiling.

It was a ballroom designed to cope with hundreds of people.

Only at that moment several clusters of extremely bored-looking women in their late twenties were standing with their hands clasped around buffet plates and wine glasses.

Every single one of them stopped talking and turned around.

And stared at her.

In total silence.

Amber had faced concert audiences of all shapes and sizes—but the frosty atmosphere in this cold elegant room was frigid enough to send a shiver down her spine.

'Look everyone. Amber DuBois made it in the end. Isn't that marvellous! Now carry on enjoying yourself. Fabulous!'

Two minutes later Amber was standing at the buffet and drinks table with a glass of fizzy water in her hand. She smiled down at her guide, who had started to chew the corner of her lower lip. 'Is everything all right?' Amber asked.

The other woman gulped and whimpered slightly. 'Yes—

yes, of course. Everything is just divine. I just need to check something—but feel free to mingle, darling…mingle.'

And then she practically jogged over to a girl who might have been one of the prefects, grabbed her arm and in no uncertain terms jabbed her head towards Amber and glared towards the other side of the room.

Amber peered over the elaborate hairstyles of a cluster of chattering women who were giving her sideways glances as though scared to come and talk to her.

This was so ridiculous. So what if she had made a name for herself as a concert pianist over the years? She was still the quiet, lanky, awkward girl they used to pick on.

And then she saw it. A stunning glossy black grand piano had been brought out in front of the tall picture windows. *Just waiting for someone to play it.*

So that was the reason her old high school had gone to such lengths to track her down with an email invitation to the ten-year school reunion.

Amber sighed out loud and her shoulders slumped down. *It seemed that some things never changed.*

They had never shown the slightest interest in her when she was their schoolmate—far from it in fact. Amber Du-Bois might have had the connections but she was not one of the posh clique of girls or the seriously academic group. She was usually on the last table and the back of the bus with the rest of the eccentrics.

Well. If there was a time to channel her inner diva, then this was it. One final performance—and the only one they would be getting from her that evening.

Cameras flashed as Amber strode, head high, canapés wobbling, across the polished wooden floor towards the ladies room.

Behind her back, Amber heard someone tap twice on the microphone but the squeaky posh voice was cut off as she stepped inside the powder room, pushed the door firmly closed with her bottom and collapsed back against it for a moment, eyes closed.

Sanctuary! If the speeches had just started she might have the place to hide out for a few precious minutes—it could even be a chance to escape.

She was just about to peek outside to check for options when the sound of something falling onto the tiled floor echoed from the adjoining powder room, quickly followed by a colourful expletive.

Amber's heels clattered on the tiles as she strolled over and peered around the corner to see where the noise was coming from.

A short brunette was standing on tiptoe, straddling two washbasins, with her arms outstretched, trying to reach the handle of the double-glazed window which was high on the wall above her. A red plastic mop bucket was lying on its side next to the washbasin.

'What's this? Kate Lovat running out on a party? I must be seeing things.' A short chuckle escaped from Amber's lips before she could stop it, and instantly the brunette whirled around to see who it was—and screamed and waved her arms about the instant she saw who had asked the question.

Which made her wobble so much that Amber rushed forwards, slid her buffet plate onto the marble counter, flipped up the bucket to create a step and then wrapped her left arm around the waist of a compact bundle of fun in a stunning cerise vintage cocktail dress.

Kate Lovat was one of the few real pals that she had made at high school.

Irrepressible, petite and fierce, Kate used to have a self-confidence which was as large as the heels she wore to push her height up to medium and a spirit to match. Today her short tousled dark hair was slicked into an asymmetric style which managed to make her look both elegant and quirky at the same time.

'Kate!' Amber laughed. 'I was praying that you were going to turn up at the reunion. You look fabulous!'

'Why thank you, pretty lady. Right back at you. You are even more gorgeous than ever.' Then Kate's mouth fell open, her eyes locked onto the floor and she gave a high pitched squeak as she grabbed Amber's arm. 'Oh my...those shoes. I want those shoes. In fact if you were not several sizes bigger than me, I would knock you down and run off with them.'

Then Kate took one step back and peered into Amber's face, her eyes narrow and her brow creased. 'Wait a minute. You look peaky. And a lot skinnier than the last time I saw you... Did I tell you that I have suddenly become clairvoyant? Because I foresee chocolate and plenty of it in your very near future.'

Then she pointed at the plaster cast on Amber's wrist. 'I have to know. Wait.' She held up one hand and pressed the fingertips of the other hand to her forehead as though she was doing her own mind-reading act. 'Let me guess. You slipped on an ice cube at some fashionista party, or was it a yacht cruising the Caribbean? It must make playing the piano a tad tricky.'

'Kate. Slow down. If you must know, I tripped over my own suitcase a couple of weeks ago. And yes, I have cancelled everything for the next six months so my wrist has a chance to heal.' Then she paused. 'And why do you need to sneak out of the window at our school reunion when you could be catching up on the gossip with the rest of our class?'

Kate took a breath, her lower lip quivered and she seemed about to say something, then changed her mind, broke into a smile and waved one hand towards the door. 'Been there. Done that. This has been one hell of a rotten day and the kidnappers have blockaded the doors to stop us from getting out.'

Then Kate lifted her chin. 'But here is an idea,' she said, her dark green eyes twinkling with delight. She gestured with her head towards the red velvet chaise at the other end of the powder room. Two buffet plates piled high with pastries and cocktail skewers were stashed on the floor.

'Who cares about them? We have a sofa. We have snacks. And the really good news is that I crashed into Saskia five minutes ago and she is now on a mission to find liquid refreshment and cake. The three of us could have our own party right here. What do you say?'

Amber's shoulders dropped several inches and she hugged her old friend one-handed. 'That. Is the best idea I have heard in a long time. Oh, I had forgotten how much I missed you both. But I thought Saskia was still in France.'

Kate winked. 'Oh, things have certainly changed around here. Just wait until you hear what we have been up to.' Then she waved both hands towards Amber and grabbed her around the waist. 'It is so good to see you. But come on, sit. What drove you out from the chosen few? Or should that be who drove you out?'

Suddenly Kate froze and her fingers flew to her mouth. 'Don't tell me that snake in the grass Petra dared to show her face.'

Petra. Amber took a sharp intake of breath. 'Well, if Petra was in there, I didn't notice, and somehow I think I would have recognised her.'

'Damn right.' Kate scowled. 'Ten years is not nearly long enough to forget that face. A friend does not jump on her best pal's boyfriend. Especially at that pal's eighteenth birthday party.' Her flat right hand sliced through the air. 'For some things there is no forgiveness. None. Zero. Don't even ask. Oh—is that a mushroom tartlet?'

'Help yourself,' Amber replied and passed Kate her plate. Strange how she had suddenly lost her appetite the moment

Petra's name was mentioned. The memory of the last time she had seen the girl she used to call her friend flittered across her brain, bringing a bitter taste of regret into her mouth. 'It takes two to tango, Kate,' she murmured. 'And, from what I recall, Sam Richards wasn't exactly complaining that Petra had made a move on him. Far from it, in fact.'

'Of course not,' Kate replied between bites. 'He was a boy and she bedazzled him. He didn't have a chance.'

'Bedazzled?'

'Bedazzled. Once that girl decided that Sam was the target he was toast.' Then Kate coughed and flicked a glance at Amber before brushing pastry crumbs from her fingers. 'He's back in London now, you know. Sam. Working as a journalist for that swanky newspaper he was always talking about.'

Amber brought her head up very slowly. 'How fascinating. Perhaps I should ring the editor and warn him that his new reporter is susceptible to bedazzlement?'

'Careful.' Kate chuckled. 'They'll be saying that I am having a bad influence on you.'

'Well, that would never do! Hi Amber,' a sweet clipped voice came from the bathroom.

'Saskia!' Kate instantly leaped up from the sofa and grabbed the plate of mini chocolate cakes that was threatening to topple over at any second. 'Look who's here.' Then she caught her breath. 'What happened to your dress?'

Saskia slid onto the sofa and lowered a screw cap bottle of Chardonnay and two glasses onto the floor in front of them so that she could give Amber a hug.

It was only then Amber noticed the red wine stain which was still dripping down the sleeve of Saskia's cream lace dress. It was almost as if someone had thrown a glass of wine at her.

Maybe things had changed? Because if Kate was the petite quirky one of their little band and Amber the lanky American, then Saskia was the classic English beauty. Medium brown hair, medium height and size. And the one girl who would never cause a scene or make a fuss.

'Excuse me for a moment.' Saskia nodded. And, without waiting for an answer, she clenched her teeth and picked up one of the paper hand towels and tore it violently into strips lengthways. Then into smaller strips, then more slowly into squares. Only when the whole towel was completely shredded into postage stamps did Saskia exhale slowly, gather up all of the pieces and toss them into the waste basket.

'Well, I feel a lot better now.' She smiled and brushed her hands off.

Kate was still choking so Amber was the one who had to ask, 'Do you want to talk about it?'

Saskia sat bolt upright on the sofa, too proud to slouch back against the cushion, and casually mopped the stain with a paper napkin. 'Apparently I am all that is bad in the world because I refused to let the school alumni committee use Elwood House for free for the weekly soiree—you know, the one I have never been invited to? You should have seen their faces the moment I mentioned the going hourly rate. That's when the abuse started.'

She sniffed once. 'It was most unladylike. Frankly, I am appalled.'

Kate pushed back her shoulders and her chin forward. 'Right. Where are they? No one disses my pal and gets away with it. There are three of us against the whole room—no contest.'

'I have just finished ten years of training as a full-on concert diva,' Amber added. 'Want to see me in action? It can be scary.'

Saskia shook her head. 'That would be playing right into their hands. They would just love it if we made a scene. It gives them something to talk about in their shallow little lives.

Let it go. Seriously. I have decided to rise above it.' Then her face broke into a smile. 'I am already having far too good a time right here. Kate. Would you be so kind as to twist open that bottle? I want to hear everything. Let's start with the obvious. My love life is on hold until Elwood House is up and running, but what about you, Kate?'

Kate looked up from pouring the wine. 'Don't look at me,' she replied in disgust. 'I seem to have an inbuilt boy repellent at the moment. One taste and they run. Unlike some people we know. Come on, Amber. What's the latest on that hunky mountain man we saw you with in the celeb mags?'

'History. Gone. Finished,' Amber replied and took a sip of wine before passing it to Saskia. 'But I live in hope. If I ever get out of this powder room I am going to start fund-raising for my friend Parvita's charity in India and, you never know, I might meet someone over the next few months. I visited the orphanage with her a few months ago and I promised the girls that I would go back if I could.' Her eyes stared over their heads at the large white tiles. 'It is the most fabulous place and right on the beach,' she added in a dreamy faraway voice.

Then her shoulders slumped. 'Who am I kidding? Heath would be furious with me for even thinking about going back to India.'

'Heath? You mean, as in your stepbrother Heath?' Kate whispered. 'Why should he object to you going to India?'

Amber took a breath and looked over at Saskia and then back to Kate. 'Because he worries about me. You see, I didn't just fall over my suitcase and break my wrist. I had just got back from India and I sort of collapsed. There was an outbreak of…'

The sound of raucous laughter cut Amber off mid-sentence as a horde of noisy chattering women burst into the ladies room. Their voices echoed around the tiled space in an explosion of sound.

Amber pressed both hands to her ears. 'Sounds like the speeches are over and I have just heard the word karaoke.' She gestured towards the entrance. 'We might be able to sneak out the side entrance if we are quick. My apartment is the nearest. Then I'll tell you what really happened in India and why Heath is as worried as I am.'

CHAPTER TWO

'Tell me what you know about Bambi DuBois.'

The question hit Sam Richards right between the eyes, just as he was swallowing down the last of his coffee, and he almost choked on the coarse grounds in the bottom of the cup.

Frank Evans strode into the corner office as though he had a hurricane behind his back and waved a colour magazine in front of Sam's nose.

Sam sniffed and gave his new boss a one-handed hat tip salute. Frank had made his name in the media company by being one of the sharpest editors in the business who only worked with the best, but Sam had already been warned that Frank had not earned the editor's desk through his personnel skills.

'And good morning to you too, Frank,' Sam replied. 'And thank you for your warm welcome to the London office.'

'Yeah, yeah.' Frank shooed a hand in Sam's direction and pointed to the desk. 'Take a seat. Monday madness. Worse than ever. You know what it's like. The chief is on my back and it's not nine o'clock yet. Time to rock and roll. You talk. I listen. Let's hear it. Show me that you're not completely out of touch with the London scene after all those years out in the wilderness.'

Sam stifled a laugh. *So much for an easy first day in the new job.*

Frank settled the seat of his over tight suit onto the wide leather chair on the other side of the modern polymer table and ran his short stubby fingers through his receding grey hair before drinking down what must now be cold milky coffee.

His cheap tie was already tugged down a couple of inches and his shirt sleeves had missed the iron, but in contrast his eyes sparkled with intelligence as he leant his arms on one of the cleanest and most organised desks Sam had ever seen.

Bambi DuBois? The shock of hearing her name kept Sam frozen to the spot, cup in hand, before his brain kicked in and he frowned as though thinking about an answer. A few manly coughs gave him just enough time to pull together a casual reply to the editor who he had previously only spoken to twice on the telephone.

The editor who had the power to decide whether he had a future career in this newspaper—or not.

This was definitely not the perfect start to his dream job that he had imagined!

Lowering his cup onto a coaster, Sam assumed his very best bored and casual disinterested journalist's face. His career depended on this man's decision.

'Do you mean Amber DuBois? English concert pianist. Blonde. Leggy. Popular with the top fashion designers, who like her to wear their gowns at performances.' He shrugged at the newspaper editor and new boss who was staring at him so intently. 'I think she was the face of some cosmetic company a few years ago. And I would hardly call Los Angeles the wilderness.'

Frank slid a magazine across the desk. 'Make that the biggest cosmetic company in Asia and you are getting close. But you seem to have missed something out. Have a look at this.'

Sam took his time before picking it up and instantly recognised it as the latest colour supplement from their main competitor's weekly entertainment section. And any confusion he might have had about Frank's question vanished into the stiflingly hot air of the prized corner office.

The cover ran a full colour half page photograph of Amber 'Bambi' DuBois in a flowing azure dress with a jewel-encrusted tiny strapless bodice.

The shy, gangly teenage girl he had once known was gone—and in her place was a beautiful, elegant woman who was not just in control but revelling in her talent.

Amber was sitting at a black grand piano with one long, slender, silky leg stretched out to display a jewelled high heeled sandal and Sam was so transfixed by how stunning she looked that it took him a microsecond to realise that his new boss was tapping the headline with the chewed end of his ballpoint pen.

International Concert Pianist Amber DuBois Shocks the Classical Music World by Announcing her Retirement at 28. But the Question on Everyone's Lips is: Why? What Next for 'Bambi' DuBois?

Sam looked up at his editor and raised his eyebrows just as Frank leant across the desk and slapped one heavy hand down firmly onto the cover so that his fingers were splayed out over Amber's chest.

'I smell a story. There has to be some very good reason why a professional musician like Amber DuBois suddenly announces her retirement out of the blue when she is at the top of her game.'

Frank aimed a finger at Sam's chest and fired. 'The rumour is that our Amber is jumping on the celebrity bandwagon of adopting a vanity charity project in India to spend her money on, but her agent is refusing to comment. As far as I am concerned, this is a ruse to get the orchestras begging her to come back with a solid platinum hello. And I want this paper to get in there first with the real story.'

Frank sat back in his wide leather chair and folded his arms.

'More to the point—I want *you* to go out there and bring back an exclusive interview with the lovely Miss DuBois. You can consider this your first assignment.'

Then Frank shrugged. 'You can thank me for the opportunity later.'

The words stayed frozen in the air as though trapped inside an iceberg large enough to sink his new job in one deadly head-on collision.

Thank him?

For a fraction of a second Sam wondered if this was some sort of joke. A bizarre initiation ceremony into the world of the London office of GlobalStar Media, and there was a secret camera hidden in the framed magazine covers behind Frank's head which were recording just how he was reacting to the offer of this amazing *opportunity.*

Sam flexed out the fingers of both hands so that he wouldn't scrunch up the magazine and toss it back to Frank with a few choice words about what he thought of his little joke, while his normally sharp brain worked through a few options to create a decent enough excuse as to why Frank should find another journalist for this particular gig.

Sam inhaled slowly as each syllable sank in. It had taken him three months to arrange a transfer from the Los Angeles office of the media giant he had given his life to for the past ten years. He had worked himself up from being the post room boy and sacrificed relationships and anything close to a social life to reach this point in his career.

This was more than just a jump on the promotion ladder; this was the job he had been dreaming about since he was a teenager. The only job that he had ever wanted. *Ever.* No way was he going to be diverted from that editor's chair. Not now, not when he had come so far.

Sam blinked twice. 'Sorry, Frank, but can you say that again? Because I think I must have misheard. I've just spent the last ten years working my way from New York to Los Angeles on the back of celebrity interviews. I applied to be an investigative journalist not a gossip columnist.'

Frank replied with a dismissive snort and he bit off a laugh. 'Do you know what pays for this shiny office we are sitting in, Sam? Magazine sales. And the public love celebrity stories, especially when it concerns a girl with the looks of Amber DuBois. It's all over the Internet this morning that orchestras have been lining up and offering her huge bonuses to come and work for them for one last season before she retires. And then there is her publicity machine. The girl is a genius.'

He raised one hand into the air and gave Sam a Vee sign. 'She has only ever been seen with two dates in the last ten years. *Two.* And not your boring classical musician—oh, no, our girl Amber likes top action men. First there was the Italian racing car driver who she cheered on to be World Champion, then that Scottish mountaineer. Climbing Everest for charity. With the lovely Amber at Base Camp waving him farewell with a tear in her eye. She is the modelling musical sweetheart and her fans love her—and now this.'

The pen went back to some serious tapping. 'Think of it as your first celebrity interview for the London office. Who knows? This could be the last fluff piece you ever write. Use some of that famous charm I've been hearing about—the lovely Miss DuBois will be putty in your hands.'

His hands? Sam's fingers stretched out over his knees. Instantly his mind starting wheeling through the possibility that someone had tipped off this shark of an editor that ten years ago those same hands had known every intimate detail about Amber 'Bambi' DuBois. Her hopes, her dreams, the fact that she always asked for extra anchovies on her pizza and had a sensitive spot at one side of her neck that could melt her in seconds. The way her long slender legs felt under his fingertips. Oh, yes, Sam Richards knew a lot more about Amber DuBois than he was prepared to tell anyone.

This job was going to make or break his career, but he had promised himself on the night they'd parted that, no matter how desperate he was for money or fame, he would never tell Amber's story. It was too personal and private. And he had kept that promise, despite the temptation—but the world he worked in did not see it that way.

Sam had seen more than one popular musician or actor pull celebrity stunts to get the attention of the media, and he had learnt his craft by writing about their petty dramas and desperate need for attention, but Amber had never been one of them. She didn't need to. She had the talent to succeed on her own, as well as a body and a face the camera loved.

Frank shuffled in his chair. *Impatient for his reply.*

Sam took one look into those clever, scheming eyes and the sinking feeling that had been in the bottom of his stomach since he had walked into the impressive office building that morning turned into a gaping cavern.

He was just about to be stitched up.

What could he do? He did not have the authority to walk into a new office and demand the best jobs as though they owed him a future. Just the opposite. But Frank might have waited until his second day as the new boy.

'I'm sure you're right, Frank. But I was looking forward to getting started on that investigation into Eurozone political funding we talked about. Has it fallen through?'

Frank reached into his desk drawer and handed Sam a folder of documents.

'Far from it. Everything we have seen so far screams corruption at every level from the bottom up. Take a look. The research team have already lined up a series of interviews with insiders across Europe. And it's all there, waiting for someone to turn over the stones and see what is crawling underneath.'

Sam scan read the first few pages of notes and background information for the interviews and kept reading, his mind racing with options on how he could craft a series of articles from the one investigation. And the more he read, the faster his heart raced.

This was it. This was the perfect piece of financial journalism that would set him up as a serious journalist on the paper and win him the editor's job he had sacrificed a lot to achieve. And it had to be the London office. Not Los Angeles or New York. London.

'Does your dad still have that limo service in Knightsbridge? We've used them a couple of times. Great cars. Your dad might get a kick out of seeing your name on the front page.'

Might? His dad would love it.

His father had sacrificed everything for him after his mother left them. He had been a single parent to a sullen and fiercely angry teenager who was struggling to find his way against the odds. Driven by the burning ambition to show the world that he was capable of being more than a limo driver like his dad.

Sam Richards had made his father's life hell for so many years. And yet his dad had stuck by him every step of the way without expecting a word of thanks.

And now it was payback time.

This promotion to the GlobalStar London office was a first step to make up for years of missed telephone calls and flying Christmas visits.

Shame that his shiny new career was just about to hit an iceberg called Amber DuBois.

Aware that Frank was watching him with his arms crossed

and knew exactly how tempting this piece was, Sam closed the folder and slid it back across the desk. This was no time to be coy.

'Actually, he sold the limo business a few years back to go into property. But you're right. He would be pleased. So how do I make that happen, Frank? What do I have to do to get this assignment?'

'Simple. You have built up quite a reputation for yourself as a hard worker in the Los Angeles office. And now you want an editor's desk. I understand that. Ten years on the front line is a long time, but I cannot just give you a golden story like this when I have a team of hungry reporters sitting outside this office who would love to make their mark on it. All I am asking you to do is show me that you are as good as they say you are.'

Frank slid the dossier back into his desk drawer. 'If you want the editor's desk, you are going to have to come back with an exclusive interview from the lovely Amber. Feature length. Oh—and you have two weeks to do it. We can't risk someone else breaking Amber's story before we do. Do we understand each other? Excellent, I look forward to reading your exposé.'

Sam rose to shake hands and Frank's fingers squeezed hard and stayed clamped shut. 'And Sam. One more thing. The truth about "Bambi's Bollywood Babies" had better be amazing or you will be back to the bottom of the ladder all over again, interviewing TV soap stars about their leg-waxing regime.'

He released Sam with a nod. 'You can take the magazine. Have fun.'

Sam closed the door to Frank's office behind him and stood in silence on the ocean of grey plastic industrial carpet in the open-plan office, looking out over rows of cubicles. He had become used to the cacophony of noise and voices and telephones that was part of working in newspaper offices just like this, no matter what city he happened to be in that day. If anything, it helped to block out the alarm sirens that were sounding inside his head.

This was the very office block that he used to walk and cycle past every day on his way to school. He remembered looking up at the glass-fronted building and dreaming about what it must be like to be a top reporter working in a place like this. Writing important articles in the newspapers that men like his dad's clients read religiously in the back seat of the limo.

The weird thing was—from the very first moment that he had told his dad that he wanted to be a journalist on this paper, his dad had worked all of the extra hours and midnight airport runs, week after week, month after month, to make that possible. He had never once doubted that he would do it. Not once.

And now he was here. He had done it.

The one thing he had never imagined was that his first assignment in his dream job would mean working with Amber.

Sam glanced at the magazine cover in his hand. And reflected back at him was the lovely face of the one woman in the world who was guaranteed to set the dogs on him the minute he even tried to get within shouting distance.

And in his case he deserved it. The nineteen-year-old Sam Richards had given Amber DuBois very good reason to never want to talk to him again.

He might have given Amber her first kiss—but he had broken her heart just as fast.

Now all he had to do was persuade her to overlook the past, forgive and forget and reveal her deep innermost secrets for the benefit of the magazine-reading public.

Fun might not be the ideal word to describe how he was feeling.

But it had to be done. There was no going back to Los Angeles. For better or worse, he had burnt those bridges. He needed this job. But more than that—he wanted it. He had worked hard to be standing on this piece of carpet, looking out, instead of standing outside on the pavement, looking in.

He owed it to his dad, who had believed in him when nobody else had, even after years of making his dad's life a misery. And he owed it to himself. He wasn't the second class chauffeur's son any longer.

He had to get that interview with Amber.

No matter how much grovelling was involved.

CHAPTER THREE

'AND YOU ARE quite sure about that? No interviews at all? And you did tell Miss DuBois who was calling? Yes. Yes I understand. Thank you. I'll be sure to check her website for future news.'

Sam flicked down the cover on his cellphone and tapped the offending instrument against his forehead before popping it into his pocket.

Her website? When did a professional talent agency direct a journalist to a website? No, it was more than that. His name was probably on some blacklist Amber had passed to her agent with instructions that she would not speak to him under any circumstances.

He needed to think this through and come up with a plan—and fast.

Sam wrapped the special polishing cloth around his fist and started rubbing the fine polish onto the already glossy paintwork on the back wheel arch of his dad's pride and joy. The convertible vintage English sports car had been one of the few cars that his dad had saved when he had to sell the classic car showroom as part of the divorce from Sam's mother.

It had taken Sam and his dad three years to restore the sports car back to the original pristine condition that it was still today. Three years of working evenings after school and the occasional Sunday when his dad was not driving limos for other people to enjoy.

Three years of pouring their pain and bitterness about Sam's mother into hard physical work and sweat, as though creating something solid and physical would somehow make up for the fact that she had left Sam with his dad and gone off to make a new life for herself with her rich boyfriend. A life funded by the sale of his dad's business and most of their savings.

But they had done it. *Together.* Even though Sam had resented every single second of the work they did on this car. Resented it so much that he could cheerfully have pushed it outside onto the street, set it on fire and delighted in watching it burn. Like his dreams had burnt the day his mother left.

In another place, with another father and another home, Sam might have taken his burning fury out in a sports field or with his fists in a boxing ring or even on the streets in this part of London.

Instead, he had directed all of his teenage frustration and anger and bitterness at his father.

He had been so furious with his dad for not changing jobs like his mother had wanted him to.

Furious for not running after her and begging her to come back and be with them—like he had done that morning when he came down for breakfast early and saw her going out of the front door with her suitcases. He had followed that taxi cab for three streets before his legs gave way.

She had never even looked back at him. Not once.

And it was all his dad's fault. The arguments. The fights. They were all his fault. He must have done something terrible to make her leave.

Sam's gaze flicked up at the thin partition wall that separated the cab office from the workshop. Just next to the door was a jagged hole in the plaster sheet the size of a teenage fist.

Sam's fist.

It was the closest he had ever come to lashing out at his dad physically.

The screaming and the shouting and the silent stomping about the house had no effect on this broken man, who carried on working as though nothing had happened. As though their lives had not been destroyed. And to the boy he was then, it was more than just frustrating—it was a spark under a keg of gunpowder.

They'd survived three long, hard years before Sam had taken off to America.

And along the way Sam had learnt the life lessons that he still carried in his heart. He had learnt that love everlasting, marriage and family were outdated ideas which only wrecked people's lives and caused lifelong damage to any children who got caught up in the mess.

He had seen it first-hand with his own parents, and with the parents of his friends like Amber and the girls she knew. Not one of them came from happy homes.

The countless broken marriages and relationships of journalists and the celebrities he had met over the years had only made his belief stronger, not less.

He would be a fool to get trapped in the cage that was marriage. And in the meantime he would take his time enjoying the company of the lovely ladies who were attracted to luxury motors like free chocolate and champagne, and that suited him just fine.

No permanent relationships.

No children to become casualties when the battle started.

Other men had wives and children, and he wished them well.

Not for him. The last thing he wanted was children.

Pity that his last girlfriend in Los Angeles had refused to believe that he had no intention of inviting her to move into his apartment and was already booking wedding planners before she realised that he meant what he said—he cared about Alice but he had absolutely no intention of walking down an aisle to the tune of wedding bells any time soon. If ever.

No. Sam had no problem with using his charm and good looks to persuade reluctant celebrities to talk to him—and he was good at it. Good enough to have made his living out of those little chats and cosy drinks.

But when it came to trust? Ah. Different matter altogether.

He placed his trust in metal and motor engineering and electronics. Smooth bodywork over a solid, beautiful engine designed by some of the finest engineers in the world. People could and would let you down for no reason, but not motors. Motors were something he could control and rely on.

He trusted his father and his deep-seated sense of integrity and silent resolve never to bad-mouth Sam's mother, even when times had been tough for both of them. And they had been tough, there was no doubt about that.

But there had always been one constant in his life. His dad had never doubted that he would pass the exams and go to university and make his dream of becoming a journalist come true.

Unlike his mother. The last conversation that they ever had was burned into his memory like a deep brand that time and experience would never be able to erase.

What had she called him? *Oh, yes.* His own mother had called him a useless dreamer who would never amount to anything and would end up driving other people around for a living, just like his father.

Well, he had proven her wrong on every count, and this editor's job was the final step on a long and arduous journey that began the day she left them.

It was time to show his dad that he had been right to keep

faith in him and put up with the anger. Time to show him that he was grateful for everything he had done for him.

All of which screamed out one single message.

He needed that interview with Amber. He knew that she was in London—and he knew where her friends lived. He *had* to persuade her to talk to him, no matter what it took, even if it meant tracking her down and stalking her. He had come too far to let anything stand in his way now.

Amber DuBois. *The girl he left behind.*

His hands stilled and he stepped back from the car and grabbed a chilled bottle of water from the mini-fridge in the corner of the workshop and then pressed the chilled bottle against the back of his neck to try and cool down. Time to get creative. Time to…

The bell over the back door rang. Odd. His dad didn't like customers coming to the garage. This was his private space and always had been. No clients allowed.

Sam turned down the radio to a normal level and was just wiping his hands on a paper towel when the workshop's wooden door swung open.

And Amber 'legs up to her armpits' Bambi DuBois drifted into his garage as though she was floating on air.

He looked up and tried to speak, but the air in his lungs was too frozen in shock. So he squared his shoulders and took a moment to enjoy the view instead.

Amber was wearing a knee length floral summer dress in shades of pastel pink and soft green which moved as she walked, sliding over her slim hips as though the slippery fabric was alive or liquid.

Sam felt as though a mobile oasis of light and summer and positive energy had just floated in on the breeze into the dim and dingy old garage his dad refused to paint. The dark shadows and recesses where the old tins of oil and catalogues were stored only seemed to make the brightness of this woman even more pronounced.

She took a few steps closer, her left hand still inside the heart-shaped pocket of her dress and he felt like stepping backwards so that they could keep that distance.

This was totally ludicrous. After all, this was his space and she was his visitor.

His beautiful, talented, ridiculously lovely visitor who looked as though she had just stepped out from a cover shoot for a fashion magazine.

She was sunlight in his darkness—just the same as she had always been, and seeing her again like this reinforced just how much he had missed her and never had the courage to admit it.

Amber looked at him with the faintest of polite smiles and slipped her sunglasses higher onto her nose with one fingertip.

'This place has not changed one bit,' she whispered in a voice what was as soft and musical and gentle and lovely as he had remembered. A voice which still had the power to make his blood sing.

Then she glanced across at the car. 'You even have the same sports car. That's amazing.'

Sam had often wondered how Amber would turn out. Not that he could avoid seeing her name. Her face was plastered on billboards and the sides of buses from California to London. But that was not the real Amber. He knew that only too well from working in the media business.

No. This was the real Amber. This beautiful girl who was running the manicured fingertips of her left hand along the leather seat of the sports car he had just polished.

Maybe she had decided to forgive him for the way they had parted.

'My dad kept it.' He shrugged. 'One of a kind.'

Amber paused and she sighed. 'The last time I saw this car

was the night of my eighteenth birthday party and you were sitting in the front seat with your tongue down the throat of my so called friend Petra. About twenty minutes after you had declared your undying love for me.'

She gave a strangled chuckle. 'Oh, yes, I remember this car very well indeed. Shame that the driver was not quite as classy.'

Or maybe she hadn't.

Sam pushed his hand down firmly on the workbench behind him.

So. *Here we go.* In her eyes he was *still* the chauffeur's son who had dared to date the rich client's daughter. And then kissed her best friend.

Goodbye editor's desk.

Time to start work and turn on the charm before she chopped him into small pieces and barbecued him on the car's exhaust pipe.

'Hello, Amber. How very nice to see you again.' He smiled and stepped forward to kiss her on the cheek but, before he got there, Amber flipped up her sunglasses onto the top of her head and looked at him with those famous violet-blue eyes which cut straight through any delusion that this was a social call.

Her eyes might have sold millions of tubes of eye makeup, but close up, with the light behind her, the iridescent violet-blue he remembered was mixed with every shade from cobalt to navy. And, just for him today…blue ice.

The contrast between the violet of her eyes and her straight blonde hair which fell perfectly onto her shoulders only seemed to highlight the intensity of her gaze. The cosmetic company might have chosen her for her peaches and cream ultra-clear complexion, but it had always been those magical blue eyes that Sam found totally irresistible. Throw in a pair of perfect sweet soft pink lips and he had been done for from the first time he had seen her stepping out of his dad's limo with her diva mother screaming out orders from behind her back.

She didn't seem to know what to do with her long legs, her head was down and she peered at him through a curtain of long blonde hair before brushing it away and blasting his world with one look.

Now she was standing almost as tall as he was and looking him straight in the eyes. The smile on her lips had not reached her eyes and Sam had to fight past the awkwardness of the intensity of her gaze.

'My agent mentioned that you were back in town. I thought I might pop in to say hello. Hope you don't mind.'

Her gaze shifted from the casual trainers he had found stuffed in the bottom of the wardrobe in the spare bedroom, faded blue jeans and the scraggy, oil-stained T-shirt he kept for garage work. 'I can see that your fashion sense hasn't changed very much. Shame, really. I was hoping for some improvement.'

Sam glanced down at his jeans and flicked the polishing cloth against his thigh. 'Oh, this little old outfit? Don't you just hate it when all of your chiffon is at the dry cleaner's and you can't find a thing to wear?' He crossed his arms. 'And no, Amber, I don't mind you popping in at all, especially since my editor has been harassing your agent for weeks to arrange an interview. He will be delighted to hear that you turned up out of the blue, expecting me to be here.'

Amber floated forward so that Sam inhaled a rich, sweet floral scent which was almost as intoxicating as the woman who was wearing it.

A whirlwind of memories slammed home. Long summer days walking through the streets of London as he memorised routes and names and places for the limo business. Hand in hand, chatting, laughing and enjoying each other's company as they shared secrets about themselves that nobody else knew. Amber had been his best friend for so long, he hadn't even realised how much she had come to mean to him until they were ripped apart.

'Don't flatter yourself. May I sit?'

Sam gestured to the hard wooden chair his dad used at the makeshift desk in the corner. 'It may not be quite what you're used to, but please.'

She nodded him a thanks and lowered herself gracefully onto the chair and turned it around so that she was facing him.

Sam shook his head. 'You are full of surprises, Amber Du-Bois. I thought that it would take a very exclusive restaurant in the city to tempt you to come out of your lair long enough to give me an interview.'

Her reply was to lift her flawless chin and cross her legs. Sam took in a flash of long tanned legs ending in peep toe low wedge sandals made out of plaited strips of straw and transparent plastic. Her toenails were painted in the same pale pink as her nails, which perfectly matched her lipstick and the colour motif in her dress.

She was class, elegance and designer luxury and for a fraction of a second he wanted nothing better than to pick her tiny slim body up and lay it along the bonnet of the car and find out for himself whether her skin felt the same under his fingertips.

'What makes you think that I am here to give you an interview?' she replied with a certain hardness in her voice which plunged him back into the cold waters of the real world. 'Perhaps I am here to congratulate you on your engagement? Has your fiancée come with you from Los Angeles and my wedding invitation is in the post? I can see that you would want to give me heads-up on that.'

He reeled back. 'My what?'

'Oh—didn't you announce your engagement in the Los

Angeles press? Or is there another Samuel Patrick Richards, investigative reporter and photojournalist of London, walking the streets of that lovely town?'

Sam sucked in a breath then shrugged. 'That was a misunderstanding. My girlfriend at the time was getting a little impatient and decided to organise a wedding without asking me first. Apparently she forgot that anything to do with weddings brings me out in a nasty rash. It's a long-standing allergy but I have learnt to live with it. So you can save your congratulations for another time.'

Amber inhaled very slowly before speaking again. 'Well, it seems that this garage is not the only thing that hasn't changed, is it, Sam? You do seem to make a habit out of running out on girls. Maybe we should all get together and form a support group.'

She raised both of her arms and wrote in the air. '"Girls Sam Richards has dumped and ran out on." We could have our own blog. What? What is it?'

Sam crossed the few steps which separated them and gently tugged at her cardigan. 'Your arm is in plaster. Hell, Bambi, what happened? I mean, you have to play the piano…'

She pulled her cardigan over the plaster, but lifted her left arm across her chest.

'I broke my wrist a few weeks ago and I'm officially on medical leave. And that is strictly off the record. My career is fine, thank you. In fact, I am enjoying the holiday. It is very restorative.'

Sam shook his head. 'Must make your daily practice interesting…but are you okay? I mean there won't be any lasting damage?'

She parted her lips and took a breath before answering, and for some reason Sam got the idea that she was about to tell him something then changed her mind at the very last minute. 'Clean break, no problem. The exercises are working well and I should be as good as new in a few months.'

'Glad to hear it. This brings us right back to my original question. What are you doing here?'

He stepped forward and stood in front of her, with one hand on each arm of his dad's old wooden chair, her legs now stretched out in front of her and trapped between his. He was so close that he could feel her fast breath on his cheek and see the pulse of her heart in her throat.

Her mouth narrowed and this time it did connect with the hard look in her eyes.

But, instead of backing away, Amber bent forward from the waist, challenging him, those blue eyes flashing with something he had never seen before. And when she spoke her voice was as gentle and soft as a feather duvet. And just as tempting.

'Okay. It goes like this. I understand that you want to interview me in the light of my recent press release concerning my retirement. I'm curious about what it is that you think you can offer me which is so special that I would want to talk to you instead of all the other journalists who are knocking at my door. You have never been the shy or modest type, so it must be something rather remarkable.'

'Absolutely. Remember that dream I used to talk about? The one where I am a big, important investigative journalist working at that broadsheet newspaper my dad still reads every day? Well, it turns out that to win the editor's desk I have to deliver one final celebrity interview.' Sam pointed at Amber with two fingers pressed tight together and fired his thumb like a pistol trigger.

Amber nodded. 'I thought it might be something like that.' Her eyebrows went skywards. 'I take it your editor doesn't know about our teenage fling?'

'Fling? Is that what you call it? No. He certainly doesn't,

or he would have sent me to your last known address with
a bunch of supermarket flowers and a box of chocolates as
soon as I walked into his office. No. That part of my life is
filed under "private". Okay?'

She gave him a closed mouth smile. 'Why? I know you
must have been tempted. I can see the headline now. "The
real truth about how I broke Amber Du Bois' heart"? Yes,
there are plenty of television reality shows who would love
to have you on their list. I could hardly sue, could I?'

'I suppose not, but let's just say that I was saving that for
a financial emergency. Okay?'

'An emergency? You were saving me to get you out of
some money crisis? I don't know whether to be flattered or
insulted. Or both. I'm not sure I like being compared to a stash
of used notes which you keep under the mattress.'

'Oh—is that where you keep yours? I prefer banks myself.
Much more secure.'

Her eyes narrowed and she licked her lower lip as though
she was trying to decide about something important.

He could remember the first time he'd kissed those lips.
They had just come out of a pizza restaurant and got caught
in a heavy rain shower. He had pulled her under the shelter
of his coat, his arm around her waist and, just as they got to
the car, laughing and yelling as the rain bounced off the pavement around them, she had turned towards him to thank him
and her stunning face was only inches away from his. And he
couldn't resist any longer. And he had kissed her. Warm lips,
scented skin, alive and pungent in the rain, and the feeling of
her breath on his neck as she rested her head on his shoulder
for a fleeting second before diving into the warm, dry car.

Not one word, but as he'd raced back to the driver's door,
there was only one thing on his mind.

She was the passenger and he was the driver. Her chauffeur. The hired help. And that was the way it was always going to be. Unless he did something to change it.

Which was precisely what he had done.

Except to Amber he would always be the rough diamond she broke her teeth on. Girls like this did not date the help.

Sam stepped back and chuckled as he tidied away the polishing kit.

'Relax, Amber. It takes a lot of hard work to become a journalist in today's newspaper business. I earned this new job in the London office. Besides, I don't need to trawl through my past history to score points with my editor. Frank Evans is far more interested in what you are doing in your life right now. Not many people retire at twenty-eight. That's bound to cause some interest.'

'And what about you, Sam? Are you interested in what I am doing in my life right now?'

He looked up into her face, which was suddenly calm, her gaze locked on him.

Was he interested? A wave of confusion and a hot, sweaty mixture of bittersweet memories surged through Sam. His breathing was hot and fast and for a fraction of a second he was very tempted to lean back and give her the full-on charm offensive and find out just what kind of woman Amber had become by being up close and personal—and nothing to do with his job.

Fool. Eyes on the prize.

'The only thing I am interested in is the promotion to the job I have been working towards for ten long years in the trenches. Sorry if that disappoints you, but there it is.'

'Ah—so your editor needs a story and you thought you could use our teenage connection to wangle the real truth from my lips. Tut, tut. What shameful tactics. And if I even hear the words "for old times' sake", I promise that I will pretend to cry my eyes out and sob all the way home to my good friend Saskia's house and my girl gang will be round with my legal team in an hour. And I will do it. Believe me.'

'Oh—cruel and unnecessary. I think I just cut myself on your need for revenge. Well, think again, because I have no intention on wandering down memory lane if I can avoid it.'

Just for a second her lips trembled and the vulnerability and tender emotion of the girl he used to know was there in front of him but, before he could explain, her lips flushed pink and she chuckled softly before answering.

'I'm pleased to hear it, because I have something of a business proposition to put to you. And it will make things a lot simpler if we can keep our relationship on a purely professional basis.'

'A business proposition? Well, there's a change. The last time we met your stepbrother and your mother were doing a fine job running your life. As I remember, you didn't have much of a business sense of your own back then.'

And the moment the words were out of his mouth Sam regretted them.

How did she do that?

He made his living out of talking to celebrities and teasing out their stories with charm and professionalism, but one look at Amber and he slotted right back into being an angsty teen showing off and saying ridiculous things. Trying to impress the girl he wanted.

Yes, Amber's mother had been furious when she found out that her musical prodigy of a daughter was sneaking out to see the chauffeur's son, but he didn't have to listen when she told him how a boy like him was going to hold her daughter back and ruin her career.

He was the one who'd taken the cheque Amber's mother had waved in front of him.

He was the one who'd marched out of Amber's eighteenth

birthday party alone, only to find a warm and receptive Petra waiting for him in the car park.

Maybe that was why it still smarted after all of these years? Because the young Sam had fallen for her mother's lies, just as she had planned he should. Because she'd been right. What hope did Amber have if she was trapped with a no-hoper like Sam Richards?

It did not excuse what he'd done. But at least her mother cared about what happened to her child. Unlike his mother.

Amber's head tilted to one side and she peered around his side to focus on the sports car that he had just been polishing before answering in the sweetest voice, 'Well, some of us have moved on in the last ten years.'

The silence between them was as rigid as steel and just as icy.

Then Amber shuffled forwards in his dad's chair and raised her eyebrows. 'Do you know what? I have changed my mind. Perhaps it was a mistake coming here after all. Best of luck with the new job and please say hello to your dad for me. Now, if you will excuse me, I have an appointment with the features editor at another newspaper in about an hour and I would hate to be late.'

She pushed herself to her feet and waved a couple of fingers in the air. 'See you around, Sam.'

And, without hesitating or looking back, Amber strolled towards the garage door on her wedge sandals, the skirt of her floaty dress waving back and forth over her perfect derrière as she headed out of his life, taking any chance of a career in London with her.

CHAPTER FOUR

'AREN'T YOU GOING to ask me what it feels like to finally work in that shiny glass office I used to drag you down to ogle every week?' Sam called after her. 'I would hate for you to stay awake at night wondering how I'm coping with being a real life reporter in the big city. Come on, Amber. Have you forgotten all those afternoons you spent listening to my grand plans to be a renowned journalist one day? I know that you're curious. Give me another five minutes to convince you to choose me instead of some other journalist to write your story.'

Amber slowed and looked back at Sam over one shoulder.

And her treacherous teenage heart skipped a beat and started disco dancing just at the sight of him.

Just for an instant the sound of her name on his lips took her right back to being seventeen again, when the highlight of her whole day, the moment she had dreamt about all night and thought about every second of the day, was hearing his voice and seeing Sam's face again. Even if it did mean sitting in the back of the limo and in dressing rooms around the country as her mother's unpaid assistant and general concert slave for hours on end.

It was worth it when Sam took her out for a pizza or a cola for the duration of the concert she had heard so many times she could play it herself note perfect.

She had adored him.

He had not changed that much. A little heavier around the shoulders and the waistline, perhaps, but not much. His smile had more laughter lines now and his boyish good looks had mellowed through handsome into something close to gorgeous. She was sorry to have missed the merely handsome stage. But, if she closed her eyes, his voice was the same boy she used to know.

And the charm? Oh, Lord, he had ramped up the charm to a level where she had no doubt that any female celebrity would be powerless to resist any question he put to them.

Sam had always had a physical presence that could reach out and grab her—no change there, but she had not expected to feel such a connection. Memories of the last time she came to this very garage flooded back. His ready laughter and constant good-natured teasing about watching that she didn't knock her head on the light fittings. The nudges, the touches, the kisses.

Until he betrayed her with one of her best friends on her eighteenth birthday. And the memories of the train wreck of the weeks that followed blotted out any happiness she might have had.

Amber turned back to face Sam and planted her left hand on her hip.

'Perhaps I am worried about all of those hidden tape recorders and video feeds which are capturing my every syllable at this very moment?'

He smiled one of those wide mouth, white teeth smiles and, in her weakened pre-dinner state, Amber had to stifle a groan. What was wrong with the man? Didn't Sam know that the only respectable thing for him to do was to have grown fat and ruined his teeth with sugary food? He had always been sexy and attractive in a rough-edged casual way, as relaxed in his body as she had been uncomfortable in her tall gangly skin. But the years had added the character lines to his face, which glowed with vitality and rugged health. Confidence and self-assurance were the best assets any man could have and Sam had them to spare.

'In this garage? No. You can say what you like. It's just between us. Same as it ever was.'

The breath caught in Amber's throat. Oh, Sam. Trust you to say exactly the wrong thing.

She flicked her hair back one-handed and covered up the bitter taste of so much disappointment with a dismissive choke. He must be desperate to go to such lengths for this interview. She had no idea how much journalists earned, but surely he didn't need the job that much?

Drat her curiosity.

Of course she remembered the way he used to talk about how he was going to work his way through journalism school at all of the top London newspapers and be the star investigative journalist. His name would be on the front page of the big broadsheet newspapers that his dad read in the car as he waited for his clients to finish their meetings or fancy events.

Maybe that was it?

Maybe he was still hungry for the success that had eluded him. And this interview would take him up another rung in that long and rickety ladder to the front page.

She was a celebrity that he wanted to interview for his paper to win the extra points he needed for the big prize. And the bigger the story the more gold stars went onto his score sheet.

And that was all. Nothing personal. He had walked—no, he had *run* away from her at the first opportunity to make his precious dream of becoming a professional journalist a reality.

She did not owe him a thing.

'Same as it ever was? In your dreams,' she muttered under her breath, just loud enough for him to hear. 'That editor of yours must really be putting the pressure on if you're resorting to that line.'

Sam shrugged off her jibe but looked away and pretended to tidy up the toolbox on the bench for a second before his gaze snapped back onto her face.

'What can I say? Unlike some people, I need the job.' Then he laughed out loud. 'You always had style, Amber, but retiring at twenty-eight? That takes a different kind of chutzpah. I admire that.'

He stepped forward towards her and nodded towards her arm, his eyes narrowed and his jaw loose. 'Is it your wrist? I know you said that it was a clean break, but…'

'No,' she whispered. 'It's nothing to do with my wrist.'

'I am glad to hear it. Then how about the other rumours? A lot of people think that you are using this announcement to start a kind of bidding war between rival orchestras around the world. Publicity stunts like this have been done before.'

'Not by me. I won't be making a comeback as a concert pianist. Or at least I don't plan to.'

Amber swallowed down her unease, reluctant to let Sam see that she was still uncertain about where her life would take her.

She had made her decision to retire while recovering in hospital and she'd imagined that a simple press statement would be the easiest way to close out that part of her life. Her agent was not happy, of course—but he had other talent on his books and a steady income from her records and other contracts—she was still valuable to him.

But the hard implications were still there on the horizon, niggling at her.

Music had been her life for so long that just the thought of never performing in public again was so new that it still ruffled her. Playing the piano had been the one thing that she did well. The one and only way that she knew to earn her mother's praise.

Of course Julia Swan would have loved her daughter to choose the violin and follow in her footsteps, but it soon became obvious that little Amber had no talent for any other instrument apart from the piano.

For a girl who was moving from one home to another, one school to another, one temporary stepdad to another, music had been one of the few constants in her life. Piano practice was the perfect excuse to avoid tedious evenings with her mother and whatever male friend or violin buff she was dating at the time.

The piano was her escape. Her refuge. It was where she could plough her love and devotion and all of the passion that was missing in her life with her bitter and demanding, needy and man-hunting mother.

So she had worked and worked, then worked harder to overcome her technical problems and excel. It was her outlet for the pain, the suppressed anger. All of it. And nobody knew just how much pain she was in.

Because there was one thing that her mother never understood—and still did not understand, even when she had tried to explain at the hospital. And then in the endless texts and emails and pleading late night phone calls begging her to reconsider and sometimes challenging her decision to retire.

Amber had always played for the joy in the music.

She was not an artist like her mother, who demanded validation and adoration. She just loved the music and wanted to immerse herself in the emotional power of it.

And Sam Richards was the only other person on this planet who had ever understood that without her having to explain it.

Until this moment she had thought that connection between them would fade with the years they had spent apart.

Wrong.

Sam was looking at her with that intense gaze that used to make her shiver with delight and anticipation of the time that they would spend together and, just for a second, her will faltered.

Maybe this was not such a good idea?

Getting her own back on Sam had seemed a perfectly logical thing to do back in the penthouse, but here in the garage which was as familiar as her own apartment, suddenly the whole idea seemed pathetic and insulting to both of them. She had made plenty of poor decisions over the past few years—surely she could forgive Sam the mistakes he had made as a teenager desperate to improve his life?

Amber opened her mouth and was just about to make an excuse when Sam tilted his head and rubbed his chin before asking, 'I suppose this is about the money?'

And there it was. Like a slap across the face.

Her lower lip froze but she managed a thin smile. 'Are you talking about the blood money you took from my mother to leave me alone and get out of London? To start your new career, of course.'

His mouth twisted and faltered. 'Actually, I was thinking more about the generous donation the paper will be contributing to your favourite charity. Although I should imagine that we are not the only ones to offer you something for your time. Not that you need the money, of course. Or the publicity.'

'You don't think that I need publicity?'

'Come on, Amber, your face was on billboards and the sides of buses, your last CD went into the top ten classical music charts and you have set new records for the number of followers you have on the social media sites. Publicity is not your problem.'

'It goes with the job—I am in showbiz. Correction. Was in showbiz. That doesn't interest me any longer.'

'Okay then. So why are you even talking to me about doing an interview? Seeing as you don't need the publicity.'

'Logistics. I thought that the press would get bored after a couple of weeks and move onto the next musician. Wrong! I was almost mobbed outside the record company this morning. So it makes sense to do one comprehensive interview and get it over with.'

She waved one hand in the air. 'One interview. One journalist.'

Sam shoved his hands deep into the pockets of his jeans, his casual smile replaced by unease.

'Wait a minute. Are you offering me an exclusive?' he asked. 'What's the catch?'

'Oh, how suspicious you are. Well. As it happens, I might be willing to give you that interview.' She cleared her throat and tilted her head, well aware that she had his full attention. 'But there are a few conditions we need to agree on before I talk on the record.'

'Conditions. This sounds like the catch part.'

'I prefer to think of them as more of a trade. You do something for me, I do something for you. And, from what I have seen so far, you might find some of them rather challenging. Still interested?'

'Ah. Now we have it. You know you have the upper hand so you decided to come down here to gloat?'

'Gloat? Do you really think I would do that?' she repeated, her words catching at the back of her throat. Was that how he thought of her? As some spoiled girl who had come to impress him with her list of achievements?

'I haven't changed that much, Sam. We've both done what we set out to do. You need an interview and I have a few things I need doing which you might be able to help me with. It's as simple as that.'

'Simple? Nothing about you was ever simple, Amber.'

Sam leaned back against the workbench and stretched out his long arms either side of him so that his biceps strained against the fabric of his T-shirt across his chest and arms. The sinewy boy she had known had been replaced by a man who knew his power and had no problem using it to get his way.

And the tingle of that intense gaze sent the old shivers down the back of her legs and there was absolutely nothing she could do to stop them. Her heart started thumping and she knew that her neck was already turning a lovely shade of bright red as his gaze scanned her face.

She could blame it on the hot May sunshine outside the garage door, but who was she trying to kid?

What had Kate said about Petra? That she had bedazzled Sam that night? Well, the Sam who was scanning her body was quite capable of doing his own bedazzling these days.

Sam had been the first boy who had ever given her the tingles and there had only been two other men in her life. All god-handsome, all rugged and driven and all as far removed from the world of music and orchestral performance venues as it was possible to imagine.

And every single one of them had swept her off her feet and into their world without giving her time to even think about what she was doing or whether the relationship had a chance. Little wonder that she had ended up alone and in tears, bewildered and bereft, wondering what had just happened and why.

But one thing was perfectly clear. Sam had been the first, and there was no way that she was going to go through that pain again, just to score a few points on the payback scoreboard.

Decision time.

If she was going to do this, she needed to do it now, and put the tingles down to past stupidity. Or she could turn around and run as fast as she could back to the penthouse and lock the door tight behind her. Just as her kind friends thought that she should. Just as she would have done only a few months earlier, before her life had changed.

'I hadn't planned to give any more interviews after the press release. That part of my life is over,' she said, her chin tilted up. 'But I have a few things you could help me with and you need this interview to impress your editor and make your mark in the London office. Am I getting warm?'

He shrugged and tried to look casual. But there was just that small twitch at the side of his mouth which he used to have when things were difficult at home and he didn't want to talk about it. 'Warm enough.'

'Warm? If I was any hotter I would be on fire. If I go to another paper, you will be waiting on the pavement for movie stars to stagger out from showbiz parties wearing their underpants as hats.'

Sam's hands gripped onto the bench so tightly that his knuckles started to turn white. 'Ah. Now I am beginning to understand. You want to see me suffer.'

Amber winced and gave a small shoulder shrug. 'You walked out on me and broke my heart. So yes, it would be a shame to miss the opportunity for some retribution. And I am not in the least bit ashamed.' She took a breath. 'But that was a long time ago, Sam. And I am keen to put that away in a box labelled "done and dusted". I think this will help me do that.'

Sam closed his eyes and shook his head from side to side before blinking awake and laughing out loud. 'Done and dusted, eh? I am almost frightened to ask what form my punishment is going to take. But please, do continue, let's get it over with.'

He stood to maximum height, pushed his shoulders back and lifted his chin. 'Hit me.'

Amber strolled into the garage and focused her attention on the sports car, her fingertips lingering on the old leather seats, her face burning with awareness that Sam's gaze was still locked onto her. 'I want to get this done as soon as I can, but time is tight. I'm redecorating my apartment and the girls want to celebrate my birthday this week.'

She almost turned around at the sound of Sam's sharp intake of breath. 'May eighteenth. Hard to forget.'

Amber flung her head up and twisted around at the waist, ready with a cutting remark, but bit it back when she saw the look on Sam's face was one of sadness and regret.

His lips twitched for a second before he replied. 'Busy week. No problem. Just give me your email address and I can send over some questions so you can work on them when you have time.'

'Email questions? Oh, no. This interview has to be in person.'

Sam coughed twice. 'Are you always so awkward?'

She tilted her head slightly to one side before replying. 'No. Just with you.'

He laughed out loud and planted a fist on each hip. 'Don't try and kid me, girl. You have been planning this for ages and are having way too much fun teasing this out.' He flicked his chin in her direction. 'You could have asked your agent to make the call and organised the interview over the phone. But that wouldn't have been nearly so satisfying, would it?'

He waved her spluttering away. 'And I understand that perfectly. Really. I do. I made a horrible mistake and treated you badly, and now you're going to make me pay.'

Then his stance softened and his gaze darted from side to side. 'I'm not proud of what happened the last time we met. Far from it. But that was ten years ago and we're different people now. At least I am. I'm not sure about you.'

'What do you mean?'

'You never had a vindictive thought in your life, Amber DuBois. So why don't you just take me through that list of little things you want me to help you with and we can get this over and done with, and we can put the past behind us?'

Amber inhaled slowly and turned to face Sam, her head tilted slightly to one side, and she carefully pushed the slip of paper deeper into the heart-shaped pocket of her dress.

'What makes you think I have a list?' she asked in the best innocent and surprised voice she could muster at short notice.

'Amber. You always had a list. For everything. A list of things to do that day, a list of how long you practised that week. You are a listy type of person and people don't change that much. So it makes sense for you to have a list of all the things I am going to have to do in exchange for one interview.'

He shot her a glance which made her eyes narrow. Why did he have to remember that small detail, of all things? There was no way she could talk him through her list now.

'I prefer to think of them as challenges. But you are right about one thing—I have thought about what you could possibly give me in exchange for an exclusive, and you can take that smirk off your face right now. You would not be so lucky. So I came up with a new approach.'

She crossed the space between them until her face was only inches away from his and licked her lips before speaking.

'Look, Sam,' she said in low, calm voice as her gaze locked onto his. 'I know people are interested in why I decided to retire when I did, but my reasons are very personal and very close to my heart.' She took a breath and swallowed before rolling her shoulders back a little. 'It would be very easy for a reporter to do a hatchet job with some crazy headline just to sell more papers. So…I need to know that I can trust the journalist I go for to give me a fair hearing.'

'That's not going to be easy,' he replied in a voice which sang with resignation and disappointment.

'I know. This is why you are going to have to prove to me

that you are the right man for the job before I say a word on the record.'

His eyebrows went skywards. 'Any ideas on how I do that?'

'Oh, yes,' she sniffed. 'You are going to have to pass an audition before I give you the job. You see, this week is crazily busy and my wrist is a problem. So I need someone to be my Man Friday for the next few days. Unpaid, of course, and you provide your own uniform. But all refreshments are provided by the management. And I just know how much Saskia and Kate are looking forward to having you around the place.'

'A Man Friday,' Sam repeated, very, very slowly. 'So, basically, I have to be your man slave for the next week before you'll even think about giving me the interview?'

Amber picked her business card out of her dress pocket with two fingers, gave Sam her sweetest camera-ready smile and looked deep into his startled eyes as she held the card high in the air. 'Well, it's good to know that your powers of deductive reasoning are as sharp as ever. The audition starts at my apartment at ten tomorrow morning. Oh—and just to make it a little more interesting, I'll have a new challenge for you every day. See you there, Sam. If you are man enough to accept the challenge.'

The air bristled with tension for all of ten seconds. Then Sam took two powerful steps forward, his brows low and dark-eyed, his legs moving from the hips in one smooth movement. Driven. Powerful.

And, before Amber had a chance to complain or slip away, Sam splayed one hand onto her hip and drew her closer to him. Hip to hip.

Amber's breath caught in her throat as his long clever fingers pressed against the thin silk of her dress as though it was not there. She could feel his hot breath on her face as she inhaled a scent that more than anything else she had seen or experienced today whipped her right back to being held in

Sam's arms. It was car oil, polish, man sweat, dust and ambition and all Sam. And it was totally, totally intoxicating.

His gaze locked onto her eyes. Holding her transfixed.

'Bambi, I am man enough for anything that you have to offer me,' Sam whispered in a voice which was almost trembling with intensity, one corner of his mouth turned up into a cheeky grin as though he knew precisely what effect he was having on her blood pressure. And there was not one thing she could do about it.

Then, just like that, he stepped back and released her, and it took a lot to stay upright.

And then he winked at her.

'See ya tomorrow—' he smiled with a casual lilt in his voice '—looking forward to it.'

CHAPTER FIVE

'No Mother. Seriously. I don't need another expert medical opinion. Every specialist I have seen recommends six months' recovery time. Yes, I am sure your friend in Miami is excellent but I am not pushing my wrist by trying to practice before it is ready.'

Amber closed her eyes and gave her virtuoso violinist mother two more minutes of ranting about how foolish she was to throw away her career before interrupting. 'Mum, I love you but I have to go. Have a great cruise. Bye.'

Amber closed the call, strolled over to the railing of her penthouse apartment and looked out over London. The silvery River Thames cut a wide ribbon of glistening water through the towering office blocks of glass and exposed metal that clung to the riverbanks. Peeking out between the modern architectural wonders were the spires and domes of ancient churches and imposing carved stone buildings that had once been the highlights of the London landscape.

Even five storeys up, the hustle and bustle of traffic noise and building work drifted up to the penthouse, creating the background soundtrack to her view of modern city life.

Everywhere she looked she saw life and energy and the relentless drive for prosperity and wealth. Investment bankers, city traders and financial analysts jostled on the streets below her on the way to their computer trading desks. Time was money.

The contrast to the tiny beachside orphanage in Kerala where Parvita was celebrating her wedding could not be greater.

The seaside village where the girls' orphanage was based had running water and electricity—most of the time.

She would love to go back and see them again. *One day*. When she was not so terrified of catching another life-threatening infection.

A cold shiver ran across Amber's shoulders and she pulled her cashmere tighter across the front of her chest.

Heath and her mother were right about one thing. *As always*. Even if she wasn't scared, she *could* raise more income for the orphanage by staying in London or Boston or Miami and fund-raising than risk returning to Kerala, where she had caught meningitis only a few months earlier.

Now all she had to do was come up with a way of doing precisely that.

Not by playing the piano. That was for sure.

No matter how much her mother nagged her to reconsider and plan a comeback concert tour. A year ago she might have gone along with it and started rigorous training but that part of her life was over now.

Wiped away by meningitis and a few months of enforced bed rest when she had to ask some hard questions about the life she was living and how she intended to spend it in the future.

Amber closed her eyes and inhaled and exhaled slowly a couple of times. *No going back, girl. No going back. Only forward. This was her new start. Her new beginning.*

The sun was warm on her face and when she opened her eyes the first thing she saw was the braided cord bracelet that

Parvita had made and woven onto her right wrist that last day she was at the orphanage.

She was so lucky.

Heath and her mother loved her and that was what she had to focus on. Not their nagging. She would go back to Boston and start work with the fund-raising committee for Parvita. Benefit concerts were always popular and between her mother and their network of professional musicians they could pull together some top name soloists who could raise thousands for the charity.

This was her chance to do something remarkable. And she was going to grab hold of it with both hands and cling on tight, no matter how bumpy the road ahead was.

First hurdle? Talking to Sam.

Amber glanced at her wristwatch and a fluttering sensation of apprehension blended with excitement bubbled up from deep inside. In another place and time she might have said that the thought of seeing him again face to face was making her nervous. That was totally ridiculous. This was her space and he was here to help her out, as he had promised.

This was not the time to get stage fright.

She was an idiot.

They had agreed to make a trade. His time in exchange for one interview. Nothing more. *What else could there be?*

Her thoughts were interrupted by a petite bundle of energy.

'One good thing came out of that whole school reunion fiasco.' Kate laughed and threw her arms around Amber's waist. 'The three of us haven't been in the same city at the same time for far too many years. And that is a disgrace. So all hail school reunions.'

Amber laughed out loud and stepped back to clink her mug of coffee against Kate's. 'With you on that. I still cannot believe that it's the middle of May already. April was just a blur.'

Kate groaned and slumped into the patio chair facing

Amber. 'Tell me about it. London might be suffering from the economic recession but bespoke tailoring is booming and I have never been so busy. It's great. Really great. But wow, is it exhausting.'

'Well, here is something to keep you going.' Saskia Elwood came out from Amber's penthouse apartment with a tray of the most delicious-looking bite-sized snacks, which she wafted in front of Amber. 'Test samples for your birthday party. I need you to taste them all and tell me which ones you like best.'

Kate half rose out of her chair. 'Hey, don't I get to try them too? I could scoff the lot. And breakfast was hours ago.'

'You're next but the birthday girl has first pick. Besides, she needs fattening up a bit. What did they feed you in that hospital, anyway? I can't have you coming to my dining room looking all pale and scrawny.'

Amber munched away on a mini disc of bacon and herb pizza and made humming sounds of appreciation before speaking between bites. 'No appetite. It was so hot and I was asleep most of the time. And the food certainly wasn't as good as this. These are fantastic.'

'Thought you would like it and there are lots more to come. So tuck in.'

Kate snatched a tiny prawn mayo sandwich and chewed it down in one huge bite before sighing in pleasure. 'Oh, that is so good. Amber DuBois, it was a genius idea to have your birthday party at Saskia's house.'

'It was the very least I could do. Ten years is a long time and all three of us have come a long way,' Amber replied and raised her coffee as a toast. 'I missed you both so much. To the goddesses.'

'The goddesses,' Kate and Saskia echoed and all three of them settled back in their chairs in the sunshine with the tray of snacks between them, hot Italian blend coffee and the sound of the city way below to break up the contented sighs.

'So what have you been up to, Amber?' Saskia asked, her eyes shielded with a hand as she nibbled on a fresh cream profiterole drizzled with chocolate sauce. 'It must get you down when you're unable to practise for hours like you usually do.'

Amber waved her right arm in the air and turned the plaster cast covering her wrist from side to side. 'Frustrating more than anything, but the exercises are keeping my fingers working and I have to get used to being one handed for a few more weeks. Only that isn't the problem. There is something missing and somehow…' Then she gave a chuckle and shook her head. 'Oh, ignore me. I'm just being silly.'

'Oh, no, you don't,' Saskia said in a low voice. 'We can tell that there is something bothering you. And you know that we're not going to let it drop until you tell us what the problem is. So come on. Spill. Out with it.'

Amber focused her gaze on the terrace. Bright flowering plants and conifers spilled out of colourful planters in front of a panoramic view across the London city skyline.

'Yesterday I was feeling down in the dumps so I pulled out my favourite music scores. If I have a spare hour or two on tour I can usually visualise the performance in my head and it is the one thing that is always guaranteed to cheer me up and have me bouncing with excitement.'

She paused and sighed low and slow. 'But not this time. I didn't feel a thing. There was nothing that made me want to tear off this plaster cast and play. *Seriously*. It's as though all of my passion for the music has gone out of the window.'

She paused and looked from Saskia to Kate and then back to Saskia again. 'And that's scary, girls. I don't know how to do anything else.'

The silence echoed between the three of them before Kate put her mug down on the metal mesh table with a dramatic thud.

'Amber? Sweetie? It might have something to do with the fact that you have just spent months in hospital recovering from the infection you caught in India. And yes, I know that it is still our secret. We won't tell anyone. But you have to give yourself time to recover and get your mojo back. Maybe even be kind to yourself and let your body heal, instead of running from place to place at top speed. How about that for a crazy idea?'

Amber blew out long and slow. 'You're right. This is the first time in years that I have been in London long enough to take stock. I just feel that I am lost and drifting on my own. Again.'

Saskia slid over to the end of Amber's lounger and wrapped her fingers around her arm. 'No, you're not. You will always have a home at Elwood House. And don't you dare forget that.'

Amber smiled into the faces of her two best friends in the world. Friends who had somehow got pushed lower and lower on her priority list over the past few years, and yet they were the very people who had come running the first time she asked.

'I don't know what I did to deserve you two. Thanks. It means a lot. But I won't put you out too much.'

'Decision made, young lady,' Saskia said in a jokey serious voice. 'You are coming to stay with me at Elwood House as my birthday present, and you are going to be cosseted, whether you like it or not.'

'Oh, that sounds good,' Kate said, and snuggled back further onto the soft cushion of the patio lounger. 'Can I come over and be cosseted in exchange for making curtains and cushions? I could use a good cosset.'

'You and your needlework skills are welcome any time.'

Saskia laughed and gestured towards Amber with her head. 'I'm going to need some help keeping this one from wearing herself out getting ready for her birthday party.'

Amber dropped her head back and closed her eyes as bright warm sunshine broke through the light cloud cover. Then she turned back to face Saskia and Kate, who were looking at her. 'It's going to be like old times. The three of us, camped out at Elwood House. But at least this time I'm not running away from home to spite my mother by eloping with Sam Richards.'

Saskia peered at her through narrowed eyes. 'Ah, yes. Sam.' She nodded. 'Were you okay? With seeing him again? Because I still cannot believe that you went there on your own.'

'Ah. So you think I would be safe from the evil clutches of the teenage boy who broke my heart and betrayed me with one of my best friends if I stayed here in my ivory tower penthouse like a fairy tale princess waiting to be rescued.'

She laughed and said with a snort, 'Not a chance, gorgeous. I refuse to be turned into some kind of recluse just because the press want to know why I decided to retire. Besides, I've been working with reporters like Sam Richards for years. He doesn't bother me.'

Kate shuffled to the edge of her seat, her bottom jiggling with excitement while Saskia just chuckled softly to herself. 'Really?'

Amber pushed out her famous moisture lipstick slicked lips. 'Oh, yes. My musician friend Parvita runs a wonderful charity in India who could certainly use the fee, only…' she sighed with a slight quiver in her voice and Saskia and Kate instantly leant closer towards her '…I've had enough of that circus who think that they can make up any kind of story and get away with it. I have helped the media sell newspapers and magazines for the last ten years. And now I'm done with it.

I am not playing that game any more. And they are going to have to get used to the idea. This time I call the shots.'

Kate's eyebrows lifted. 'I knew it! You're going to charge them megabucks for a full page nude shot with you sitting at a white grand piano with only discreet pieces of sheet music and fabulous jewels to cover your modesty? That could be fun.'

Amber and Saskia both turned and stared at Kate in silence.

'What? So I have a vivid imagination?' Kate shrugged.

Amber frowned at Kate for a moment and then blinked. 'Not exactly what I had in mind and no, it wouldn't be fun, not even for the megabucks. But do you know what? The more I thought about it, the more I got to thinking that maybe Sam does have something we can trade with after all.'

Kate drew back and squinted at her suspiciously. 'Go on.'

'I need to get the past off my back. Parvita's charity and my birthday party are going to take all of my time and energy, and the last thing I need is a troop of paparazzi making my life even more of a nightmare.'

'You really are serious about retiring?'

'Totally,' Amber replied and smiled at Saskia. 'But talking to you two has reminded me where my real priorities lie.' And then she reached out and squeezed Saskia's hand for a second. 'Your aunt Margot gave me a sanctuary at Elwood House, and I haven't forgotten it. I owe you. This is why I'm thinking of doing something rather rash.'

'What do you mean by rash?' Saskia asked in her low, calm, gentle voice.

Amber took a long drink of coffee, well aware that both of her friends were waiting for her to speak.

'When you told me all about your plans to convert Elwood House into a private meeting and dining venue I was amazed that we hadn't thought about it before. Your dining room is stunning.'

Her voice drifted away dreamily. 'I gave my first piano recital in that house. I'll never forget it. The crystal chandeliers. The flickering firelight. It was magical. This is why I want to do as much as I can to help make Elwood House a success.'

Saskia shook her head. 'You have already invited half the fashion models in London, their agents, their posh friends and the music industry to your birthday party this week. I couldn't ask for better publicity.'

'And yet you still don't have a decent website or booking system or photo gallery to showcase the house. And that. Is where I come in. And you can stop shaking your head; I know that you won't take my money. So I am going to ask a professional photographer to come over and put together your full marketing package and organise the website. Free. Gratis. Won't cost you a penny.'

'Really?' Saskia replied and lifted her mug towards Amber in a toast. 'That's fantastic. Is he one of your fashion pals?'

Amber licked her lips and took a sip of water before answering.

'Not exactly. I think Sam Richards is calling himself a photojournalist these days. More tarts, anyone?'

Amber paused and looked at Kate, who was groaning with her head in her hands. 'Don't worry about Sam. He knows that he has to be on his very best behaviour if he has any chance of that interview. Saskia needs those photos and Sam seems to know which end of a camera to point. And no, I haven't forgiven him yet. Think of this as part of the payback. So please don't kill him. At least not in front of the party guests. Saskia does not want bloodstains on her nice carpet.'

The words had barely left Amber's mouth and the shouts were still ringing in her ears when the oven timer bell rang and Kate shook her head slowly from side to side before diving back into the kitchen to get fresh supplies of snacks.

'Don't burn your mouth by eating them straight out of the

oven,' Saskia called out to Kate, but then her mouth relaxed into a half smile. 'Payback. I suppose that is one way of looking at it and I have no doubt that he would do a good job. But sheesh, Amber. I am worried for you.'

Amber was just about to rattle off a casual throwaway remark, but instead she paused before answering one of her few real friends in the world. The old Amber would have laughed off her friend's concern with a flippant gesture as some sort of silly joke, but the new Amber was slowly getting used to opening up to people she loved and trusted. 'You always did like Sam, didn't you?'

Saskia gave a brisk nod. 'I suppose so. Not in any sort of romantic way, of course, nothing like that, but yes, I did. His dad had driven my aunt Margot around for years and sometimes he brought Sam along with him. I suppose that's why I suggested that your mum use his limo service to take her to venues.'

Saskia lifted one hand. 'I think I might even have introduced you. So blame me for what happened. But yes, I thought he was okay.' Her brow squeezed together. 'Why do you ask me that now?'

'Because it was so weird. Over the years I sometimes imagined what I would say if I met up with Sam unexpectedly at some airport or hotel, or if he came to one of my performances. But when I saw him yesterday? All those clever, witty put-downs just fled. He was still the same Sam, working in his dad's garage. And I was right back to feeling like a gawky, awkward, six feet tall seventeen-year-old with big feet who was trying to sound all grown-up and clever around this handsome, streetwise city boy.'

Amber looked up at Saskia and shrugged. 'I trusted him then and he let me down just when I needed him the most. How do I know that I can trust him now? The orphanage in India is too important to me to see the real message buried under some big celebrity exposé which is around the world in seconds. Can you imagine the headlines? "Brave Bambi DuBois cheats death from meningitis. Career in tatters." Oh, they would love that.'

'Which is why you are taking control. Maybe there is too much history between the two of you for him to be objective. But we agreed that we would give him an audition for the job, and that is what we are going to do. Okay?'

'Absolutely okay. If he can stand it, then so can I.'

'Right. And on the way you can make sure that Sam gets the message that you have moved on to even more handsome and successful boyfriends. But fear not. Kate and I will make sure that we rub it in at regular intervals that he made a horrible mistake when he let you go and you are so totally over him.'

'Saskia! I didn't say anything about being cruel. And as for being over him? Sam only had to smile at me yesterday and I got the tingles from head to toe. Which is so ridiculous I can hardly admit it. The last time that happened I ended up on a plane to Kathmandu with a suitcase full of evening wear and piano music and no clue about what I was going to do when I got there.'

'Mark the mountaineer?'

Amber nodded. 'And three years before that it was Rico. Racing car driver. One kiss on the cheek and a cuddle in the pits and I smelt of diesel fumes for months.'

Amber sighed dramatically and slumped back. 'I am a hopeless case and I know it. I mean. *A mountaineer*? What was I thinking? I got the tingles and that was that.' She blinked a couple of times. 'The only scientific explanation is that I was cursed at birth. You know how it goes. The good fairy godmother blesses me with some musical talent, and the evil one says, "Oh, that's sweet, but in exchange you are going to fall for men who will only ever be interested in their obsession. So you had better get used to the idea."'

'You weren't thinking. You were taking a chance on love with remarkable men,' Saskia replied wistfully. 'You know. Not all of us have had a chance to be cuddled by racing car drivers or kissed at Everest base camp. I envy you for having the courage to take that risk.'

Amber instantly sat up and wrapped her arm around Saskia's shoulder. 'You'll meet someone—I'm sure of it. Especially now you're opening up Elwood House. Think of all the handsome executives who will be queuing up to sample your tasty treats.'

'From your lips… But in the meantime, where does that leave our Sam Richards? Because, to me, this little plan of ours could go in one of two ways. Either you keep your cool and freeze out his tingle power so that you can finally get Sam out of your system and your life. Or…'

Saskia smiled and pushed out her lips. 'You might be tempted to try out the new and improved version to see if the quality of those tingles has improved over the years. And don't look at me like that. It's a distinct possibility. Dangerous, scary and not very clever, but a possibility…and that worries me, Amber. I know how much you cared about Sam. I was there, remember? I don't want to see you running back to Elwood House in tears over Sam Richards.'

'Sam?' came a squeaky voice from the bedroom and a second later its owner appeared on the patio and she was not carrying more snacks.

Kate was wearing a huge fascinator in the shape of a red tropical flower on her head and several strings of huge beads cascaded below bundles of silk scarves. 'You don't have time to think about boys, woman!'

Kate gestured with her head towards the dressing room, which had long since given up any hope of being used as a second bedroom. 'Amber DuBois, you are officially one of the worst hoarders I have ever seen. And I make clothes for women who are still wearing their mother's hats. You have been crushing stuff into those cupboards for years. I am frightened to open those wardrobes in fear of avalanche.'

Amber waved one slender hand in the air. 'I know. I spent most of yesterday trying to root out casual day clothes to wear and ended up going to the shops. I have got so used to just dumping my stuff here that when I want something I cannot find it.'

Amber frowned and pushed her lower lip out. 'Is it normal to have more performance dresses than pants? I love dressing up for my audiences, but I find it so hard to refuse when designers start giving me free gorgeous things to wear. Most of those dresses have only had to survive one recital. It does seem a shame to just stash them until they gather dust. Unless, of course…'

She grinned and looked from side to side. 'Ladies. I have been looking for some way of raising funds. What do you say to a spot of dressing up in the name of decluttering? I am talking Internet auctions and second-hand designer shops.' A wide grin creased her face as she was practically deafened by shrieks from Saskia and Kate. 'I'll take those screams as a yes. Right. Then let's get started on those ball gowns. But girls—there is one condition. You do not touch the sacred shoes. Okay? Okay. Let's do it. I'll race you.'

CHAPTER SIX

SAM RICHARDS LEANT against the back wall of the elevator, propped his camera bag against his foot and crossed his arms as he enjoyed the view.

Two tall, very slender brunettes dressed from head to toe in black had rushed in at the last minute from the cream and caramel marble reception area to Amber's apartment building, gushing thanks and flooding the space with giggling, floral perfume and an empty garment rail which took up the whole width of the elevator. Judging by their sideways glances, indiscreet nudging and body language, they were not too unhappy with being crushed into the space with him, and any other time and place he might have started chatting and enjoying their company.

But not today.

His morning had already got off to a poor start when his dad had phoned from France saying that he was going to stay on a few more days because for once the weather in the Alps was perfect for a spot of touring.

Perhaps it was just as well. His dad had not exactly been sympathetic when Sam had told him about Amber's little scheme. In fact he had laughed his head off and told him to behave himself.

As if he had a choice.

Sam pressed his hands flat against the cool surface of the elevator wall.

Amber had the upper hand and he was going to have to go with it, but it didn't mean to say that he liked it. One. Little. Bit. He had stopped being at other people's beck and call the day he'd left London and there was no way he was going to step into the role of Amber's fool and like it.

But he would get through it and move on. He could survive being pulled back into Amber's high class life as a diva for a few days.

If she could stand it—then so could he.

Sam inhaled the perfumed air, which was suddenly overheated and cloying. He had no interest in this world of fashion and celebrity—he never had. The A-list party and clubbing circuit had long lost their appeal for him. It was his job and he worked hard to create something interesting and new out of the same old shallow gossip and the relentless need for fame and riches fuelled by the public obsession for celebrity—an obsession he helped to foster, whether he liked that fact or not.

Past tense. He had paid his dues and earned the right to sit behind that editor's desk, doing the job he had been trained for. And he wasn't going to let that slip away from him without a fight.

He had come a long way from the raw teenager with a fire in his belly that Amber had known.

Man enough for the job? Oh, yes, he was man enough for the job all right.

Even if he had no clue what the actual job was. Her text message had asked him to bring his camera bag and a screwdriver over and they were all the clues she had given him.

Sam rolled his shoulders back as the elevator slowed and the girls starting fidgeting with the clothes rail.

The elevator doors slid open on the floor number Amber had given him but, before he could stride forward with his bag, the girls swept out into the wide corridor of pale wood and pastel colours.

Interesting.

Unless, of course...

With a tiny shoulder shrug Sam slowly followed the girls towards the penthouse apartment. Lively disco dance music drifted out through an open door towards him, the beat in perfect tune with the rattle of their high heels on the fine wooden floor.

Disco music? If this was Amber's place, she must be out shopping for the morning. The only music Amber DuBois liked was written by men with quill pens and dipping ink hundreds of years ago.

The girls rolled the garment rail into the apartment, waved at someone inside, then swept back past Sam out into the hall-way, arm in arm in a flutter of perfume and girly giggles.

He paused for a second to admire them, then turned to face the door.

This was it. Show time. He took a deep breath, pushed the door open another few inches, stepped inside the apartment and instantly went into sensory overload.

What looked like the entire contents of a large fashion boutique was scattered over every surface in the living room. Handbags, shoes, hats and assorted female fripperies were draped across sofas, chairs and tables in a wild riot of colours and patterns, illuminated by the daylight streaming in from the floor to ceiling patio doors at the other end of the room.

His first reaction was to step back into the corridor and call the whole thing off. Right then and there. Apparently there were some men who enjoyed going clothes shopping with their wives and girlfriends. He had never understood how they could do that. There was probably medication for that kind of mental self-affliction.

He had never done that kind of crazy and he had no intention of starting now.

But he couldn't leave. And she knew it. Which meant that Amber had to be here to witness the payback in person.

Time to get this over with.

Sam sniffed, pushed his shoulders back, stashed his bag behind the sofa so that it was out of the mayhem and by stepping over the entire contents of a luggage department, he wound his way through the obstacle course that was the corridor towards the source of the disco music.

He had been on racing circuits which had fewer chicanes than this room.

Sam paused at the open bedroom door and leant casually on the door frame, his arms crossed.

It was a long, wide room but surprisingly simply furnished with a large bed with an ivory satin quilt, a small sofa covered in a shiny cream fabric with flights of butterflies painted on it and a wide dressing table next to more patio doors.

One complete wall was covered with a floor to ceiling mirror.

And standing in front of the mirror were three girls he had last seen together at Amber's eighteenth birthday party, what felt like a lifetime ago.

Amber, Saskia and Kate were wearing lemon-yellow oversized T-shirts with the words 'ALL SIZES' printed on them in large black letters. Kate was in the middle, moving her hips from side to side and jiggling along to the disco music and holding a hairbrush to her mouth as a microphone. Saskia and Amber were her backup singers. Kate could not be more than five feet four inches tall in heels, Saskia was a few inches taller in flat shoes and Amber—Amber had been six feet tall aged sixteen.

It stunned him to realise that he could recognise Amber's voice so easily. She could sing like an angel and often had at

Christmas concerts and birthday parties. Kate was the best singer in their little schoolgirl clique so Amber had left her to it and stayed on the keyboard, but she had such a sweet, clear voice. He had missed that voice. And whether he liked it or not, he had missed the sound of Amber whispering his name as she clung on to him with her arms looped around his neck.

Sam pressed back against the door frame.

A memory of those same three girls wearing those same yellow T-shirts at Margot Elwood's house came drifting back. It was someone's birthday party and the girls had put together a little musical routine for Saskia's aunt and Amber had asked Sam to join in the fun. Strange. He had not thought about Elwood House in years.

These three girls looked the same—but he knew that they had all changed more than he could have imagined. But these three girls? In those T-shirts? It was a blast from a happier time when they all had such wonderful dreams and aspirations about what they were going to do with their lives.

This was a bad time to decide to become sentimental. Time to get this started.

He banged hard on the door with the back of his knuckles and called out in a loud voice, 'Is the lady of the house at home? The help has arrived.'

They were so intent on singing along to the words of some pop tune from the nineteen nineties that it was a few seconds before Saskia even glanced in his direction.

She instantly stopped dancing, put down her can of hairspray microphone and nudged Amber in the ribs before replying, 'Hi, Sam. Good to see you.'

'Hey. We were just getting to the chorus,' Kate complained, then turned towards him and planted a fist on each hip and tutted loudly, but Sam hardly looked at the support band.

His whole attention was focused on the girl who was peeking out at him over the top of Kate's head.

In contrast to the fresh, floral Amber who had waltzed into his dad's garage, this version of Amber had donned the uniform of the full-on casually elegant fashion world.

The T-shirt was V-necked and modest enough to cover her cleavage but fashionably off centre so that a matching azure bra strap was exposed over one shoulder as she moved. Her collarbone formed a crisp outline.

Amber had never been overweight, but it seemed that she was paying the price of working with fashion designers.

She was too skinny. *Way too skinny.*

She had tied her broken wrist into a long blue scarf with pink and gold threads which ran through it to form a kind of halter neck.

The shade of blue matched the colour of her violet eyes. Perfectly. And, without intending to, Sam's gaze was locked onto those eyes as though he was seeing them for the first time.

Her hair was clipped back behind her head in a simple waterfall. She wasn't wearing any make-up from what he could see and did not need any.

He wondered if she realised how rare that truly was. Yes, he had met stunning girls in Los Angeles—the city was full of them.

But Amber DuBois was the real deal.

No doubt about it.

The lanky, awkward girl who had never known what to do with her long legs and arms and oversized feet was gone.

For good.

Replaced by a woman who looked totally comfortable and confident in her own skin.

This was the Amber he had always known that she would become one day, and he was suddenly pleased that she had realised just how lovely she truly was. And always had been.

Now the world had the chance to see Amber the way he

had once seen her. As a beautiful, confident woman with the power to take his breath away. Just by looking at her.

'Hi, trouble,' she replied casually with a bright smile as though she were greeting an old friend, which was about right. 'You are right on time.'

He gave her a mock salute. 'Reporting for duty as ordered.'

Her small laugh turned into a bit of a cough, then she turned back to Kate and Saskia and pressed her cheek lightly to each of them in turn. 'Thanks, girls. I'll see you the same time tomorrow. Oh—and don't forget to check online about the shoes. Bye. Bye for now.'

Amber stepped past Sam and waved to Kate and Saskia as they carefully wove their precious cargo of bags and suit carriers down the hall towards the front door, laughing and chatting as they went, with only the occasional backwards scowl from Kate over one shoulder to indicate how *pleased* they were to see him again. *Not.*

Only then did Amber turn back to face Sam, her hand resting lightly on one hip.

'I cannot believe that you actually came.'

'So you weren't serious about the audition? Great!' Sam replied, pushing himself off the door post and dusting his hands off and patting his pocket. 'Shall we get started now? I have my trusty tape recorder right here.'

Amber exhaled explosively and held up both hands. 'Not so fast. I was perfectly serious—you have to audition for this gig.'

Sam lifted both hands as he grinned at her.

'Well, here I am. This is me proving that you can trust me to keep my word and do whatever it is you need me to do. Your personal slave is ready for action. So let's get started.'

'Oh, now don't tempt me,' Amber murmured under her breath, then she lifted her chin and peered at him through creased eyebrows. 'You had better come into my bedroom.'

Sam blinked several times. 'I am liking the sound of this already.'

She closed her eyes and shook her head. 'And I am regretting it already. Do not even try and flirt with me because it won't work. Okay?'

'Methinks the lady doth protest too much,' Sam replied, then winced at the searing look she gave him. 'Okay, I get the message. I am a snake who cannot be trusted. So. Let's get this game of charades started. What is the first thing on that long list of yours?'

Amber pressed her forefinger to her full, soft pink lips and pretended to ponder.

'You may have noticed that I am having a bit of a declutter at the moment.'

'Declutter? Is that what you call it? I have to tell you that, despite reports to the contrary, my knowledge of female clothing is not as great as you might imagine. So if you are looking for fashion advice…'

Amber jabbed her finger towards the bedroom wall right in front of them, which was covered with a framed collection of artwork, portraits of Amber and old sheets of music manuscripts.

'I need someone to take my pictures down so I can decorate. It is a bit tricky one-handed and some of them are quite valuable. I vaguely recall that you can handle a screwdriver. Think you can manage that?'

Sam stepped forward so that they were only inches apart.

'Bambi, I can handle anything you throw at me.'

She took a step closer, startling him, but there was no way that he was going to let her know that.

'Oh, this is only the start. I have a very, very long list.'

'I expected nothing less.'

He turned to go back into the living room, and then looked back at Amber over one shoulder. 'And don't worry. I won't tell anyone that you couldn't wait to drag me into your bedroom the first chance you could get.' He tapped one side of his nose with his forefinger. 'It will be our little secret.' And with that he strode away from Amber, leaving her wide-mouthed with annoyance, delighted that he had managed to squeeze in the last word.

CHAPTER SEVEN

TWO HOURS LATER Sam had taken down the framed pictures from the walls of two bedrooms, a kitchen and a hallway, covered them in bubble wrap and packed them into plastic crates already stacked two high along the length of Amber's hall, before starting on the living room.

The barrage of noise, telephone calls and visitors had slowly faded away as the morning went on so that by the time he had unscrewed the last of the huge oil paintings and modern art installations in the living room, he didn't have to worry about stepping on Amber's peep toe sandals as she worked around him, or accidentally brushing plaster dust onto some fabulous gown which had been casually thrown over a chair or garment rail.

It took superhuman effort but for most of that time he kept his eyes on the rawl plugs and loose plaster behind the pictures instead of the long, lean limbs of the lovely woman who brushed past him at regular intervals in the hallway, leaving a trail of scented air and a cunning giggle in her wake.

Decluttering? When he'd cleared out his furnished Los Angeles apartment, he had walked out with two suitcases and a laptop bag. The same way he had found it. All of his car magazines and photos were safely scanned and digitised. The rest had been recycled or passed on to his pals. He never had to go through this palaver.

Sam stood back and tilted his head to look at a pair of large oil paintings made up of small shapes inside larger shapes inside larger shapes which was starting to give him a headache.

And some of the picture frames had sticky notes on the front with the letter S written in purple marker pen. Purple, he snorted. What did that mean?

Right. Finish this little collection. Then it was time to go and find the lady and find out.

No need. Here she was, ambling towards him. Head down, a large garment bag over one shoulder and a cellphone pressed against her ear, oblivious to his presence.

From the corner of one eye he watched her flip the phone back into her pocket and pick up several scarves from the top of the piano. Then Amber paused and ran two fingertips along the surface of the keys without pressing them firmly enough to make music.

Only as he watched, her lovely face twisted into a picture of sadness and regret and pain that was almost unbearable for him to see.

He turned around to face her, but it was too late—the moment was lost as Amber suddenly realised that she was being observed. A bright smile wiped away the trauma that had been all there to see only a few seconds earlier, startling him with how quickly she could turn on her performance face, and she lowered the lid on the piano. 'Plaster dust,' she whispered. 'Not a good idea.'

'Don't let me put you off playing,' Sam quipped and gestured towards the piano with his screwdriver. 'I brought my own earplugs in case you were holding a rehearsal session.'

'Very funny, but your ears are safe. I am not playing today.' She took a breath and raised her plaster cast towards him. 'My wrist is hurting.'

Her chin lifted and she angled her head a little. 'You can

tell your lovely readers that I simply cannot tolerate second best. My standards are just as high as ever.'

'Yeah.' He nodded. 'Right. It's just weird that you haven't even tried to play. It used to be the other way around. I spent a lot of time trying to drag you away from the nearest keyboard.'

Sam looked into her face with a grin but her gaze was firmly fixed on the scarves in her bag.

'That was a long time ago, Sam. People change.' And with that she turned away and strolled back to her bedroom. In silence.

As he watched her slim hips sway away from him, every alarm bell in his journalist's mind started ringing at the same time.

Music used to be the one thing that gave Amber joy. She used to call it her private escape route away from the chaos that was her mother's life.

Well, it didn't look like that now.

Something was not right here. And it was not just her wrist that was causing Amber pain.

And, damn it, but he cared more than he should.

Amber ran her fingers over the few dresses still left in her wardrobe and stifled a self-indulgent sniff. She had loved wearing those evening gowns which were now on their way to a shop specialising in pre-loved designer wear. But she had plenty of photos of the events to remind her what each dress had looked like if she wanted a walk down memory lane.

Which she didn't.

She had never been sentimental about clothes like some of the other performers. There was no lucky bracelet or a corset dress which was guaranteed to have her grace the cover of the latest celebrity magazine. They were just clothes—beautiful clothes which had made her feel special and beautiful when she had worn them. But clothes just the same.

So why did it feel so weird to know that she would never wear them again?

Amber sniffed again, then mentally scolded herself.

This was pathetic! She was still Amber Sheridan DuBois. She was still the girl with the first class degree in music and the amazing career. The same Amber who had flown so very high in a perfect sky which seemed to go on for ever and ever.

Until she had gone to India and fate had sent her tumbling back down to earth with a bang.

The sound of an electric screwdriver broke through her wallow in self-pity and Amber shivered in her thin top. All in the past. She was over the worst and her wrist would soon be better. She was lucky to have come through the infection more or less intact, and that was worth celebrating.

So why did she feel like collapsing onto her bed and sleeping for a week?

She was overtired. That was it. *Idiot.* The doctors had warned her about overdoing it, then her mother and Heath and now so had Kate and Saskia—and Parvita, who had offered to delay the wedding because she felt so guilty about inviting her friends to perform a concert at the orphanage. She had had no clue that there was a meningitis outbreak sweeping across Kerala.

Of course she had told Parvita not to be so silly—the astrologers had chosen a perfect wedding day and that was precisely what Parvita was going to have. A perfect wedding back in her home village without having to worry about an exhausted concert pianist who should be in Boston resting in glorious solitude at her stepbrother's town house.

Pity that she had not factored in the mess in her apartment, and surviving a birthday party at Elwood House. And then there was the ex-boyfriend who had suddenly popped into her life again.

Yes. Sam might have something to do with her added stress levels.

Good thing he had no idea how her body was on fire when he was in sight or she would never live it down.

He had no idea that she had tossed and turned most of the night with an aching wrist, wondering would have happened if she had fallen into Sam's arms that night of her eighteenth birthday. Would they still be together now? Or would their relationship have fizzled out with recriminations and acrimonious insults?

She would never know, but there was one thing she was sure about.

Ever cell in her body was aware that Sam Richards was only a few feet away from her in the next room. His boyish grin was locked into her memory and, whether she liked it or not, her treacherous body refused to behave itself when he was so close. Her hands were shaking, her legs felt as though they belonged to someone else and it had nothing to do with the fact that she was supposed to be resting. Nothing at all.

All she had to do was survive a few more days and Sam would be out of her life.

Amber rolled her stiff and sore shoulders and rearranged her sling.

Shaking her head in dismay, she stretched up to tug at the boxes on the top shelf of her dressing room but they slid right back into the corner and out of her reach.

Grabbing the spare dining room chair Kate had used earlier to find the hat boxes, Amber popped the headphones of her personal stereo in her trouser pocket over her ears, and hummed along to the lively Italian baroque music as she jumped up onto the chair and stretched out on tiptoe to reach the far back corner of the shelf.

She had just caught hold of the handle of her old vanity case and was tugging it closer when something touched the bare skin below her trouser leg.

As she whipped around in shock, her left hand tried to grab the chair, which had started to wobble alarmingly at the sudden movement, throwing her completely off balance. The problem was that her fingers were already tightly latched onto the vanity case and as it swung off the shelf it made contact with the side of Sam's head as he stepped forwards to grab hold of her around the middle and take the weight of her body against his.

She dropped the case, and it bounced high before settling down intact.

Not that she noticed. Her fingers were too busy clutching onto Sam Richards as she stared into his startled face.

Time seemed to stand still as she started to slide down the front of his hard body, her silky top riding up as she did.

Sam reacted by holding her tighter, hitching her up as though she was weightless, his arms linked together under her bottom, locking her body against his.

'Sorry about that,' she said, trying to sound casual, as though it was perfectly normal to have a conversation while you were being held up against the dusty T-shirt of the man who had once rocked your world. 'Good thing I didn't hit anything important.'

He bit his lower lip, as though he was ready to hit back with some comment and then thought better of it, then one corner of his mouth turned up and he slowly, slowly, started to bend his knees until her feet were on the floor. But all the time his arms were locked behind her back as though he had no intention of letting her go.

Why should he? Amber thought. Sam was having way too much fun.

Strange that his breathing seemed to be even faster than

hers, if that was possible, and she could see the blood pulsing in his neck. Hot and fast.

His wide fingers slid up from her hips to her waist, holding her firm, secure, safe but being careful not to crush her plaster cast.

Amber inhaled the warm spicy aroma of some masculine scent that had a lot of Sam in the blend and instantly became aware that she could feel the length of his body pressed against hers from chest to groin.

His breathing became stronger. Louder. And his fingers stretched to span the strip of exposed skin below her top, gently at first and then moving back and forth just a little against her ribcage. Amber felt like closing her eyes but didn't dare because his gaze had never left her face.

He felt wonderful. He smelt better.

Sam tilted his head and looked at her. Really looked at her. Looked at her with an intensity that sent shivers and tingles from her toes to the ends of each strand of hair.

It had been such a long time since any man had held her like this, with that fire in his eyes.

Bad fire.

Bad tingles.

Bad, bad heart for wanting him to finish what he had started.

It would be so easy to kiss him right now and find out if his kiss was still capable of making her weak at the knees.

Bad Amber for wanting him, when that was the worst thing that could happen to either of them.

Her back stiffened and she lifted her chin slightly.

'You can put me down now if you like,' she said in a jokey voice which sounded so false and flat. Her words seem to echo around the narrow dressing room until they found their target.

'And what if I don't like?' Sam replied and leant closer to

breathe into her neck while his fingers moved in slow circles at her waist.

Suddenly Amber wished that she had installed air conditioning in the apartment because the air was starting to heat up far too quickly in this small space. And so close to her bed...

Amber lifted her hand from Sam's shoulder and reached behind and gently slid her fingers around his wrist and released him.

And, just like that, the connection was broken, leaving her feeling dizzier than she wanted to admit.

Without his support, her legs felt so wobbly that she had to swivel around and sit down on the chair—anything but the bed. That would be far too dangerous with this man around and she would hate to give him ideas.

His brow creased and Sam crossed his arms in front of his chest as he stared at her, his legs wide, his shoulders back and squared, his gaze locked onto her face. As he stared his eyes narrowed as though they were concerned about something. And her foolish girly heart gave a little leap at the idea that he might still care about her.

'Hey, Bambi. I thought we had a deal. It's time you kept to your side of the bargain.'

'Will you please stop calling me Bambi? Yes, I know you came up with the name in the first place, but Amber will do fine. And what do you mean? My side?'

'Okay, then. Amber, I brought my own work uniform...' Sam waved a hand down his clothing.

'But you promised me refreshments. So far all I have seen are a small plate of girly mini cupcakes and one mug of weak Earl Grey tea.'

He winced and shook his head slowly from side to side. 'That. Is not refreshments as I understand them. What's more, I have just raided your refrigerator and there is nothing more than a couple of low fat yoghurts and some supermarket ready meals.'

He stood back and ogled her, then reached out and pinched her arm.

She wriggled away. 'Hey. Ouch. What was that for?'

'Too skinny and too pale and wobbly. By far. That decides it. We, young lady, are going out to get some food. What is your fancy? Mexican? Pub food? Take your pick.'

Amber looked around the bedroom in horror at the debris.

'I can't leave now. The flat is a mess and it will take me ages to tidy it up.'

'But the girls have gone for the day…right?'

'Well, yes. I don't have any more appointments.'

'Good. Because it is two o'clock in the afternoon and neither of us have eaten since breakfast. Right?'

Amber sighed and checked her wristwatch, and then her shoulders sagged. 'I am flagging a bit. I suppose it would make sense to eat some late lunch…and what are you doing?'

'Looking for your coat. And which one of these is your handbag? Come on, girl. The sun is still shining and there is nothing fit to eat in this apartment. What do you say? We get some lunch and I volunteer to carry your shopping home from the supermarket on the way back. You can't get a better offer than that.'

'Can't I?'

Amber leant backwards and pulled out her mobile phone from her trouser pocket and was about to sling her cashmere wrap over one shoulder when Sam stepped behind her and wrapped it around her shoulders, gently pressing the collar into her neck, his fingertips touching her, and she blinked in delight then cursed herself for being so needy.

'Actually, I might have a better idea, but I need to make a phone call. This restaurant can get extremely busy around lunchtime.'

Sam groaned. 'I might have known. How many awards does it have? Because I have to tell you—I am not in the mood for mini tasting portions served on teaspoons made out of toast.'

She sniffed dismissively. 'Several. But wait and see. You might just like it. And the table has the most amazing view over London.'

'I don't believe that you ordered home delivery,' Sam exclaimed and put down his screwdriver as Amber sauntered into the kitchen swinging a large brown paper bag. 'Don't tell me that the famous Amber DuBois has suddenly got cold feet about being seen out in public. Or were you worried that I would make you pay the bill?'

Amber sniffed dismissively in reply. 'Well, someone has a very high opinion of themselves.' Then she sighed in exasperation and gestured with her head towards the cabinets. 'Only now I am out of hands. Would you mind bringing the plates and cutlery? Have a rummage in that drawer. Yep. That's it.'

'You are avoiding my question,' Sam said as he followed Amber out onto the sunlit terrace and spread the picnic kit out onto the table, where Amber was already pulling out foil containers. 'Why not go out to some fabulous restaurant so the waiters can fawn all over you?'

She looked up at him and gave a half smile. 'Two reasons. First, I want some peace and quiet to enjoy my meal, and the restaurant this food came from is always crushed jam-tight. And secondly—' she paused and looked out towards the skyline '—I have only used this apartment on flying visits these past few years and never stayed long enough to enjoy the view.' She nodded towards the railing. 'Feel free. This is your city, after all. And I know how much you love London.'

Sam took the hint and walked the few steps over to the railing. And exhaled slowly at the awe-inspiring scene spread out in all directions in front of him. The stress of the past few days melted away as he took in the stunning view over the Thames and along both sides of the river for miles in each direction. His eyes picked out the locations which were so familiar they were like old friends. Friends like Amber had once been.

'You always were the clever one. This is a pretty good view, I'll give you that. And yes, London is my city, and it always has been. And what is that amazing smell?'

He turned back towards Amber and instantly his senses were filled with the most amazing aromas which instantly made his mouth water.

'Are those Indian dishes? You used to hate spicy food.'

'That was before I tasted real southern Indian food like this. Home-cooked traditional recipes from Kerala. The restaurant doesn't usually do take out but I know the owner's cousin. Willing to risk it?'

'Are you kidding me?' Sam replied and flung himself into the seat. 'I loved living in Los Angeles, but you cannot get real Indian food unless you cook it yourself. Pass it over and tell me what you ordered.'

'Vegetable curry, chickpea masala, coconut rice and a thick lamb curry for you. And just this once we are allowed to eat it using a fork and plates instead of fingers and a banana leaf. Go ahead and tuck in. I ordered plenty. What do you think?'

Sam held up a fork and dived into the nearest dish, speared some lamb and wrapped his lips around it.

Flavour and texture exploded on his tongue and he moaned in pleasure and delight before smiling and grabbing each dish in turn and loading up his plate with something of everything.

'This is seriously good. But now I'm curious. How do you know the owner of a Keralan restaurant in London? That doesn't seem to fit with a career musician.'

Amber swallowed down a mouthful of vegetables and rice and gave a tiny shrug before taking a sip of water.

'The orchestra I tour with has an amazing cellist who has become one of my best friends in the business. Parvita is one of those totally natural talents who has been winning awards all over the place—but it was only when I got to know her that I found out just how remarkable she really is.'

Amber topped up her plate as she spoke, but there was just enough of a slight quiver in her voice to make Sam look at her as he chewed. 'Parvita was left at an orphanage for girls when she was only a toddler. Her widowed mother was too poor to feed another daughter. She needed her boys to work their farm in Kerala and knew that the orphanage could give a little girl an education and a chance to improve her life.'

Amber chuckled. 'I don't think that Parvita's family were expecting her to win scholarships to international music schools and then build a career as a concert cellist. But she did it, against all of the odds.'

Amber raised her water glass. 'And along the way my friend introduced me to real home-cooked food from Kerala. The chef who runs this restaurant is one of her cousins and is totally passionate about fresh ingredients and cooking with love. I think it shows.'

Sam lifted his fork in tribute. 'This is probably the best Indian food that I have ever eaten. Although it does make me wonder. Aren't you going to miss your friend Parvita? Now that you have decided to retire?'

Amber closed her lips around the fork and twirled it back and forth for a second before replying. 'Not at all. She is still my friend so I will make the effort to keep in touch. She even invited me to her wedding next week and sent me a fabulous hot pink sari to wear.'

'Now that is something I would like to see. Just tell me which fabulous and exclusive London venue is having the privilege of hosting this happy event and I'll be right there with my camera.'

'Oh, she isn't coming to London. The wedding party is in Kerala. I've already sent my apologies—' Amber shrugged '—but the newlyweds will be passing through London in a few weeks, and we can catch up then.'

'So you are not going to the wedding after all?'

She shook her head as she chewed and pointed to her plaster.

'That's interesting.' Sam nodded. 'If one of my friends was getting married I wouldn't let a simple thing like that stop me from going. Unless, of course, there is more to it than that. Hmm?'

Then he leant back and crossed his cutlery on his plate and shook his head from side to side.

'Well, well. Why do I get the feeling that some things have not changed that much after all? Let me guess. Your mother ordered you not to go, didn't she? Or was Heath Sheridan worried that his little stepsister is going to get sunburnt if she goes to India? How is your stepbrother doing these days? Still trying to interfere in your life? Um. I take that glaring scowl as a yes.'

He sniggered off her rebuke, and dived back into his food. 'You surprise me, Amber. You're twenty-eight years old, with a brilliant career, an international reputation and the kudos to match, and you still cannot get out from under their thumb, can you? Well, shame on you, Amber DuBois. I thought you were better than that.'

CHAPTER EIGHT

'SHAME ON ME? Shame. *On me*?'

Amber felt the heat burn at the back of her neck which had nothing to do with the Indian food and she crashed her hand down onto the table hard enough to make both Sam and the plates jump, and leant forwards towards him.

'*How dare you?* How dare you tell me that I should be ashamed of the fact that my family love me and care what happens to me? No, I don't always agree with what they tell me, but at least they make an effort to be part of my life. But you know all about that, don't you? How are you getting on with your dad these days? And remind me of the last time you saw *your* mum?'

The words emerged in harsh outbursts which seemed to echo around her patio and reflect back from the stone-faced man sitting opposite. And she instantly regretted them.

It shocked her that Sam was capable of making her so spiteful and hard. She was one of the few people who knew how hard it had been for him when his mother abandoned her husband and son. But that didn't mean that she had to throw his pain back in his face.

She was better than that. Or at least she was trying to be.

'In fact I don't know why I am even listening to you in the first place.' She blinked and tossed her head back and calmly sipped her water. 'You are hardly qualified to take the moral high ground. I certainly don't need a lecture on making decisions from you, Sam. Understood?'

'Perfectly.' Sam nodded, then leant forward and rested his elbows on the table while his gaze locked onto her face. 'Is your little tantrum over now, Miss DuBois? Because I would really like to get this so called interview over and done with as soon as possible. I have a real assignment waiting for me back at the paper, so can we move on, please?'

'Absolutely,' Amber replied, trying to calm her heart rate and appear to be more or less in control again. 'But it does make me wonder. What are you *really* doing back here in London? Because whatever it is must be very important to persuade you to go through with this little game of charades.'

Sam tried to savour more of the delicious food as slowly as he could while his brain worked at lightning speed, trying to form an answer, but his appetite was gone and he pushed his meal away.

Amber had fired her arrow and hit her target right in the centre.

Strange how this girl was one of the few people alive who knew just what his emotional hot buttons were and was not afraid to press them down hard when she needed to.

Just as he had pressed hers.

That was the problem with working with people who understood you.

Touché Amber.

If this was a game, then it was one point to each of them.

Sam sat back in his chair and watched Amber as she turned away from him and looked out over the city, all joy in her food and apartment forgotten.

The warm sunlight played on her pale skin and delicate features. Up close and personal, she was even lovelier than the girl on the magazine cover. Her chest rose and fell and he could sense the emotional strain these last few minutes had cost her.

Strain he was responsible for.

Shame on him.

Amber DuBois was gunpowder and those few minutes they had just shared in the dressing room had proved just how explosive getting within touching distance could be.

Any ideas he might have had about staying distant and professional had just gone out of the window the instant his fingers touched her skin.

He might be over his teenage crush but this woman he was looking at now had the power to get under his skin and bother him.

Bother him so badly that suddenly it felt easier to keep his change of heart towards his father to himself. If she had a whiff that he was some sort of self-sacrificing martyr who desperately wanted to make it up to his dad for all those angry years, she would never let him forget it.

A few days. He could stay cool and professional for a few days for his dad's sake.

His eyebrow lifted. 'I told you. I need the promotion and the boss made it clear that I will only get that if I come back with an exclusive from, and I quote, "the lovely Miss DuBois". That's it, job done,' and Sam went back to the food.

No way was he going to fall into Amber's trap and start spouting on about how guilty he felt about leaving his dad all alone for years on end while he lived the high life in California. This was Amber he was talking to. She would be only too ready to believe that he was a heartless son who had only come back to London for the job and the status.

After what had just happened in the dressing room he intended to keep as far away from her as physically possible.

He had to keep up the pretence that he was still the self-absorbed young man who would let nothing come between him and his career. Which was not so far from the truth. Happy families were for other men. Not men like Sam Richards.

'Job done. Right,' Amber replied and picked up her water glass. 'Come on, Sam. Out with it. From what I hear, you can get a job anywhere you like. Why here? Why now? And why do I suspect that there is a lovely lady involved in the answer?'

'You think I came back to London for a woman? Oh, no. Sorry to burst your romantic bubble, but this was strictly business all the way.'

'Um,' Amber replied. 'Pity. I could have given her a few tips. Such as run for the hills now, before he breaks your heart. That sort of thing. But not to worry, it will keep for another time.'

And she smiled sweetly at him over her water glass. 'But do tuck into your lunch. You are going to need it for this afternoon's opportunity to shine.'

'More pictures?'

'Yes, but that is for later when you deliver the paintings to Saskia and hang them up for her,' Amber replied. 'But in the meantime I have something which is much more suited to your…talents.'

She narrowed her eyes and rested her elbows on the table so that she could support her chin with one hand. 'Did you bring your camera and tripod? I'll take that nod as a yes. Super. My shoes really do need the right angle to look their best.'

Sam spluttered into his water glass. 'Shoes? You want me to photograph your shoes?' he asked in complete disbelief.

'Eighteen pairs of designer loveliness.' Amber sighed. 'Worn once or not at all. Gorgeous but unloved. Kate wanted them but she has tiny feet so I am selling them on the Internet.'

'You are selling your shoes.' Sam snorted and tossed his

head with a sigh. 'Things must be desperate. Cash flow problems?'

Her tongue flicked out and she licked her lips once. And right there and then he knew that she was keeping something from him.

'Don't try and hide your enthusiasm. I knew that you would be excited by the opportunity. This is just part of the modern girl's annual clearing out of last season's couture so that she can buy new ones to take their place—and all the money goes to charity. Oh—and tomorrow gets even better. The lovely Saskia is trying to launch Elwood House as a private dining venue and her online presence is just not cutting it. She needs a professional writer to redesign the website and create a whole new photo gallery—and it has to be complete in time for my birthday party on Thursday.'

'Is there any good news in all of this?' he spluttered, while shovelling down more chickpeas and rice.

'Of course. You have a front row seat at my birthday party, hobnobbing with the great and good of the London scene. Even if you are taking the photographs for Saskia's website at the same time.'

Sam blew out slowly. 'I am so grateful for your kind consideration. So that's Saskia covered. Are you sure that Kate Lovat wouldn't like me to stand in her shop window modelling a tartan dinner suit in my copious spare time?'

'Hey, that's not a bad idea. You might be able to fit it in after you have cleaned the spiders and mouse droppings out of her attic tomorrow. Oh. Didn't I mention that? Silly me. And after you have sorted the ladies out, then you can pop back here. By then I should have sorted out my unwanted lingerie. I am sure you can come up with some suitable slogan like "as worn by Amber" when you put together the adverts for the Internet auction.'

Amber tilted her head to one side as he glared at her through slitted eyes.

And this was the girl he was thinking of asking to be his friend.

'Not lingerie. Shoes I can understand. But I draw the line at photographing lingerie unless you intend to model it in person.'

'But this is your audition, sweetie. Have you forgotten so quickly? Of course, if you are refusing to carry out my perfectly reasonable requests, well, I shall have to phone the journalist on the other paper and see if she is still interested… And no, my modelling days are over.'

She leant her chin on the back of one hand and fluttered her eyelashes at him.

'You're looking a little hot under the collar there, Mr Richards.' Amber smiled. 'How about some ice cream to cool you down? It's delicious with humble pie.'

'Well. What do you think? The emerald and diamond drop necklace or the sapphire white gold collar?'

Amber held one necklace then the other to her throat, slowly at first, then faster and then faster, using two fingers of her plastered wrist to prop them up against her skin.

'Hey. Slow down, I'm still thinking about it.'

Kate sat back against Amber's bed pillows in Saskia's best spare bedroom and stretched both arms out above her head.

'Decisions, decisions.' Then she sniffed. 'The sapphires. They are absolutely perfect with that dress. Although, if it was me, I would wear both and go totally overboard on the bling. Especially since you won't be wearing either of them again.'

Amber smiled and dropped the emerald necklace, which had been a present from a fashion designer who had been trying to woo her into being their cover girl, back into the velvet tray. 'True. But the way I look at it, some other girl has the chance to enjoy them and the charity gets the loot. The last thing I need is a load of expensive jewellery in a safety deposit box which has to be insured every year at huge expense. It makes sense to sell it back to the jewellers while it is still in pristine condition.'

Kate shuffled to the edge of the bed. 'Don't let the spy hear you say that. Can you imagine the headlines? "Injured pianist forced to sell her jewellery to make ends meet".' Then Kate pushed herself off the bed. 'Here. Let me help with the earrings. I'm thinking some serious dangle and maximum sparkle and that is a tricky thing to pull off one-handed.'

She peered into the tray and pulled out a pair of chandelier diamond and sapphire drops. 'Ah. Now we are talking...' Then she took another look at the maker on the box and blew out hard. 'Wow. Are these for real? My fingers are shaking. I never thought I would be holding anything from that jeweller. Oh, Amber.'

Amber reached up and wrapped one arm around Kate's shoulders but, as her friend laughed and reached up to fit her earrings, she shook her head. 'Not until you have tried them on first. Go on. I want to see you wear those earrings—and that necklace.'

'What? My neck is too short and my ears are tiny. Nope. These are serious jewels for serious people. I'll stick to my pearls, thanks all the same.'

'Kate Lovat, I won't take no for an answer. I know that my clothes and shoes are huge on you, so please, just this once, be nice and do what I ask. It is my birthday.'

Amber pushed her lips out and pretended to sulk.

'Oh, stop it,' Kate replied with a dramatic sigh. 'You are ruining your make-up and it has taken me the best part of an hour to make it look natural. Okay, okay, I'll try the jewellery on. But only because it's your birthday, Look, I'm doing it. And... Oh, Amber.'

Kate stepped behind Amber and rested her head on her shoulder as Amber smiled back at her. 'Absolutely gorgeous. Told ya. Right, that's sorted. You're wearing the jewels that Heath gave me. Done. Or do you want them to sit in the box up here in the bedroom unused and unloved because you have rejected them?'

Kate replied by reaching for a tissue. 'Oh. Now look what you have made me do. Pest.'

Then Kate peered at herself in the mirror. 'Do you think that Heath would like me in these?'

'Pest right back. And he would definitely like you in those earrings,' Amber replied and wrapped her arm around Kate's waist. 'Does Heath still hold the prize for the best emergency school party date a girl could hope for?'

Kate rested her head on Amber's shoulder before answering with a small shrug. 'Absolutely. Which must make me the stupidest girl in London. Here I am, surrounded by loads of handsome boys, and the only one who comes close to being my personal hero is living in Boston and doesn't remember that I even exist unless you are around. Mad just about describes it.'

'Oh, Kate. Don't worry. You'll find someone special, I know you will.'

Kate grinned and ran a tissue across the corner of both eyes. 'Damn right. Who knows? My soulmate could be on his way to this very party this evening. How about that?'

'Absolutely. Now shoo. I have to finish getting ready and you need to show your loveliness to all and sundry. Go. Have fun at the party. And Kate...make sure that Sam the spy takes your picture. You can't miss him—he'll be the one with the camera around his neck.'

'You've got five minutes, young lady—then the posse will be up here to drag you downstairs.'

'I would expect nothing less,' Amber replied and waved to

Kate as she waltzed across the carpet on her tiny dainty heels and the bedroom door swung closed behind her.

Only when she heard Kate's sandals on the marble floor of the entrance did Amber feel it was safe to flop back down on her bed.

So her best friend Kate was still in crush with her step-brother Heath. Oh, Kate. Maybe it was a good thing that Heath had already spoken to her from his lecture tour in South America and was not turning up for this party after all. He might have brought his lovely girlfriend Olivia with him. Not good. *Not good at all.*

Her wrist was aching, her head was thumping and she could quite easily pull the quilt over her legs right then and there and sleep for days. But she couldn't. She might have organised her birthday party at the last minute, but she was still the star of the show—and she had to make her appearance.

Time to turn up and give the greatest performance of her life.

All smiles and confidence and clear about what she was doing and why. Exploring. Taking a break. Enjoying herself. Fund-raising for charity. What fun!

That was the official line and she was sticking to it. She could count the number of people who knew the truth on one hand—and that was how she wanted it to stay. Until she was ready. And then she would have to add Sam Richards to the list.

Sam.

What was she going to do about Sam?

Was he Sam the spy as Kate called him? Could she trust him again?

He had kept his side of the bargain and worked hard at every ridiculous task that the three of them had thrown at him over the past few days without much in the way of complaint.

He could never know that she had spent two nights tossing and turning in her bed as his words roiled in the pit of her stomach. She did listen to Heath—she always had and probably always would. He was her sensible older stepbrother. But these past two days, every time he had told her to do something rather than ask or suggest, she kept thinking about what Sam had said. Maybe she was still under his thumb more than she liked? Maybe he had a point.

Of course going back to Kerala would be scary. She would be a fool not to be worried. But she had made a vow in hospital that her life would be different from now. She *wanted* to see Parvita married and share her happiness.

She *wanted to* go back and yet it was so risky. Doubt rolled over Amber in waves, hard and choppy, buffeting and threatening to weaken her resolve.

Turning her life around was harder than she had expected.

The jewel tray was still open on the dressing table and Amber slithered off her bed and lifted out the top tray. Hidden inside a tiny suede pouch at the very bottom was a small gold heart suspended from a thin gold chain.

Sam had given it to her at her eighteenth birthday party, just before they had escaped out of the kitchen door and taken a ride in his dad's vintage open top sports car.

Amber smiled as she let the chain slip between her fingers. Sam had let her stand up tall on the passenger seat with her arms outstretched to the sky as they rode through the London streets—the wind in her hair and the sound of their laughter and the hoots from passing motorists reverberating through every bone in her body.

She had been so very, very happy, and she should be grateful to Sam for showing her what true happiness felt like. It was a joyous memory.

The sound of party music drifted up the stairs and Amber grinned. She had survived meningitis more or less intact, she had friends waiting for her downstairs and more on their way.

She looked at herself in the mirror and, without another moment of hesitation, she winked at her reflection and dropped the gold chain back into the pouch and closed the lid down on the box with the rest of her past.

She was a lucky girl.

Time to rock and roll and *enjoy herself.*

Taking a deep calming breath, Sam Richards strolled across the luxurious marble-floored hallway of the Victorian splendour that was Elwood House.

He paused to check his reflection in the Venetian hall mirror above a long narrow console table, and lifted up his chin a little to adjust his black bow tie.

Not bad. Not bad at all.

For a chauffeur's son from the wrong part of London.

At least this time he had been welcomed at the front door!

Which had certainly not been the case ten years ago when he had stood in the hallway of another house and another birthday celebration.

Amber might have invited him to her eighteenth birthday party but her mother had taken one look at him standing on her front doorstep, snorted and closed the door in his face. Just to make sure that he got the message loud and clear.

Sam Richards was not good enough for her daughter. Oh, no. Nowhere near.

Of course he wasn't going to put up with that—he had plans for Amber's birthday and there was no way that her mother was going to thwart his little scheme.

So he'd climbed over the garden fence and sneaked in through the conservatory where the young people were having fun.

Suddenly there was the tinkle of laughter from the kitchen and Sam grinned as he strolled into the warm, light, open space of the huge kitchen sun room that Saskia's aunt Margot had built. Every worktop was covered with plates and bowls and platters of foodstuffs—but his attention was focused on the two women who were walking towards him.

Here come the girls.

Saskia's arm was around Kate's shoulder, which was not difficult, considering that Kate could just about make five feet four inches if she stretched. Although tonight she looked stunning in a dark green taffeta cocktail dress with real jewels. Saskia was in midnight-blue crushed velvet with a real pearl choker and gorgeous lilac kitten heels.

They were like dazzling stars transported from a catwalk fashion show into this London kitchen. English style and elegance. Not too much flesh on show, and all class.

Kate hissed at him, but Saskia nudged her with a glare and moved forward to shake his hand.

'Hello, Sam. Nice to see you again. I appreciate your help with my website—it's ten times better than I could have thought of on my own. We're having a few drinks on the patio before the hordes of locusts arrive. Why don't you come and join us?'

'Perfect. Thanks. And I'm pleased I could help.'

'You go ahead. One more thing to bring out of the oven,' Saskia replied, and waved Kate and Sam onto the terrace.

The second they were out of sight of the kitchen, Kate grabbed Sam's sleeve, whirled around and planted a hand on each hip as she stared up at him with squeezed narrow eyes.

'I'm watching you, Sam Richards. If you step out of place tonight or do anything to spoil Amber's evening I'll be on to you like a shot.'

He raised both hands in surrender.

'I came here to work. And help Amber have a good time along the way. Okay?'

Kate replied by jabbing her second and third fingers towards her eyes then stabbed them towards his face, then back to her eyes.

'Watching you,' she hissed, then broke into a wide-mouthed grin and popped one of Saskia's mini tomato tarts into her mouth and groaned in pleasure as Saskia strolled up with the most delicious-smelling tray.

Kate raised her glass of white wine in a toast. 'Fab. You always know exactly how to pull off the perfect party, Saskia. Always have.'

'Hold that thought, gorgeous. Special order for the star of the show. Mini pizza. Extra anchovies. Okay?'

'Did someone say mini pizza?'

Amber sidled up to Saskia and kissed her on the cheek before biting into the crisp pastry and nodding. 'Delicious.' Only then did she look across at Sam and smile. 'Hello, Sam. What perfect timing.'

And she took his breath away.

Her long sensitive fingers were wrapped around the stem of a wine glass which Kate was topping up with sparkling tonic water rather than wine. A diamond bracelet sparkled at her wrist and flashed bright and dazzling as she moved in the sunlight.

But that was nothing compared to the crystal covered dress and jewelled collar she was wearing.

Sam dragged his eyes away from Amber's cleavage before Kate noticed and stabbed him with the corkscrew.

Her earrings moved, sparkling and bright, and helped him to focus on her face. Stunning make-up showed her clear, smooth complexion to perfection, and her eyes glowed against the dark smudge of colour. Her lips were full, smooth. Her whole face was radiant.

Amber had never looked so beautiful or more magical.

This was the Amber he had always imagined that she

would look when she was happy in her own skin—and she had exceeded his wildest imagination.

He had often wondered over the years if Amber had stayed the sweet, loving girl that he had fallen for, under the surface gloss and razzmatazz, and it only took a few seconds of seeing her now with her friends to realise that she had somehow managed to keep her integrity and old friendships alive.

Now that was something he could admire.

He would give a lot to be here as her date this evening. To know that those lovely violet-blue eyes were looking at him with love instead of tolerance.

He had walked away from a great love.

Maybe his only love. And certainly the only girl that he had ever truly wanted in his life.

Which made him more than a fool. It made him a stupid fool.

The best that he could do was try and capture this moment for ever. So that when they were back in their ordinary worlds on other continents he had something to remind him of just how much he had lost.

She was the star. And he was a reporter who was working for her.

Because that was what he was here for, wasn't it? To work?

Not as one of the guests.

Oh, no.

The likes of Sam Richards did not come to these events as a guest. He was the one parking cars and taking the coats.

Strange to think that he had some standing on the A-list circuit in Los Angeles. But it took London to put him right back in his place.

As one of the help.

Pity that he had no intention whatsoever of fitting in with someone else's idea of who and what he was. He was here because they needed him as much as he needed Amber.

An equal trade. Yes. That was better. He could work with that. He was done with being second best. To anyone.

Instantly Sam smiled. 'You look lovely, Amber—and not a day over twenty-eight. In fact, you ladies look so stunning as a group that I think this would make a charming example of a perfect summer drinks party. Early evening cocktails for a private party? So if you could just hold that pose? Lovely. And a little more to the right, Kate? Gorgeous—and don't forget to smile, Kate. Much better than sticking your tongue out at me. That's it.'

Sam stepped back and by the time the girls had straightened their dresses and rearranged the canapés his digital camera had already captured the trio from several angles, taking in the conservatory, the lovely sunlit garden and the happy women enjoying themselves.

Of course Amber had no idea that he had taken several shots for his personal album. And every one of them was of Amber.

'Fantastic. And a few more with you choosing something from the tray and pouring more wine. Excellent. Now. Saskia. How do you want to showcase the patio? With or without the food?'

CHAPTER NINE

FIVE HOURS LATER, every canapé, savoury and dessert that Saskia had served had been eaten, empty bottles of champagne stood upside down in silver wine buckets and the eighty or so guests had been entertained by some of London's finest musical talent.

One Spanish musician had even brought along a classical guitar and Amber had kicked off the flamenco dancing with great gusto and much cheering. It was amazing that the glass wear had survived the evening.

He had taken hundreds of photographs in every public room, with and without guests, from every possible angle. But there was no doubt who was the star of the show.

Sam could only watch in awe as Amber laughed and chatted in several languages to men and women of all ages and dress styles. Some young and unkempt, some older and the height of elegance, but it did not seem to matter to her in the least. The fashion models and media people were introduced to classical artists and quite a few popular musicians with names that even he had heard of.

Everyone from the costume designers to hairdressers and international conductors were putty in Amber's fingers. He had never expected to hear a sing-song around the grand piano where four of the world's leading sopranos improvised a rap song with an up-and-coming hip hop star.

It took skill to make a person feel that they were the most important person in the room—and Amber had that skill in buckets.

He was in awe of her.

It was only now, as Saskia and Kate chatted away to old friends and lingering guests, that he realised that Amber had already slipped away into the kitchen before he had a chance to thank her and say goodnight.

He quickly scanned the kitchen for Amber and waved to the waiting staff that Saskia had set to work on the washing-up. He had just turned away when he saw a splash of blue on the patio and slowly strolled out of the hot kitchen into the cool of the late May evening.

Amber was sitting on the wooden bench on the patio, humming along to the lively Austrian waltzes being played on the music system in the conservatory only a few feet away.

Her eyes were closed tight shut and her left hand was twisting and moving as though it was dancing in the air, her right arm waving stiffly along in time, the plaster cast forgotten.

Her face was in shadow but there was no mistaking the expression of joy which seemed to shine from inside outwards, illuminating her skin and making it glow.

She was happy. Beautiful. And content. And he yearned to be part of that happiness and share that little window of joy with this amazing woman.

This was the Amber he had fallen in love with ten years ago and then fallen in love all over again in the first ten seconds when she'd walked into his dad's garage and knocked his world off its axis.

And the fact that he had been in denial until this moment was so mind-boggling that all he could do was stand there and watch as she sang along to the music, all alone in the light of the full moon and the soft glow streaming out from the conservatory where the last guests were mingling in the hallway.

He stood in the shadows, watching her for minutes until the music changed to a new track and she dropped her hands onto her lap and clasped hold of her knees and blinked open her eyes.

And saw him.

'Hi, Sam,' she said, and her eyes met his without hesitation or reluctance. Almost as if she was pleased to see him there. 'Are we on our own?'

Sam swallowed down the lump in his throat and strolled over to the bench in the soft light and lifted up her feet and sat down, her legs on his knees, well aware that he probably had a huge man crush grin all over his face.

'More or less. The girls are seeing the last of the guests out. It was a great party. Did you have a good time?'

Amber sighed and snuggled sideways on the arm rest. 'The best. Even though I am now completely exhausted. How about you?'

Sam half turned to face her and as she shuffled higher, her legs resting on his thighs and her arm on her lap, he inhaled a wonderful spicy, sweet perfume that competed with the full musk roses and lavender which Saskia had planted behind the bench. It was a heady, exotic aroma that seemed to fill his senses and make him want to stay there for as long as Amber was close by.

He wanted to tell her that she looked beautiful.

But that would be too close to the truth. So he covered up his answer and turned it into something she would be expecting him to say.

'I had an interesting evening. Your guest list was inspired. I suspect the birthday present swag will be excellent.'

'Birthday presents? Oh. No, I only had a few. I asked people to make a donation to Parvita's charity instead.'

She looked at him. Really looked at him. Her gaze moved so slowly from his feet upwards that by the time it reached his face Sam knew that his ears were flaming red.

'Nice suit. You look positively dangerous. Was it safe to let you out on your own? I'm sorry I didn't have much time to talk. Did you get all of the shots Saskia needs?'

'I can usually be trusted to behave myself if the occasion demands. And yes, I think I can do something creative for a website and make the most of the venue.'

'Really? That almost sounds professional. Then things truly have changed. And not just the suit.'

'Oh, no compliments, please; you'll have me blushing.'

'I noticed you working the room with your camera. Hasn't Saskia done a lovely job?'

'I have been to this house so many times with my dad but I'd forgotten how stunning it is. Judging from some of the comments from your guests, I think she might be on to a winner.'

Amber hunched up her shoulders. 'I hope so. She's had a rough time since her aunt Margot died. This is why it's important to me that you do a good job and help Saskia out. Elwood House is her home but it's also her business. She needs a decent marketing and promotional campaign to get it off the ground.'

'There are expert companies out there who could make it happen.'

'Yes, there are. And they cost serious amounts of money. And Saskia won't accept my help. I have plenty of colleagues and casual friends in my life. You met some of them this evening. But nobody comes close to real friends like Kate, Saskia and her aunt Margot. They made me believe that, despite everything that happened with my mother, I could make a real home in London and create something close to a normal school life for myself. And that was new.'

'I know, I was there. Remember?'

Then she laughed out loud. 'Oh, yes, I remember very well indeed. But I refuse to be angry with you on my birthday. Life really is too short. I have had enough of all of that. And yes, you can record that little snippet on your handy pocket tape recorder and do what you like with it.'

He patted his pockets. 'Oh, shame. I seem to have left it at the office. Fancy that. The last time I came to your birthday party I had to climb over the garden fence. It makes a nice change to come in through the front door.'

She chuckled before answering. 'How could I forget?' She laughed out loud. 'You strode into my eighteenth birthday party as though you were the guest of honour and hadn't just climbed over the fence to avoid the security on the front entrance. And then you kidnapped me when my mother was in the salon with all of the stuffy, important guests she had invited who I had never met, and you whisked me away in your dad's sports car. It was magical and you were the magician who made it possible. It was like some happy dream.'

She shook her head, making her chandelier earrings sparkle, and brought her knees up to her chest. 'My mother still hasn't forgiven you for the fact that I missed my own birthday cake, eighteen candles and all. Heath had to blow them out for me.'

'Your mother is a remarkable lady. As far as she is concerned, I will always be the chauffeur's son, but do you know what? I am proud of the fact that my dad used to drive limos for a living before he moved into property. I always have been. No matter what you and your family think.'

Amber inhaled sharply and tugged her hand away from his.

'Wait a minute. Don't you dare accuse me of treating you differently because your dad was our driver. Because I didn't. I never did, and you know that. You were the one who was always defending yourself. Not me.'

'Your mother...'

'I'm not talking about my mother. I'm talking about you and me. I would never, ever have looked down on you because of the job you did. And maybe it's about time to get over that stupid inferiority complex of yours so that you can see all of the amazing things you have achieved in your life.'

'You mean like being an international concert pianist who is able to perform in front of thousands of people? Or my wonderful career as a fashion model and cosmetics guru? Is that what you mean?'

'I was in the right place at the right time and I got lucky. And you are insufferable.'

'And you are deluded.'

Amber glared at him for several seconds before she took a slow breath and shook her head slowly from side to side, before flicking her long hair back over her left shoulder.

'Parents. They have a lot to answer for. And that includes mine as well as yours. It's a good thing that we have both been able to rise above them to become so independent and calm and even-tempered.'

'Isn't it just.'

Amber slowly lowered her legs to the floor and shuffled closer to him on the bench so that there were inches and ten years of lost time between them. So close that he could hear her breathing increase in speed with his.

'Which reminds me...' Sam smiled and released her to dive inside his jacket pocket and pull out a long slim envelope which he passed to her. 'Happy birthday, Amber.'

And, without waiting for her to reply, he leant forwards

and kissed her tenderly but swiftly on the cheek. Lingering just long enough to inhale her scent and feel her waist under his fingertips before he drew back.

She looked at him with wide, startled eyes. 'Thank you. I mean, I wasn't expecting anything. Can I... Can I open it now?'

'Please. Go ahead.'

Sam looked around the garden for the few seconds it took for her to slide a manicured fingernail under the flap of the envelope and draw out a slim piece of faded paper.

'Sam? What is this? It looks like...' And then she understood what she was holding and her breath caught at the back of her throat.

'Is this what I think it is?'

Then she shook her head and sat back away from him, head down, reading the letters in the dim light before speaking again. And this time her voice came out in one long breath.

'This is the cheque my mother gave you to leave me alone.'

She looked up at him and her gaze darted from the cheque to his face and then back to the cheque again. 'I don't understand. She told me that she had offered you enough cash to take you through journalism school.'

Amber dropped the cheque into her lap and took hold of his hand, her eyes brimming with tears. 'Why? Why didn't you use this money, Sam? The damage had already been done.'

Sam raised his hand and stroked her cheek with his fingertips, until they were on her temple, forcing her to look into his eyes.

'Your mother knew the real thing when she saw it. I was dazzled by you, Amber. Dazzled and scared about how deep I was getting into a relationship I never saw coming. She took one look at me and saw a terrified young man who had barely survived his parents' divorce and was determined not to make the same mistake myself. She knew that we cared about each other very much. Too much. You were so beautiful and talented and for some crazy reason you wanted to be my friend and were even willing to sacrifice your music scholarship to stay in London with me. She couldn't let that happen.'

Sam made a slicing motion with the flat of his hand through the air.

'So she did the only thing she knew. She used my feelings for you to break us up.'

The air was broken by the sound of Amber's ragged breathing but Sam kept going. If ever there was a time and a place for the truth to come out, this was as good as any.

'All she had to do was put the idea in my head that you were looking for a ring on your finger and a house and two kids and that was it. She didn't need to spell it out. Staying with me would mean the end of your career as a concert pianist and my grandiose fantasy scheme to be an intrepid international reporter.'

Sam turned to face the garden so that he could rest his elbows on his knees, only too well aware that Amber's gaze would still be fixed on his face.

'That was the weird thing. I didn't believe her at first. I kept telling myself that she simply wanted me to leave you alone because she didn't think that I was good enough or ambitious enough for you.

'The problem was, when I went back into the party, you were talking to your rich friends from the private school who were all in designer gear and real jewels, chatting away about yacht holidays, and the more I thought about it, the more I realised that maybe she had a point. What future did we have together? If you stayed with me, I would be holding you back. You would be better taking the scholarship and spending the next three years in Paris with people who could further your career. People who sat in the back of limos. Not in the driver's seat.'

'Sam—no!' Amber exploded. 'How could you even think that? Why didn't you come and talk to me about what she had said? I would have put that idea out of your head right then and there.'

He shook his head. 'Clever woman, your mother. She knew that my dad was on his own because my mum had walked out on us. All she had to do was plant the idea in my head that if I wasn't good enough for my own mother—then how could I possibly be good enough for her beautiful and talented daughter who deserved the very best in life? The big chip on my shoulder did the rest.'

Amber took his hand in hers and squeezed but he dared not look at her. Not yet. 'It was all too much; my head was thumping with the champagne and I couldn't deal with everything with the sound of the party going on around me. So I slipped out of the kitchen door and into the car park to get some air.'

Sam looked up into the sky, where the stars were already bright. 'And you know who was there, waiting for me in the convertible?'

'Petra,' she replied in a shaky voice.

He nodded. 'She had a bottle of champagne and two glasses and my mind was so racing with all the possibilities and problems and options that it never even occurred to me to wonder why she was outside in the first place. It was only later that I found out—Petra knew that I was going to be coming outside.'

'My mother sent Petra out to wait for you? Is that what you're saying?'

Sam nodded. 'Petra called a few days later to tell me that her folks were taking her to their villa in Tuscany for the whole of the summer before finishing school in Switzerland. I think she was genuinely sorry that she had been used the way she was, but by then it was too late. You had already left for Paris. It was too late. She had done it. She had broken us up.'

Amber pushed off the bench and walked across the patio to the flower beds and stood with her back to Sam, her shoulders heaving up and down with emotion.

Every word that Sam had said echoed around inside her head, making it impossible for her to reply to him.

Her good arm wrapped tight around her waist, trying to hold in the explosion of confusion and regret that was threatening to burst out of her at any moment.

And not just about what had happened on her eighteenth birthday.

She had been so totally trusting and gullible! But the more she thought about it, the more she recognised that Sam was right. She was still dancing to her family's tune eleven years later—and the worst thing was, she was the one who was allowing them to do it.

So much for her great plans to make a new life for herself!

She was still too afraid to make her own decisions and follow her heart.

No longer.

That ended tonight.

From now on, she chose what to do and where. And who with.

Starting with Parvita. She wanted to see her friend get married so very much and that was precisely what she was going to do. Risk be damned.

Before Amber could calm her beating heart, she sensed his presence and seconds later a strong hand slid onto each side of her waist, holding her firm. Secure. She breathed in his aftershave, but did not resist as he moved closer behind her until she could feel the length of his body from chest to groin pressed against her back.

She had not even realised that she was shivering until she

felt the delicious warmth and weight of Sam's dinner jacket as he dropped it over her shoulders.

Sam's arms wrapped tighter around her waist, the fingers pressing oh so gently into her ribcage and Amber closed her eyes, her pulse racing. It had been a long time. And he smelt fabulous. Felt. Fabulous.

Sam pressed his head into the side of her neck, his light stubble grazing against her skin, and her head dropped back slightly so that it was resting on his.

Bad head.

Bad need for contact with this man.

Bad full stop.

One of his hands slid up the side of her neck and smoothed her hair away from her face so that he could press his lips against the back of her neck.

'It was all my fault,' he said, and his low, soft voice sounded different. Strained. Hesitant. 'I was trying to do the right thing and in the end I caused you pain. I'm so sorry.'

Amber sighed and looked up at the twinkling stars in the night sky, but sensed her shoulders lift with tension.

'There's nothing for you to be sorry about. It was eleven years ago and we were both so young and trying to find our way. It's just…it never crossed my mind that you were trying to do the noble thing by walking out on me. I wasted a lot of angry tears. And that is just sad, Sam.'

Sam continued to breathe into her neck, and one of his hands slid up from her waist to move in small circles on her shoulders under his jacket, and Amber suddenly began to heat up at a remarkably rapid rate.

'I know you're tired. No wonder. I've watched you dance the night away and I'm glad that I was here to see that. So thank you again for inviting me. Although Kate was watching me like a hawk to make sure that I wasn't making any moves on you.'

And that did make Amber grin. 'Kate the virtue keeper. I like that.'

Sam said nothing, but the hand tracing circles slid down her arm from shoulder to wrist, and he moved impossibly closer, his hand moving slowly up and down her arm.

'And necessary. You look very beautiful tonight.'

Amber smiled wide enough for Sam to sense her movement. 'Thank you. And thank you for finally telling me the truth about what happened.'

She slowly lifted one of Sam's hands from her waist and pushed gently away from him, instantly sorry that she had broken the touch, but turned back to face him.

'It's gone midnight. And I have had a very bad year, Sam. In so many ways. I don't want to start the next year of my life with regrets and bitterness.'

The smile on his lips faded and his upper lip twitched a couple of times. Amber knew that move. He couldn't be nervous. *Could he*?

She looked into his face and smiled a closed mouth smile. 'We both made mistakes. And I'm the last person who should be judging anyone. So how about starting the next year of my life as we mean to go on? As old friends who have just met up again after a long break. Can you do that?'

'Old friends,' he replied and lifted her fingers to his lips, his eyes never leaving hers. 'I'll drink to that. How about…'

But, before Sam could finish speaking, a fat lounger cushion whacked him on the side of the head. And then a second time.

'You can stop that right now, Sam Richards. I mean it. Stop or I'll go and find the rolling pin and wrap it around your ears.'

'It's okay, Kate.' Amber sighed and rolled her eyes. 'Sam has just passed the audition. He'll be coming to India to interview me next week. You can put the pillow down.'

Sam stopped ducking his head and whipped around. 'What did you just say?'

'I have changed my mind about going to Parvita's wedding.' Amber smiled, her eyebrows high. 'Isn't that exciting?'

CHAPTER TEN

From: Amber@AmberDuBois.net
To: Kate@LondonBespokeTailoring.com; Saskia@Elwood-House.co.uk
Subject: Sam Report
Hey Goddesses

Greetings from another gorgeous day in Kerala. The girls are still trying to settle down after all of the excitement of Parvita's wedding so lots to do, but my wrist is feeling a lot better today—despite all of the sitar playing!

Sam's flight was an hour late leaving London so he won't arrive until very late in the evening, which is probably a good thing considering this pre monsoon heatwave. No doubt he is bursting to get this interview over and done with so he can get back to his nice cool London office. Especially since I asked the janitor to pick Sam up at the airport in his rusty old motor, which is definitely on its last legs. Just for Kate.

Will report back tomorrow. Have fun. Amber

SAM RICHARDS SLID his rucksack off his shoulder and mopped the sweat from his brow and neck with one of his dad's pocket handkerchiefs as he strolled up the few steps to the single storey white building. If it was this hot at dusk he was dreading the midday temperature. But he would find out soon enough.

Great! *Not.*

The school janitor, who had picked him up at the airport,

had pointed him towards the main entrance to the girls' home but Sam had barely been able to hear what he said since he kept the wreck of a car engine going just in case it broke down before he made it home.

The last hour had been spent in a bone-shaking car from the nineteen-sixties driven by a friendly janitor who seemed oblivious to the fact that he was hitting every pothole on the dirt road between the local airport and the girls' home in a car with bald tyres and no suspension.

Sam was amazed that the patched up, barely intact motor had lasted the journey without breaking down in a coconut grove or rice paddy. But it had got him here and for that he was grateful.

Slipping his sunglasses into his shirt breast pocket, Sam stretched his arms tall and tried to take in the sensory overload that was the Kerala coastline at sunset.

And failed.

The sea breeze from the shockingly beautiful crescent shaped bay was blocked by the low brick wall which formed the boundary of the property, creating a breathless oasis of fruit trees, a vegetable garden and exotic flowering plants which spilled out in an explosion of startlingly bright colours from wooden tubs and planters.

The immaculately kept gardens stretched down to the ocean and a wide strip of stunning white sand which glowed in the reflected shades of deep rich apricot, scarlet and gold from the setting sun. His view of the lapping waves was broken only by the thin trunks of tall coconut palms, banana plants and fruit trees.

It was like a poster of a dream beach from the cover of a holiday brochure. Complete with a long wooden fishing boat on the shore and umbrellas made from coconut palm fronds to protect the fishermen and occasional tourists who were out on the beach this late in the evening.

Coconuts. He was looking at real coconut palm trees. Compared to the grey, drizzly London Sam had left the previous afternoon the warm breeze was luxuriously dry and scented with the salty tang from the sea blended with spice and a tropical sweet floral scent.

A great garland of bougainvillea with stunning bright purple and hot pink flowers wound its way up the side of the school entrance and onto the coconut fibre roof, intertwined with a wonderful frangipani which spilled out from a blue ceramic pot, attracting bees and other nectar-seeking insects to the intensely fragrant blossoms. The perfume almost balanced out the heavy red dust from the dirt road and the bio odours from the cows and chickens who roamed freely on the other side of a low coconut matting fence.

He loved writing and his life as a journalist. He always had, but it was only when he came to villages like this one that it really struck home how much of his life was spent in open plan offices under fluorescent light tubes.

Even the air tasted different on his tongue. Traffic from the coast road roared past. Trucks in all colours, painted auto rickshaws and bright yellow buses competed with birdsong and the chatter of people and motor scooters. Everywhere he looked his eyes and ears were assaulted by a cacophony of life.

But as he relaxed into the scene, hands on his hips, the sound of piano music drifted out through the partly open door of what looked like a school building to his left and Sam smiled and wandered over, his shirt sticking to his back in the oppressive heat and humidity.

Amber was sitting on a very frail looking low wooden bench in front of an upright piano which had definitely seen better days. The polish was flaking off, the lid was warped and, from where he was standing, it looked as if some of the black keys were missing at the bottom of the scale.

But it didn't matter. Because Amber DuBois was running the fingers of her left hand across the keyboard and suddenly the old neglected instrument was singing like a nightingale.

She was dressed in a blue and pink long-sleeved cotton tunic and what looked like pyjama bottoms, her hair was held back by a covered elastic band and, as her feet moved across the pedals, he caught a glimpse of a plastic flip-flop.

And, for the first time in his professional life, Sam Richards did not know what to say.

Amber DuBois had never looked more beautiful in her life. Exotic. Enchanting. But at that moment there was something else—she was totally and completely relaxed and content. Her eyes were closed and, as she played, she was humming along gently to the music as it soared into flights of soft and then dramatic sections of what sounded to Sam's uneducated ears as some great romantic composer's finest work.

Her shoulders lifted and fell, her left arm flowing from side to side in brilliant technique while her plastered hand moved stiffly from octave to octave. But that did not matter—the music was so magical and captivating that it reverberated around this tiny school room and into every bone of his body.

The tropical garden and birdsong outside the window disappeared as he was swept up in the music.

This was her joy and her delight. The thing she loved most in the world.

He was looking at a completely different woman from the one who had flounced into his dad's garage, or the fashion model who had haughtily gossiped with the designer goddesses as she decluttered her apartment.

This was the real Amber. This was the girl he used to know. The girl whose greatest joy was playing the piano for her own entertainment and pleasure.

She was back!

And Lord, the longer he looked at her and listened to her

music, the more he liked what he saw and the more he lusted. The fire that had sparked the second his fingers had touched her skin in that ridiculous penthouse dressing room suddenly flared right back into a blazing bonfire.

The heat and humidity of Kerala in May was nothing compared to the incendiary fire in his blood which pounded in his neck and ears.

Did she know? Did Amber have any clue that when she played liked this she was revealing to the world how much inner passion was hidden inside the cool blonde slender frame?

He had thought that he had been attracted to her before, but that was nothing compared to the way he felt now.

He wanted her. And not just in his bed. He wanted Amber in his life, even if it was only for a few days, weeks or months. He wanted to be her friend and the man she wanted to share her life with. The music seemed to soak into his heart and soul and fill every cell with a fierce determination.

Somehow he was going to have to find a way of winning her back and persuading her to give him a second chance, or risk losing her for ever.

His bag slumped onto the floor.

Sam walked slowly into the room and slid next to Amber on the very end of the child-sized wooden bench. She did not open her eyes but smiled and slowly inhaled before giving an appreciative sigh.

'They say you can tell a lot about a man from the aftershave he has chosen. Very nice. Did you buy it at the airport?'

Her hands never missed a note as he gave a short dismissive grunt in reply. 'Then you won't mind if I move a little closer.'

Sam was blatantly aware that the fine wool cloth of his trousers brushed against the loose cotton trousers Amber was wearing as he slid along the shiny wooden surface until the whole side of his body seemed to be aligned against her.

'Hello. How was the flight?'

He started to say something, changed his mind, and left her staring at his mouth for just a few seconds too long. Much too long. His eyes scanned her face as though he was trying to record the images like a digital camera in his memory.

He had been worried about how awkward this moment was going to be. But, instead of watching every word, it was as though he was meeting one of his best friends in the world—and his heart lifted.

'You're playing nursery rhymes. From memory.'

She shook her head slowly from side to side. 'It sounds terrible and I am totally out of practice.'

'But you are trying. In your apartment last week, I couldn't help wonder if the old piano-playing business had lost its appeal. Am I right?'

Her fingers slowed down but did not stop. 'Full marks to the man in the sweaty shirt. You're right. I didn't want to play. No. That's wrong. I didn't want to perform.' She gave a little giggle and her left hand played a trill. 'This is not performing. This is having fun. And I have missed that. Do you know what I spent this afternoon doing? Making up tunes and songs around nursery rhymes these girls have never heard before. We had a great time.'

'Wait a minute. Are you telling me that you don't enjoy performing? Is that why you decided to retire? Because you do know that you are brilliant, don't you? I even splashed out and bought your latest album!'

She stopped playing, sat back and smiled, wide-eyed.

'You did? That was very kind.'

'No, it wasn't kind. It was a delight. And you haven't answered my question.'

Her gaze scanned his face as though looking for something

important and Sam suddenly remembered that he needed a wash and a shave. 'That depends on who is asking the question,' she replied in a low, soft voice with the power to entrance him. 'My old pal Sam who I used to trust once upon a time, or the newest super-journalist at GlobalStar Media who I am not sure about at all.'

He swallowed down a moment of doubt but made the tough choice. Editor be damned. 'Let's try that first option.'

'Okay. Let's.' She looked down at her left hand and stretched out the fingers on the piano keys. 'Well. *Off the record.* These past few years have been very hard going. I haven't given myself enough time to recover from one tour before launching into rehearsals for the next. Combine that with all of the travelling and media interviews and suddenly I'm waking up exhausted every morning and nothing I do seems to make any difference.'

Her gaze shifted to his eyes and locked on tight. Shades of blue and violet clashed against the faint golden tinge to her skin. 'Every night was a struggle to make myself play and dive into the music to try and find some energy. I lost my spark, Sam. I lost my joy.'

'That's not the girl I used to know talking.'

'I'm not that same girl any more.'

'Aren't you?' Sam replied and reached up and touched her cheek. 'Are you quite sure about that? Because when I came in just now you had that soppy girly look on your face like you used to have when you sat down at a piano.'

'What do you mean, soppy?'

'Soppy. It means that you are your old self again—and I am very glad of it. This place seems to be doing you a lot of good.'

He glanced down and shocked her by gently lifting up her left hand and turning it over, his forefinger tracing the outline of the beautiful scrolls and flowers drawn in henna on the back of her hand.

'Take this, for example. I've never seen anything like it. Totally amazing. How was the wedding?'

His fingers stroked her palm, then lifted the back of her hand to his lips so that he could kiss her knuckles and was rewarded with an intense flash of awareness that told him that she knew exactly what he was saying. It was not the henna he found amazing.

She tutted twice, took her hand back then turned to face him. 'It was a fabulous wedding and I wouldn't have missed it for the world.' She gestured with her head towards the window. 'Parvita's family organised a flower arch in the garden and the service was so simple. A few words spoken by a man and a woman from completely different worlds, and yet it was totally perfect. There was not a dry eye in the house.'

'You cried at your friend's wedding? Really? And there is no such thing as a perfect marriage, just a decent wedding day.'

'Yes, I cried, you cynic,' Amber replied and scowled at him and pulled her hand away. 'Because this was the real thing. They didn't need a huge hotel with hundreds of guests who they would never have a chance to meet and talk to. All they wanted was their friends and family to help them celebrate. The little girls were all dressed up and throwing flowers. It was perfect. So don't mock.'

Sam held up both hands in surrender.

'Hey. Remember my ex-girlfriend who tried to lure me into a wedding without asking me first? Not all of us believe in happy endings, you old romantic.'

Amber thumped him on the arm. 'Well, that is just sad and pathetic.'

'Maybe you're right,' Sam replied and looked around, suddenly desperate to change the subject. 'Is this one of your school rooms?'

She nodded. 'The building work is going flat out before the

monsoon rains so this is a temporary teaching room. I like it but I can't wait until the new air conditioned school is ready.'

'Have you decided on a name for the school you are paying for?' Sam asked as he picked up his bag and they strolled out into the evening air. 'The DuBois centre? Or the DuBois School for Girls. What is it to be?'

'Oh, you would like that, wouldn't you? No. I suggested a few names to the board of governors and they came back with one winner: the Elwood School.'

'Elwood? You named the school after your friend Saskia? Why did you choose that name?'

Amber leant back and gestured towards the girls who were playing on the grassy lawn under the mango and cashew nut trees. 'Do you see these lovely girls? They are so talented and bursting with life and enthusiasm. And yet not one of them has a home to go to. They are not all orphans as we would define orphans—far from it. Most of them have parents who cannot look after them or there were problems at home which mean that they only see their parents for a few months every year. But one way or another they have found their way here to this girls' home, where they can feel safe and protected by people who love them.'

Amber turned back to Sam with moisture sparkling in the corners of her eyes and when she spoke there was a hoarseness in her voice which clutched at Sam's heart and squeezed it tight. 'Well, I know just what that feels like. Saskia and her aunt Margot gave me a safe refuge when I needed to get away from my mother and whatever man she was living with who struggled to recall my name.'

Then she shook her head with a chuckle. 'They even let me stay with them after the mega-row I had with my so called parents after the disaster that was my eighteenth birthday party.'

Sam coughed, twice. 'You had a fight with your mother? I haven't heard that part of the story.'

She sniffed. 'I had no idea that those particular terms of abuse were in my vocabulary until I heard them come out of my mouth. Harsh words were exchanged about the expensive education I had been subjected to. It was not my moment of shining glory. And then I stomped out of the house with only my handbag and walked around to Elwood House. And Saskia and her aunt Margot took me in and looked after me as though I was one of their own.'

Amber sat up straight and curled her right hand high into the air with a flourish. 'Ta da. Elwood School.' Then she blinked and gave a curt nod. 'It may surprise you but I do have something in common with Parvita and these girls.'

Then she shivered and chuckled. 'Well, I did tell you that this article was going to be a challenge. I cannot wait to see what you do with that little insight, if it was on the record.'

'Any more like that?'

'Plenty. Just wait and see what tomorrow brings.'

CHAPTER ELEVEN

From: Amber@AmberDuBois.net
To: Kate@LondonBespokeTailoring.com; Saskia@Elwood-House.co.uk
Subject: My fiendish plan

Well, this is turning out to be a very odd week.

I came out first thing this morning to find Sam halfway up a jackfruit tree tossing fruit down to the girls below. He claims that he couldn't sleep because of the heat but he is now their official hero in long pants and is mobbed wherever he goes. I have just peeked outside and he is showing his little gaggle of fans the slideshow of photos on his digital camera. Amazing!

He even had me playing Christmas carols and nursery songs to amuse the girls during meal times in exchange for helping to organise the juniors. They adored him. I think he may never be allowed to leave!

My fiendish plan is to steal Sam away long enough for a walk along the beach at dusk and talk him into working on Parvita's story instead of mine. It is worth a try. Otherwise I don't know how long I can keep him hanging on.

The good news is that my wrist is feeling a lot better and I am enjoying playing for the first time in ages.

Cheers from Kerala. Amber

From: Kate@LondonBespokeTailoring.com
To: Amber@AmberDuBois.net

Subject: Sam Report
Sheesh, that man has no shame when it comes to charming the ladies. Don't be fooled. Glad that your hand is feeling better. Don't forget to drink plenty of water. Love ya. K

SAM WIPED THE spark plug from the janitor's ancient motor
car on a scrap of cotton and held it up to the fading sunlight
before deciding that the plug had lived a very long life and
needed to take retirement, as of right now. He had managed
to find one replacement at the bottom of a tool kit which was
so rusty that it had taken hours to clean the tools to the stage
where he could use them to service what passed as a car.

But at least the work had kept him close to Amber.

They still had a lot of work to do to rebuild that fragile
friendship but she had seemed genuinely delighted when he
helped her collect the girls together and keep them in one
place long enough for her to explain about the keys on the
piano and what the notes meant. With a bit of help from a
couple of coconut shells, three tin buckets and a wrench.

Weird. He had surprised himself by actually enjoying playing on a makeshift set of drums.

The only thing they were not doing was talking about her
career.

She might have trusted him enough to take the risk and invite him here to his magical place to see what she was doing
with her life but that was as far as it went.

So far there had always been some excellent excuse why
this was not a good time to record an interview and after three
days he had all the background photos he might need but not
the exclusive extra material he needed to create a compel-
ling story—her story.

So what was the problem?

The sound of female laughter echoed out from the school
room and he peered in through the window just in time to

see Amber conducting a mini orchestra of five girls playing wooden recorders in tune with some Italian baroque music which blasted out from a cheap cassette player perched on the teacher's desk.

He smiled and dropped back down before she saw him.

It might have been his idea for her to play a few simple tunes, one note at a time, but once she got started the girls and teachers had begged her for more and now there was no stopping her.

Amber had a way with the girls that was nothing short of astonishing. It was as if they knew that she understood what they were going through and wanted to help them any way she could.

And it had nothing to do with her musical talent, although she was playing more and more every day.

Amber was giving these girls the kind of unconditional love he hadn't seen in a long time.

Seeing her with the children, it was obvious that Amber would make a wonderful mother—but how did that happen? Her own parents certainly had not been good role models. No. This came from her own heart and her ability to reach out and touch a child's life and make a little girl laugh.

Perhaps it was a good thing that Amber had thrown herself into working with the girls at the orphanage. Because the longer he spent with her and listened to her sweet voice and shared her laughter, the harder it was to kid himself that he could control this burning attraction to her.

He was falling for Amber DuBois all over again.

And that had to be the craziest thing that had happened to him in a long time.

But the worst thing that he could do right now—for either of them, was tell her how he felt. He had to be patient, even if it killed him.

Somehow he had to stay objective and cool enough to write

an exclusive celebrity interview which gave no hint of how badly he wanted to be with the celebrity, talk to her and tell her how much she meant to him.

No. Forget wanted. Make that *needed* to be with her while he had the chance.

In the past few weeks he had seen Amber the cold, snarky concert pianist, Amber the fashion designers' favourite model, who happened to love Indian food as much as he did, and now he was mending the janitor's car while a stripped down, enchanting Amber taught small girls with bangles on their wrists all about Italian baroque.

And guess which version of Amber was capable of rocking his world just at the sight of her?

Every day she spent here seemed to make her even more relaxed and at ease. Happy and laughing. Enjoying her music again with every note she played and loving every minute she spent with these girls. And she could teach—that was obvious, even if she did roll her eyes at him every time he applauded after a class.

He must have told her a dozen times how good it was to hear her play with such delight—even if it was with one hand and a few fingertips, and his message seemed to be getting through. She had actually admitted over breakfast that she had never enjoyed music so much in a long time.

Maybe retiring from concert performances was not such a bad idea for Amber DuBois?

Everything he had seen and heard so far told him that she was serious about turning her back on the offers streaming in from orchestras all over the world. Frank had got that wrong. She was a lot more interested in the girls here than a prestigious career—for the moment, at least.

Sam jumped into the broken driver's seat and listened as the engine reluctantly kicked into life.

The problem was that after listening to Amber's countless

stories about how wonderful her friend Parvita's wedding had been, it was fairly obvious that her idea of a happy relationship meant a ring on her finger and a house and a garden with children to play in it.

What was it with women and weddings? Why couldn't two people accept that they wanted to share their lives and be happy at that?

A few months before his ex-girlfriend Alice took the initiative in Los Angeles, they had travelled to New York for her cousin's wedding and over a very long weekend at grandiose parties he had fended off at regular intervals the constant ribbing from her relatives about when they were going to make an announcement about their wedding. Alice had done the same, only with a twist. 'Oh, Sam is not the marrying type. You can take a horse to water, but you can't make him drink. Isn't that right, Sam?'

And he had smiled and replied with yet another joke, just a bit of fun to amuse the other guests. Alice had known, even then, that they would never be together long-term, and he had been too complacent to talk to her about it. Too content to accept second best and go with the flow. Until she'd decided to take the initiative and organise the wedding on her own. And he had bolted.

Coward. After he'd left, Alice had found someone she wanted to spend the rest of her life with.

Amber was bound to do the same. She was beautiful, funny and talented and she deserved some happiness in her life. With a man who could give her what she wanted.

He wanted Amber to be happy—why wouldn't he?

The problem was, he had broken the unwritten rule. He cared about Amber. If he went back to London without telling her how he felt he would be walking away from the best thing in his life. And breaking both of their hearts all over again. And that truly would make him a coward.

'Hey there. Good news. You have just won the prize for inventing a new musical instrument. Coconut shells and buckets filled with different amounts of water make different sounds when you hit them with a wrench. Who knew? The girls loved it! What made you think of that?'

'Ingenuity. And drumming on oil cans in my dad's garage. I thought it might work.' Sam chuckled up at Amber, who was waving goodbye to the girls who were streaming out from her classroom. 'Failing that, I could always play the spoons. But I am saving that for an encore. I live in hope.'

Amber gave a small shoulder shrug. 'Either one of those would work for me. It seems that you have hidden talents after all. Are your mum and dad musical?'

'Not a bit. Nobody in our house could sing a note in tune but I like the drums. Not exactly the most subtle of instruments and my mum couldn't stand me making a noise in the house so my dad let me make loose on the oil drums. I hope I didn't scare the girls.'

'Not a bit and I was impressed. But, speaking of hope, are you free to come down to the beach for a stroll before it gets dark? It's lovely and cool down there.'

'Five minutes to wash my hands and I'll be right with you. That's the best offer I have had all day,' he replied with a sexy wink.

'Keep that up and it will be the only offer you have. Meet you under the palm tree. Second from the left.'

'It's a date,' he whispered and was rewarded with a definite flush to her cheeks before she lifted her chin in denial, rolled her eyes in pretend disgust and strolled down the lawns towards the bay.

In the end it took Sam ten minutes to wash then extricate himself from the gaggle of girls who clutched onto his legs as he made his way across the gardens towards the beach.

But it was worth it.

Sam reached for his small pocket digital camera so that he could capture the lovely image of the woman who was sitting on the edge of an old wooden fishing boat on a wide stretch of the most incredible fine golden sand, on a beach fringed with coconut palms.

She looked up as he took the shot and gave him a warm smile which came from the heart.

And he knew. Just like that. This was the photo he would use on the cover of his article—and keep in his wallet for rainy days back in London when the office got too much.

She was wearing a simple tunic and trousers, the plaster cast on her wrist covered with children's names, and her hair was tied back with a scarf. And in his eyes she was the most beautiful woman that he had ever seen in his life.

And then he saw it. Nestling at her throat. It was a gold heart shaped pendant that had cost him every penny of the money that he had been saving for spare tyres for the car his dad was working on for him.

He had given her the necklace in the car the evening of her eighteenth birthday the moment before he had turned the key in the ignition. And it had been worth every penny just to see her face light up with joy and happiness at that moment.

It was the first time she had kissed him without him prompting—and it meant the world to him.

He couldn't drag his eyes away from it. Of all the jewels she must have collected she had chosen to wear his necklace tonight. Had she chosen it to provoke him, or, and his heart swelled at the thought, to show that she had not forgotten how very close they had been?

Sam shuffled closer to her, stretched out his hand and, with two fingers, lifted the gold chain clear of her remarkable cleavage and dangled the heart pendant in the air.

'Nice necklace.'

'Thank you. It was a gift from a boy I was in love with at the time. I wear it now and again.'

'To remind yourself that you were loved?'

'To remind myself that love can break your heart,' Amber replied and reached up and took hold of Sam's fingers in hers. 'And that I was loved. Yes, that too.'

And she took his breath away with the honesty.

So much so that, instead of sitting next to her, Sam knelt down on the sand in front of Amber and looked deep into her surprised eyes before asking the question which had been welling up all day.

'Why are you avoiding our interview, Amber? What is it that you are so afraid of telling me?'

Her reply was to break off eye contact and look out over his shoulder to the sea in silence.

'We were such close friends once,' he went on. 'We used to talk about everything. Our hopes and our dreams. Our great plans for the future. *Everything*. I don't think you have any idea how much it hurts me that you find it so impossible to get past the mistake I made when I listened to your mother and walked out of your birthday party that night.'

She glanced back at him, reached out and plucked a leaf from his shoulder. 'I thought that you were the one who had thrown our friendship away as though it didn't matter.'

'You were wrong. So *wrong*. I was confused about where we could go as a couple—but never about that. You were always the friend I came to when I needed someone. Always.'

His gaze scanned her face from her brow to her chin and back again. 'You were the only real friend I had. Oh, I know that you and your pals thought that I was the popular boy around town, but the truth was harder to accept. I knew everyone in my area, played football and talked big, but I was still too raw from my parents' divorce to talk about what really mattered to anyone at school. So I kept my deep feelings to myself. Even if that meant being lonely.'

'Was that why you talked to me, Sam? Because I was an outsider?'

'Maybe.' He shrugged. 'I may also have noticed that you were not hard to look at. But hey, I was a teenage pressure cooker of hormones and bad skin. Nothing special about that.'

'Yes, you were. You were always special. To me at least.'

'I know.' His brows squeezed together. 'I think that was what scared me in the end, Amber.'

'What do you mean?'

'You took me seriously. You listened to me babbling on about what a successful journalist I was going to become and actually encouraged me to stick my neck out and pass the exams I needed to go to university. You believed in me. And that was one of the reasons why I fell in love with you.'

He heard her sharp intake of breath but ignored it and carried on. 'And it terrified me. I had seen my parents fall apart from all of the fights and arguments which they tried to keep from me, but failed miserably. You were not the only one to be dragged around from new house to new house as your mother found a new partner. I refused to go to see my mum the minute I turned eighteen but she still had the power to make my life miserable.'

Sam paused. He had not thought about that in years. Strange. 'And then you stepped out of a limo with your mother one evening. Amber Sheridan DuBois.' He grinned up into her face. 'And suddenly my life was not so miserable after all. And I will always be grateful to you for being the friend that had been missing from my life and I hadn't even realised that fact. Always. I couldn't have been happier that last year.'

'Until we became more than friends. Is that what you are saying?'

Sam nodded, lips pressed tight together. 'That night of

your eighteenth when we got back to your house after our mini tour of London, and I told you that I loved you—I meant it, Amber.'

He pushed himself to his feet. 'That is why you asked me to come out to Kerala instead of giving your interview in London or over the Internet. You knew that I loved you but I still walked away. And now you are the one with the power to walk away and leave me behind.' Sam shook his head and half turned to look out across the sands to the gaggle of children playing in the surf. 'Strange,' he chuckled, 'I never thought that you would turn out to be such a diva.'

Amber gasped so loudly that Sam whirled back to look at her.

'A diva?' she repeated in a horrified voice. 'You think I am behaving like a diva? Oh, Sam. You have no idea how hurtful it is for me to hear you say those words. A diva?'

She shook her arm away as he reached out to take it and stood up. 'A diva is the very last thing I ever wanted to be.'

Sam started to follow her onto the sand, but she whirled around to face him, her hand clenched into a tight fist by her side. 'I thought that you, of all people, would understand why I despise the very word. That was what they used to call her. Remember? "The loveliest diva in the music business". Julia Swan.'

Sam groaned. 'Yes. Of course I remember. Your mum used to relish it. But I thought…I thought you wanted star billing and your own dressing room. You have worked so hard for so many years as a soloist. Doesn't that go with the territory?'

'Of course it does. And I have worked hard. So very hard. But you still don't understand, do you?'

She stepped up to him and clenched hold of his hand. 'That wasn't what I wanted. It has never been what I wanted. I loved the music. That was the important thing.'

She released him and turned sideways to stand with her

arm wrapped around her waist and look out over the ocean. 'You asked me the other day why I wanted to retire. It wasn't the work. It was me.'

Her voice faded away as though the breeze was carrying it out to sea. 'I didn't like what I was becoming, Sam. And this last tour of Asia was the final straw.'

She flung back her head so that the breeze could cool her neck. 'By the time we got to India, I started demanding things like my own dressing room and quiet hotel rooms and white cushions and stupid things like that. My pals on the tour said that it was because we were all so tired but when we got to Kerala and took a break from the tour I realised that the concert organisers were wary of me—they expected me to be demanding and difficult.'

As Sam watched, Amber closed her eyes. 'And the worst thing was that the complaining and the headaches—they had nothing to do with the love of the music and everything to do with the stress of the performances and the touring. Somewhere along the way my passion for the music had been buried under the avalanche of photo shoots and the press parties and the dresses and I hadn't even noticed. And that was so wrong.'

Amber half turned to look at Sam and she felt the tears prick the corners of her eyes even before she said the words. 'I was turning into my mother and it was killing the one thing that I had loved. I was terrified of becoming that sad and bitter and lonely diva that was Julia Swan. That's when I decided to retire, Sam. I was terrified that I was turning into my mother.'

CHAPTER TWELVE

'No,' SAM REPLIED, resting the palms of his hands on Amber's shoulders and drawing her back to the boat to sit down. 'That was never going to happen. Never.'

His gaze locked onto her lovely eyes and held them tight. 'I've spent the last three days watching you connect with these girls. Where did you learn those skills? Not from Julia Swan and certainly not by being some diva.'

She smiled back at him but her eyes were suddenly sad. 'I can say the same thing about you. Those girls love you. But you don't understand. It had already happened. And do you know the worst thing? The moment it hit me what I was doing was when I finally understood her. After all of these years I finally understood that my mother didn't hate people—she hated her job. She hated it but she didn't know anything else, so she took her frustration out on everyone around her.'

'You might be right. But what did you do? Just walk off the tour?'

She flashed him a look. 'Hardly. No. My friend Parvita had organised a series of charity concerts in small towns and school halls in Kerala and Goa. Until then I had always said that I was too busy, but at the very last minute their solo pianist had to go to New York and Parvita asked me to take his place.'

She raised her hands then dropped them to her lap. 'What

can I say? India knocked me sideways. I love everything about it. The heat, the colours, everything. We travelled with a group of incredible sitar players, and we had the best tour of our lives. And the very last day was a revelation. Can you imagine—the whole musical troupe was in a rickety bus, dodging the potholes, in the middle of nowhere heading for a string of orphanages for abandoned girls?'

She looked at Sam and managed a smile.

'Nothing can prepare you for what we found here. I thought I had seen it all. Wrong again. Same with my friends. I think I cried every night. It was tough going but Parvita worked her magic and for a short while we had a real working music school right here in this village. We had planned to do two nights at the orphanage before heading back to the airport. We stayed a week! Can you imagine? By working all around the area, we raised enough money to pay for hospital treatment for the girls with enough left over to give them a decent meal every day for a month. These girls. Oh, Sam. These amazing girls.'

She broke into a wide grin. 'You wouldn't believe the fun we all had. It was crazy. They are living in the worst conditions and they found happiness. It was very precious. I'll never forget it.'

'I can see how important it is to you. Is that why you decided to come back here for Parvita's wedding?'

Amber nodded. 'Parvita wants to create the music school but she needs help to pay the teachers' wages and keep things going. So when she left on her honeymoon I offered to stay on and help in the school before the monsoon hits.'

She paused and her eyes flicked up at Sam as he held his breath for what she was about to say next. 'I have had the most amazing fun here. You were right when you told me that I seemed happier here. The problem is—until I came here I had no idea how shallow and self-indulgent my life as a concert performer was. These girls have given me a new insight into my life.'

'You worked your whole life for your success, Amber. Hey, wait a minute. Last summer you were the new face of a huge cosmetics campaign. How does that fit in?'

Amber screwed up her face and Sam could almost see hear her jaw clench. Her face creased into a grimace. 'It was a tricky decision. My agent was thrilled and suddenly I had all of these glamorous people telling me what an asset I would be for their cosmetics. But that was not why I did it. Of course my first reaction was to laugh it off as some big joke. But then they offered me a sum of money that made my head spin. A wicked amount of money. Criminal, really. And once I had that sum in my head, it wouldn't go away. I kept thinking about my friend Parvita and all of the fund-raising work she was doing for the charity. And the more I thought about it, the more I realised that what I was actually saying was that my pride was more important than these girls having an education and healthcare. All I had to do was sit there wearing a lovely dress while make-up experts, hairdressers and lighting engineers worked their magic. This was ridiculous. I couldn't walk away from that opportunity to do something remarkable for the sake of a few hours having my photograph taken. That would be so selfish I wouldn't be able to live with myself.'

She chuckled. 'I knew that I would get a terrible kicking from the media. And I did. You and your colleagues were not very kind and it upset me at the time, but do you know what?'

Amber smiled and dropped her shoulders. 'It was worth it. I had to weigh up every cruel comment from the music press and every sniping gossip columnist against seeing a real school going up in place of the slum ruin that was here before.'

'Why didn't you tell them? That the money wasn't going into your own bank account?'

Amber turned to face him. 'You know why, Sam. How long

have you been interviewing television personalities and so-called celebrities? Years, right? And how many times have you ridiculed the charity work that people do with their time and money? It doesn't seem to matter if a famous basketball player wants to visit a hospice for the day to cheer up the boys. Or a bestselling novelist donates a huge amount to a literacy campaign. They are all accused of having so much money that they can splash out on some charity or other for tax reasons and to make them look good.'

She shook her head. 'That's not for me, Sam. I wanted this project to be part of my private life, away from the media and the cameras and the concert halls. It is too personal and important. The last thing I want is my photo with the girls to be splashed over the cover of some celebrity gossip magazine. I would hate that to happen.'

'Now that I simply do not understand. Yes. Those articles help to sell newspapers and magazines, and the charity gains some free publicity at the same time. Don't you want that for the girls?'

He looked back up the hill towards the school. 'They still have a long way to go. And your name could help them get there.'

Amber started chewing on the side of her lower lip. It was an action that he had seen her do a hundred times before, usually when her mother was nagging.

'I know. And I have turned it over in my mind so many times but, in the end, it all boils down to this.'

Her gaze locked onto his face. 'I need you to write a feature article about the orphanage. And if that means using me as a hook to get readers interested—' she took a breath '—then okay, I will have my photo taken in India and splashed all over the internet and wherever the article reaches—as long—' she paused again '—as long as the article makes it clear that I am supporting the charity set up by my friend,

Parvita. I'm just one member of the team working on fund-raising and teaching the pupils for free—and there is a whole long list of other professional musicians who are involved. Small cog. Big charity project. Only...'

'Only?' he asked, his head whirling with what she was asking him to do.

'I have to trust you to tell the truth about why I chose to spend my time teaching here with Parvita instead of performing in some huge concert hall, without turning it into some great fluff piece about how I am lowering myself to be here. And not one word about my mother. Can I do that? Can I trust you, Sam?'

'Amber, you don't know what you're asking. My editor, Frank, is not interested in an in-depth article on a charity in India. He wants celebrity news that will sell papers in London. And if I don't deliver, that editor's desk will go to another hungry journalist and I'll be back at the bottom of the pecking order all over again.'

She closed her eyes and his heart surged that he might be the cause of her pain. She had offered him the truth—now it was his turn.

Reaching out, he took her left hand and held it tight against his chest, forcing her to look at him.

'I need this job, Amber. My dad isn't getting any younger and I've hardly seen him these past ten years. I made his life hell after my mother left us and he had to take the blame. But do you know what? He believed in me when my mother made it clear that I was a useless dreamer who would never amount to anything. And now I have proven her wrong. That's special.'

'Your dad. Of course. How stupid of me. You finally did it. You got there. And I'm not so stupid that I can't see how much of your dad has rubbed off on you. You are terrific with the kids. But...' her brow screwed up '...now it's my turn to be confused. You always said that you wanted to write the long feature articles on the front page, and wouldn't be happy until your name was right there. On the cover.'

Then she shook her head. 'But that was years ago. I probably have got it wrong.'

Sam took a breath. 'You didn't get it wrong. I simply haven't got to the front cover yet.'

'But you will, Sam,' Amber breathed, her gaze locked onto his face. 'From the moment I first met you, I knew that you had a fire in your belly to prove your talent and were determined to be the best writer that you could be. Your passion and energy drove you on against the odds. And you have done it. Your dad should be proud of you. In fact, am I allowed to be proud of you too?'

He felt his neck flare up red in embarrassment but gave her a quick nod. 'Right back at you.'

'Thanks,' she sniffed and then lifted her chin, eyebrows tight together. 'In that case, I have an idea.'

'You always have an idea. Go on.'

'Simple. Write two articles. I will give you enough quotes for a celebrity piece about my broken wrist and taking time out with my friend at the music school—and you have those shots from my birthday party to show me in full-on bling mode. But...' her voice dropped '...the real interview starts here. At the orphanage for abandoned girl children in a wonderful country bursting with potential. You were the one who saw that they needed a teacher more than they needed a fund-raiser this week. *You get them. You understand.* That could be the feature which takes you to the front page, Sam.'

'You think I am ready for those dizzy heights?'

'I know that you have the talent—you always did have. But what do you think, Sam? You have been writing fluff pieces for years, languishing in the middle ground and peeking out now and again to write about the bigger world. Are you ready to show Frank what you are truly capable of? That is what he wants, isn't it? Or are you too scared to stick your head out above your comfort zone and take a risk in case you are shot down and rejected?'

She stepped forward and pressed her hand flat against Sam's chest. 'You have an amazing talent. I still believe that you can do this. And do it brilliantly. Do it, Sam. Do it for me, but most of all, do it for yourself.'

CHAPTER THIRTEEN

From: Amber@AmberDuBois.net
To: Kate@LondonBespokeTailoring.com; Saskia@Elwood-House.co.uk
Subject: Sam Report

Sam has just let me read his article about Parvita and it is fantastic! My boy done good! In return I have posed for some cheesy photos on the beach under the palm trees and answered lots of questions about my last concert tour and the building plans for the new school I have decided to fund here at the orphanage. I am calling it the Elwood School—I think that your aunt Margot would have approved, Saskia.

There is so much to do here and the builders are pestering me with questions and paperwork, I am really flagging. Good thing that Sam has been here to help with the tradesmen and architects.

I am going to miss him when he goes back tomorrow. And so will the girls.

This is his last evening. So it is time to have that talk I have been putting off.

Wish me luck. Amber

From: Saskia@ElwoodHouse.co.uk
To Amber@AmberDuBois.net; Kate@LondonBespokeTailoring.com;
Subject: Elwood School

Oh, you wonderful girl—Aunt Margot would have loved it, and I have just spent five minutes blubbing into my tea.

Re Sam the friendly spy. I think it could be time to ask that young man his intentions!

Take a chance on happiness Amber. And tell Sam that he is welcome here any time.

Good luck. Saskia

From: Kate@LondonBespokeTailoring.com
To: Amber@AmberDuBois.net
Subject: Sam Report

Love, love, love the name of the school. Do they need a needlework teacher next winter? You should tell Sam what happened pronto. Who knows? He might be okay now you have worn him down a bit with tropical beaches and hot curries.

Big might. Still scared for you.

Best of luck, gorgeous. Kate

AMBER DROPPED DOWN onto the fallen tree trunk that lay among the driftwood on the shore and pressed her hand flat against the weather-smoothed exposed wood before closing her eyes. The warm wind was scented with spices from exotic flowering shrubs and the tang of the ocean waves as they rolled up on the sand in front of her. White foamed and fresh and cool, their force broken by the shallow rocks and reefs under the sand.

Which was pretty much how she was feeling at that moment. Like a spent force.

She desperately needed to calm down and focus on the coming days ahead. But her mind was still reeling from the thousand and one things on her to do list. And Sam.

Maybe things could have turned out differently for them if her mother had not scared him away.

Would they have stayed together in London and stuck it out through university and her concert tours? It would have made a difference to know that she had someone who loved her back in London, waiting for her. Someone who she could give her heart to and know that it was safe and protected.

The sound of children playing made her open her eyes as a group of boys ran across the beach, wheeling a rubber car tyre with a stick, laughing and dancing in and out of the surf. Their mothers strolled along behind them, barefoot, bright in their lovely gold braid trimmed colourful saris and sparkling bangles. Chatting like mothers all around the world.

And somewhere deep inside her body her need to have her own family contracted so fast and so painfully that she wanted to whimper with loss. Being with these girls had shown her how much she loved to share her life and her joy with open minds.

She would willingly give up her slick penthouse for a small family house with a garden and a loving husband who wanted children with her.

Sam was right. Her parents—and his—were hardly the best examples that they could have, but she still wanted to give some love to children of her own one day. At least she knew what *not* to do.

As for Sam? Sam would make a wonderful father given the chance.

'A penny for your thoughts.'

Sam!

Amber whipped around on the sun-bleached tree trunk so fast that her tunic snagged. But there he was. Sam Richards. This man who had come back into her life just when she'd least expected it, and was just as capable of making her head and body spin as he had ten years earlier.

It staggered her that one look at that tanned handsome face could send her blood racing and her senses whirled into a stomach-clenching, heart-thumping spin.

How did he do it? How did he turn back the clock and

transform her back into a schoolgirl being taken out for a pizza and a cola by the chauffeur's son?

But those were on dull evenings back in London. She could never have dreamt that she would be with Sam on a sandy tropical beach with the rustle of coconut palms and tropical birdsong above her head.

Sam grinned and strolled along the sand towards her.

He was wearing loose white cotton trousers and a pale blue linen shirt which matched the colour of his eyes to perfection. He looked so confident and in control it was ridiculous. He moved from the hips, striding forward, purposefully, with his head high. Even on a remote beach in Kerala, Sam managed to look like a journalist ready to interview a big movie star or show business personality for the next big news story.

The Sam she was looking at belonged in the world she had left behind—the world he would be going back to in only a few hours, while she stayed behind.

Was that why she longed to hold him closer and relive the precious moments when he had held her in his arms in the apartment? To feel the tenderness of his lips on hers for one last time before they parted?

No—she dared not think about that! Amber smiled back and patted the log.

'I've saved you the best seat in the house but the show has already started.'

But when she looked up into Sam's face as he drew closer, his ready smile seemed to fade and he stopped and shrugged, almost as if he was wondering what to say to her.

His gaze locked onto her face and the look he gave her sent her body past the tingling stage and way over into melting.

'Sorry to keep you waiting. I have just been phoning London.'

'Parvita told me that you had emailed her with a few questions, even though she was on her honeymoon,' Amber said, trying her best to appear calm and unruffled. 'But you couldn't promise her much in the way of publicity.'

She peered into his face. 'Was that what you were trying to tell me yesterday, Sam? That Frank might not want to know about two crazy women who are trying to build a music school in Kerala? Especially when you are handing over the exclusive on how brave Bambi has survived her terrible trauma of being forced to play on out of tune pianos in the back of beyond?'

'Not exactly. I have just got off the phone with Frank and offered him a very interesting feature for the paper's new current affairs magazine on how girls are still being given up by their parents in some parts of India but are now being trained to be part of the technology boom. Giving them a great education and a future. And do you know what? He loved it. Two sides of an amazing developing country. In fact he loves it so much he wants to bring it forward to next month's magazine, complete with photographs and quotes from the lovely Parvita.'

Amber laughed out loud and gave him a quick one-handed hug. 'Wow. That's amazing! Congratulations. Your first feature in the London paper. And it couldn't be better publicity for what we are trying to do here. Thank you. Thank you, Sam. It means a lot—to all of us.'

Sam tilted his head sideways and grinned. 'My pleasure. And don't make me out to be some kind of hero—it's my job to spot a great story and run with it.'

Then her face relaxed into a smile. 'Of course. You were simply being a professional reporter. So the girls didn't have any effect on you at all. Of course they didn't. You were just doing your job.'

He nudged her with his elbow and she nudged him back.

'What does it feel like to be a feature writer at long last, oh, great journalist?'

'It feels okay. No. Better than okay. It feels grand. Just grand.'

He took a breath. 'There is one thing. Frank gave me a heads up on a couple of rumours flying around the Internet that you have just spent time in hospital in Boston recently.'

The cool breeze on Amber's shoulders suddenly felt icy and threatening.

Boston. Of course. Someone had tipped off the newspapers. Probably one of the hospital team back in Boston. Heath had warned her that she wouldn't be able to keep her hospital visit a secret for long and it looked as though he was right.

Great.

She inhaled slowly, then pushed down hard on the log.

His whole body stilled and he reached out and took her hand in his. 'You are still underweight, still pale despite this glorious sunshine and the other day I felt every one of your ribs. And yes, I know how hard you are working to make this new school possible before the rainy season, but there is more to it than that. Isn't there?'

Amber looked into Sam's face and saw genuine concern in his blue eyes. It was almost as if he was scared of hearing her answer.

Squaring her shoulders, she stared directly into his eyes and said, 'They are right, I was being treated for an infectious disease, but I am absolutely fine now.' She rushed on as Sam tensed up. 'Seriously. I had the all clear before I left London and don't need to take any more antibiotics.'

Then she paused and licked her lips.

'Amber. Just make it fast and tell me. Because my imagination is going wild here and you are killing me. Just how bad was it?'

Taking a deep breath, she met his gaze head-on. This was it. This was what the whole interview jag had been building up to. 'It was bad,' she whispered, her whole body trembling with the emotion and the relief that came with finally being able to tell him the secret that she had been keeping from him. She turned her head and rested her forehead against his, feeling his hot, moist skin against hers and soaking up the strength she needed to say the words.

'The last time I came to Kerala I caught meningitis. And I almost died, Sam. I almost died.'

CHAPTER FOURTEEN

THE SOUND OF motorised rickshaws and the relentless battle of car horns and truck engines from the village road rumbled across the beach towards Amber and Sam but she did not hear them. She was way too busy fighting to keep breathing, as she desperately scanned his face, which was pale and white with shock.

Sam turned sideways, lowered his body onto the log next to her and stretched out his long legs, his arms out in front of him, hands locked together, his chin down almost to his chest.

One side of his throat was lit rosy pink by the fading sun as he twisted his body around from the waist to face her, apparently oblivious to the damage he was causing to his trousers, which stretched to accommodate the muscled thighs below.

The look on that face was so pained, so tortured and so intense that Amber could barely look at him for fear that she would burn up in the heat.

They sat in silence for a few seconds but she could hear each slow, heavy quivering breath that he took, his chest heaving as his lungs fought to gain control.

His fingers reached across and took hers and held them tight to his chest, forcing her to look up into his face.

'Oh, Amber,' he said, his pale blue eyes locked onto her face, his voice low and intense, anxious. 'Why didn't you tell me that you had been so ill?' Then he exhaled very, very slowly. 'You knew where I was working. All you had to do was ask Heath or one of your friends to lift the phone and I would have flown over to see you. Spent time with you. Help you through it, read you books, tell you crazy stories and the latest gossip from Hollywood. Anything. Anything at all.'

She swallowed down hard and took a long juddering breath. 'You would?'

'In a heartbeat, you foolish, stubborn woman,' Sam answered with a faint smile, and reached up and stroked a strand of her hair back over her ear, his fingertips gently caressing her forehead as he did so.

His touch was so tender and so very gentle that Amber almost surrendered to the exhaustion that keeping her secret from Sam had caused.

'You might be right about the stubborn bit. I had intended to tell you before you left,' she whispered through a throat that felt as though she had swallowed a handful of sharp gravel, 'but there never seemed to be a good time. But I had to be sure, Sam. Really sure, before I told anyone the truth.'

'Sure of what? That I would do a good job telling your story? Or that you could trust me enough to be honest with me?'

His brows screwed together and for a terrifying moment Amber thought that he was going to jump up and walk out on her. But instead, Sam closed his eyes and when he opened them she was stunned to see a faint gleam of moisture in the corners.

Moisture she was responsible for putting there by her selfish behaviour.

And the sight sucked the air from her lungs, rendering her speechless.

'That was why you decided to retire,' Sam said, his gaze scanning her face.

All she could do was nod slowly in reply. 'I was already

back in Boston when I collapsed. I don't remember breaking my wrist when I fell over my suitcases. And I only have snatches from that first week in the hospital. I think I scared the hell out of Heath.'

'I'm not surprised. You are doing a pretty good job with me right now,' Sam replied with a tremble in his voice that she had never heard before.

'The doctors told him that I was in danger for the first twenty-four hours—but when I was in the ambulance I made Heath promise not to tell anyone. This was one time I did not want the media following every second of my life. I couldn't hide the fact that I had broken my wrist—but I could hide the fact that I broke it when I collapsed. I don't want the world to feel sorry for me. Pity me. Can you understand that?'

'Not a bit. Why not?' Suddenly Sam's voice switched from desperate and sad to excited and enthusiastic. 'Let me tell the world how you survived this trauma and came out of the other side with a new purpose in life. That's an amazing story. Inspiring. You could do a lot of good for the children's home if you went out and promoted it.'

'Promoted? You mean talking about the trauma of those weeks in hospital on TV chat shows and breakfast television? No. Not for me, Sam. I'm done with talking about how great I am. Because I don't feel brave or inspiring or any of those things.'

She dropped her head backwards, closed her eyes and inhaled slowly several times before going on. 'I remember the afternoon I was discharged from hospital and Heath drove me to his house and I looked out of the window in awe and astonishment. The colours were so vibrant it made me glad to be alive. The air smelled wonderful, fresh, clean, invigorating—especially compared to the hospital. Everything looked amazing, as though I was seeing the streets and the cars and even Heath's old stone house for the very first time.'

Amber raised her hand then dropped it again onto Sam's lap. 'And waiting for me was all of the clutter and admin and mess of details that comes with being a public performer.'

She shrugged. 'And do you know what? I didn't want any of it. The little things didn't matter any longer. All that mattered was being with my friends again. Living my life the way I want. In a world full of colour and hope and laughter and enthusiasm for life. That was what mattered to me now. And I knew that was not in Boston with Heath in stifling luxury, or in Paris with my dad and his new family, or in Miami with my mother on a cruise ship somewhere.'

Amber winced and pinched off a flower blossom from the tree by her side and inhaled the fragrance. 'I wanted to go where I felt at home and loved and welcome. I wanted to come here. Doing what my heart tells me is right, and not what other people and my fears tell me to do. Not any longer.'

Sam shook his head. 'I cannot believe that you came back. Hell, Amber, the same thing could happen again. Or there could be another tropical disease.'

'Or I could get knocked over by a London bus. It happens. And I'm okay with that—because this is where I want to be, Sam. This makes me happy.'

Her fingertips stroked his cheek before she tapped him on the end of his nose. 'I could have woken up with permanent brain damage or deafness, but I didn't. I don't know what I am going to do with the rest of my life but I know that I cannot go back to the life I had been living. I am so grateful for every new day that I am alive.'

She gestured towards the coconut palms. 'I have a roof over my head and food I can pick off the trees if I get hungry. And there is enough work here to last a lifetime.'

'You want to stay here? For good?' Sam asked with a look of total astonishment and disbelief.

'I've decided that I want to be happy. I choose to be happy.

Whatever problems I have in my own life—sharing the magic and beauty of music with these girls and seeing the glow of excitement in my students' eyes makes everything worthwhile again. Small gestures. A hug. A smile. A kiss. A surprise when they are least expecting it. That is how I want to spend my life.'

Amber stopped talking and grinned at him as Sam sighed in exasperation.

'And I have you to thank for all of this, Sam. Now, don't look so surprised. Remember what you said over lunch at the penthouse? You challenged me to come here for Parvita's wedding and somehow I found the courage to take that first step and make it happen. Thank you. It's been a long journey, Sam.'

'Right back at you. We've both come a long way to get to this place.'

Then he looked around him, from the coconut palms to the beach, and laughed out loud. 'And what a place. You always did have great taste, girl, but this would take some beating. In fact, this village had got me thinking.'

'And I thought the burning smell was from the road. What are those trucks burning? Cooking oil?'

'Funny girl. And yes, they might be burning cooking oil, but actually I was thinking more along the lines of a series of articles about regional development and the culture of Southern India. What do you think? It could be a winner and the paper would cover all of the costs. Providing, of course, I could find someone who was willing to put me up around here. Know any local hotels or guest houses?'

Sam was so close that all she could focus on was the gentle rise and fall of his chest and the caress of the warm breeze on her skin. Time fell still so that she could capture the moment.

'What do you say, Amber?' he asked, his pale blue eyes smiling into hers, and with just a touch of anxiety in his voice.

'Could you put up with me if I came back here to stay for a while? Say yes. Say that you will let me be part of your life. And you know that I am not just talking about a few weeks. I want to be with you for the long haul.'

Say yes to having Sam in her life? Here in India at the school?

'Are you sure?' she asked, her voice hoarse and almost a whisper. 'I thought that your life was going to be in the London office from now on. It's your dream job. Don't you want that editor's chair any more?'

Sam replied by sliding his long, strong, clever fingers between hers and locking them there. Tight. His smile widened as his gaze scanned her face as though he was looking for something, and he must have found it because his grin widened into an expression of such joy and happiness that was so infectious that she had to smile in return.

'A clever woman has shown me that it is possible to go beyond your dream and never stop following your passion until you know what you finally want. I like that idea. I like it a lot. Almost as much as I like those girls of yours.'

He snorted out loud. 'You never thought that you would hear me admit to loving kids. But there is something about this place. And about you, Amber DuBois. In fact, this might not be the comfiest chair I have ever sat on,' Sam said as he patted the log, 'but I do know what I want. And I'm looking at what I want at this very minute.'

And just to make sure that she got the message, Sam bent forward and tapped her on the end of the nose with the soft pad of his forefinger.

'That's you, by the way,' he said in a voice that could have melted an iceberg, 'in case you're not keeping up.' And then he sat back up straight and winked at her.

Amber blinked and tried to take it all in.

The school.

Her dream.

Her Sam.

This was a chance of happiness with this man who she thought she had lost ten years ago. This amazing man who had come back into her life only a few weeks ago, and yet at that moment she felt even more connected to him than she had ever done before.

She felt as though they were two parts of one whole heart and soul. She had known happiness in her music and her teaching but nothing compared to this.

Could she do it? Could she take him back and take a risk on heartbreak?

Sam was holding her dream out to her, and all she had to do was say yes and it would be hers.

And that thought was so overwhelming she faltered.

Amber inhaled a deep breath and tried to keep calm, which was rather difficult when Sam was only inches away from her, the fine blue linen of his shirt pressed against her tunic, begging her to hold him and kiss him and never let him go.

'Why me? We tried to be together once before and it didn't work. And we both know how hard long distance relationships can be.'

Amber let out a long slow breath as his fingertips moved over her forehead and ran down through her hair, sliding off her hair barrette before coming to rest on her shoulder.

'You're right. We would be spending time apart. But it would be worth it.'

His forehead pressed against hers. 'You are the only woman I want in my life. I lost you once, Amber. I can't stand the idea of losing you again.'

'I know. And I want you too. Very much. It's just…'

'Just what—go on. Please, I want to know what is holding you back and what I can do to help you.'

'It has taken me ten years to build up all of these heavy

barriers around my heart to protect it from being broken again by being rejected and abandoned. You were the only man that I ever let into my world. The only one. I fell in love with your passion and your fire and I was pulled towards you like a moth to a flame. Rico and Mark had that same spark and I knew that I could get burnt, but I couldn't help but be drawn to them. You had ruined me for ordinary men, and I have only just realised it. I want to give you my heart, Sam. *Truly.* I do. But I'm scared that it would never recover if it was broken again this time. That's why I'm scared of making this leap.'

'All or nothing. It's the same for me. So here is the plan. We both know what hard work is like. So we work at our relationship and make our love part of the joy we find in everything that we do. We might not be in the same room or even the same country but we would still be together. We can make this work. I believe it.'

'*All or nothing.* Oh, Sam.'

Suddenly it was all too much too soon to take in.

She looked across at the new school building and was instantly transported into what life could be like. The school. Her concerts. And then, maybe, the tantalising prospect of playing with the girls in the lovely garden of the orphanage with Sam by her side.

By reaching up and taking hold of Sam's hand in hers, she managed to regain some control of herself before words were possible. His fingers meshed into hers, and he raised one hand to his lips and gently kissed her wrinkly dry-skinned knuckles before replying.

'I know a good opportunity when I see one and, from what I've seen, we would make a great team. You can do this, Amber. You can teach and run this school. I know you can.'

The pressure in her chest was almost too much to bear as she looked into his face and saw that he meant it. He believed in her!

'You would do that? You would fly back to India just to be with me now and then?'

'If it meant I could be with you and the girls? In a heart-beat. You are bound to spend some time in London, especially over the monsoon season. And the rest of the time we have these amazing new-fangled technical inventions which mean that I can see you and talk to you any time I want. In fact I intend to make myself the biggest pest you could imagine.'

His presence was so powerful, so dominating, that she slid her fingers away from below his and pushed herself off the log and onto the hot sand on unsteady legs. Sam was instantly on his feet and his fingers meshed with hers and held them to his own chest as it rose and fell under her palm.

She forced herself to look up into his face, and what she saw there took her breath away. Any doubt that this man cared about her flashed away in an instant.

No pity, no excuses, no apologies. Just a smouldering inner fire. Focused totally on her. She could sense the pressure. Trembling, hesitant, but loving.

He was the flame that had set her world on fire. Nothing would ever be the same again.

Which was why she said the only words she could.

'Yes, Sam. Yes. You are the only man I want in my life—the only man that I have ever wanted in my life. I want you and I need you and I never want us to be torn apart again. Never again. Do you understand that?'

Sam looked into those perfect violet-blue eyes which were brimming with tears of joy and happiness and fell in love all over again. All of the clever and witty things he had intended to say to make her laugh and look at him drifted away onto the sea breeze, taking doubt and apprehension with them.

This was it. He had finally found a woman he wanted to be with. As a girl, Amber had taught him what the overwhelm-ing power of love could be like. But Amber the woman was a revelation. She was so beautiful his breath caught in his throat just at the sight of her.

And now this woman, this stunning, clever, open and giving woman, had just told him that she wanted to be with him as much as he wanted to be with her.

And, for once, words failed him.

How could he have known that the path to happiness led right back to the first girl that he had ever kissed and meant it? How ironic was that?

Frank Evans and that editor's desk were not important any longer.

All that mattered was this woman, looking at him with tears in her eyes. This was where he wanted to be. Needed to be. With Amber.

He dared not speak and break the magic of that moment, that precious link that bound him to Amber for this tiny second in time. But he could move closer, closer, to that stunning face. Those eyes filled with the love and tenderness he had only imagined was destined for other men. And now she was here. And he loved her. This was no teenage crush but a tsunami of love which was more shocking and startling but destined to last.

He. Loved. Her.

Finally. It had happened. He had known lust and attraction. But the sensation was so deep and overwhelming that the great loner Sam Richards floundered.

He was in love.

The lyrics of every love song he had ever heard suddenly made perfect sense.

Without thinking, his hands moved slowly up from her arm to her throat, to cradle her soft and fragile face, gently, his fingers spreading out wide. As her eyes closed at his touch, he had to blink away his own tears as he moved closer, so that his body was touching hers, his nose pressed against her cheek, his mouth nuzzling her upper lip, as his fingers moved back to clasp the back of her head, drawing her closer to him.

She smelt of every perfume shop he had ever been into, blended with spice and vanilla and something in her hair. Coconut. The overall effect was more than intoxicating; he wanted to capture it for ever, bottle it so that he could relive this moment in time whenever he wanted.

And then her mouth was pressing hotter and hotter into his, his pulse racing to match hers. Her hand was on his chest, then around his neck, caressing his skin at the base of his skull so gently he thought he would go mad with wanting her, needing her to know how much he cared.

Maybe that was why he broke away first, leaning back just far enough so that he could stroke the glint of tears away from her cheeks with the pads of his thumbs.

'Why didn't you tell me that you were still recovering from meningitis when you came to my dad's garage in London? I could have swept you away to a long holiday in California.'

Amber grinned despite the turmoil inside her heart. 'Each day is a new day for me. A new start. It could have been a lot worse. Instead of which, I am here with you. Who needs a holiday? I am just grateful to be in one more or less working piece.'

She pressed her head into his shoulder as his arms wrapped around her body, revelling in the touch of his hands on her skin, the softness of his shirt on her cheek, and the way his hand moved to caress her hair.

'Me too. I understand that you want your independence. I get that. But when you need help, you have to know that I am right here. I am not going anywhere without you in my life.'

He was kissing her now, pressing his soft lips over and over again against her throat, and tilting his head so he could reach the sensitive skin on her collarbone without crushing her plastered wrist and hand.

His mouth slid slowly against her hot, moist skin and nuzzled away at the shoulder strap of her dress. Her eyes closed and she leant back just a little further, arching her back against his strong arm, which had slid down her back to her hips.

Amber stopped breathing and inwardly screamed in frustration when his lips slid away and she could no longer inhale his spicy aromatic scent.

His hot breath still warmed the skin on one side of her neck, and she knew that he was watching her. And her heart and mind sang.

Amber closed her eyes tight shut and focused on the sound of her own breathing. Only it was rather difficult when the man she wanted to be with was holding her so lovingly.

Tempting her. Tempting her so badly she could taste it. She wanted him just as much as he wanted her.

His voice was hoarse, low, intense and warm with laughter and affection, and something much more fundamental.

'I have an idea.'

'Umm,' was all she could manage. His fingers were still moving in wide circles on her back.

'Let's hold our own private concert. Just the two of us. Your place is closer. I'm sure the girls would understand. But, one way or another, we need to get off this beach before we get arrested for bad behaviour and setting a bad example for the girls.'

The girls! The concert!

Amber opened her eyes, shook her head once from side to side and chuckled into his shoulder. 'Are you mad? They would never forgive us! I promised them a little Mozart if they had done their piano practice.'

Then she raised her eyebrows coquettishly as Sam groaned in disappointment.

'Maybe—' she took a breath '—you could escort me home afterwards, Mr Richards?'

The air escaped from his lungs in a slow, shuddering hot breath against her forehead, and he lowered both hands to her waist.

'It would be my pleasure. Do you think they would notice if we skipped dessert? My stomach is not used to those syrupy sweets yet.'

'That sounds wonderful. Although I will have to insist on having an early night.'

The brilliant grin grew wider, although she could still sense the thumping of his heart in tune with hers. 'I'm sure we could manage that.'

Then the reality of what he was asking hit her hard. 'Oh, I'm sorry, Sam. I completely forgot. I arranged a meeting with the local governors after the concert. They are keen to organise some legal guardians for the new babies who are still being brought in every week. They are so adorable I'm tempted to offer to put my name down. But that wouldn't be fair on them with my life being so unsettled at the moment. Looks like I shall have to wait to have my own children.'

As soon as the words left her mouth, she regretted them. 'But we have a few hours tomorrow before you fly back, and I'll be in London in a few weeks. The time will fly by.'

The man who had been holding her so lovingly, unwilling to let her move out of his touch, stepped back. Moved away. Not physically, but emotionally.

The precious moment was gone. Trampled to fragments.

His face closed down before her eyes. The warmth was gone, and she cursed herself for being so clumsy. She had lost him.

It took her a few seconds to form the words of the question she had to ask, but was almost too afraid what the answer would be.

'You don't want children, do you?' Her voice quivered

just enough to form the syllables, but she held her breath until he answered.

Sam shook his head slowly as his chin dropped so their foreheads were touching. His breath was hot against her skin as the words came stumbling out. 'No, my darling, I have never wanted a family. I want you, and only you. Can you understand that?'

Amber took a slow breath and squeezed her eyes tight shut, blinking away the tears. 'And I want you. So very much. I had given up hope of ever finding someone to love. Only I so want to have children of my own. You would be a wonderful father, Sam, and I know that we could make a family. Besides, you're forgetting one big thing. We aren't our parents. We're us. And we can make our own happiness. I just know it.'

'A family? Oh, Amber.'

'I saw you working with the girls, Sam,' Amber replied with a smile. 'You were wonderful and I know that any child would be lucky to have you as their dad.'

His back straightened and he drew back, physically holding her away from him. Her hands slid down his arms, desperate to hold onto the intensity of their connection, and her words babbled out in confusion and fear.

'Let's not talk about it now. You are going to have a busy few days at the paper. And your dad will be back from holiday. That is something for you to look forward to.'

He turned away from her now, and looked out onto the shore and the distant horizon, one hand still firmly clasped around hers.

'Children need stability and love. I saw what happened when my parents divorced and so did you. The kids always suffer when a relationship breaks down and I would hate that to happen to us.'

The bitterness in his voice was such a contrast to the loving man she had just been holding. The world stilled, and the temperature of the air seemed to cool, as though a cold wind had blown between them.

She stepped back and wrapped her arm around her waist, closing down, moving away from the hot flames that would burn her up if she kissed him again, held him close to her again.

'Oh, Sam. Are you really telling me that you don't believe that we could stay together and make our marriage work?'

'I love you so much and I don't want to lose you. But I can't wipe away twenty years of resentment in a few days. Maybe you're right but it's going to take me a lot longer than that. We have each other. We don't need a piece of paper or children to make us a couple. You are all I need.'

She raised both of her hands in the air so that Sam couldn't grab hold of them.

'You're breaking my heart, Sam. Is it wrong to give a child a loving home with two parents, in this hard and cruel world? Can't you see that is part of my new dream?'

'Amber! I need some time.'

She paused and spoke very slowly, with something in her voice he had never heard before and did not ever want to hear again.

'Oh, don't worry. I'll get through the concert tonight and see you off at the airport tomorrow with a smile on my face. I care about you so much, but I have to protect myself from more heartbreak down the road. So it might be best to stop this now. You have your life thousands of miles away, but this in my new home and I don't want to give it up. If you care about me, then let me go, Sam. Let me go.'

The only thing that stopped Sam from running after her was the heartbreak in her words and the unavoidable truth that he did care about her enough to stand, frozen, and watch her walk away across the sand.

CHAPTER FIFTEEN

From: Amber@AmberDuBois.net
To: Kate@LondonBespokeTailoring.com; Saskia@Elwood-House.co.uk
Subject:
Sam left this morning. And I miss him. So very much. Can't talk about it. A

SAM WAITED IMPATIENTLY in the baggage reclaim area as more bags were unloaded from his flight. He slung his laptop bag over one shoulder and rolled back his shoulders as the time difference and lack of sleep started to kick in.

The huge echoing hall was jam packed with families and people of all shapes and sizes from his flight, all jostling to find their luggage and get back to their normal lives.

He closed his eyes for a moment, then blinked them open again. He was used to air travel—that was part of his job, but that didn't mean to say that he liked it.

Especially not tonight.

It was hard to believe that only sixteen hours earlier he had been sitting on the beach looking out over the ocean with the morning sun on his face and the colour and life and energy of India whizzing around him. Now he was back in this white, cold, sterile land in a city of stone and glass which he called home.

And he had never felt as lonely in his life.

Amber had kept her word and travelled with him to the airport but her forced smile and tense face only served to make him feel even more uncomfortable and awkward. Their easy friendliness and connection felt strained to the point of snapping completely.

When he wrapped his arms around her to kiss her good-bye, Amber's gentle tears had almost broken his resolve. It would have been so easy to forget all about the flight and the London job and find some way of working as a freelance in India. Other people did it and so could he.

But how would that change the way he felt? Staying would only prolong the agony for both of them. It was up to him to have the strength to walk away.

Over the past ten restless hours in the cramped aircraft seat where sleep was impossible, he had come to the conclusion that Amber was the strong one. She had the courage to change her life for the better and do something remarkable that she was passionate about, and he couldn't be more proud of her. He counted himself lucky to know her. Care about her. Love her.

He had loved working with those girls at the orphanage. Loved being part of Amber's life and sharing her world.

The fact that she actually cared about him in return was something he was still trying to deal with.

So what was the problem?

He was scared of not being worthy of her love.

Scared about not being the man and husband she wanted and needed.

He was scared of letting her down.

He cared enough for her to leave her and walk away from the pain he would cause if he stayed—but he already missed her more than he'd ever thought possible. An Amber-shaped hole had formed in his heart and the only person who could fill it was thousands of miles away, teaching little girls how to make music.

A huge over-stuffed suitcase nudged his foot and Sam turned around to see a gorgeous toddler grinning up at him, followed by a laughing man about his age who swung the giggling child up into his arms and hugged him and hugged him again then apologised profusely but Sam let it go with a smile and jogged forwards to grab his bag off the belt before it went around again.

He had to smile because at that moment his throat was so tight he wouldn't have been able to talk even if he had wanted to.

That was the life that he had turned his back on.

He glanced back over one shoulder. A pretty pregnant blonde girl had her arm looped around her lucky partner's waist. And just for a second she looked like Amber, and his heart contracted at the sight of her.

Amber wanted to be a mother so much. And she would be.

How was he going to feel when another man had made her his wife and given her children, when he knew that Amber had loved him and offered him her life and her soul?

And he had turned down the chance of a family life with the only woman he had ever loved. Why?

The answer screamed back at him so loudly that he was surprised that the other passengers didn't hear it above the sound of the tannoy.

Because he was a coward.

Which made him the biggest fool in the world.

Sam strolled out through the customs area and peered around the cluster of people waiting impatiently in the arrivals hall at Heathrow Airport, looking for the familiar face of his father. And there he was, one hand raised in a friendly wave.

Sam had never been so grateful to see a friendly face after a long exhausting flight.

A quick back slap and a greeting and they were on their way to the car park and a small family hatchback that Sam had never seen before.

'What's this, Dad? Don't tell me that you have finally got around to buying yourself a little runabout to take you to the supermarket? About time.'

'Don't be so cheeky. No, I borrowed it from your Auntie Irene.'

'Auntie Irene? I thought my lovely godmother was living in France these days?'

'She moved back to London about six months ago, so she's renting out her house in the Alps as a holiday let. And it's a great place. I know I enjoyed it. The views are unbelievable.'

'Ah, so that was why you chose the Alps. And here I was thinking it was all about driving around those hairpin bends and mountain roads. You don't get a lot of that around London. Or are you getting too long in the tooth for that kind of driving?'

His dad snorted a reply as he loaded Sam's bag into the boot and closed down the lid. 'Hey. Watch it on the "too old" bit. And, as a matter of fact, we did squeeze in a driving tour around the lakes, then went over to Switzerland for a few days. We had a great time.'

Sam's eyebrows headed north as he fitted his seatbelt in the passenger front seat. 'We? I thought you went on your own.'

His father started to say something, then paused. 'I'll tell you about that when we get home,' he replied and reached forward to turn the key in the ignition.

Sam rested his hand lightly on his father's wrist and looked into his startled face.

'Dad, I have just had a very long flight after an exhausting few days with Amber DuBois. And I have come to one very startling conclusion. If you need to say something, then just say it. Please. So. What is it? What do you have to tell me?'

'Okay, son,' his dad replied with just enough lift in his chin for Sam to inhale slowly so that he was prepared for whatever was coming.

'It's your Aunt Irene. Over these past few months we have been seeing a lot of each other one way or another. She needed someone to help her settle into the town house I had just renovated and it's just two streets away from the garage, so it made sense for me to show her how things have changed around our part of London in the past twenty years.'

He took a breath and licked his lips before going on.

'Do you remember when Irene used to come around to the house to see your mum and take you out when you were little?'

'Auntie Irene. Yes, of course. She was mum's best friend. I always knew that we weren't related but she liked being called Auntie Irene and I didn't have any other aunties or uncles. I missed her when she went to France. And I still don't see where this is going.'

'Then I'll make it clear. Irene invited me to stay at her home in France to have a bit of a holiday and, well, when we were away, she finally confessed to me that she had been in love with me for years. Before I married your mum we all used to go out in a big group of friends together. But she knew that I only had eyes for your mum, so she didn't tell me how she felt. But in the end it was too hard to watch our marriage fall apart so she moved away.'

He shot Sam a glance. 'She hated leaving you. But she couldn't stay.'

Sam blew out a long whistle. 'Is that why she never married? I always wondered if she had a secret boyfriend in France somewhere.'

'She had a couple of relationships but never met anyone else.'

'So Auntie Irene has been burning a candle for you for thirty years. Did you know? Or even suspect?'

His dad nodded quickly. 'About a year after I divorced your mum, Irene turned up at the garage one day out of the blue. She cooked us both that lovely French meal. Do you remember that? After you had gone to bed, she asked me if I wanted her to stay and take your mother's place. And I said no.'

'You turned her down,' Sam said in a low voice.

'Wrong time. I was still hurting and you needed me to be there for you. So I sent her back to France.'

He banged the heel of his hand against his forehead.

'I was a fool. I lost the woman who loved me and who had always cared about me as a friend. I have spent the last years alone when I could have shared them with Irene and had some happiness. But these past few weeks have shown me that it's not too late. She is a wonderful woman, Sam, and I have decided to take a chance on love for the second time in my life. I hope that is okay with you.'

'Okay? You don't need to ask my permission. I think that it's fantastic. Good luck to you. Good luck to both of you.'

'Thanks, son. Right. Let's get this car started. Because I want to hear exactly what you have done this time to mess up your chance of happiness with Amber. And I won't take no for an answer. Oh, and you had better get used to seeing Irene around—she's moving in. So. Start talking. And there's your first edition of the paper if you want to catch up with the latest. I think I saw something about Amber in it.'

'What?' Sam picked up the paper and turned the pages until he found it. It was the photo he had taken of Amber on the beach.

His blood ran cold and the more he read the more chilled he became.

It might be his photograph but he had not written one word of this article.

Frank had given the fluff piece to someone else to write. And that was so wrong that he didn't even know where to start.

He snatched up the paper and started reading, desperate to find out how bad it was.

He couldn't believe it. Frank had taken the quotes and twisted them around to portray Amber as a shallow, selfish woman who was creating a vanity project for her own glory—just the opposite of what Sam had intended. His idea had been twisted around to focus on Amber and how foolish she was to risk her health and try to teach with a broken wrist.

'Son, are you okay? What's happened?'

'Frank Evans has sold me out,' Sam replied in a low voice, the paper on his lap. 'This is not about Amber, this is about rumours and lies and half-truths for a headline. And it makes me feel sick to my stomach.'

He looked up at his father and took a breath. 'Dad, I need your help. But before that I need to say something and say it now. I was a brat when Mum left. And I am sorry for making your life such a misery. I truly am. Can you forgive me for that?'

His dad shook his head and smiled. 'I've waited a long time for you to grow up. Looks like it's finally happened. Past history. What do you need?'

Sam exhaled long and slow and stared out of the car window. 'A family house with a garden where Amber can play with our kids.'

The silence in the car was so thick that it was hard to breathe, but it was his dad who finally broke it by asking, 'Do you love Amber that much?'

'She is the only woman I have ever loved and ever will love. It has taken me ten years to realise that. I can't lose her again now.'

The instant the words came out of his mouth Sam realised

what he had just said and chuckled. It was the truth and he had been a fool to pretend otherwise.

'Then I have just the house for you. Welcome home, son. Welcome home.'

CHAPTER SIXTEEN

From: Amber@AmberDuBois.net
To: Kate@LondonBespokeTailoring.com; Saskia@Elwood-House.co.uk
Subject: On my way back to London
The June monsoon rains came! At last. And how. We are flooded out and the girls have either been sent home for a few weeks or moved to the old school further inland. Any building work has stopped and the lads have taken off.

I am just waiting for my connecting flight back to London and should be with you for breakfast tomorrow. Cannot wait to catch up. See ya soon. Amber

From: Kate@LondonBespokeTailoring.com
To: Amber@AmberDuBois.net
Subject: On my way back to London
Brilliant—but do not read the newspaper at the airport. Seriously. Don't. We need to talk first. K

AMBER STROLLED INTO Saskia's kitchen conservatory room, yawning loudly, her good hand stretched tall above her head. There was no sign of Kate or Saskia but, instead, stretched out on a lounger with his feet up and a steaming cup in his hand was Sam Richards.

He looked as casual, cool and collected as if he had just

come from a business meeting. Come to think of it, he was wearing a suit and a shirt with a tie.

Amber glanced back towards the hallway. 'How did you get in? Saskia is going to have a fit if she sees you here, drinking her coffee.'

'I climbed over the garden gate,' Sam replied with a quick nod. 'They might want to think about making it a little taller. I can still clamber over, even at my age. Although I probably have dirt on my trousers.'

'Which you are now putting onto her favourite lounger. Sheesh. What cheek.'

Amber peered at his jacket, then physically recoiled. 'Has anyone ever told you that you have the worst taste in suits? Our Kate needs to take you in hand.'

He smiled up and waved his coffee mug in her direction.

His gaze slid up from Amber's unpainted toenails to the tip of her bed-head and gave a low growl of appreciation at the back of his throat to indicate how much he liked what he saw.

Amber instantly tugged the front edges of her thin silk pyjama jacket closer together as her neck flared with embarrassment.

'A lovely sunny good morning to you too. And thank you for a warm welcome. And, as for the lovely Miss Lovat? Kate may have called me to let me know that you have come back to escape the monsoon rain, but Kate is not the woman I want to take me in hand,' he whispered, and then spoilt the moment by wagging his eyebrows up and down. His meaning only too obvious.

Amber's heart soared but her head took over.

He seemed determined to make leaving him even more difficult than it would be already.

'Are you always this much trouble in the mornings?' she asked.

'Want to find out?' he replied in a low husky voice.

Amber dropped her head back and rolled her shoulders.

'What? No. You do not do this to me on my first morning back from India. Especially when I am not awake yet.'

She blinked several times. 'Wait a minute. Did you just say that Kate called you? That is not possible. Because you are officially off our nice man list. You snake. Your magazine did a real hatchet job on me. You have no right to interfere with my head like this. In fact, I shouldn't even be talking to you.'

'Of course you should. I am the new media and fund-raising manager for the Elwood School.'

'Oh, no, you are not. We don't need a media… Wait a minute, okay, maybe the school does need a fund-raising manager but the last person I would choose would be an investigative journalist with a chip on his shoulder the size of a pine tree who delights in stitching me up. Sorry.' She peered at him and sniffed. 'Nice tie. Best of luck with your job interview. Are you going to your newspaper today?'

'Already been. I had a little chat with the editor in chief and we agreed that I should leave the magazine to explore creative opportunities outside of GlobalStar Media.'

Her eyes shot open and she slumped down on the edge of the sofa. 'Oh, no, Sam. You've been sacked.'

'Actually, I resigned. I didn't like the way they changed the meaning of your article without asking me first. Let's just say that we had an honest and open discussion.'

'You stomped out.'

Sam touched two fingers to his forehead. 'I stomped out.'

'Oh…but what are you going to do? Your dad is so proud of your new job—this is what you've been working for.'

'My dad is back home and when I left this morning my godmother was making him breakfast and giving him a cuddle. My dad is in heaven and loving every minute of it—and my lovely Auntie Irene is the wealthiest woman I know. The last thing he needs is an out of work layabout of a son cluttering up his love life.'

'Oh, I am pleased; I like him so much. He deserves some happiness.'

Sam raised both hands and gave a flourish from his lounging position.

'At last we have something we both agree on. And in case you were wondering, he has always liked you too. You should be grateful, you know. There are plenty of other job opportunities for a man of my experience in this town. I could even work with my dad in his new property development business. But no, I came here to offer you my services before anyone else snapped me up.'

She flashed him a freezer stare but it was obvious from his smug smile that Sam had no intention of doing anything other than what he wanted or letting her get a word in sideways.

'Your ploy to drive me away will not work. Not listening. We are officially working on this together. Full-time job. Sorted. You see, I have been thinking about our last discussion—' he nodded, his brows tight together '—and it seems to me to point one way.'

'Ah. Thinking.' Amber smirked and pretended to waft away some horrible smoke from in front of her face.

'Funny girl. But not always a clever one. In fact, after several hours of deep consideration, I have come to a serious conclusion.'

Sam swung his legs off the sofa and pointed to Amber. 'Amber DuBois, I have decided to appoint myself the job and save you the time and effort in advertising and then going through a series of tedious interviews before deciding that I am the one and only candidate.'

He flung one hand towards her, palm upwards. 'I know. It is not a job for the faint of heart, and it would mean giving up my dream of joining the astronaut programme, but I am willing to take on the task. I am the man to do it. Starting today.' He beamed a wide-mouthed grin. 'What do you think of that?'

'What do I think?' Amber replied and started pacing the floor, her eyes wide. 'I think you need to cut down on the dose of whatever you are taking because it is making you quite delusional. I have never heard such arrogance in my life—and I'm used to working with prima donnas in major orchestras.'

'It's okay, you can thank me later.' Sam shrugged.

'Thank you? Oh, I don't think so. Now, listen to me when I explain, Are you listening? Good. First, I do not need help finding a project manager. Full stop. I am quite capable of taking care of myself and when my wrist heals I shall be back on fighting form. And second, you never had any intention of joining the astronaut programme. You only sent off for the forms from NASA so that you could impress your science teacher with your knowledge of hydrogen and hydrazine.'

'You remembered—' Sam grinned '—how sweet.'

'Of course I remembered. I think you only did it because Heath was thinking of being a pilot for all of two days and the girls in my school thought that was amazing. Astronaut, indeed. As if anyone would be impressed by that.'

'Did it impress you?'

Amber paused just long enough for Sam to sit back smirking. 'I thought so. And you're missing the point. You need someone to take care of the business side of the project because you are going to be busy with Parvita and the other girls in the school.'

'We already have cooks and housekeepers and an office receptionist, thank you. I'm not sure how many, but plenty.'

'Ah, I had better add that to the job description.' He tugged a smartphone out of his pocket and began keying in as he spoke. 'Sort out staffing. Got it.'

'Job description? What job description?' Amber asked, blinking in confusion.

'The one I came up with during my thinking session—you know, the one you should be writing if you were not so very confident that you can do everything yourself.'

'What makes you so sure that I can't do everything myself? I have managed very well so far, thank you.'

'Have you? Have you really, Amber?' He pointed to her wrist. 'Look at you. Your hand is hurting and you're hardly sleeping. You are worrying like mad about the girls in Kerala, even though you talk to them every day, and now you are intent on going over there and making things worse by barging in with the best intentions when your architect is quite capable of sorting things out himself.'

'What?' Amber called out and raised her hand into the air in a rush, blinking and shaking her head in disbelief. 'He has problems and is asking for answers based on out of focus photographs. I feel so accountable. I need to go there and see for myself and take responsibility for the project. I have to make sure the money isn't wasted on work that has to be repeated and…oh.'

She only wobbled for a fraction of a second before Sam took her hand and half tugged, half helped her across to the dining table.

'Sit. Head between your knees. Deep breaths. Then breakfast. Here. Finish my coffee.'

'Well, this is embarrassing.' She sniffed as she lowered her head and tried to stop feeling dizzy.

'Not for me. It's actually rather satisfying.'

Sam slid onto the fine oak floor and sat cross-legged so that his face was more or less in line with hers.

'Now. About this job interview. I may have just proved my point that you need someone to help talk to the architects and works manager and all of the suppliers and the like while you do what you do best. Teach. Play your piano and fill those girls' heads with the sounds of wonderful music that they will never forget. Because that is what happens when I hear you play. You transport me to a better place. A place where I want to stay and never leave.'

'I do?'

'Every time. You always did. Probably always will. Those girls are going to have a wonderful teacher. The best. And I want to help you to make that happen. If you will let me.'

He turned his head and flashed her a full strength beaming smile. 'Will you let me, Amber? Will you let me work with you and travel with you and be part of your life?'

He nodded towards the sofa. 'I have my laptop in my brief-case and can print out my resumé if you like.'

'You might get bored without your career,' Amber countered. 'It's been your life.'

'No chance. Not around you. And look who's talking.'

Amber sat up slowly in her hard dining chair and stretched out both hands and took hold of Sam, who stayed exactly where he was.

She could tell that his breathing had speeded up to match hers.

This was it. This was where she had to make the decision.

'You know that I want to take over from Parvita some time soon. After what happened…are you ready to move away and be accountable for a whole school-load of children? Because I don't want to bring you into their lives only for you to take off. That wouldn't be fair, Sam. On them or you. On any of us.'

'I know,' he replied in a serious voice that she had never heard him use before. 'And I wouldn't be offering unless I was in it for the long haul. I mean it, Amber. I want to help you run this school. You can do it on your own, I have no doubt about that, but with the two of us…we could achieve some remarkable things.'

'Are we still talking about the project manager's job?' she asked, smiling.

'What do you think?'

'I think that you care about me, but I would need a lot more than that.' Amber took a breath. 'I need to know how you feel before I agree to have you in my life. Working with you is one thing, but more than that is just setting me up for heartbreak, and I don't know if I am up for it.'

'Hate to break the news to you, gorgeous, but I am already in your life. And I am not going anywhere. From the second you walked into my dad's garage that day I have felt an overwhelming sense of recognition and connection. I have absolutely no intention of letting you go again. And, from what I saw, that orphanage needs someone who is handy with a car repair kit and those girls could use someone to teach IT and my version of English. I can probably fit all of that in around my freelance writing work.'

'I'm scared, Sam.'

Sam silenced her by pressing his fingertips to her lips. 'I know. But you haven't heard the rest of the offer. My dad has just finished renovating a sweet little two bedroom terraced house within walking distance of where we are sitting.' His lips turned up into a smile. 'The whole place is about the size of your penthouse living room. But it has a garden. A garden fit for children and pets. And all it needs is a little love to make it a family home. It's ours. All you have to do is say the word.'

He stood up and pressed one hand onto each of her shoulders.

'I should be going. My dad needs me to help him plaster a wall. But you know where to find me when you decide that you are crazy in love with me after all. And Amber, don't wait another ten years. Be seeing ya.'

And, before Amber had a chance to reply or even move from her chair, Sam had started walking back into the kitchen.

He was leaving.

And this time it was through the front door.

Amber shuffled off her chair and opened her mouth to reply, then closed it again. This was it. Decision time. She had to take Sam as he was, faults and all, or risk losing him for ever.

Wait a minute. He had just offered her a home. A real home. *Their home. With a garden fit for children and pets.*

He understood. He understood everything.

She did need him. But she wanted him more.

'Sam. Wait.'

His steps slowed until he was more shuffling forward instead of striding.

'Stay. Please. Stay.'

Sam turned around just in time to catch her in his arms as she flung herself at him, her arms around his neck.

Her feet swung up into a perfect curve as he lifted her high off the ground, his arms wrapped tight around her waist as he pressed his lips to her forehead, eyes, then onto the waiting hot lips with all of the tender passion that Amber had been dreaming about most of that night.

The energy and passion of his kiss sent her reeling so hard that Amber had to step back and steady herself before leaning into his kiss, focusing her love into that single contact as she closed her eyes and revelled in the glorious sensation.

When she eventually pulled away her eyes were pricking with hot tears.

'It's okay, darling,' Sam laughed. 'It's okay. I'm not going anywhere without you ever again. You want to go to India, I'll go to India. Timbuktu, I'll be there. There's no way you are going to get rid of me.'

She replied with a wide-mouthed grin and her heart sang at the look of love and joy on Sam's face.

'Timbuktu wasn't on my list before but it sounds good to me. Anywhere with you. Oh, God, Sam, I love you so much. I don't care what happens any more. I just know that I love you.'

The tears were real now, her voice shaking with emotion as she forced out the words he needed to hear, afraid that they were getting lost in his shirt as she slid to the ground.

One arm unwound and lifted her chin high enough for their eyes to meet, and her heart melted at what she saw in his eyes as he grinned down at her, eyes glistening in the bright sunlight.

'I've loved you since the moment you stepped out of the limo with your mother at your back all of those years ago. It just took a while for it to sink in.'

He took her face in between the palms of his hands and confessed, 'I never imagined that I could love another human being on this planet as much as the way I feel at this moment. Come here.'

Somewhere close by was the sound of whooping and hooting from Saskia and Kate but Amber didn't care who saw her kissing the man she loved and would go on loving for the rest of her life.

* * * * *

TOO CLOSE FOR COMFORT

HEIDI RICE

Special thanks go to fellow authors Scarlet Wilson
and Libby Mercer for their help in making my Scottish
heroine and my Californian hero sound real (I hope).

And to the lovely Roberto, who gave me
an invaluable insight into the culture and traditions
of California's Mexican-American community—
any mistakes in the portrayal are entirely mine.

CHAPTER ONE

'HEY, MITCH, WAS there anything on a kid in Demarest's file? About five-two or-three, hundred and ten pounds?'

Zane Montoya squinted into the shadows of the motel parking lot, trying to make out any other usable details. But whoever the kid was, he was being real careful not to stray into the pools of light cast by the streetlamps, making the fine hairs on Zane's neck prickle. He'd been staking out Brad Demarest's motel room for five hours—taking over right after Mitch had called in with the flu—and Montoya Investigations had been on the guy's tail for six months now. Getting the tip that this by-the-hour motel on the outskirts of Morro Bay was Demarest's latest bolt hole had been their first break in weeks. And his gut was telling him the kid was casing the joint. And he didn't like it, because if Demarest showed up the last thing Zane needed was some little troublemaker alerting the guy to their presence—or, worse, spooking him before they could do a citizen's arrest.

'Is this kid a girl or a boy?' Mitch's voice croaked.

'Don't you think I would have…?' Zane's frustrated whisper cut off as the kid stepped back and the yellow glow of the streetlamp illuminated a sprinkle of freckles, vivid red-and-gold curls springing out from under a low-riding ball cap and the curve of a full breast beneath the skintight black tank she wore over camo trousers and boots. 'It's a girl.'

A girl who had to be up to no good. Why else would she be dressed up like GI Jane?

'Make that a young woman—eighteen to twenty-five—Caucasian with red shoulder-length hair.'

The girl melted into the shadows as he tried to picture the intriguing features he'd glimpsed on a mugshot.

'She doesn't look familiar,' he murmured, more to himself than Mitch.

He'd reread Demarest's file while gorging himself on the endless supply of junk food Mitch had stashed in the glove compartment, but he couldn't remember any of Demarest's known associates fitting her description.

Mitch gave a weighty sigh. 'If she's hanging round his motel room, she's probably another mark.'

'I don't think so—she's too young,' Zane replied. *And way too cute.* He cut off the thought. If she was mixed up with Demarest, she couldn't be that cute. A one-time B-movie producer who'd taken a brief detour into porn before finding a more lucrative income duping rich women by promising to make them movie stars, Demarest was a typical LA parasite. But this kid with her pale skin, her freckles, her silicone-free breasts and her furtive activities looked anything but his typical mark.

'Don't be too sure,' Mitch replied. 'The guy cast a wide net and he wasn't choosy.'

'Oh, hell,' Zane muttered as the girl approached the door to Demarest's room. 'Call Jim for back-up,' he added sharply. 'And get him over here now.'

'Has Demarest showed up?' Mitch's croak rippled with excitement.

'No.' *Thank God.* 'But Jim'll have to take over the surveillance. We've got trouble.' He glared across the lot, his irritation levels rising as his stomach sank. 'Because whoever the heck she is, she's just broken into his motel room.'

He shoved the cell into his back pocket as he lurched out of the car and headed across the parking lot.

Just what he needed after five hours sitting in a damn car—A GI Jane lookalike with freckles on her nose screwing up a six-month-operation.

Iona MacCabe eased the door open, and clutched a sweaty palm around the skeleton key she'd spent a week doing the job from hell to get hold of. The tiny strip of light coming through the curtains was alive with dust motes, but didn't give her much of an idea of the room's contents bar the two queen-size beds.

Her heart pounded into her throat at the footstep behind her, but as she whipped round to slam the door a tall figure blocked the doorway.

Brad!

Her stomach hit her tonsils as the apparition shot out a hand and wedged the door open.

'I don't think so,' came the gruff voice—tight with anger. *Not Brad.*

The knee-watering shaft of relief was quickly quashed as an arm banded round her waist. Her back hit a chest like a brick wall, knocking the wind out of her, as he lifted her off her feet.

'Let go,' she squeaked, her reflexes engaging as the shadow man hefted her backwards.

'What the hell do you think you're doing?' she yelped as he kicked the motel door shut and carted her across the parking lot to who knew where.

The muscular arm tightened under her breasts and her lungs seized as she figured out that getting abducted might actually be worse than being caught by Brad—the thieving love rat.

'I'm stopping a felony in progress,' the disembodied voice

growled. 'Now shut up, because this'll go a lot worse for you if someone spots us.'

She grabbed his arm and tried to prise it loose, but he was holding her too tightly for her to get any leverage. The tensile strength under her fingertips made the panic kick up a notch. She heard the heavy clunk of a car door opening and began to struggle in earnest. He was kidnapping her.

No way!

She'd come five thousand miles, lived on her wits for a fortnight, been cleaning toilets for a week in the grottiest motel in the world and hadn't had a decent meal since the day before yesterday, only to get murdered by a nutjob in a motel car park a few feet from her goal.

Fury overtook the panic. 'If you don't put me down this instant I'll yell my head off,' she whispered, then wondered why she was whispering—and why she was giving him a warning.

She drew in a breath and a callused palm slapped over her mouth. The ear-splitting scream choked off into an ineffectual grunt.

She kicked furiously, but only connected with air, as the scent of something clean and intensely male cut through the aroma of rotting garbage that hung in the night air.

He doesn't smell like a low life.

The thought disconcerted her long enough for him to twist round and dump her into the passenger seat of the car.

With his hand no longer cutting off her air supply, she hitched in a shaky breath—only to have the palm cover her mouth again. His forearm held her immobile.

She tried to bite him, but her jaws were wedged shut. His dark head loomed over her, the features still disguised by the shadows—and her heart battered her ribs with the force of a sledgehammer.

The enticing scent enveloped her as he hissed next to her ear. 'You let out a single sound and I'm going to arrest you on the spot.'

Arrest.

Her mind grabbed hold of the word.

He's a cop. He won't kill me.

But while her heart stopped pummelling, the panic still crawled across her skin and made sweat trickle between her breasts.

Not being murdered thousands of miles from home was good. But getting caught by a cop breaking into Brad's room was definitely bad. The temporary work visa she'd spent two months getting a hold of would be revoked. She could get deported and then she'd have no chance of getting even a fraction of the twenty-five thousand pounds of her dad's money Brad had absconded with.

'Nod if you understand me?' he said again, low and apparently seriously pissed off.

She nodded, her fingers curling around the key she'd used to get into Brad's room. She slid the key under her bottom.

He lifted his hand and she sucked in a deep breath.

'Why didn't you identify yourself as a cop sooner?' she demanded in a furious whisper, deciding attack was the best form of defence—and a good way to distract him until she could get away from him. 'You scared ten years off my life.'

'I'm not a cop, I'm a private investigator.' He tugged something out of his back pocket and flipped it open. She guessed the card he was showing her was some form of ID, not that she could see it any better than she could see him in the darkness.

'Now put your seatbelt on, we're leaving.'

Outrage welled up her throat as he shut the car door, skirted the bonnet, climbed into the driver's seat and turned on the ignition.

He's not even a proper cop?

She grasped the dash as the car reversed out of its slot. 'Hang on a minute—where are you taking me?' Maybe she'd been a bit hasty assuming he wasn't a kidnapper.

'Put the seatbelt on now or I'll put it on for you.'

'No, I will not,' she announced as he drove down the block of doorways and braked in front of the motel office. 'I have a room and a job here. I'm not going anywhere. And if you're only a fake cop you can't make me.'

She reached for the door handle, intending to dive out. But he leaned across her, the roped muscle of his arm skimming her breast, and clamped his hand over hers on the door handle.

'You're not staying here any more.' The menacing growl was so full of suppressed anger she flinched. 'And I *can* make you. Just try me.'

She tried to flex her fingers, the iron-hard grip merely tightened.

'Let go now,' he murmured, his minty breath feathering her earlobe and making her nape tingle. 'Or so help me, I'm calling this in and to hell with the investigation.'

'I can't,' she snapped back, her anger not quite as controlled as his. 'You're holding on too tightly.'

He released her hand and she let go of the handle, shaking her numb fingers in a bid to restore the blood supply before she got gangrene. 'That hurt. I think you may have crushed a finger.'

The huff of breath suggested he didn't care if he had.

A large, square open palm appeared under her nose. 'Now hand over the key.'

'What key?' she squeaked, struggling to sound innocent while the key burned into her left bum cheek.

'The key that's under your butt.' He snapped his fingers, making her jump despite her best efforts to remain aloof. 'You've got ten seconds or I'm going to get it myself.'

And then he started to count. Her nipples tingled at the memory of his forearm wedged under her breasts.

She retrieved the key and slapped it into his palm, conceding defeat at the unpleasant thought of those long, strong fingers delving under her bottom.

'There, fine, are you satisfied now?' she asked, disgusted

with herself as well as him. 'I had to scrub fifty toilets to get that. And believe me, the toilets in this dump need more than their fair share of elbow grease.'

The scoffing sound sent another inappropriate prickle of reaction shooting up her spine.

What the heck was wrong with her? This guy was the opposite of sexy. Clearly a fortnight spent living on a shoestring budget doing dead-end jobs in an alien, unfriendly country had melted her brain cells.

'Don't go anywhere,' he said, getting out of the car. 'You won't like me if I have to come get you.'

She folded her arms across her chest, tense with indignation. 'I don't like you now.'

He gave a humourless chuckle.

Iona glared at his back as he walked into the motel office and indulged in a brief fantasy of running off into the night. But as his tall frame stepped into the office—and the lean athletic build rippling under a tan polo shirt and dark trousers became apparent under the harsh strip lighting—she let the fantasy go.

After a ten-minute conversation with Greg, the night clerk, he strolled back towards her, silhouetted by moonlight again. As he approached she became painfully aware of the mile-wide shoulders, narrow hips, long legs and the predatory stride.

Flipping heck.

Whoever this guy was, he was a lot stronger and bigger than she was—and she already knew he didn't mind using his physical advantage. Which meant she was going to have to wait to make a clean getaway.

He paused next to the car and pulled out a smartphone. As he talked into the device, the blue light from the neon Vacancy sign hit his face.

Iona gasped. Her abductor could make a living as a male supermodel.

A bubble of hysteria built under her breastbone as she stared at the firm sensual lips, the aquiline nose with a slight bump at the bridge, the sculpted angular cheekbones, the olive-toned skin and the shadow of stubble on his jaw. He glanced towards her and her lungs stopped as she absorbed the deep sapphire-blue of his eyes and the unusual dark blue rim around the irises. Was that a trick of the light? Even Daniel Craig's eyes weren't that blue. Surely?

He finished the call—not a word of which she'd managed to catch due to the loud buzzing in her ears from a lack of oxygen—and slipped the smartphone back into his pocket.

He settled into the driver's seat, thankfully casting his stunning face into darkness again.

She looked away and concentrated on breathing. So what if he was better looking than Adonis? He was still a bullying jerk.

She repeated the mantra in her head as he drove off without acknowledging her.

'If it's not too much to ask,' she said as they left the motel's lot, 'where exactly are you taking me? Because my purse, my passport and all my worldly goods happen to be in room 108. And I don't want someone to nick them.'

Not that she had a great deal of money in her purse, or many worldly goods, but her credit card was kind of important, and her passport if she was ever going to get out of this Godforsaken country.

'That's cute, coming from you,' he said as he flipped the indicator and turned onto Morro Bay's main street.

She bristled. 'I'm not a thief, if that's what you're implying.'

'Uh-huh. So what were you doing in Demarest's room? Planning to scrub his john after hours?'

The mention of Brad's name had her bristling even more. So he knew Demarest? Or knew of him? She tried to decide whether this was good or bad.

'This is the way it's gonna work,' he said, his voice

domineering—and deadly calm. 'Either I report you to the Morro Bay PD and they put you in a cell to keep you out of my way or you do what I say and tell me everything you know about Demarest.'

His thumb tapped rhythmically against the steering wheel as the car drifted out of the small town—taking her farther away from her goal, and her passport.

'It's not stealing if someone's already stolen from you,' she offered, after considering her options. She didn't plan to tell this arrogant stranger anything but she didn't want to end up in a cell either.

His thumb tapped three more times. 'No, actually, technically it's still stealing.'

Great, the man wasn't just a bullying jerk, he was a self-righteous bullying jerk—with eyes bluer than Daniel Craig. Her pulse spiked.

Get over the eyes. Looks can be deceiving—you know that.

'How much?'

'How much what?' she asked, confused by the question.

'How much did Demarest take you for?'

The toneless enquiry had all the pain and humiliation charging up her throat and threatening to gag her. She swallowed down the bitter taste. So she'd made a mistake. A stupid, selfish mistake by believing in a guy who had never been what he seemed. But she'd spent the last two weeks trying to put that mistake right—that had to count for something.

'Not me, my father.' She stared out of the window into the darkness. The car had reached the bluff over Morro Bay and even though she couldn't see the ocean, she could sense it.

She hit the button to slide down the window, suddenly desperate for the scent of fresh air. The dry ache in her throat caught her unawares as the musty scent of earth, and sea and tree sap brought with it a vivid picture of Kelross Glen. The little Highland town in the foothills of the Cairngorms she'd spent the first twenty-four years of her life trying to escape.

And every second of the last two weeks wishing she could return to.

She hit the up switch, sealing out the painful memories. She couldn't go back, not until she made amends for Brad and the childish wanderlust that had drawn her to him in the first place. She had to get at least some of her father's money back. And if that meant tracking Brad the Cad through every dive on California's coastline—and putting up with the arrogant guy seated beside her—she'd do it.

'How much did he take your father for?' The sharp question jolted her out of her thoughts.

'Twenty-five grand,' she said. Her dad's life savings. Peter MacCabe had believed he was giving Iona a shot at her dream—but Brad's promises of setting her up as a wildlife artist in Los Angeles had been as false and shallow as he was.

She pushed out a shaky breath.

Stop being a drama queen.

Once she'd given Detective Sexy the slip and worked out a way to get back into Brad's room, she'd finally be able to look for her dad's money.

'You don't seriously think he's got twenty-five grand in Irish bills stashed in his motel room do you?'

The incredulous statement had her head whipping round. And her eyes narrowing.

'I'm not Irish, I'm Scottish,' she said, indignation ringing in her voice—how come no one in California knew the difference between a Scottish and an Irish accent—hadn't any of them ever watched *Braveheart?* 'And I don't see where else he would put the money. He's not likely to be using a bank account, is he?'

'When did he hit your old man?'

'December.'

December the twenty-third, to be precise. What a merry Christmas that had turned out to be. To think she'd actually believed the story he'd told her about popping over to Inverness to get her and her father a Christmas present. Until her father had dropped the bombshell about cashing in all the bonds he owned to 'give you a chance at happiness with your new young man.' She hadn't even had the heart to tell him she and Brad were hardly a love match.

'That's three months ago.' She heard the note of pity in the detective's voice, and hated him for it. 'The money's long gone by now.'

It couldn't *all* be gone. Not all twenty-five grand. 'How? He's not exactly spending it on his accommodation.'

'He's got a cocaine habit. He could lose that much up his nose in a weekend.'

'But…' A cocaine habit? Was that why he'd seemed so fragile and vulnerable when he'd walked into the Kelross giftshop?

'I'm taking it he kept that quiet while he was in…' The detective paused. 'Where are you from?'

'The Scottish Highlands,' she said absently.

'So that's why he disappeared from our radar for a couple of months,' he murmured more to himself than her. 'I figured he might have skipped town to avoid his marks, but I didn't think he had the imagination to skip all the way to Europe.'

'He has other marks?' she said dully.

'*Querida,* he's a high-end hustler with a class-A habit— where do you think I come in?'

'I don't know, where *do* you come in?' she snapped. Did the guy really have to be quite so patronising?

'My name's Zane Montoya. I own and operate a private investigations firm based in Carmel. We've been investigating Demarest for six months. Gathering evidence, witness statements, establishing a money trail, all on behalf of an insurance company who made the mistake of insuring some of his victims.' He waited a beat as she struggled to absorb the information.

So her father hadn't been the only one who'd fallen for

Brad's clever lies? This hadn't been some arbitrary, opportunistic con? Her stomach pitched at the thought.

Had she really believed this couldn't get any worse?

She'd got over her ludicrous fantasy that Brad Demarest cared about her and admired her artwork—enough to help her get out of Kelross Glen—months ago. But Montoya's revelations felt like the final rusty nail in the rotting coffin of her pride and self-respect.

'A complex, high-level investigation,' Montoya continued. 'That your dumb stunt came close to screwing up tonight.'

She ignored Montoya's irritation. If he expected an apology for her 'dumb stunt,' he'd be waiting until they were serving snow cones in hell. She couldn't care less about him or his anonymous insurance company or his complex, high-level, 'almost screwed up' investigation.

All she cared about was her father.

Peter MacCabe was a good man, who'd wanted to give her a dream. A dream she'd destroyed by letting a professional conman into their lives.

They rode in silence for the next few miles. Iona stared into the darkness and tried to get her head around what she was going to do next. It had taken her over two weeks to track Brad this far, in the hope she could get some of the money back. But if all the money was gone, was there even any point in confronting him? The hopelessness of the situation felt debilitating.

The lights of a strip mall shone in the distance as they approached another seaside town, but her mind had gone numb and she simply could not get it to engage.

Even her bones felt tired. She'd been running on adrenaline since she'd got to California, trying to live on as little as possible while she waited for Brad to return to the motel she'd had staked out. Tears of frustration and weariness pricked her eyes. She sucked them up. Crying never solved anything.

The yellow sign of a fast-food franchise flickered on the

side of the road. Her stomach protested audibly and the hot flush of shame fired up her neck. Seemed the coffin of her self-respect hadn't completely rotted away because she'd be mortified if Montoya had heard her hunger pains.

No such luck.

The car bounced across the cracked pavement in the fast-food restaurant's forecourt, then stopped at the drive-through window.

He slanted a look at her belly. 'What do you want?'

'Nothing, I'm good,' she said, even though she hadn't eaten since the coffee and doughnut she'd splurged on at breakfast. She'd rather die of starvation than accept charity from this jerk.

'What'll it be, sir?' The teenage girl in the drive-through window blushed profusely before letting out a choked sigh— clearly suffering from the same asphyxiation problem Iona herself had had after her first good look at Detective Sexy.

He glanced at her over his shoulder and she got another unwelcome eyeful of that staggering face. An alarming series of pinpricks shimmered across her nerve endings.

'You sure?' he asked.

'Positive.' She lifted her chin.

The flat line of Montoya's lips curved up at one end, sending a dimple into his cheek. The pinpricks gathered and concentrated in all sorts of inappropriate places.

A dimple? Seriously? Give me a break.

The hint of a smile was more rueful than amused, but there was no denying the spectacular blip in Iona's heart rate—or the loud answering growl of the lion in her stomach still hoping to get fed.

'Suit yourself.' He turned back to the blushing teen. 'I'll have two double cheeseburgers with a couple of large fries and a chocolate malt, Serena,' he purred, reading her name off the badge pinned to her heaving bosom.

'Yes, sir, coming right up.' The girl jumped to attention. 'That'll be six dollars fifty, sir.'

Iona rolled her eyes. What was with the sir? Couldn't Serena see Detective Sexy already had an ego the size of Mars? Stroking it would turn it into a supernova.

He paid for the food, thanked Serena with what Iona guessed must have been the full dimple effect—because the girl's face went radioactive—then drove to the pick-up window.

'Here, hold these.' He passed her the two grease-spotted paper bags.

The delicious aroma of grilled meat and freshly fried potatoes swirled around Iona as he steered the car to a parking space one-handed while taking a loud slurp of his malt.

A giant chasm opened in her stomach and began to weep as she thrust the bags back as soon as the car was stationary. 'Why did you get two?' she snapped, drool pooling under her tongue. 'I told you I'm not hungry.'

Was he trying to torture her?

'They're both for me.' He patted what appeared to be a washboard-lean stomach, the rueful twist of his lips mocking her. 'Stake-outs are hungry work and all I've had since lunch is ten Twinkies and a gallon of Dr Pepper.'

She glared across the console. 'My heart bleeds for you.'

The mention of the sugary treats was torturous enough, but then he produced an enormous cheeseburger from one of the takeout bags.

The lurid orange substance that passed for cheese dripped from the sesame-seed bun as the savoury scent filled the car. The chasm in Iona's stomach yawned as his Adam's apple bobbed up and down while he demolished the cheeseburger, then made equally fast work of the fries. The crunch of crisp golden potato and the heady fragrance sent her taste buds into overdrive.

He balled up the empty bag and flipped it into a bin outside the car window. She licked her lips as her stomach rolled into her throat.

One down, one to go.

He peered into the second bag, lifted out the last cheeseburger. Wrapping the serviette round one half, he brought it to his lips in slow motion.

'Wait.' Her hand shot out to grab hold of one thick wrist as the lion howled.

'Something you want?' His tone sounded strangely alluring in the darkness. Her tortured gaze met his mocking one.

'Yes…I…' Her tongue swelled, the drool choking her. 'Please.'

One dark eyebrow lifted. 'Please, what?'

The bastard was going to make her beg.

'Could I have a wee bite?' She begged, ready to sacrifice her pride, her self-respect and anything else he might want for one little nibble.

The intensely blue gaze dipped as her teeth dug into her bottom lip—and the pinpricks radiated up and out from all those inappropriate places. She dismissed her response. It had to be some weird physical reaction brought on by starvation.

She waited, ready for him to torture her some more, but to her relief his lips quirked—making the damn dimple wink at her—and he handed over the precious burger. 'Knock yourself out.'

She paused for a second as her fingers sank into the spongy bun, then ripped off a huge chunk with her teeth.

Her taste buds sang a hallelujah chorus as the meat juices and the creamy, salty cheese caressed her tongue. A low moan of gratification eased out round the mouthful of burger and his gaze locked on her mouth, the mocking smile gone.

She swallowed quickly and took another massive bite. She could feel the disturbingly intense gaze as she stuffed the rest of burger in—but she didn't care.

Let him be as appalled as he liked by her terrible table

manners. She hadn't had a decent meal in days. And it hadn't been her idea to get kidnapped.

Why did that look so damn hot?

Heat shot into Zane's crotch as the wide full lips shone from the coating of grease.

'Slow down, you'll make yourself sick,' he murmured.

She peered at him, her expression wary as she continued to devour the burger like a ravenous wolf. He shifted in his seat, suppressing the urge to lick off the trickle of juice dribbling down her chin. She swiped the back of her hand across her mouth, wiping off the trickle, but the tug of arousal made it impossible to drag his gaze away.

I must seriously need to get laid.

Had it been six months since he'd had that weekend fling in Sonora with Elena, the public defender? Six months wasn't that unusual for him—he'd always been choosy about his sexual partners—but this time the abstinence had to be messing with his radar.

The girl was cute, no question. The slanting chocolate eyes, thick red-gold curls, her wide kissable mouth and pale freckled skin made a unique package—but cute was hardly his type. And then there was the biggest turn-off of all. He was involved with her in a professional capacity. She was definitely a witness, possibly even a perp. And he never crossed that line. Ever.

The heat subsided as he watched her gulp down the last of the burger as if her life depended on it. Exactly how old was she? With that petal-soft skin it was hard to tell, but she could be a teenager.

He forced his gaze from her lips as he lifted the bag of fries off the dash, and passed them to her. 'How long's it been since you had a decent meal?'

She stiffened. 'Not long,' she said grudgingly but took the bag.

Yeah, right.

She popped the fries into her mouth, but continued to watch him, as if she expected him to snatch them back at any moment.

He suppressed the dart of compassion.

Grab a dose of reality, Montoya.

She's no damsel in distress—she's a resourceful little operator with her own agenda. Getting a job at Demarest's motel had been a neat trick. And how the hell had she tracked the guy from Scotland, when they'd had trouble tracking him across California? Until he had the full story of how she fitted into the picture with Demarest, he didn't plan to trust her an inch.

But that didn't solve his immediate problem. What to do with her tonight? He hadn't planned much past getting her away from Demarest's motel.

He couldn't take her back to Morro, and booking her into another motel wasn't an option either, because she'd skip.

Of course he could dump her on the cops. But while handing her over would 'contain' the problem, he couldn't quite bring himself to do it.

'So how did you find out Demarest had a room at the Morro, Iona?' he asked, deciding it was about time he started interrogating her properly—and stopped fixating on those damn lips.

She stopped shovelling fries into her mouth. 'How do you know my name?' she said in that lilting Celtic brogue.

'The motel clerk was real talkative when I told him about your crime spree with his key.'

Her rich chocolate eyes went squinty with temper. 'You told him? How could you? I'll lose my job.'

'You're not going back there anyway,' he said, dismissing the prickle of guilt. He wasn't the one who'd decided to indulge in some after hours B and E. 'I don't want you alerting Demarest to our presence.'

'I'm not going to alert him. Why would I?' She sounded aggrieved. 'How am I going to pay my bill now? They probably won't even give me the wages they owe me.'

'I settled your bill.' He'd also paid the clerk to keep her valuables in the motel safe. If Demarest showed up tonight, he might not need the bargaining chip Iona's ID documents represented, but he had a feeling it wasn't gonna be that simple. Because nothing about this damn case had been simple so far.

And the biggest complication of all was sitting right in front of him.

A complication made a whole lot worse by his perverse reaction to her.

He'd never before got a kick out of manhandling a woman—even on the force he'd earned the nickname Lancelot, because of his preference for using persuasion and persistence when interrogating female suspects, instead of threats and intimidation.

But there was no getting away from the fact that when he'd caught her in Demarest's room tonight—he'd noticed the generous breasts propped on his forearm and the fresh, subtle fragrance of her hair. And while he might have been able to ignore that momentary loss of control—because it had been six months since he'd had a woman, any woman in his arms— that excuse was nowhere near good enough to explain why he'd come close to getting a hard-on just watching her eat.

'But you can kiss your paycheck goodbye,' he said, making sure the chill stayed in his voice.

Her big brown eyes widened, making him feel as if he'd just kicked Bambi.

'Now stop arguing with me or I'll kick you out of the car and leave you in the middle of nowhere.'

It was an empty threat, he wouldn't do that to any woman, especially not one who had no money, no ID, who'd just devoured a burger as if she hadn't eaten in days and who had eyes like Bambi.

But instead of being cowed, she stuck her chin out. 'Fine, dump me here if you want. I've no got a problem with that.'

Damn, she was actually serious.

What kind of guys had she been dealing with? Then he thought of the seedy motel, and her connection to Demarest and had a pretty good idea.

'Yeah, well, unfortunately I do.'

'Then take me back to the motel. I'll get my stuff and stay somewhere else. I won't interfere with your case, I swear. I want Brad caught as much as you do.'

Maybe it was the flinty determination in her voice or the way her gaze never wavered. But he wanted to believe her.

Which only made him sure he shouldn't. Ten years on the force had taught him that trust was a dangerous thing—and following your gut instead of having proof could get you killed.

He slid the car into reverse. 'Forget it. You're staying where I can keep an eye on you.'

'Why?' she said, the hitch in her voice telegraphing her shock. 'This is ridiculous. You dislike me as much as I dislike you.'

Unfortunately he didn't dislike her nearly as much as he should, but he let the observation pass.

Her brow creased. 'All you have to do is trust me a little bit and we never have to lay eyes on each other again.'

'Trust you?' He sent her a long look. 'You think?'

'Oh, for Pete's sake,' she hissed. 'I already told you Brad stole money from my father.'

So it was Brad now.

'I was trying to get it back,' she finished, crossing her arms, and making her breasts plump up under the scoop neck of the tank.

'Yeah, but I don't have a heck of a lot of proof.' He dragged his eyes away from her cleavage. Annoyed with himself. And her. Was she doing that on purpose? 'And until I do, we're stuck with each other.'

He reversed out of the lot, deciding the argument was over.

'Now hang on,' she piped up. 'If you don't trust me, why the heck should I trust you? You say you're a private investigator, but for all I know you could be an axe-murderer.'

'I showed you my licence,' he said, humouring her.

'Which you could have had forged for you by axe-murderers.com.'

His lips quirked at her tenacity, but he bit back the chuckle. The accusation wasn't funny, it was insulting.

He braked and pulled out his smartphone, then keyed in the number for the LAPD. He passed the phone to her as it started ringing. 'Ask for Detective Stone, or Detective Ramirez in Vice, whichever one is on shift. They can vouch for me.'

He waited while she spoke to the dispatcher, and spent some time verifying that she was talking to a genuine LAPD officer—and not one of his axe-murdering pals.

Smart girl.

'Excuse me, Detective Ramirez,' came her smoky voice when she got his former partner on the line. 'My name is Iona MacCabe and I'm here with a man called Zane Montoya. He says he's a private detective and that you know him. Is that true?' She listened for a moment, her teeth releasing her bottom lip as she nodded. 'Can you tell me what he looks like?' Her gaze roamed over his face as she listened to Ram's reply. Her scrutiny was sharp and dispassionate, and so unlike the glassy-eyed stares he had come to expect from women that something perverse happened. His nape heated, triggering a flash back to high school, when those glassy-eyed stares had allowed him to charm any girl he wanted into his bed—or more often the back seat of his uncle Raoul's Chevy.

He rubbed a hand over the back of his neck.

Damn it, Montoya. Get real. You're not in high school

any more and you don't want Iona MacCabe in your bed, or anywhere else.

'All right, I guess this is the same guy,' she murmured, that smoky accent only making him more uncomfortable. 'And you're sure he's no an axe-murderer?'

Her eyebrows inched up her forehead and then she laughed, the sound low and amused and so unexpected it arrowed right through him.

He didn't even want to think what Ram had said. His ex-partner had a sense of humour coarsened by twenty-five years spent in a squad car and a locker room. It wasn't exactly subtle.

At last she passed him back his phone. 'Okay, you check out,' she said a little grudgingly. 'The detective wants to speak to you.'

Terrific.

'Hey, Ram,' he said without a lot of enthusiasm. He usually enjoyed shooting the breeze with the guy, but not now, not with this woman in the car—who was becoming way more of a complication than he needed.

Ramirez's amused voice boomed down the phone. 'Lance-lot, man, who's the *chiquita*? She sounds cute.'

Zane kept his eyes on Iona, and hoped she hadn't heard the dumb remark. 'I'm on a case, man,' he said sternly, relieved when Iona broke eye contact and stared out of the window, ignoring him.

'I'll bet.' The rusty laugh caused by two packs a day wheezed out as Ram replied. 'What happened, man? You finally find one you can't charm out of her panties with that pretty face of yours?'

'I appreciate you vouching for me, Ram,' he said, wishing to hell it had been Stone on the late shift tonight—whose sense of humour was about as animated as his name. And ended the call.

He dumped the smartphone on the dash, tunnelled his fingers through his hair. This night had started badly and gone downhill from there.

'Satisfied?' he asked Iona.

'I guess so,' she said, sounding snotty again.

She wasn't the only one in a snit now, though.

He started the car and pulled out.

'You still haven't told me where we're going.'

'Monterey,' he said, being as vague as possible. 'It's about two hours' drive so you might as well get comfortable.'

'And why are we going there?'

'I have a friend who owns some vacation rentals in Pacific Grove,' he said, remembering the key he still had in his glove compartment to Nate's property, which he'd stayed at a month ago while his kitchen was being remodelled. He could stash her in the picturesque little cottage for tonight, then review his options.

Without a car, or any cash or ID, she wouldn't be able to get far. And it was close enough to his place on Seventeen Mile to be convenient.

'You can stay there tonight—and I'll bring over your stuff tomorrow.'

When he planned to interrogate her—and find out exactly what she knew about Demarest.

It had been on the tip of his tongue to tell her he was taking her back to his place for the night. He had five bedrooms in the timber-and-glass beach house he'd bought a year ago, and it was a little more remote than Pacific Grove. But he'd kicked the idea into touch almost as soon as it had occurred to him.

He rarely did sleepovers, even with women he was dating. And he'd sure as hell never had one he was planning to interrogate stay over. Plus, given his unpredictable reaction to Iona already, having her under his roof had the potential to turn a complication into a catastrophe.

'And what if I don't want to stay at your friend's vacation rental in Pacific Grove?' she demanded.

'I turn you over to the cops,' he said, not sure why he wasn't doing that already. 'Your choice.'

The weighty silence told him what his passenger thought about the proposed sleeping arrangements.

'Why are you even giving me the option?' she said at last, the note of caution making it clear she'd accepted the lesser of two evils. 'I could wreck the place to spite you.'

Good question, and not one he wanted to answer.

'True enough, but you'd be facing a lot more than a B and E charge when I caught you.' He slanted her a long look, frustrated that he trusted her even though he didn't want to—and letting every ounce of that frustration show. 'And I would catch you.'

Her musical voice didn't pipe up again until they hit the coastal highway.

'Fine, I'll stay where you put me—until tomorrow. But only because I don't have a choice.' The Celtic mist of her accent did nothing to disguise the annoyance. 'But I'm not your *chiquita*. So don't get any funny ideas, Lancelot.'

Zane's fingers tensed on the wheel until he could feel the stitching on the leather biting into his palms.

Gee, thanks, Ramirez.

CHAPTER TWO

THE VICARIOUS PLEASURE at getting the final word didn't last long when Montoya's only response was the creak of leather—as he held the steering wheel in a death grip.

Way to go, Iona. Why not draw attention to his reputation for charming women out of their knickers? Because that's just what you want, to make this encounter personal.

'Did Ram say something dumb about me?' he asked after twenty seconds that had stretched over several lifetimes.

Iona risked a glance at him. His eyes remained fixed on the road as if he were trying to burn off a layer of tarmac.

'Maybe,' she said carefully, feeling increasingly awkward. Why hadn't she kept her smart mouth shut?

With a face like that, the guy probably got hit on by supermodels—despite his less-than-charming personality—which meant snide remarks about being indifferent to his charms probably made her sound delusional.

He sighed. 'Ram's got a big mouth and he gets a kick out of busting my balls. Don't pay any attention to him.'

The knot of tension in Iona's stomach released. He didn't sound angry; he sounded embarrassed.

'So you don't have a reputation for charming the *chiquitas* out of their panties?' she said, intrigued by his reaction.

Instead of taking the bait, he laughed. The low rumble of

amusement shivered down her spine and re-ignited the stupid pinpricks she'd been trying to forget.

'I do,' he conceded. 'But I didn't do a whole lot to earn it.'

She didn't believe him. Either he was being falsely modest, or he was lying. From the lazy, casually seductive tone he'd slipped into so effortlessly, she'd bet he could charm the average *chiquita* out of her panties from five hundred paces.

'Ramirez tends to exaggerate my exploits.' He protested a bit too much. 'Because he's been happily married for twenty-five years.' He sent her a dimpled smile and the pinpricks were toast. 'Don't worry, Iona, you're safe with me.'

The pulse of awareness that warmed the air at his softly spoken guarantee had her nipples hardening under the thin black camisole. She folded her arms over the tell-tale buds and cursed the knee-jerk thought that she wouldn't completely object to a little danger.

'Good to know,' she replied, trying to convince herself she was grateful he had no designs on her panties.

Given her disastrous relationship history, the last thing she needed right now was to develop some ridiculous crush on Detective Sexy. She was already at enough of a disadvantage with the man.

'So how did Demarest manage to relieve your old man of twenty-five grand?' he asked, sliding effortlessly from charm offensive back to cop mode.

'Why do you ask?' she said, attempting to deflect the question. While she'd much rather be dealing with Montoya the cop, than Montoya the pantie charmer, she had no intention of revealing the grim details of her affair with Brad.

'It's not Demarest's usual MO.'

'What is his usual MO?'

He paused, and she had the uneasy feeling he had seen right through the stalling tactic. 'All the victims we questioned were women, mostly over fifty, recently divorced or widowed. He poses as a producer, gives them a line about casting them in his latest movie, sweetens the deal with a little recreational sex and then asks for an investment.'

The flush spread up Iona's throat at Montoya's matter-of-fact statement. But she managed to choke back the urge to correct him.

Sex with Brad had been the opposite of recreational, at least in her experience. He'd been rough and demanding, but because he'd been her ticket out of Kelross Glen, she'd wanted to please him. Her stomach sank to her toes, her scalp burning at the memory of how hard she'd tried. Hard enough to persuade herself she actually liked Brad.

When Brad had dangled the carrot of knowing a wealthy benefactor in LA who might be keen to commission her artwork, she'd had no qualms about mentioning the opportunity to her Dad. But while her gullibility made her sick with shame, it was the way she'd let Brad use her in bed that made her feel sordid.

'Demarest's a sick bastard,' Montoya continued. 'The money's not the main kick for him, it's sleeping with the women he's exploiting,' Montoya hesitated. 'Which is why I'm wondering how your old man fits into that? Where was the kick?'

She flinched at the perceptive comment. Montoya wasn't buying it. Had he guessed her father hadn't been the real mark? And why did the thought that he might find out the truth only make her feel a thousand times more unclean?

It really shouldn't matter what this man knew or didn't know. He was a stranger. And she didn't even like him. In anything other than a hormonal sense, she added grudgingly.

But somehow it did matter.

'Demarest was going to make a tourist film for my dad,' she said, remembering one of Brad's earlier carrots—that her father hadn't taken. 'We have a gift shop in Kelross. Demarest suggested making a movie about the history of the place for US investors,' she added. It had *almost* been true.

'How long was this movie going to be?'

'I'm not sure…' She scrabbled around trying to remember if Brad had even got that far with the con. 'An hour, maybe.'

'An hour? For twenty-five grand?' He gave an incredulous laugh. 'Your old man sounds like an easy mark.'

Iona bristled, knowing she'd been the easiest mark of all. 'He just doesn't know much about movie making.' And unfortunately neither did she.

'Although it still seems kind of weird,' Montoya murmured, the continued scepticism making her tense. 'For there not to be a woman in there somewhere.' He bumped his thumb against the steering wheel, the insistent tapping making Iona feel like Captain Hook listening to the tick-tock of the approaching crocodile. 'What about your mother? Where does she fit into the picture?'

The question was so unexpected, she answered without thinking. 'Nowhere. She ran off when I was small. We haven't seen her since.'

The recently eaten burger turned over as the ugly truth made her feel suddenly vulnerable, scraping at an old wound. A scabbed over, forgotten wound that she thought had healed years ago.

'That's tough.' Montoya's gruff condolence only made her feel more exposed.

'Not that tough. I can barely remember her,' she lied, ashamed of having revealed too much, too easily.

She curled away from him, gazed at the stars sprinkled over the dark line of the cliffs, and closed her eyes, trying to shut out the memory of her mother—so beautiful, so careless and so indifferent.

Don't think about her. You've got quite enough to deal with already.

Fatigue made her eyelids gritty. She blinked furiously, determined to stay awake. She couldn't afford to give into sleep yet, because that would mean trusting Montoya and she'd known ever since she was a child she shouldn't trust anyone.

And her experience with Brad had only confirmed that.

Montoya didn't offer any more useless platitudes or ask any more probing questions. Something she was pathetically grateful for as she pressed her cheek into the soft leather, listened to the soothing hum of the car's engine—and plummeted into a dreamless sleep.

Zane braked gently in the driveway of the small cottage—and studied his sleeping passenger.

She'd dropped off like a stone an hour ago, and hadn't made a sound since. The engine stilled and the only sound was the chirp of crickets and night crawlers and the distant hum of a passing car. He unclicked her seatbelt, eased it over her bare shoulder and got a lungful of her scent.

The fresh fragrance of baby talc and some flowery soap mixed with the sultry scent of her invaded his senses, and the inevitable pulse of arousal hit.

He tensed, annoyed with his inability to control the response. The cottage's nightlight illuminated her pale face and the varying shades of red in her unruly hair. The thick lashes resting on her cheeks and the even breathing made her look impossibly young. The heat subsided as he imagined her as a kid, losing her mother. The dart of sympathy was sharp and undeniable.

What would he have done if Maria had abandoned him? And she'd had more cause than any mother.

He shook his head, to dispel the thought.

Don't make this personal, Montoya. You're having enough trouble keeping a professional distance.

He didn't even know how old she was. Or how much of her story was true.

And exactly how mixed up with Demarest was she? She'd lied to him about the con. He'd spotted it straight away, the hitch in her breathing, the hesitation as she stumbled over the explanation. Had she been the mark all along? Was that why she'd been so determined to get her father's money back? Because she felt responsible for the loss? Exactly how much danger had she put herself in, while tracking Demarest?

And why did the thought of that bother him so much?

She wasn't his problem, not in the long-term.

He retrieved the key buried in the glove compartment. Then thrust a hand through his hair as it occurred to him he was glad she was here tonight, and under his protection, instead of back at that seedy motel.

He got out of the car, walked around to the passenger door and stared at her cuddled into the seat. He should shake her awake, get her to go into the cottage under her own steam, but she looked so peaceful, he couldn't do it.

Without giving himself too much time to think, he scooped her into his arms.

The sultry scent enveloped him as he carried her onto the cottage's porch. She let out a puff of breath and her soft hair brushed against his chin as she burrowed into his chest like a thrusting child.

He fumbled with the key, pushed the door open with his foot and stepped into the dark interior, an emotion he didn't like banding across his chest.

She didn't stir as he placed her on the small queen-size in the cottage's only bedroom, untied the laces on her combat boots and slipped them off, then covered her with the throw before he got fixated on the slow rise and fall of her breasts beneath the tank.

He found a note pad in the kitchen, scribbled a note and pinned it to the corkboard above the fridge. Unplugging the phone and tucking it under his arm, he walked out of the door, closing and locking it behind him. Then dropped the key through the letter slot.

As he drove back to his place he sent a voicemail to Nate's business line, to inform him of his new house guest, and left one with his PA.

If they didn't pick up Demarest tonight, he was diverting every free man he had to the case tomorrow. He needed to get this damn case closed, before it got any more complicated.

CHAPTER THREE

*Stay put, I'll be back tomorrow to tell you what's going
to happen next.*
Montoya

IONA RAN HER fingers through her damp curls, tucked the towel
between her breasts and glared at the thick black writing—
particularly the shouty capitals.

Where did Detective Sexy get off giving her orders like
a pet dog?

No one told her what to do. She'd been taking care of herself since she was ten years old. And taking care of her dad
too. And okay, maybe she hadn't exactly been doing a stellar
job of it of late, but that hardly gave him the right to treat her
as if she were his to command.

And what exactly did he mean by *'to tell you what's going
to happen next'*?

She struggled to hold on to her indignation and ignore the
little blip of disappointment at the fact that so far the only
person she'd seen was one of his detectives. A rotund guy
called Jim with a gruff but friendly manner, who'd woken her
up an hour ago to deliver a bag of groceries, her rucksack—
conspicuously minus her purse and passport—and the news
that Mr Montoya was busy with the case but would be in
touch later in the day.

Pulling the note off the corkboard, she scrunched it up and dumped it in the kitchen bin. Well, hooray for Mr Montoya—it must be nice to get to order everyone around like a demigod.

Goosebumps rose on her arms. She marched back into the cottage's tiny living area and grabbed fresh underwear, jeans and a T-shirt from her rucksack. He'd better bring her passport when he showed up or there would be trouble. Returning to the compact bedroom, she hunted around for her boots, then stopped dead when she spotted them—placed neatly together on the rug by the bedside table, the laces undone.

Her heartbeat bumped her throat as a picture formed in her mind's eye. The picture she'd been holding at bay ever since she'd been woken up by the sound of knocking at the front door, snuggled cosy and content and well rested under a clean quilt that smelled pleasantly of fabric conditioner.

The picture of Montoya carrying her into the cottage, taking off her boots and then covering her with said quilt.

The pulse of reaction skittered up her spine, making the pinpricks shimmer back to life and party with the goosebumps.

She swallowed heavily, trying to ease the ache in her throat.

The thought of being fast asleep in his arms was disturbing enough, but much worse was the thought of him putting her to bed so carefully.

When was the last time anyone had bothered to treat her with that much care and attention? Her father had been unable to care for himself after her mother left, let alone her. So at ten years old, she'd become the parent—caring for both of them while he struggled to pull himself back from the brink of depression. She'd had a few boyfriends before Brad, but they'd been young and reckless—providing nothing more than the easy thrill of youthful companionship. And as for her brief liaison with Brad, well Brad had been a user, always quick to take, never willing to give.

Big deal. He just took your boots off for you.

Perching on the edge of the bed, she grabbed one of the boots and shoved it on, staunching the ridiculous tide of her thoughts.

Zane Montoya didn't care about her; he just cared about his case. And she didn't care about him either. So why was she turning one moment of consideration into a primetime drama?

She returned to the kitchenette and began taking the groceries out of the brown paper bag Jim had delivered, determined to put the moment of vulnerability behind her and concentrate on finding a solution to her situation.

She almost wept with joy when she found a tin of coffee. She filled the kettle, looking out of the window to find a sweet little patio garden carpeted with climbing vines. As the rich smell of brewing coffee filled the kitchen, a strange contentment settled over her.

The cottage was tiny, but so clean and pretty—and completely adorable compared to the dives she'd been forced to stay in of late. Pouring herself a steaming cup, she smiled as a hummingbird fluttered into view and settled over the bright yellow pegonias in the window box, and began gathering nectar in its long beak. Putting down the mug, she rushed back into the living room and dug out her art supplies, her palms itching to detail the blurred lines of the bird's movement in the static medium of paper and graphite. Settling in front of the kitchen window, she sketched furiously, trying to capture as much as she could before the bird disappeared. As the hummingbird flitted from flower to flower and the clear lines began to form on the heavy paper the leaden feeling of failure that had bowed her shoulders for so long began to lift.

She relaxed as the bird flew off, and gazed at her drawings. More than enough to create a detailed watercolour later. Refilling her now lukewarm coffee, she took a muffin out of the deli-bag on the counter and realised that for the first time in a long time she felt the bright sheen of possibility peeking out from under the dead weight of failure.

And she had Detective Sexy to thank for that.

When he appeared, she would be conciliatory instead of combative. The truth was, she'd been aggressive and unnecessarily snotty with him last night. Because she'd been exhausted, hungry and terrified—she might as well admit it. But she'd had her first full night's sleep in weeks. Which meant she owed Montoya—however high-handed he'd been with his little note.

But once she'd thanked Montoya and was on her own again, the bigger picture was more complicated. Still, now she was well rested her prospects didn't seem nearly as bleak as they had seemed last night.

She had some money left and a work visa that lasted another five months. There was no reason why she couldn't look for a better place to live now, away from the seedy motels Brad frequented. And perhaps sell a few more sketches. She'd managed to sell all the hand-painted postcards she'd produced in the cafés along Morro Bay's Main Street, but keeping an eye on Brad's motel room had meant she hadn't had time to replenish her work. But now she was free of Brad-surveillance she could actually devote herself to finding a decent job and spend her evenings sketching. Monterey was supposed to be arty and bohemian—as well as being a tourist mecca. Surely there were bound to be places she could sell her stuff and look for a job. The summer season was only weeks away, so casual work shouldn't be too hard to find.

The most important thing of all, and the main reason she'd come to America to track Brad, was to stop her dad from ever finding out that he'd been conned again by someone he trusted. And while she most likely wouldn't be able to get him his money back, she could still achieve that much.

She'd told her father she was travelling to LA at Brad's invitation, that her 'new man' had come through with his promises of a showcase for her work. Even though the lie had nearly choked her at the time, it had kept her father happy.

And while getting a gallery showing had always been a foolish pipe dream, in five months if she worked hard and applied herself she might be able to return home with at least some money to replace what her father had lost—and a small degree of success to show for his bogus investment.

She frowned as she grabbed another muffin. But first she had to convince Montoya she was of no significance to his case. To do that, she needed to be polite and cooperative—and keep things impersonal.

Wiping the crumbs off the surface and rinsing out her coffee mug, she picked up her sketch pad again, feeling almost euphoric. Until Montoya arrived, she planned to indulge herself and do what she loved for a change.

Zane tucked the cottage's phone under his arm and rapped on the front door. The early evening light beamed off polished wood but as he peered inside it was obvious there was no one in the front room.

He rolled his shoulders as the muscles cramped. He hoped she'd done as she was told and stayed put. After the day he'd put in already, the last thing he needed now was to have to scour Pacific Grove for her.

The original plan had been to swing by first thing that morning. But after having his night's sleep disturbed by way too many sweaty dreams involving firm breasts, wide caramel-coloured eyes, worn tank tops and full kissable lips glossy with burger grease, he'd held off, and sent Jim to deliver the groceries instead.

Iona MacCabe had an unpredictable effect on him, and until he figured out what—if anything—he was going to do about it, keeping his distance was the smart choice.

Then the case had exploded at ten when Demarest had shown up at the Morro Motel—and all hell had broken loose. Zane had been tied up with the Morro Bay PD for the rest of the day, handing over the case files and contacting the LAPD to make sure Demarest got transferred there before the day was out. As a courtesy, Stone and Ramirez had let him observe their interrogations. He massaged the back of his neck to ease the tension headache that had been building ever since.

Just as he'd guessed after their original profiling, in the interview Demarest had been slick and supremely arrogant. But he soon lost control under pressure, and proved how volatile and dangerous he was.

Zane shuddered. What the hell had Iona been thinking breaking into the guy's room? What would have happened to her, if it had been Demarest who'd caught her last night and not him? At some point he planned to give her a damn good talking to about personal safety.

The thought of any woman being at the guy's mercy had sickened him—but worse had been the moment when they'd questioned Demarest about his trip to Scotland. Demarest had laughed and boasted about the Scottish girl who'd been 'begging for it' and Zane had been forced to walk out—the urge to leap through the mirrored partition and strangle the guy triggering the sickening memory that had haunted him most of his adult life.

He eased the kinks out of his shoulders and rapped again.

He should be feeling great now. Six months' work had finally paid off and Montoya Investigations was in line for a nice fat bonus payment. Plus his firm had been instrumental in catching one of the nastiest and most parasitic low lives in California and bringing him to book. But somehow it didn't feel like enough—because it could never undo the damage the bastard had done.

He squinted through the clouded glass again, and a little of the tension dissolved as he spotted the petite silhouette coming to the door from the back of the house. Then the door swung open and the punch of lust hit full force.

The setting sun glinted on her hair, highlighting the different shades of red, and making her skin almost transpar-

ent. Her rich caramel eyes glowed with energy, and, while the
wary caution of the night before was still there, the bruised
shadows underneath were gone. In a pair of old jeans and a
T-shirt that hugged the generous breasts he recalled a little
too well pressing against his forearm, her feet encased in the
boots he'd taken off her the night before, she should have
looked like a tomboy. She didn't.

'Hello, Mr Montoya. Sorry I didn't hear you knocking—
I was in the back garden.' The Celtic lilt and the hitch in her
breathing called to his inner caveman.

*Down, Montoya. You're here on business. Not pleasure.
However tempted you might be to stray over that line.*

He noticed the pad under her arm, which was covered in
a series of intricate drawings of a small bird.

'You're an artist?' he asked, although the answer was obvious from the quality of the work.

'Yes, I…' She shrugged. 'I specialise in drawing flora and
fauna. It's a passion of mine.'

She stumbled over the word *passion* and two pink flags
appeared on her cheekbones, making the sprinkle of freckles
on her nose more vivid.

'A passion, huh?' he said, not quite able to hold back the
grin when she squirmed. So he wasn't the only one struggling
to remain professional.

Good to know.

'Come in, Mr Montoya,' she said, the cool, polite tone
disconcerting as she stepped back and held the door open.
He wondered what had happened to the firebrand he'd met
last night.

'The name's Zane.' He dumped the phone on the coffee
table. 'I brought this in case you want to call your father. You
got the groceries okay this morning?'

'Yes, you should tell me what I owe you for them,' she said,
the cool tone turning chilly. 'Although it's going to be hard
to pay you without my purse.'

He tugged her purse and passport out of his back pocket. But when she reached for them, he lifted them above her head. 'Not so fast. I'll need your word you're not going to run off.'

The beguiling almond-shaped eyes narrowed. And the firebrand came out of hiding.

'And what would you be needing my word for?' she asked, propping her hands on her hips and making her breasts flatten against the tight T-shirt. 'If you don't believe a single thing I say?'

'It'll go some way to putting my suspicious mind at rest,' he said, enjoying the view probably a bit too much.

The fire in her eyes flared. 'Is it just me you don't trust?' she asked her tone dripping with sarcasm. 'Or do you have this low an opinion of all women, Mr Montoya?'

He choked out a laugh. No one had ever accused him of that before. Especially not a woman. But then Iona MacCabe was turning out to be an original in more ways than one.

His gaze wandered over her face and he watched with satisfaction as her cheeks pinkened. 'On the contrary, I have a very high opinion of women.'

The pulse of awareness warmed the air as her cheeks heated to a dull red. And pert nipples protruded against the T-shirt.

It was a crisp spring evening outside, but the sun shining through the cottage's front window meant the atmosphere was warm and close.

She crossed her arms to cover the stiff buds.

Too late, your secret's out, querida. You're no more immune to me than I am to you.

'In fact,' he added, 'I can't think of a single thing about women I don't enjoy.'

Professionalism be damned. Iona McCabe was too cute to resist flirting with.

'So perhaps we should start over—and forget about last night.' He held out his hand. 'Zane Montoya, at your service.'

Suspicion clouded her eyes, but then she thrust her slim hand into his much larger, much darker one. He clasped her fingers for barely a second, the handshake quick and impersonal, but the cool, soft touch of her skin contrasted sharply with the arrow of heat that darted straight to his groin.

She stuffed her hand into the back pocket of the jeans. But her pupils dilated with something he recognised only too well, before her gaze flickered away.

You felt it too.

Endorphins flowed freely through his system. He'd always been a connoisseur of women, in all their myriad and wonderful varieties. Which was why he didn't have a type. But for some reason, this girl hit all his happy buttons, without even trying.

And he was through fighting it.

As of today, Demarest was in a cell and would be for a very long time. The case was closed as far as Montoya Investigations was concerned. So there was no professional reason why he shouldn't push a few of her happy buttons right back.

'I've got some news on the case, Iona,' he said, planning to ask her if she wanted to discuss it over dinner, but before he could say any more her head shot up.

'News about Brad?'

He frowned, his happy buttons not feeling all that happy any more. 'We picked him up at ten this morning. He's in a cell facing more charges than he can count.'

'I see.' Her voice sounded casual, but then she fixed him with that cautious gaze and he knew it wasn't. 'Did he have any of my dad's money on him?'

He shook his head and her face fell.

'Right.' She looked down, but not before he saw the shadow of distress.

He shoved his hand into his pocket, resisting the urge to run his finger down her cheek, and stroke the distress away.

For one tense moment he thought she might cry. But then she seemed to pull herself back from the brink.

'Well, I guess this is where we part company, then, Montoya,' she murmured.

Something tugged hard under his breastbone. And that surprised him.

The threat of female tears didn't usually faze him, but there was something about Iona McCabe's stoicism—and those sultry eyes, so large and wary in her small face—that *had* fazed him.

She let out a weighty sigh. 'Do you think it would be okay for me to stay here another night? I could pay any rent that's due.'

His sympathy dissolved. She looked scared but defiant, like a puppy who expected to be kicked but was determined not to yelp.

He didn't deserve that.

He trusted her. In fact, she sort of fascinated him. She was feisty and unpredictable and refreshingly transparent and he hadn't been able to get his mind off her, even though he'd tried. But it was real clear that however attracted she might be to him, she didn't trust him. And while he'd understood her animosity last night, he was finding it hard not to take it personally now.

'Damn it, Iona, you can stay here as long as you need.' In fact, he planned to insist on it. She might think she was safe, but he knew different. A woman alone was always vulnerable, but especially a woman as impulsive as her. 'And there's no charge—the place was empty anyway.'

'Why would you do that? I'm not your responsibility.' She sounded genuinely confused, making his annoyance increase.

'Because, weirdly enough, I'm not the kind of guy who kicks women when they're down.' *Unlike your pal Brad.*

'Okay, well, thank you, I appreciate not having to leave

tonight,' she said. But then her chin stuck out in a stubborn show of strength. 'But I'll make sure I'm gone by tomorrow.'

I don't think so. Not until I'm sure you'll be safe.

He bit back the retort, seeing the mutinous expression on her face. In his experience, pushing her only made her push back. And anyhow, he didn't want to argue with her. Not tonight.

'How about we talk about it over dinner in Santa Cruz? I know a place that does the best enchiladas on the West Coast.'

Her face went completely blank for a second and she blinked, her eyes going round with astonishment.

That had sure shut her up.

'You're n-not serious?' she stammered, her accent thickening.

Damn, she's even cuter when she's flustered.

Had Detective Sexy just asked her on a date? Or was she hallucinating?

'I'm always serious about Manuel's enchiladas,' he replied, while the tempting glint in his eye implied the opposite. 'My treat,' he continued, apparently not the least bit bothered by her shock.

But then she suspected he was probably used to that reaction from women.

What with that devastating face—not to mention that subtle I-can-have-you-any-time-I-want-you smile—she already knew he was an expert at charming women out of their panties. She'd only got a glimpse of his charm the night before—but she was standing in the full glare of it now, and getting a little light-headed.

Then she made the mistake of drawing a breath into her lungs. The fresh scent of laundry soap, a zesty hint of aftershave and something musky and entirely masculine drifted up her nostrils.

Good Lord, he's got so many let's-get-naked hormones pumping off him, I can actually smell them.

She pressed her arms into her breasts as her traitorous nipples began to ache.

'But why…?' she began, struggling to come up with a coherent response.

He leaned forward and whispered, 'Because I'm starving, *querida*. Aren't you?'

His breath feathered her earlobe and sent the pinpricks careering down her neck and straight into her nether regions. She drew her head back, and got fixated on those penetrating blue eyes. She didn't answer the question, because she was fairly certain they weren't talking about enchiladas any more.

His smile widened—and the nuclear blush radiated up her neck.

'Well, I…?' she began again, fighting to stem the tide of brain cells leaking out of her head.

He chuckled. 'Say yes, Iona. They really are the best. I don't lie to women.' He winked, the playful gesture as dazzlingly sexy as that azure gaze. 'It's one of my many charms.'

He probably lied to women all the time, but the firm 'no' that should have been hovering on the tip of her tongue wasn't.

Taking Detective Sexy up on his offer of a dinner date was probably not a smart move. Especially as she might end up getting zapped to a crisp by his let's-get-naked hormones. She'd promised herself she'd be polite and sensible and keep her interaction with him impersonal. But as soon as she'd opened the door, and seen him standing on the porch, a sunbeam spotlighting that blue-black hair and breathtaking face, she'd had to concede that impersonal was always going to be a hard sell. And then he'd started talking, in that patronising but oh-so-sexy way and polite and sensible had taken a nosedive too.

Plus she finally had something to celebrate. The news that Brad Demarest was out of her life for ever. It had been a blow to discover her father's money really was gone, but she wasn't going to worry about that. If she could make a go of her artwork in Monterey, at least something good might come of the loss.

And then there was the fact that she hadn't been out on a date in—well, for ever. The boyfriends she'd had in Kelross had never been able to stretch to much more than a visit to the local chip shop. And Brad had only ever been interested in getting her naked and then getting the sex over with as soon as he was satisfied.

She blitzed the thought.

Do not go there. Concentrate on the enchiladas—the best on the West Coast no less—they sounded delicious. And being in the company of a guy who made her pulse vibrate, instead of one who made her feel as if she didn't have a pulse.

Plus there was no danger of her doing anything stupid, no matter how much her pulse vibrated. Because post-Brad she was pretty sure she was man-proof—or at the very least man-averse—with or without the pinpricks.

And Montoya was probably only asking her because he felt bad about threatening to have her arrested last night. So this had to be a pity date.

'Okay, you're on,' she said, reckless excitement thrumming through her veins.

Brad had destroyed her confidence in ways she hadn't even realised. And she'd let him. But she couldn't think of a better way to get some of it back. If ever there was a cure for a woman's shattered ego, it had to be spending an evening with someone as drop-dead gorgeous as Detective Sexy.

CHAPTER FOUR

IONA TIED THE silk scarf around her head as Zane's vintage convertible bulleted down the coast road. She gazed out across the dark blue expanse of the Pacific Ocean. The rolling breakers created a mighty backdrop to the soft tangerine glow of sunset hitting the low cliffs. The zing of exhilaration made her pulse throb, especially as the dramatic splendour of Monterey Bay wasn't the only spectacular view on offer.

'Exactly how many cars have you got?' she shouted, stealing a glance at the man beside her.

He'd rolled up his shirt sleeves, giving her a gratifying glimpse of tanned forearms dusted with dark hair while he negotiated the road's hairpin bends. His dark hair ruffled in the wind around his face and made him look relaxed and gorgeous. A bit too gorgeous, really. Nerves fluttered.

Relax. Pity date, remember. Absolutely no call to panic.

The quick grin gave her a flash of even white teeth in his darkly handsome face. Designer sunglasses hid those diamond-bright eyes from view, thankfully, but she could still sense the twinkle of amusement. 'Several.' He glanced at her. 'Automobiles are a passion of mine.'

She stroked the shiny red paintwork, and laughed at the way he'd emphasized the word *passion*. He was definitely flirting with her. Which felt ridiculously good.

'So how did you get into drawing flora and fauna?' he asked.

'There happens to be a lot of it about in Kelross Glen, so it was a no-brainer really,' she replied.

'Kelross Glen? That's the town you're from in Scotland, right? What's it like?'

'Small,' she said—but decided not to elaborate. That was more than enough about her.

During the half-hour drive along the coast road, Zane Montoya had used those killer looks and that killer smile to prise information out of her about everything from her childhood, to her education, to her father's depression, to her job in the gift shop her dad owned in Kelross Glen, while at the same time neatly sidestepping any personal questions about himself. She'd basically undergone a charm offensive that Lieutenant Columbo would be proud of. No wonder the man made a living as a private detective.

But she was wise to his tactics now. And she wasn't going to divulge another iota of information about herself, until she managed to get him to reciprocate—because all the things he wasn't saying were making her unbearably curious.

The car slowed as they entered the city limits of Santa Cruz. The engine noise dropped to a well-oiled hum as the open road gave way to neighbourhoods of brightly painted clapboard houses with their obligatory picket fences. Teenagers skateboarded on sidewalks whooping out the joys of spring while grey-rinse cyclists thronged the bike paths leading to the boardwalk. Everything was so safe and normal and non-seedy it was enchanting.

The scent of sea salt and fish was a pungent reminder of the beach community's nearby marina. But instead of heading towards Santa Cruz's famous funfair, or the historic Main Street she'd read about in the guidebooks, Zane took a small side road, which wound its way down to a sandy cove.

The restaurant came into view perched on a bluff. A large

wooden terrace packed with Friday-night diners jutted out over the ocean. The fairy lights strung from its canopy twinkled festively in the gathering dusk. Cars lined the narrow access road. The joint was jumping and Iona wondered where they were going to park. Her question was answered when Zane drove round to the back lot and slotted his convertible into the only available space under a huge yellow sign that read in ominous black letters: 'Unauthorized Vehicles WILL BE Towed, 24 Hours A Day.' And then underneath scrawled in red graffiti: 'Don't even think about it, Amigo.'

'Shouldn't you think about this, Amigo?' she asked, pointing to the sign as Zane opened the passenger door. He sent her a rakish grin. 'You're worried about me.' He offered her his hand as she climbed out. 'I'm touched.'

'I'm more worried about your beautiful car, actually,' she said, her pulse skipping pleasantly as his palm settled on her hip. His fingers slid against the linen of the short shift dress she'd changed into as he directed her to the restaurant's entrance.

The slope of her back felt as if it were being stroked with a low-voltage cattle prod, the sensation a little shocking and a lot exhilarating.

'And how I'm going to get home if it gets towed,' she finished, trying not to make too much of the possessive touch. He wasn't deliberately trying to electrocute her erogenous zones, it was all in her head.

His low chuckle rumbled through her, upping the voltage.

'Don't worry, I have connections.' He caressed the words the same way he was caressing her back, his palm skimming under the denim jacket she'd worn to ward off the spring chill. 'One of my *primos* owns the place,' he added. 'The Mustang will be safe.'

She shivered and he rubbed gently, the absent caress instantly chasing away the chill. The electrical tingles morphed into tantalising zaps of energy and her nipples drew into tight buds, trapped against her bra.

And she wished this date weren't as safe as his Mustang.

'You're cold.' His gaze dipped to her cleavage as he led her past the queue of people waiting in line for a table. 'Let's grab a booth inside.'

She spotted the booths against the back wall in the darkest part of the restaurant. Their high leather backs and the tea lights flickering on the tables made them look intimate and inviting—and a bit too romantic.

'I'm not that cold. Let's sit outside, over the ocean.' Sharing a booth with him and his let's-get-naked hormones would be risky. She might well get high on them and start purring, especially if he touched her again. And that had the potential to be embarrassing.

His brow quirked, the sceptical smile calling her on her cowardice. 'You sure about that? It's chilly tonight.'

'Absolutely, positively,' she said, determined to avoid purring at all costs.

Montoya's questions in the car and the light flirtatious banter had made her feel important and special. Even if it was a routine he used with every woman he met, her battered ego appreciated the boost. Not only that, but the restaurant was fabulous, the smell of roasting meat and Mexican spices almost as delicious as the lively buzz of friendly people having friendly conversations—and not shouting out obscenities at the top of their voices in the middle of the night.

She felt safe here and really rather fabulous under Montoya's attentive gaze—but she didn't want to get carried away.

A young waiter with bright ginger hair and an eager smile greeted Zane like an old friend and showed them to a table tucked at the end of the terrace.

Iona absorbed the sound of the waves lapping on the beach

below and the glittering lights of the funfair across the bay, her stomach grumbling.

As pity dates went, this was shaping up to be one of her best.

Get your eyes off her butt.

Zane lifted his gaze from Iona's perfect rear end as Benji pulled out their chairs.

He kept his gaze above her waistline as he held her chair. But then she smoothed her dress over that delicious tush and planted it on the seat. And his blood pressure shot up another notch.

So now you're a butt man—when did that happen?

Then again, Iona McCabe had a lot of exceptional parts he decided as a gust of sea air plastered her dress against her breasts. Benji handed them both menus and Zane took in a lungful of the salty breeze to calm himself down. This was supposed to be fun and flirtatious—and a fact-finding mission. He wasn't planning on taking things any further till he knew a lot more about her. She'd relaxed on the drive up and he'd managed to get some details out of her, but she'd clammed up again before he'd even got to talking about her association with Demarest.

So he needed to relax, turn up the charm and stop fixating on her assets, or he was never going to find out what he wanted to know.

Benji filled their water glasses. 'Welcome to Manuel's Cantina.' He nodded at Zane. 'I'll tell Mani you're here, Zane.'

'Don't bother, Benj—I'm sure he's busy,' he said, tensing up at the thought of seeing his *primo*. He liked Mani well enough, and the food here was terrific, but he never felt comfortable pretending their family connection meant something.

'No problem,' Benji remarked, before reeling off the specials and then leaving them to decide.

'That all sounded delicious.' Iona picked up the menu, and

he was struck again by how young she looked. He knew now she was twenty-four—he'd checked out the birth date on her passport—but she looked younger. The image of Demarest sitting behind the mirrored glass with a cruel smile on his face made his stomach knot.

Forget it. Whatever the guy had done to her, she was safe from him now. He put his menu down on the table. 'So, Iona, what do you want?' he asked, making an effort to keep his tone G-rated.

'Quite a lot actually,' she murmured, the sparkle of flirtation in rich caramel making the knot sink lower. A lot lower.

'Uh-huh, well, why don't I help you to decide?' He stretched out his legs, rested his forearms on the table—and forced himself to ignore the insistent pulse of heat.

He never slept with a woman on a first date, no matter how much he desired her, because it meant making demands that might be misconstrued later. He respected women, he enjoyed their company, but if sex was going to happen it would be on his terms and at his pace.

'My personal favourite is the blackened catfish enchiladas with green chilli salsa.'

Her lips quirked. 'Are they now? And why's that?'

'Because they've got heat and spice—which is the way I like my enchiladas.'

She tilted her head to one side, propped her elbow on the table and ran her tongue over her bottom lip, torturing him. 'Sold, Montoya.'

'Call me Zane.'

'Yes, Zane.' The quick smile became astute. 'Tell me something, do you date a lot of women?'

'Why do you ask?' That was a lot more direct than he was used to.

'Because you're very good at it. And you haven't answered my question.'

'I never date more than one at a time,' he replied, not wanting to tell her it had been six months since he'd dated—and give this evening more significance than it deserved.

'You're very cagey. Is that part of the detective code? Not divulging personal information?'

'No.' He gave a half laugh, as if he didn't know what she was talking about. But he knew he'd been busted, and he wasn't sure how to deal with it. Women generally enjoyed it when you made them the focus of the conversation. He'd sure as hell never had one turn the tables on him this fast.

'I'm an open book,' he lied smoothly. He leaned back in his chair—the picture of relaxed indifference. 'What do you want to know?

'Why *did* you ask me out tonight?'

'For all the usual reasons,' he said carefully. Was that a trick question? No way was he going to tell her about his recently acquired butt-fetish.

'Which are?' she prompted.

The confusion cleared and he relaxed for real. She was looking for a compliment. Not surprising, given her recent association with Demarest. He leaned forward, happy to oblige.

'You're cute and tenacious. I admire your spirit—even if you do need a keeper when it comes to your personal safety—and I wanted to get to know you better.'

Truth was, he wanted to get to know her a lot better, but no need to go there yet.

Instead of her looking pleased with his answer, though, the light in her eyes dimmed and the colour in her cheeks bloomed. She stared out to sea for a moment, her smile pensive and more than a little sad. And he wondered where she'd gone.

'You're really a nice guy, aren't you?' she said at last. 'I'm sorry I was so rude to you yesterday—you didn't deserve that.'

Nice? What the hell?

Zane bristled, the spurt of irritation catching him off guard. No one had ever called him nice before. But before he could think of how to respond, a huge hand clasped his shoulder, and he glanced round to find his *primo* Manuel—the last person he wanted to see—standing by the table.

'Great to see you, *compadre,*' Manuel boomed, the hearty smile making Zane tense even more. 'Welcome back to my humble cantina.'

Cute!

Wasn't that what Brad had once called her? And she'd despised it even then. Why couldn't she be sexy, or, better yet, irresistible?

Iona let the grudging disappointment melt away as she listened to Zane's friend Manuel wax lyrical about the blackened catfish enchiladas, which she already knew were Zane's favourites. Her stomach rumbled loudly and the excitement of the evening seeped back.

Enough with the pity party. If you didn't want to know, you shouldn't have asked.

And cute was better than what she'd begun to fear. That the only reason he'd asked her here was to interrogate her about her association with Brad. As long as the man sitting opposite never found out the truth about that, she could live with cute.

'They sound ravishing, Manuel,' she said, smiling when the proprietor's warm mahogany eyes lit with enthusiasm. 'But I already know how good they are from Zane's sales pitch.'

Manuel beamed at Zane. 'You like them? I didn't know that.'

'It's hardly a secret how much I like the food here. I come here often enough.'

The statement was brusque, and lacked Zane's usual charm.

'And I appreciate your custom, cousin,' Manuel replied.

Her curiosity was piqued. How odd—why did Zane seem so tense if Manuel was his cousin?

'Enjoy your meals.' Manuel pasted the smile back on,

smoothing over the discomfort. 'I'll see you Saturday, Zane, at Maricruz's *quinceañera.*'

A muscle in Zane's jaw jumped. 'Yeah, sure.' But from the look on his face as his cousin left, Iona didn't think he was looking forward to it at all. Which only piqued her curiosity more.

'Who's Maricruz?'

Zane watched Iona lick the salt from the rim of her margarita glass and tried to focus on the question, instead of the coil of desire descending south.

Their enchiladas had come and gone, and he'd discovered that watching her eat was as erotic as it had been last night. He'd never given it much thought before, but far too many of the women he'd dated in the past had picked at their food, or worse insisted on ordering nothing more exciting than a salad—usually because they had some dumb idea they were fat.

But not Iona. She'd closed her eyes and hummed with pleasure while swallowing her first bite of the spicy enchilada. The husky groan had arrowed right through him, and he'd been struggling to keep his mind on their conversation ever since.

'She's my cousin, like Manuel,' he clarified. 'And most of the rest of Santa Cruz.'

'How many cousins do you have?' She put down her margarita, her voice hushed in awe.

'Last count? Twenty-eight.' Or was it twenty-nine? It wasn't something he kept abreast of.

Her eyes widened. 'But that must have been fabulous growing up,' she said, the words overflowing with enthusiasm. 'Having such a huge family?'

Not especially, he thought, annoyed to feel the old anger and resentment resurfacing.

'It was just me and my dad growing up,' she added, and he

remembered what she'd told him about her mother. 'Do you have lots of brothers and sisters too?'

'No. There's only me,' he said, the soft brogue of her accent wrapping around him like a caress. 'My mother married a great guy ten years ago. They wanted more kids, but—' He stopped abruptly, astonished he'd let that piece of information slip out. 'But it didn't happen.'

Maria had never blamed him, never even mentioned it, but he knew having him had screwed up her chances of having more children. So he always avoided the subject.

'That's a shame,' Iona murmured, the genuine sympathy in her tone soothing, even though he'd cauterised the wound years ago. 'But I guess at least you had all those cousins.'

'We didn't see much of each other as kids,' he said, careful to stop short of explaining the reason why this time. He'd let go of the anger a long time ago, when his grandfather Ernesto had finally been forced to admit that Maria's *gringo* son could amount to something. But that didn't mean he wanted to talk about it.

'So what's a *quinceañera?*' Iona swirled the straw in her margarita and then placed it in her mouth.

Plump lips sucked on the thin plastic. 'It's a girl's fifteenth birthday party. In the Mexican-American community, that's when her family celebrates her coming of age.'

'And Maricruz's *quinceañera* is this weekend?'

'Yeah, I guess so.' How come they were talking about Maricruz and her party? He jerked his gaze off her lips, which had mesmerized him again. And struggled to get the conversation back where he wanted it. 'So how did Demarest get so friendly with your old man?'

Her smile faltered and then disappeared. 'That's a bit of a non-sequitur.'

'I'm curious.' He forced himself not to care when she stiffened. She owed him. He'd already told her more than he would usually tell a date about his mother's family, but she had a way of questioning him that made him forget to be cautious.

His gaze strayed to the snug bodice of her dress. Not to mention her other distracting qualities. He took a swig of his *cerveza.*

Behave.

'Why don't you want to tell me? Have you got something to hide?' he asked.

'He came into our gift shop,' Iona replied, her face a rigid mask.

'You told me you were the one who worked in the gift shop,' he said, and knew he had her when she flushed. 'Why didn't you tell me about you and Demarest, Iona?' He pressed his advantage, despite the tremble in her fingers as they clutched the stem of her margarita glass.

It was what he was trained to do. And he wanted to know. Suddenly it seemed vitally important to hear the truth from those lush lips.

'Why didn't you tell me about what Demarest did to you?'

She remained rigid in her chair, her eyes glassy with shock.

'Did you think I would judge you?' he added, softening his voice.

A lone tear spilled over her lid, shocking him.

Hell. Had it been worse than he thought?

She brushed the tear away with her fist and stood up.

'You can go right to hell, Montoya,' she whispered, her whole body vibrating with tension.

The show of temper was a relief after the moment of anguish. But his relief was short-lived, when she threw her napkin on the table and rushed off through the crowded tables towards the exit.

'Hey, come back here,' he shouted, making the nearby diners turn and stare at him, but she didn't even slow down.

Tugging his wallet out of his pocket, he threw a wad of bills on the table and headed after her.

Where the hell was she going?

Iona burst out of the restaurant into the night, ignoring the queue of people staring at her and Zane's shouted demand to slow down.

She wanted to throttle him. She would throttle him, if he so much as touched her.

'Madre de Dios.'

She heard the muffled curse only moments before a hard forearm wrapped round her waist, halting her getaway as his lean body butted against her back.

She swung round but he grabbed her bunched fist in his hand, and stopped her from socking him on the jaw.

'Calm down, damn it.'

'No,' she shouted, the word whipping away on the wind as the fury rose up to mask the pain and humiliation.

She'd let her guard down, had started to believe that this might be more than just a pity date. That he'd actually meant what he said about wanting to get to know her better—which only made the humiliation worse. 'Don't touch me,' she said yanking her hand out of his.

The tightening in her breasts, and the slow pulse of arousal in her belly that she had no control over, only added insult to the injury.

'Miss, is everything all right?' The tentative question had both her and Zane turning to stare at the older man who had come to her rescue. 'Is this man bothering you?' he asked, not looking quite so confident about the gallant impulse when Zane glared at him.

'She's great,' Zane ground out, before she could think of what to say. She knew she wasn't in any physical danger from Zane Montoya, but didn't emotional danger count? 'I'm a cop.'

'Okay.' Her Sir Galahad nodded quickly. 'Sorry to bother

you, Officer.' He hurried back to join his wife in the queue—
the impulse to rescue her hastily abandoned.

'You're not a cop,' she snapped as Zane hauled her into the
car park, away from the ocean and out of sight of the other
customers. 'You're a fake cop, remember.'

She kept her voice down. She was perfectly capable of
fighting her own battles. Especially now she'd got a good
head of steam.

'I used to be a cop,' he shot back, sounding as furious as
she felt. 'Now shut the hell up before you cause any more
trouble.'

'Me?'

He'd ambushed her, when she hadn't been prepared for it.
She should have guessed he'd been a cop—he certainly had
one hell of an interrogation technique. He'd let her think she
mattered, that even though this might be a pity date, it had
potential. She'd been flirting with him, the buzz of the margaritas making her bold as they devoured the food and she
lapped up all that focused attention. And then he'd shown his
true colours and ruined it all. And for what? So he could get
information out of her that she hadn't wanted him to know.
That he had no business knowing. The case was over, Brad
was in jail where he belonged—what had been the point of
humiliating her further? Had he wanted to punish her? Who
gave him the right to do that?

'Yeah, you,' he snarled. 'You don't see me trying to punch
anyone, do you?'

She wrestled her arm out of his grip, but as she turned to
face him he backed her against the sand-washed brick of the
restaurant wall.

'You deserved it.' She hurled the words at him, angry that
her shiver of reaction had nothing to do with the chilly sea air
and everything to do with his nearness. She raised her arms
to shove him away but he captured her wrists, held her hands
easily by her side to hold her still.

'Let go of me.'

'Not until you settle down,' he said in that firm, domineering voice that made her feel like a six-year-old.

'How could you do that?' she asked, her voice breaking on the accusation and making blood surge into her cheeks.

'Do what? Ask you about Demarest?' he replied, his face shadowed by the moonlight. 'Because you lied to me last night.'

'So what? I knew this was a pity date. I knew it,' she ranted, determined that he would never know how easily he'd primed her with his let's-get-naked hormones. She yanked her wrists free, wedged her hands against his chest.

'A pity date! What the hell…?'

'Oh, come on, Montoya. I knew you were patronising me. I figured you had an ulterior motive.' How could she have lost sight of that so easily? 'But I never thought you'd stoop that low.' The more she thought about it, the more outraged she became. He'd taken advantage of her inexperience and her vulnerability. Just like Brad. 'Did you learn that in cop school? How to flirt women into a coma, and then go in for the kill?'

'What the hell are you talking about?'

'I'm talking about how you played me.' As if he didn't know. 'All those smouldering looks. All the flirtatious words and clever little touches—as if you wanted me. When we both know all you really wanted was to question me about Brad.'

'Are you nuts?' The rising fury and frustration in his voice made her pause for a moment. 'You think I was faking that?'

'I know you were,' she shot back—not prepared to fall for the soft words and flirtatious tricks all over again. Even if the tone wasn't all that soft now.

He swore under his breath. Then murmured, 'To hell with this.'

Grasping her cheeks in callused palms, he slanted his lips across hers.

Shock came first, the gasp of surprise giving him the access he needed. His tongue delved into her mouth, firm and seeking and hungry. The shudder of arousal bolted down to her core. She squirmed, easing the ache against the hard wall of his chest. Rough palms trailed down, his thumb stroking the pounding pulse in her throat as he framed her face and angled her head, to take more.

The blast of need burned through her system as her tongue tangled with his. And the fast, furious exploration turned to slow, insistent strokes. He tasted delicious, the hot spice of heat and lust and man making her head spin. She reached for him, her fingers fisting in cool linen and feeling the flex of muscle beneath.

He lifted his head at last, his breathing as harsh as hers.

His hips trapped hers, and the ridge in his pants prodded her belly. 'You think that's fake?' His eyes glittered in the streetlight.

She shook her head, unable to speak as her tongue had gone numb.

'I've been sporting that most of the night,' he continued. 'Ever since you licked the salt off the rim of your first margarita.'

Iona blinked, desire unfurling in long ribbons of need.

'It appears I may have misconstrued your motives,' she choked out in a husky whisper.

His eyebrows shot up and then he laughed, the sound amused and arrogantly male. 'Yeah, just a little.' He dropped his forehead to hers, let out an unsteady breath, his thumb tracing the line of her collarbone in an absent caress. 'I shouldn't have made this about him. Because it's not,' he murmured. 'I screwed up and I'm sorry.'

'I accept your apology,' she replied breathlessly, the magnificent erection cradled against her belly.

He stepped back and her eyes darted down to the bulge of their own accord.

Oh, my!

Her tongue wasn't numb any more; it had swollen to twice its normal size—along with a few other parts of her anatomy. 'I stand corrected. That certainly doesn't look like pity,' she murmured.

He let out a strained laugh as he led her to the Mustang and opened the door. 'I better take you home.'

She climbed into the car. Home? He was taking her home? Now?

He climbed into the driver's seat, switched on the engine and crunched the gear shift into reverse.

'Excuse me for asking,' she protested, having found her voice at last as the car trundled down the access road, 'but why are you taking me home?'

He sent her another of those penetrating stares as the sheen of something dark and dangerous lit up those striking blue eyes.

'Because no way in hell are we ending this date in a parking lot.'

CHAPTER FIVE

A PITY DATE!

Zane kept his eyes locked on the road, the headlights slicing through the dusky dark.

'What made you think this was a pity date?' he asked over the rushing wind. Had Iona really been that clueless about how much he wanted her? How was that even possible?

'No particular reason,' she said, but he could hear the lift in her voice that signified she was lying.

'Sure there is.'

She glanced across the console and he slowed the car, so that he could divide his attention between her and the road.

A long-suffering sigh gushed out. She crossed her arms over her waist in a defensive gesture that would have been cute, if it weren't so distracting. 'You called me *cute*.'

'Only because you are.'

'No, I'm not. Babies are cute. Puppies are cute. I'm a grown woman and I'm not cute.'

He smiled. He couldn't help it—the snippy tone only made that do-or-die accent all the cuter.

'Puppies, huh?' he said, not quite able to resist the urge to tease. 'Have you ever owned a puppy?'

She slanted him a quelling look. 'It's not funny, Montoya.'

'I'm guessing that's a no, then,' he continued when she maintained a stony silence. 'Because if you had, you would know that puppies are not cute. I rescued a six-week-old lab cross from the pound a year ago. She ate a six-hundred-dollar pair of shoes, peed in my closet, drank from my john and tried to lick me to death. And that was all in the first day.' He pictured the love of his life, who'd nearly killed him this morning by sticking her wet snout in his ear while he was in the middle of his morning reps on the bench press. 'Not cute at all.'

'You didn't send her back, did you?'

The concerned tone tempted him to tease her some more. He resisted.

'Nah, we came to an understanding. Now she only chews her toys and she knows peeing in the closet is out unless it's on fire.' He looked her way, enchanted by the smile edging her lips. 'We're still working on the other two.'

'What's her name?'

'C.D.'

'You called your dog Compact Disc? What a dreadful name.'

'It's not short for Compact Disc. It's short for Cookie Dough.'

'You're joking.' She giggled, the sound light and so sexy he began to wonder how they'd ended up talking about his dog.

'Hey, it's my favourite flavour,' he said in his defence. 'And C.D.'s kind of the same colour, so it fit.'

'Now it all makes perfect sense,' she replied, the tentative smile turning into something warm and appealing.

Time to change the subject. And get this seduction back on track.

'The point is,' he began, because there had been a point in there somewhere, 'when I called you cute, I wasn't picturing you peeing in my closet or drinking from my john.'

She snorted out another laugh. 'That's a relief.'

He chuckled back, despite the heat now pounding in his abdomen like a nuclear reactor. He swung the Mustang onto her street, pulled into the driveway next to the tiny vacation rental and switched off the transmission. 'But I could probably live with the puppy analogy.' He slung his arm over the back of her seat, touched his knuckle to her cheek and watched her smile falter. 'If you had the sudden urge to lick me to death.'

Her pupils dilated and the freckles on her nose stood out against the flush of colour. He ran his knuckle across the soft skin, hooked a curl behind her ear.

Her tongue flicked out to moisten her bottom lip as those big almond eyes dipped to his mouth.

Cradling her cheek, he leaned across the stick shift and pressed his lips to hers. Determined to keep it slow this time, and easy.

She gasped, a soft sob that filled the air with the sweet scent of margaritas and desire. He swept his tongue across her lips, tempting her to open her mouth—knowing her taste was more intoxicating than that first sip of cherry cola on a sweltering summer day.

'Or I could just lick *you* to death,' he murmured, finally letting go of the pretence that he didn't want to devour her in a few greedy bites. 'Your call?'

Iona dragged herself back from the warm touch of his fingers on her cheek, transfixed by the low murmur of his voice. She sucked in air past the constriction in her throat and got a lungful of his light spicy cologne tempered by the salty sea scent in his hair.

He wanted to lick her to death.

The hot ball of desire plunged, sending ripples of sensation radiating out.

'What do you say, Iona?' The husky tone made the desire ignite. 'It's your choice, no pressure. But I'd like to take this further.'

Yes, please.

The thought shot into her mind and spilled out of her mouth. 'Me too.'

His quick smile made her breath catch. Then he kissed her again. The press of lips hot and firm, the lingering touch of his tongue brief, subtle and not nearly enough. 'Let's take this inside.'

She nodded. But as she stepped out of the car and he clasped her hand and led her to the postage-stamp-size porch her mind began to race through all the things that could go wrong. She fumbled to find her keys as his palm rested on the slope of her back and rubbed.

Zane Montoya was hot and sexy and a bit too overwhelming What if she tensed up? What if, beneath that seductive charm, he was as rough and impatient as Brad?

She rushed ahead of him into the dark interior, heard the door close behind him, the thrum of purpose and possibilities tempered by the shot of panic.

His footsteps followed her into the galley kitchen. She dropped her keys and purse on the table, crossed to the sink and poured herself a glass of water. Her fingers trembled on the tumbler as he wrapped warm hands round her waist and enveloped her in that delicious scent again.

His lips traced the arch of her neck and she tilted her head, instinctively giving him access despite the tangle of nerves.

'You taste great, *querida*.' Hot breath nuzzled her neck as the forceful imprint of his erection pressed into her buttocks. 'As great as cookie-dough ice cream with extra chocolate chips.'

A desperate little laugh came out at the silly compliment, but then his large palms settled on her waist. She stiffened as the heat spread.

He moved his hands to her hips, turned her gently to face him. Lifting the forgotten tumbler out of her numb fingers, he placed it on the countertop.

'Iona, if you've changed your mind, you only have to say so.' The words were tight, a little strained, but there was no edge to them.

She raised her gaze and what she saw made her heart ricochet. The dramatic planes and angles looked even more breathtaking gilded by moonlight.

She shook her head. 'I haven't changed my mind. I'm nervous, I guess.'

He rested his hands on her hips, caressed the cotton. 'Why nervous? Is it too soon? After Demarest?'

She heard the controlled anger in his voice. And realised he thought she'd been a victim. That Demarest had traumatised her. When the truth was a lot more sordid.

'He didn't force me, Zane...' She felt the furious blush set fire to her scalp but soldiered on. 'We only did it a couple of times and then he got bored with me.' She stuck her chin out, made her gaze meet his. She had to stop feeling ashamed about this. 'Turns out, I'm not a natural at this.' She coughed, reached for her glass and took a quick sip to swallow down the frog that had lodged in her larynx.

'Not a natural at what? Sex?'

He sounded so incredulous, she got a little peeved. Was it really so hard for him to understand? Surely she wasn't the only woman he'd ever met who wasn't that into sex? But then she thought of the giddy rush that she'd been struggling to suppress most of the night—and realised she probably was.

'Yes...I get tense and flustered and I can't relax and then the moment's gone.'

His forehead creased. And the arousal fizzled and died.

Terrific, Iona, that was way too much information. Why not kill the mood completely?

'And Demarest made you think that was your fault?' he asked in a stiff voice.

She hitched her shoulder in a non-committal shrug, determined not to be defensive. Not every woman could be multi-orgasmic. 'Possibly,' she said, the hairs on the back of her neck stinging with humiliation.

'And you believed him, why exactly?'

'Because I don't exactly have a lot of other testimonials,' she blurted out, getting more peeved by the second.

'What are you saying—that he was your first?' He sounded incredulous again.

'Maybe.' She looked down at the floor, her humiliation complete. 'That's not to say I haven't had boyfriends. I've had lots of boyfriends.' *Two.* 'But it never... It never quite... There isn't a big array of possible... Kelross Glen is a small place and...' She trailed off.

Great, now he knew just how pathetic she was.

Warm hands still on her hips, he tugged her close, nudged her hair with his lips. 'That really sucks.'

'Don't I know it.'

He tucked a finger under her chin, lifted her face. 'So I'm assuming you've never had an orgasm while making love?' The question was asked in a gentle coaxing voice that belied the intensity in his gaze.

She bit into her lip. Good Lord, how had they ended up talking about this? 'I'm really not comfortable discuss—'

'I figured as much.'

'I never said—'

'Shh...' He touched his thumb to her lips. 'No more talking, Iona. You talk too much anyway.'

Indignation flared. 'Now wait a—'

His lips covered hers, silencing the protest, and the need raged back to life, the dance of lips and tongue so erotic she could scream as he held her head and explored in slow, deliberate strokes.

He eased back and clasped his hands round her waist. He hauled her up as if she weighed nothing and deposited her on the countertop. Her bottom landed on the cold formica.

She clung on to his shoulders for balance, felt the bunch of muscle and opened her mouth to say something. Anything. But nothing came out as hot palms edged up her thighs under the dress, shocking her into silence.

'You know what we're going to do now, Iona,' he said
slowly, his fingers drawing tantalising circles on her naked
thighs.

She shook her head, having lost the power of speech for the
second time in one night, which had to be a record.

'We're going to forget about him, undo all the bad stuff he
did—and make this your first time.'

Something tight banded around her heart. 'I'm not sure
that's entirely necessary—'

'It isn't hard to bring a woman to orgasm,' he interrupted.
'Not if you pay attention and take the time and trouble to do
it right. If he didn't do that, it was his fault not yours.'

The blush crept up her throat. She'd known that, of course
she had. She'd known as soon as she'd lost her virginity to
him and he'd laughed at her inexperience that Brad was a selfish lover as well as a nasty man, but she'd been so desperate
to believe his lies she'd allowed herself to bury her growing
dislike of him. And that had been her fault, not his. Even if
he had been a liar and a thief.

Wiggling out of Zane's hands, she jumped down from the
countertop. Maybe if the cracked linoleum could swallow her
whole, she could get out of this situation without making it
any worse. She grasped her glass from the countertop, took
a fortifying gulp and kept her back to Zane.

'Do you mind if we take a rain check?' *At least until the
turn of the next millennium.* 'I'm not really in the mood any
more.'

Instead of his taking the hint all she heard was a low
chuckle. And then his thumb cruised under her hairline. 'You
really want to give him all the power? Even now?'

She swung round, dislodging his thumb—which unfortunately did nothing to dispel the sizzle of sensation. 'This has
nothing to do with him.'

'Uh-huh.' A sceptical eyebrow rose up his forehead. 'Then
why don't you prove it?'

'And how exactly do you propose I do that?'

He braced his hands on the countertop, caging her in, and making her breathing accelerate. 'It's real simple, Iona. Stop blaming yourself—and get back on the horse.'

'You're not serious?' She propped her forearms against his chest, wanting to be outraged at the offer—but the surge of sensation as his hands came around her waist and he nudged her closer made it kind of hard to muster the required indignation.

'Try me.' The smile in his bright sapphire eyes twinkled with mischief.

'What? So you're offering your services, now.' She paused for effect. 'As my personal stallion?'

Instead of his looking affronted or even abashed, the smile only got naughtier—the slow twist of his lips as disarming as it was amused. 'Stallion might be overselling myself a bit. But, hey, I can go with that analogy if you want. I'm not as picky as you.'

A laugh choked out without warning as her eyes dipped to his pants and she spotted something that made her think stallion would not be overselling him one bit. 'You're incorrigible.'

'Well, hell, Iona.' He edged closer, his hands firm on her hips, the impressive erection nudging her belly as he smiled. 'That's the nicest thing you've ever said to me.'

The full-bodied laugh bubbled out, breaking the tension. She didn't know how he'd done it, but she didn't feel self-conscious any more, or guilty. She felt relaxed and sexy, desire pumping through her like a heady drug.

'Here's the way it plays for me,' he said, angling his head to nibble kisses under her chin. 'We take it slow. And we focus on pleasure. Your pleasure.' He lapped her collarbone with his tongue. 'No conditions. And no talking allowed.'

'Why no talking?' she asked, trying not to let her mind

snag on the rough cadence of the word *pleasure*. And the riotous sensations shivering up her neck.

'Because you talk too much.'

'You are so cheeky.'

'Guilty as charged.' He chuckled, his fingers edging under the strap of her dress to send sensation skittering across her shoulder blade. 'So no talking, except to tell me what you like and what you don't like.'

'Considering there are supposed to be no conditions,' she teased, 'there seems to be an awful lot of them.'

He hoisted her into his arms. 'Put your legs round my waist,' he demanded, strong hands gripping her bottom.

'See, there's another one!' she said, clasping her arms round his shoulders as her legs hooked his waist.

'Stop being so damn literal,' he said on a rueful laugh as he carried her into the shoebox-sized bedroom.

'And yet another condition, already,' she said, amusement loosening the flood of heat.

'Enough, woman,' he announced, surprising a laugh out of her as he dumped her on the bed. 'I forgot this bedroom's smaller than my closet,' he added, glancing round the room. 'Next time we do this at my place.'

The offhand mention of a next time had warmth wrapping around her chest, followed by the pinch of regret. There wouldn't be a next time. This was strictly a one-night fling. She wasn't going to make the mistake of thinking this meant more than it did. She wasn't that needy, insecure girl any more.

He stripped off his shirt, kicked off his shoes and climbed onto the bed beside her. Her vision blurred, dazed by the glorious display of muscles and sinews and bronzed skin in the moonlight. He looked magnificent, the masculine perfection of his chest almost as arresting as that incredible face. She placed her open hand on his sternum, explored the dark nipples nestled in the sprinkle of hair, and then let it drift down to the ridges of his six-pack.

He quivered beneath her palm and his hand covered hers, halting the descent. Her gaze rose, and she marvelled at the cleft in his chin defined by the hint of stubble, the dramatic slash of his cheekbones—the dark intensity of those sapphire eyes.

Thank you, God.

She whispered the silent prayer in her head as her heartbeat sped up to dizzying speeds. If one night was all she could risk with this man, she intended to make the most of it.

'I'm feeling kind of underdressed here,' he murmured.

She laughed at the wry note as his hand skimmed over her shoulder. He propped himself up to lean over her and she heard the sibilant crackle of the zip releasing. The bodice of the dress drooped and he nudged down the straps, revealing the pink lace of her bra.

'Cute,' he murmured, amused, and she huffed out another chuckle. She certainly didn't feel like a puppy dog any more.

'I thought I told you not to call me that.'

He tumbled her back onto the bed, straddling her before his hands swept down her body peeling the dress down to her waist. 'And I thought I told you not to talk.'

She wriggled but he held her still, hoisting her arms above her head, then pinned her wrists to the bed in one hand as he bent to press his lips to her collarbone. The trail of kisses dipped to her breasts, and he teased the edge of her bra cup with the rough stroke of his tongue. Her cleavage heaved against the confining lace, her body bucking against his hold.

'You like that, huh,' he said, gruff and amused.

It didn't sound like a question, but she answered anyway. 'I'm not allowed to talk.'

The wicked grin had the fire igniting. 'Now she remembers.'

He released her arms, but as soon as she dropped them

sure, steady fingers slipped the bra straps off her shoulders, and her breasts spilled out. She moaned as he cupped the heavy flesh, flicked his thumb across the beaded nipple. He grappled quickly with the hook, stripped away the pink lace and moulded both breasts in his palms, then bent forward to take one straining nipple into his mouth.

She groaned, the sound deep and primal, as his lips suckled and the melting sensation became a hot, hard yank of need.

She arched into his mouth, her fingers clutching the bedspread, the riot of sensation new and overwhelming. How could so little make her feel so much?

He lifted his head, blew on the wet nipple, watching intently as it puckered even more. 'Good?'

'Hmm,' she rasped, her throat dry.

His gaze stayed transfixed on her naked breasts. 'They're gorgeous,' he said, and warmth flooded through her. 'Especially when they're begging for attention like that.'

Then the exquisite torture continued.

He licked at the areola, nipped and teased the tender tip, sending a new shockwave of need hurtling down to her core. Desire built as he feasted on first one breast then the other, the blinding pleasure warring with a foolish wave of gratitude. She felt powerful, important, irresistible, the need flooding between her thighs and making her sex ache. She curled her fingers into the short hair at the sides of his head, pulled his face up. The harsh look of arousal only made her more grateful. 'That feels so good,' she said. 'Thank you.'

Lifting up, he took her chin in his fingers. The kiss was hard, fast and demanding. 'You're welcome, Iona. Now stop distracting me.'

She laughed, delighted with the strain in his voice. Then gasped as he turned his attention back to her breasts while knowing fingers slid up under her dress, the heel of his hand pressing against the mound of her sex.

She launched off the bed, the sudden contact shocking as he cupped her through the silk of her panties.

'Easy, *preciosa*,' he murmured, his thumb brushing against the tight bundle of nerves at her centre in deliberate circles.

She writhed, seeking the exquisite touch and yet scared of the force of her need.

She gripped his forearm. 'Please…that's…too—' The words choked off on a sob as his fingers dipped beneath the gusset and found the hot wet heart of her.

Pleasure gripped like a silken fist, and her body bowed as his fingers played.

'There?' he asked as his sure, steady touch triggered a sharp, painfully exquisite sensation.

She nodded, cried out as he rubbed, circled, stroked her clitoris. Pleasure rippled and zapped across her skin in a billion sparkles of light—and then pulled hard. She sobbed, teetering on the high ledge for one tantalising second and then cried out—the cascade hurtling her over.

'Oh. My. Goodness.' Iona panted as she drifted back to full consciousness. Gradually she became aware of the cramp in her fingers as they dug into the sinews of his forearm, and the large, rough hand trapped down her knickers.

She released his arm instantly, worried she might have left bruises, and clamped her knees together as quickly and discreetly as possible.

He eased his hand out of her knickers, and grinned down at her as she shivered, still a little shocky from the strength of her climax.

Good Lord, the man has magic fingers.

'What did I tell you? Not hard if you pay attention.'

The smug, almost boyish look of satisfaction on that too-handsome face had her coughing out a laugh.

'That was…' *Awesome.* The word echoed in her head, but she stopped herself from saying it—and fought the sting of tears. This was only sex, she shouldn't make too much of it. 'Thank you,' she managed at last, not sure what else to say.

His grin widened and he placed a possessive kiss on her nose. '*Querida,* the pleasure was all mine.' He let his hand settle on her stomach, and she felt the outline of his erection against her hip. 'You look real cute when you come.'

She gave him a playful slap on the arm. 'Stop it.'

'And so damn sexy, I almost came myself.' He kissed her, the smile on his mouth as potent as the soft, sure touch of his lips.

She shifted as he raised his head, and, feeling bold, caressed the hard shaft through his trousers.

He tensed, let out a strained laugh. But when she reached for the zip to release him, he covered her hand, and stopped her. 'Don't…' He touched his forehead to hers. 'We can't take this any further.'

'Oh, okay.' She tugged her hand out from under his, the sudden sense of failure so intense it hurt. 'I'm sorry.'

'Why are you sorry?' He slipped a knuckle under her chin. 'I'm hoping like hell we can still take a rain check.'

She shook off his hold, gathered her dress to cover her breasts and sat up. 'All right,' she said dully, knowing a charity case when she saw one.

'Damn it…' He gripped her shoulders, dragged her round to face him, the spark of anger confusing her. 'I don't have any protection with me,' he said, his voice hoarse with exasperation.

'That's the reason you wanted to stop?' she asked, the fury in his eyes more exalting than the feel of his rigid flesh moments before.

'Damn straight it is. If I had a condom with me, I'd be inside you right this second.' He cursed viciously. 'I want you so badly I'm in agony here, and trying real hard to be smart about this, so don't you dare look at me as if—'

'There are condoms here,' she cut in, deciding to intervene

before he got any madder. While the sound of his frustration was boosting her fragile ego into the stratosphere—she didn't want him to explode before they got to the main event. 'In the bathroom. I saw them yesterday.' She bounced off the bed, buoyant with pleasure that the moment of rejection was nothing more than a stupid misunderstanding. 'I'll go get them, shall I? Put you out of your agony,' she finished unable to resist the urge to tease him.

'No, wait.' He grasped her arm, drew her back. He wrapped his arms around her waist, buried his face in her hair. The deep breath he blew out brushed against her nape and sent awareness skittering down to her toes. 'I shouldn't have lost my temper,' he said, sounding serious. 'I apologise.'

'If you think that's losing your temper, you ought to meet a Scotsman.'

'Yeah?' He gave a rough chuckle, as she'd hoped he would. 'It's just you've got me so…' He sighed, the hesitation so endearing, and so unlike him, her heart pounded heavily. He let go of her waist, rubbed his open palms down her upper arms. 'I'll get the condoms.'

'But you don't know where they are,' she said, chewing on her lip to stop the smile as he climbed off the bed. Affection bloomed alongside her lust. She didn't know why it felt so good to see that super-confident mask of his slip. But it did.

He glanced over his shoulder on his way to the door. 'I shouldn't have too much trouble.' He winked. 'I'm a trained detective. Detecting stuff is my profession,' he said as he left the room.

She collapsed onto the bed, her hands still clasping her dress, and took in a shuddering breath.

His head popped around the doorframe, making her jolt upright. 'But while I'm gone, lose the dress and panties.'

She gasped at the audacious command as excitement and anticipation soared. 'Well, really!'

'Well, really,' he purred in a surprisingly good imitation of

her Scottish accent. The roguish smile came back full force.
'I want you ready for round two when I get back, lady.'

She scrambled out of her clothes as his bare feet padded
down the corridor, and shouted after him, 'Conditions! Conditions!'

CHAPTER SIX

NOT COOL, MAN. Not cool at all.

Zane glared at the cracked bathroom mirror, taking in the dull colour on his cheeks, and the crater-like furrows on his brow.

He'd almost lost it, again.

He released his death grip on the sink and glanced at the pounding erection confined in his pants, which had been so hard for so long it was starting to hurt. And had his answer.

He adjusted his pants to ease the ache. Something about Iona had really got to him.

Her honesty, her openness and the ease with which he could read every single expression on her face, made her more vulnerable than any other woman he'd ever seduced. And when you added what she'd revealed about her run-in with Demarest, he felt responsible for her in a way he never had before in a relationship. The guy had taken her virginity and given her nothing in return. Less than nothing.

But instead of her inexperience putting him off, which by rights it should have, it only made her live-wire response to the simplest of caresses seem that much more irresistible— bringing out the hunger he'd thought he'd satisfied years ago.

Tonight, he'd been less in control of himself than he'd been since he was a teenager, banging pretty much anyone who offered, and as a result he'd almost blown the stringent rules he'd imposed on his sexual appetite ever since.

When she'd come apart in his arms, the soft sobs of her surrender spurring his own arousal to fever pitch, and then held him through his pants, her face flushed with arousal, for one brief agonizing moment he'd almost snapped, consumed by the need to thrust deep inside her.

Thank God that burning need had only lasted a split second, and he'd come to his senses in time. But it had still been deeply disturbing. His control had almost shattered—giving him a connection he didn't want to contemplate to the man who had fathered him.

How could he be entirely free of that legacy, and even for a second have considered taking a woman without due care and attention? Without even the proper protection? Simply to satisfy his own lust?

He took two deep breaths, let them out as steadily as he could.

Don't overreact.

He rolled his shoulders, pulled on the mirror to check the bathroom cabinet and spotted the box of condoms, still wrapped in cellophane, on the top shelf.

His breathing slowed as the insistent ache subsided a little.

The thing to remember was, he hadn't snapped—he'd held it together. And he'd apologised to Iona. From her sweet, funny reaction it was clear she hadn't had a clue how close he'd come to losing it. Which was great, because now he had the chance to make it up to her—to finish what they'd started and do it right. The way he'd promised her he would.

He lifted the box off the shelf, ripped the seal.

Only three! Who the hell buys condoms in boxes of three? That's not even enough for...

He clamped down on the thought, let out another calming breath.

Hold it together.

Three was good. Three was enough. Three was more than

enough for them to take the edge off their hunger and have a good time, before they went their separate ways.

He closed the cabinet, dumped the box in the trash and stuffed the condoms in his back pocket before splashing some water on his face, determined to be grateful for the three condoms if it killed him.

But as he walked into Iona's bedroom, and she smiled at him, the sheet stretched across her breasts, her dress and panties by her bra on the floor and her face flushed with anticipation, the hunger coiled hard, taunting him.

'Did you find them?' she asked, the eagerness in her voice making the erection pound.

He slung the condoms on the bed. 'I told you, I'm a trained detective.'

He eased the zip down on his pants and her gaze followed the movement. He shoved his pants and boxers off, and her upper lip curled into her full bottom lip, her gaze now riveted to his groin.

'That's impressive,' she whispered, the Scottish burr low with fascination.

He tore open the first foil package as his erection hit critical mass—and admitted there was no freaking way three condoms was ever going to be enough.

Goodness.

Iona studied the long thick erection jutting out proudly from the dark hair at Zane's groin as he rolled on the condom with practised efficiency. Heat swelled in her abdomen, her heartbeat ricocheted into her throat and her breathing sped up.

She let her gaze drift back up his body, past the ropes of muscle that defined the V above his hip bones and up the thin trail of hair that bisected the flat ridges of his six-pack and then bloomed around his pecs.

She reached his face at last, her heart pounding so hard now it was practically choking her. 'You're gorgeous all over.'

He laughed but it sounded strained as he lifted the sheet and tugged it off. She lay still, the heavy beat of her heart plunging into her sex. Her skin tingled and tightened as his gaze roamed in return.

Just when she thought she couldn't stand the intense scrutiny a moment longer, his eyes finally lifted to her face. 'Not as gorgeous as you.'

Climbing onto the bed, he settled beside her, his flesh hot where it touched her thigh as he swept his hand over her in a tender caress, following the curve of her body to her breasts. He stroked the underside, then rolled the engorged tip between his thumb and forefinger. He bent to flick his tongue across the swollen peak and she jolted in his arms.

'Sweet,' he muttered, then suckled hard.

The choked sob of pleasure was almost animalistic as the prickle of need arrowed down. He took one breast then the other into his mouth, gorging himself on her and making the heat and pleasure race across her skin and tug hard in her sex.

'You're so responsive, you're killing me,' he rasped in her ear as he grasped her leg, lifted it over his hip and brought her sex into sudden contact with the large head of his erection. 'I'm not sure I can wait much longer.'

She gripped his shoulders, clinging on to sanity, and arched into him. 'Don't wait.'

He muttered something in Spanish, then grasped both her thighs and rolled, holding her open, until he was poised above her. Then he sank into her in one long, slow, all-consuming thrust.

She tensed at the shock of penetration, her body shuddering as she struggled to adjust to the invasion.

'Shh,' he soothed, his voice tense with the effort to hold still. 'Just breathe—it'll take a moment. You're so tight.'

Then his thumb traced across her hip and found the place where their bodies joined. She bucked beneath him, cried out as he touched the sensitive nub. Then he started to rock inside her, pulling out, thrusting back, gradually at first, and so gently. Then faster. And harder.

The full-stretched feeling gathered and intensified, the incendiary stroke of his thumb radiating outwards and shooting like lightning through her body. She moved with him, instinctively angling her hips to take him deeper, racing towards that glorious oblivion that beckoned just out of reach.

The brutal orgasm hit in a bright, beautiful, never-ending wave, crashing over her and then rising up to crest again. She heard her thin cry of desperate pleasure matching his harsh grunt of release as the wave crashed through that final barrier, hurtling them over together.

Iona couldn't seem to keep her eyelids from drooping to half-mast as he tucked her under his arm and gathered her close. She settled her head on his shoulder, breathing in the spicy scent of his skin and the clean musk of fresh sweat—the slight soreness between her thighs nothing compared to the slumberous afterglow of spectacular sex and the sweet, serene feeling of achievement.

He brushed a strand of hair off her forehead and smiled. 'Good?'

She smiled back. 'Very.' And ignored the rush of tenderness as her heartbeat evened out and her eyelids grew heavy.

'Get some sleep, *querida*.' His lips brushed against the top of her hair. 'We're not finished yet.'

'We're not?' she asked, around a huge yawn, trying to keep a lid on the rush of excitement, and the swell of longing.

'Of course not. We've got two condoms left.'

She huffed out a laugh, and snuggled against him as she drifted into sleep—refusing to regret the fact that once they'd used those two condoms and the night was over, he would be gone.

CHAPTER SEVEN

IONA BLINKED AT the business card perched on her nightstand. Sitting up in the empty bed, she picked up the card and flicked it over, to find a note scribbled in black ink.

Hey Sleepyhead,
I had to go let C.D. out before she starts figuring my closet is on fire!
Call me.
Zane
PS. You look real cute when you're sleeping—even when you snore.

'I do not snore,' she whispered, sputtering out a half laugh. She rubbed her thumb across the embossed writing on the front of the card and felt the lump lodged in her throat sink to the pit of her stomach and land like a lead weight. She stared at Zane's name and his contact details framed next to the geometric drawing of an office building—which was probably his firm's headquarters in Carmel—and then concentrated on the 'call me' scribbled in his looping scrawl on the back.

She set the card on the nightstand. Their fling had been amazing, but now it was over and mooning over him, or thinking they could take this any further, would be silly.

She needed to find gainful employment and a cheap place

to stay—not get mixed up with a sex god like Zane Montoya. The man was way too distracting.

Getting out of bed, she stretched, feeling all the little aches and pains and tender spots Zane had left behind to remember him by.

He'd woken her twice during the night, both times bringing her expertly to orgasm before finding his own release. He'd located and exploited every erogenous zone she had, with the focused, thorough precision of a man who knew his way around every inch of a woman's body.

But each time she'd reached for him, eager to explore his magnificent body and exploit his limits in return, he'd distracted her, by swirling his tongue or stroking his finger across some super-sensitive part of her anatomy, or simply insisting that he'd never last if he let her have her way with him. And while that might very well have been true—she certainly hoped so—the last time she'd collapsed into his arms, dawn peeking through the pretty gingham curtains, she'd fallen into an exhausted sleep feeling sated and sexy—and the tiniest bit disappointed.

She examined her face in the bathroom mirror, the reddened patch of whisker burn under her chin and the sleepy afterglow still making her eyes shine.

Get away with you, woman.

How typically Celtic of her, somehow managing to find fault with the most stupendous sex she'd ever had.

She should be thanking the man, and rejoicing in the generosity of his lovemaking, not criticising him for his perfection. If it hadn't been for Zane she would have continued to believe that her experience with Brad was as good as it got.

Reaching into the shower cubicle, she turned on the tap full blast, set the temperature a notch below scalding and stepped under the stream.

And anyway, she was never going to see Zane again, so none of this mattered… She'd made a promise to him, and herself, to be out of the cottage today and the quicker she packed her stuff and got going, the better.

But as she shampooed her hair and soaped the scent of Zane Montoya, Latino-Lover Extraordinaire, off her skin she knew in a tiny part of her heart what he had done to her, and for her, all through the night, would always matter—even if she hadn't been able to do the same thing for him.

By mid-afternoon she'd showered, made herself a hearty meal—most of which she hadn't eaten—laundered the bed linen, scrubbed out the kitchen and phoned her father to tell him she was great and everything was going brilliantly. At least that wasn't as much of a lie now as it had been in the last few weeks.

And now she was ready to move on. Almost.

She flipped Zane's card over in her fingers. And stared at the phone. Should she call him? To say goodbye, and thanks? It seemed like the polite thing to do.

The heavy weight that she'd been busy ignoring all day rose up her throat. She placed the card by the phone, pulled the sketch she'd made of the hummingbird the morning before out of her rucksack and scribbled a note on the back in pencil. She then counted out twenty dollars from her purse and placed it with the sketch beside his card, her fingers trembling.

She stared at the meagre offerings, and knew she was taking the coward's way out, but she simply couldn't afford the luxury of a goodbye. It was always better to be self-sufficient. The blockage in her throat already felt suspiciously like an emotional involvement that had snuck up on her when she wasn't looking—and she mustn't pander to it.

Zane wasn't responsible for her, she was responsible for herself—and while last night had been wonderful, it wasn't only the sex that had been spectacular. The feeling of safety and security as she'd fallen asleep in his arms had been even more seductive, but she couldn't afford to count on it, or him.

Hefting the rucksack onto her shoulders, she turned to leave, when the loud rap on the door startled her.

Zane. Bugger.

She debated pretending she'd already left, but decided that was too cowardly, even for her. She dropped the rucksack, and opened the door.

Her heart thundered as she stared at the man leaning casually against the doorframe, wearing dark trousers, a pristine white shirt and a seductive smile she knew only too well. The lead weight in her throat expanded alarmingly.

'You didn't call,' he said.

'I know. I didn't have time.'

'Yeah?' He pushed away from the frame, his eyes fixed on her face for several potent seconds, before his attention strayed to the rucksack—and the sketch and money she'd left by the phone. He brushed past her, the spicy scent she remembered doing strange things to her insides.

'What's this?' he asked, picking up the sketch and then flipping it over.

She closed the door—and realised her clean getaway was history.

After reading the note, he glanced at her rucksack and the small pile of crumpled bills again. Then the narrowed gaze returned to her.

'Thanks for the picture—it's really cool,' he said, the tone measured, but she could see the muscle twitching in his jaw. 'But you're gonna have to explain the rest.' He held up her note. 'Were you about to run out on me?'

Shame mixed with the hormones raging in her belly, making her voice come out on a husky whisper. 'I told you I was leaving today. I didn't think you really wanted me to call you.'

His brow shot up, the muscle clenching tight. 'After what we did last night? What kind of jerk do you think I am?'

She flinched at the show of temper, but worse was the shadow in his eyes. Had she hurt his feelings somehow? She hadn't intended to, hadn't even thought she could. But the truth was, she hadn't even considered his feelings.

'I'm sorry, I didn't think…' She stared at her toes.

'Damn it, Iona.' The words came out on a soft sigh, the anger gone. 'Just because one guy's a deadbeat,' he said, 'it doesn't mean we all are.'

She nodded, feeling about two inches tall.

He cradled her cheek in one rough palm and her thoughts scattered.

'Where were you planning to run to?' he murmured as his hand tugged through her hair and brushed the curls behind her ear.

She shrugged, trying to gather the will to pull away from his touch—and that piercing blue gaze. 'I figured Monterey? I need to find a cheap place to live and a job.'

'Accommodation in Monterey's not cheap. And why would you go looking for a new place to stay, when I told you that you can stay here for free?'

'But that was before…' The blush crept up her neck as his hand trailed down and settled on her collarbone.

'Before what?'

She pushed out a breath. The yearning to stay and take him up on his offer was so intense it was almost painful. But with the intense yearning came the kick of panic. She shouldn't want this, and certainly not this much. They weren't a couple, they weren't even an item, they were a one-night fling and wanting it to be more than that was dangerous—because it implied an intimacy that went way beyond sex. 'Before last night.'

His hand dropped to his side. 'You figure because we slept together, you can't stay here? Why not? One thing hasn't got a damn thing to do with the other.'

'It wouldn't feel right.' She felt her own temper kicking in. Why was he making this so hard? 'It would feel like I was taking advantage of you.'

'You…? You're kidding, right?' The incredulity was bad enough but the rough chuckle that followed had her glaring at him.

'What's so funny?'

'You are, Iona. How would staying here be taking advantage of me? This place isn't even mine—it belongs to a friend of mine.'

'Then I'd be taking advantage of your friend, wouldn't I?' It all seemed perfectly obvious to her. Why was he being so obtuse?

'Settle down.' He grasped her wrist, drew her back towards him. 'The guy owns half of central California, so you staying here rent-free for a few weeks isn't going to bankrupt him.' He rested his hands on her hips, the confident, sexy smile firmly back in place—and having a predictable effect on her hormones. 'And you didn't sleep with him, you slept with me, so it's kind of beside the point.'

She pulled out of his arms. 'I fail to see why you—'

'Iona, I want you to stay here,' he interrupted, the determination in his voice neatly cutting off her tirade.

'Why?' she asked, wrapping her arms round her waist as her belly churned with a confusing mix of need and panic. They were strangers, despite what they'd shared last night—couldn't he see that?

'Because it's important to me.'

'Why?'

Her arms tightened, the churning getting worse. How could she be terrified that he was going to say she mattered to him—and equally terrified that she might not?

Zane saw the puzzled arousal and confusion in her caramel eyes and felt the answering pulse of heat, but steeled himself against the urge to scoop her up, carry her down the shack's corridor to her bedroom and show her just how important it was to have her nearby.

He wasn't here for sex. Or not only for sex.

She was probably dealing now with the same misgivings he'd wrestled with all day. When he'd wanted to call, but convinced himself it would be better to let her make the next move. But after a long torturous morning of waiting for the phone to ring, he'd had enough of waiting. Although he still couldn't quite believe she'd been about to skip out on him.

Seeing her backpack by her feet, and the guilty flush on her cheeks had been more than enough to have his temper straining, but it had taken a Herculean effort of will not to start yelling when he'd read the note she'd written on the back of her drawing:

Zane,
Please accept this sketch as a small thank you for all your help. The money is to pay for the groceries and the phone call I made to my dad in Scotland. I hope it's enough?
All the best, Iona

Not one mention of last night. He'd had her sobbing out her release in his arms less than eight hours ago and now he didn't get a decent goodbye?

Cool it, don't get too worked up.

He didn't want to spook her. Or give her the idea this was more than it was. So he needed to be careful.

He lifted both palms up, and kept the nonchalant smile in place. 'Because I need to know you're safe. I used to be a cop, remember.'

'That's the only reason?' Her cheeks turned a charming shade of magenta and he felt the answering spike of lust. Damn, he'd forgotten how much that easy blush turned him on.

'Yeah, what else?' he said, more than happy to oblige if she suggested she wanted a little more than that.

It occurred to him in that moment that this would be the perfect opportunity to give Iona The Speech.

The one about how he wasn't a good bet for the long haul, how he wasn't looking for anything too heavy, but how he really liked her in the here and now. He'd given The Speech to every woman he'd ever dated since leaving high school, usually long before they slept together, so it was already overdue.

But as he waited for her reply The Speech sat on the tip of his tongue like a bad taste—and he realised he didn't want to give it to her.

Not that he wanted anything heavy with her. He didn't. Exposing yourself to that kind of commitment simply wasn't in his make-up. He enjoyed the chase way too much, the challenges and the flirting and the non-stop sex that came at the beginning of a relationship—and the cooling-off period afterwards, when he had discovered all of a woman's secrets and she started nagging him to return the favour, a whole lot less.

He'd had some sticky moments in his twenties, when he'd been less aware of who he was and what he wanted, and he'd made the mistake of lingering too long. But since then he'd become an expert in reading the signs, getting his timing right and letting the women he dated down gently before they got the wrong idea.

But then Iona had thrown his usual dating routine totally out of whack right from the start and not one single thing had gone according to plan since. When was the last time he'd slept with a woman on a first date, or effectively been a woman's first lover? Because he wasn't counting what had happened with that deadbeat Demarest.

And then there was yesterday night. When was the last time he'd had to stop a woman touching him, simply so that he could keep a lid on his own desire? Not since he was a teenager.

But last night, he'd had to practically tie her down to stop her from tipping him over the edge.

She'd confused things again today, by not calling—leaving the need for her burning hot and hard, and forcing his hand. And now, for the first time ever, The Speech felt kind of redundant.

With all the whys and why nots and what the hells fogging up his mind as he waited, he didn't hear her muffled reply.

'What was that?'

She lifted her head and stared straight at him. 'I think you're right, Zane.'

'About what?'

'That it's better if we don't sleep together again.'

'Huh?' *When did I say that?*

He stared at her, dumbfounded, The Speech forgotten.

'I had fun last night,' she continued in the same steady serious voice. 'You were...' her blush brightened '...completely amazing.'

'Thanks,' he said flatly, more irritated than flattered. He'd been praised before for his skills in the sack, and it had always given him a nice little ego-boost, but it didn't feel like much of an achievement now. Did she think she owed him something, because the man who'd taken her virginity had been such a selfish jerk?

'But I don't want to complicate things,' she continued as he tried to concentrate on what she was saying and not the low level irritation grinding in his gut. 'Especially if I'm going to stay here.'

Okay, that did it.

'Sex doesn't have to be complicated,' he said. 'Not if we keep things casual.'

'But it doesn't feel casual, if you feel responsible for me.'

'Iona, it feels casual to me.' Or it would, once he'd made certain she was safe.

'Are you sure?'

'Sure I'm sure. Look, why don't you unpack, get settled,

check out the job situation in Monterey and then give me a call in a couple of days when you're ready?'

The suggestion tasted like ash on his tongue. He didn't want to leave—or stay away until she was ready to call him. But he needed to get this fling back on track. And this was exactly how he would have played things in the past.

'I'd like to see you again,' he continued. 'And I've got the weekend free.' His first in months, he thought, looking forward to the chance to see her again already. 'But it's your call, okay?'

Iona was right; last night had been spectacular—but neither one of them wanted this to be anything other than casual. Which meant he needed to back off, and get over the urge to take her to bed right this second. This had to be her choice. Not his.

'Okay, that would be lovely,' she said, the smile in her eyes turning the caramel to a rich chocolate. 'And you're sure it's okay with your friend for me to stay?'

He sent her a long-suffering look.

'All right, great. And thanks.' She gave a little sigh of relief, the movement making her breasts move under her T-shirt.

The desire to cup the ripe flesh in his palms and tease the nipples into tight buds with his teeth was so acute he could taste her. He forced his gaze back to her face and watched the lids on her sultry golden eyes go heavy with the same longing.

'Good luck with your job hunt,' he murmured. 'But don't forget to call me this time.'

Three days, Montoya. You can last till Saturday. Then she can call you, and there won't be any more confusion about just how casual this is.

He picked up her sketch, but left the crumpled bills beside the phone as he crossed to the door.

'But what about what I owe you?' she asked as he opened the door.

'We can settle up once you've got a job.' Or more like when hell froze over, but that was an argument for another day.

'Okay, if you're sure.'

'I am.' Cradling her cheek, he gave her a light teasing kiss, but forced himself to pull back when her lips parted, inviting him in.

Not yet, but soon.

He brushed his thumb across her chin, enjoying the look of stunned passion. 'I'll see you Saturday.'

Her lips curved, the smile quick and spontaneous.

'I'll be looking forward to it,' she said, the burr of her accent smoky with need.

Not as much as I will be, querida.

CHAPTER EIGHT

'ZANE, YOU'RE HERE.'

Zane's gut tightened as he lifted Iona's fingers to his lips and buzzed a kiss across her knuckles. 'I thought we had a date.'

Colour flared in her cheeks and he grinned.

'Oh, yes, now I remember,' she said, the coy words somewhat contradicted by the dancing light in her eyes.

What the heck had possessed him to suggest they go for a drive? After three torturous days of waiting to have her again?

'I'll get my coat,' she said.

He watched her collect the denim jacket. She'd added gloss to her mouth, and there was something dark and sultry smudged around her eyes. Beaded sandals, a vivid pink scarf tied round her shoulder-length hair and a thin gold ankle chain completed the outfit. She looked chic and sexy and cute enough to eat.

But it wasn't until they'd climbed into the car, and he got a lungful of her scent, that the hunger really started to eat at him.

'So where do you want to go?' He laid his arm across the back of her seat, and played with the curl that had escaped from her scarf.

'You decide? I'm easy.'

He laughed. 'I certainly hope so. I've been in agony for the last three days.'

She giggled; the light flirtatious sound had the heat twisting and turning. 'Haven't you ever heard of deferred gratification?'

'I've heard of it,' he said as he backed out of the drive. 'I've discovered I'm not real wild about it.'

Her smoky laugh drifted on the wind but when he stopped the car to lean across the console, ready to suggest they give in to instant gratification—and leave the drive till later—his cell phone buzzed.

Iona touched her finger to his lips. 'Uh-oh, saved by the bell.'

'Not really.' He nipped her finger. 'I'm gonna give the caller some deferred gratification. See how they like it.'

But when he touched his lips to hers, she wriggled out from under him. 'You should answer it. It might be important.'

He sent her a long-suffering look, but lifted the phone off the dash, stabbed the caller ID. Seeing his mother's number, he sighed. Maria rarely called him, and, although it was unlikely to be life or death, if she wanted to speak with him she'd only call back—better to get this over with.

'Hold that thought,' he said as he took the call.

It was only when his mother's voice rang out in his ear at top volume that he realised he'd forgotten to take the cell off speaker phone. 'Zane, where are you? The *quinceañera* started two hours ago. You promised you'd come this time.'

He stabbed the button to turn down the volume, but one glance at Iona told him the damage had already been done. She'd heard that loud and clear.

'I can't make it. I'm sorry.'

'Why not?' his mother asked in her typically pragmatic way.

'Something came up at the last minute.' He shifted, stupidly embarrassed by the double entendre he hadn't intended—and had to bite down on the flicker of annoyance when Maria continued to harass him about the party. She knew he didn't like spending time with her family. Why couldn't she let this drop?

'How about if I get Maricruz a present, make it up to her later?' he asked, trying to get out of the situation gracefully. He would do pretty much anything for his mother, but not this.

'It's not enough. You need to come. Why is it so hard for you to be a part of this family?' He flinched at the accusation—and the knowledge that he could never tell her the reason why.

He felt the light touch of fingers on his arm, and turned to find Iona looking at him, her eyes bright with sympathy. She mouthed something to him.

'Just a minute, Maria,' he said, and covered the handset.

'Is this your cousin's party? You should go,' she said as soon as he turned his attention to her. 'You can come back afterwards,' she said, the sincerity in her eyes crucifying him. 'I'll still be here.'

No way.

Everything inside him rebelled against the idea of leaving her alone for the evening. After waiting three days to see her, it wasn't just the sex he'd been anticipating.

But then she said, 'I don't feel right about keeping you away from your family,' and he knew he was sunk.

'Okay, great,' he said grudgingly. 'I'll go, but you're coming with me.' If she was going to guilt him into this, he didn't plan to be the only one suffering.

'Don't be silly. I can't go, I hardly know…'

Ignoring her protests, he put the phone back to his ear. 'We're on our way,' he added, blanking the gasp of annoyance from the passenger seat.

'We? Who's we? Are you bringing a date?' His mother sounded so surprised, and pleased, it suddenly occurred to him all the ways in which this could go wrong.

He never talked to his mother about his love life, to avoid

any awkward conversations. And she hadn't met any of the women he'd dated since he was sixteen. 'I'll be there in about half an hour,' he replied, deliberately ignoring the question.

He switched off his cell. And raked his fingers through his hair.

Hell, the evening he'd had planned featuring some flirting, a little foreplay and lots of hot sex had already taken a turn he didn't like. But if Maria met Iona it could get a lot worse. His mother would be bound to overreact—totally screwing up the whole 'casual sex' vibe he'd just spent three days of abstinence to establish.

'Buckle up,' he said to Iona, who still looked mutinous about the invite. 'You wanted deferred gratification. You've got it.'

'That's enchanting.' Iona sighed, feeling more than a little overwhelmed by the dazzle of lights as the car approached the huge estate on a hill carpeted by rows of ripening vines.

The sun was slipping behind the Santa Cruz mountains, haloing the majestic hacienda on the brow of the hill in the golden glow of twilight. As they approached she realised the lights were lanterns, suspended from the porch railings and shining in the red, green and white livery of the Mexican flag.

What looked like fifty cars were crammed in the driveway, parked on the verges and squeezed under the towering oaks that edged the fields. Ornamental rose bushes and showy oleander vied for attention with wild flowers and ferns in the flowerbeds that framed the house. A band of teenagers hung out on the porch, the girls looking like beautiful peacocks in their elaborate ballgowns and the boys lanky and uncomfortable in matching tuxedos.

'I think we're a little underdressed,' Iona murmured as they walked towards the house, tugging down the hem of her minidress. As if it weren't bad enough that she'd been forced into coming, now she felt like a hooker. 'You could have mentioned the dress code.'

'Why? It's not like we had any time to change,' he replied, holding her hand as he led her towards the house.

She felt herself starting to pout. Hating the fact that he had a point. What had she been thinking suggesting he come? It was just that the woman on the phone had sounded so upset, it had made her feel guilty for thinking prurient thoughts about him, while he was supposed to be at a big family event.

But she was so over that now.

'Hey, don't sweat it.' Zane squeezed her hand, taking pity on her. 'The Queen of England would look underdressed at this thing. We won't stay long.'

The romance of fiddles and guitars played energetically in the background competing with the lively hum of conversation as they mounted the steps to the house. Someone shouted a greeting in Spanish to Zane as he led her past the group of teens. Her hand felt clammy in his wide palm, the nerves buzzing in her stomach like hyperactive bees as dark eyes settled on her, most staring with open curiosity.

Zane didn't pause, but led her round the deck to a huge landscaped garden at the back of the house festooned with more lanterns. The remains of an elaborate banquet lay on trestle tables while suited waiters dispensed sparkling wine and beer to the groups of guests crowded into every corner. A band of musicians played in front of a dance floor set up beside a glorious infinity pool. Numerous people in their finery waved at them or shouted greetings at Zane, which he returned with a perfunctory salute.

Then the crowd parted and a young woman dressed in beaded white lace like a Disney Princess raced towards them.

'Zane, you came!' She grasped the tiara on her head under the waterfall of artfully arranged curls before throwing her arms around Zane's neck.

Iona stepped back as he held the teenager for less than a

second before depositing her back on ice-pick heels. *'Feliz cumpleaños, Maricruz.'*

She did a twirl, making the fanciful tiers of white lace shimmer. 'What do you think?'

'You look great,' Zane replied. 'All grown up.'

She grinned, her face flushed with excitement and the blush of pleasure. 'Maybe now you'll stop treating me like a *niña.*'

The flirtatious sparkle in her glorious brown eyes was unmistakeable and Iona wondered if Zane knew his fifteen-year-old cousin had a crush on him. Was that the reason he looked so uncomfortable?

'Maricruz, I want to introduce you to my date, Iona.' Reaching behind, he grabbed her wrist and dragged her forward, tucking her against his side.

'Oh, hello.' Maricruz looked stunned for a moment—and not particularly pleased to see her.

'It looks like a wonderful party,' Iona said, grateful for the weight of Zane's arm round her shoulders.

'Thanks,' the girl said a little sulkily, then beamed another winning smile at Zane. 'Will you dance with me, Zane? Later, there are going to be some more waltzes.'

'Sure, if we're still here,' he said.

'You will?' The sulkiness disappeared as quickly as it had come—and Iona felt a little sorry for the girl, guessing she hadn't heard Zane's qualification.

'Yeah.'

She sent Iona an impish grin that suddenly made the beautiful young woman look like an excited child. 'I love your dress. Where did you get it? It's so funky.'

Iona felt the tension in her stomach ease at the girl's open expression. 'From a little shop in Edinburgh.'

'What's your accent? It's way cool?'

'Scottish.'

'Awesome, like *Braveheart.*'

Iona grinned back. At last, an American who knew a little about her homeland—even if it was based on Hollywood folklore. 'Uh-huh. Among other things.'

'Do the men really wear skirts there?'

'Kilts,' she corrected. 'And yes, sometimes, although usually only for special occasions. They can be a bit draughty.'

Zane tightened his arm round her shoulders. 'Enough with the questions. Iona's from Scotland, not the moon.'

'If you think I'm bad, wait till you introduce her to the family. Forget questions, it's going to be the Mexican Inquisition.' Maricruz sent Iona a conspiratorial smile. 'Zane never brings dates to family events.'

The startling announcement had the bees buzzing back to life in Iona's stomach.

'You are gonna be the hot topic of conversation for months,' the girl added.

'We need to go get some food,' Zane cut in. 'We'll see you later, Maricruz,' he said, deliberately steering them away from the inquisitive teen.

'I'll save the next waltz for you,' she called after Zane before being swallowed up again into the gaggle of teenage girls preening by the pool.

'That's not true, is it?' Iona whispered above the music from the Mariachi band. She'd just started to feel a tiny bit more relaxed about coming, and now this?

Taking her hand, Zane led her around the edge of the dancers towards a long table laden with food. He passed her a china plate and a cloth napkin. 'Let's grab some food before it goes—and then get out of here.'

'I'm serious, Zane. I'm not really the first date who's ever met your family, am I?' she asked, holding the plate limply as he proceeded to heap it with food from the tureens.

'Ignore Maricruz—she's teasing you.'

'That's not an answer,' she countered.

He sent her a deliberately sexy smile, and her heartbeat

skipped into her throat. 'I don't bring dates because I don't usually come to these things if I can avoid them.'

'Why would you want to avoid them?' she asked, the panic replaced by confusion. Maybe the party was a little overwhelming, for a stranger. But he wasn't a stranger, he was part of this family and, from what she'd seen so far, everyone seemed very warm and welcoming.

He scooped up a generous helping of a fragrant rice and chicken dish. 'Because I usually have a lot of other stuff I'd rather be doing, like tonight,' he said, those striking blue eyes promising all sorts of heady excitement later in the evening.

The heat that was never far from the surface flared to life. 'I see.'

He chuckled, the sound rich and confidently male. Then leaned close, and let his lips linger over the sensitive spot below her ear. 'Now stop asking dumb questions and eat your *arroz con pollo* so we can get out of here.'

As it turned out, getting away from Zane's family was easier said than done. Before the two of them had managed to finish the delicious banquet leftovers, they had already been accosted by a parade of his relatives.

The succession of *tias* and *tios, primos* and *primas* ranging in age from teens to pensionable age whose names and places in the Montoya family tree Iona would need a wall chart to keep straight soon began to blur into one. But two things became obvious very quickly—every one of them was overjoyed to see Zane at the party, and Zane was a lot less than overjoyed to be there.

After close to twenty minutes of non-stop introductions, Iona was exhausted from all the attention they'd received—but also enthralled by Zane's close-knit and affectionate family, and his place within it. Why was he so tense and uncommunicative with people that obviously loved and cared for him?

Both questions she planned to ask him, the minute they

managed to escape from their latest interrogator—his statuesque Tia Carmen, who if Iona's memory was correct was married to Zane's uncle, Carlos.

When Carmen finally paused for a breath, Zane grasped Iona's hand and butted in. 'We need to go, Carmen. I'll see you around.'

Carmen's mouth opened, as if she wanted to say more, but Zane was already dragging Iona away.

'Shouldn't we stay a little longer? We've been here less than an hour,' Iona asked above the swelling music as the smooth strains of a waltz began and couples flooded past them onto the dance floor.

He paused, quirked an amused eyebrow. 'Hell, no. I think we've handled enough of the Mexican Inquisition for one night, don't you?'

'It wasn't that bad. They've all been very sweet and very polite.'

He gave a harsh laugh. 'You call Roberto's interrogation about where your family come from polite?'

'I didn't mind. He obviously cares about you—they all do.'

He cupped her elbows, drew her towards him. 'Will you stop being so damn earnest? It just makes me want you more.'

She frowned at the deliberate evasion. 'I'm serious. It's nice to have people care about you that much. Why wouldn't it be?' How many times as a child had she gone to bed at night, wishing that her own mother could have given that much of a damn about her?

The thought of all those unanswered prayers made her a little sad, even a little annoyed that Zane seemed determined to shun the family he had.

He kissed her nose, gave a rough chuckle and then whispered against her ear. 'Maybe because my life is none of their damn business.'

He rubbed her arms, then took her hand in his. 'We've only got a small window of opportunity. Let's go.'

But as they headed for the deck Iona noticed Maricruz, standing by the edge of the dance floor, watching them leave, her hands clasped in front of her and a defeated expression on her face.

'No, wait, Zane.' She yanked on his hand to stop him. 'Maricruz's waltz, you promised. And I think she's waiting for you.'

Raking his hand through his hair, he looked over her shoulder and swore softly, obviously spotting the girl—and her anxious expression.

'It's her special day—you must.'

His gaze locked on hers and she could see that he was fighting a losing battle with his conscience. 'Fine, I'll do it,' he said at last. Then gripped her upper arms. 'But wait for me here, and don't move a damn muscle. I'll be back in ten minutes. Twenty tops? And then we're leaving.'

'Yes, Zane, although not moving a muscle may give me a cramp,' she teased, stupidly touched that he'd opted not to break the promise he'd made to his cousin, however reluctantly.

'Ha ha.' Cupping her cheeks, he planted a hot, firm kiss on her lips—her insides churned with a potent mix of heat and embarrassment. 'Stay put,' he said, the command in his voice unequivocal. 'Or there will be trouble.'

'I certainly hope so,' she chirped as he left.

She wrapped her arms round her waist, her lips lifting as she saw him stop in front of Maricruz. The girl dropped into a low curtsy in her ballgown, her forlorn expression turning to one of unadulterated glee. The girl laughed, her joy painfully transparent as he led her onto the dance floor and her Court of Honour cheered.

Iona sighed as she watched them together. Zane in his white shirt and dark trousers looked tall and impossibly dashing despite the fact that he was the only man on the floor not wearing a tuxedo. Perhaps it was his height—at six feet two or three he had several inches on the legion of teenagers dancing with their dates. Or maybe it was the tanned, chiselled features shadowed with stubble marking him out as a man and not a boy. Or maybe it was simply the effortless way he glided across the floor, his steps perfectly matched to Maricruz as he led the beaming girl in a series of perfectly executed twirls and dips. But as the romantic music swirled around her Iona realised it was more than Zane's height or his looks or his dance skills that made him stand out so much: it was that aura of tension and distance that he wore like a cloak.

No wonder Maricruz had a major crush on him. Iona could just imagine herself at that age. There was an air of danger about Zane, that lurked just beneath the surface of that lazy charm.

'Hello, I'm Juana.'

Iona jerked her gaze off Zane and his dance partner at the softly spoken interruption, to find a pair of astute coffee-coloured eyes studying her. 'I'm one of Zane and Maricruz's *primos segundos*. A second cousin,' she clarified. 'You're Zane's *novia?*'

'Yes, that's right, my name's Iona. Iona McCabe,' Iona replied politely, and offered her hand in greeting, even though she figured *novia* was a bit of an exaggeration—but she could hardly tell a girl who didn't look much older than Maricruz that she wasn't Zane's girlfriend, she was simply his casual-sex fling. 'Nice to meet you.'

The girl grinned, then turned her gaze back to the dance floor. She held a palm to her chest and sighed. 'Zane's so awesome. What's it like dating him? Is it really cool?'

So Juana was another of Zane's fan club.

'It's…' Iona stumbled—cool didn't quite cover what they'd done on their one date. 'Yes, it's pretty cool.' *And way hot.*

'I'm so glad he came, Maricruz would have been heartbroken if Zane didn't show.' The girl gazed at her. 'So thanks for letting him.'

'You're welcome,' Iona mumbled, confused. 'Although it didn't have much to do with me.'

The girl smiled and shrugged. 'It's still nice that you're not as stuck up as the rest of them.'

'The rest of who?'

'We think Zane only dates spoilt stuck-up women who don't want him to mix with his family.' The contempt in the girl's voice spoke volumes. 'Not that you're one of those. You seem really nice,' Juana added, her eyes widening as she realised she might have insulted Iona.

'What makes you think those are the only women he dates?' Iona asked, more curious than insulted. Juana was turning out to be a font of all knowledge.

'Because of his father.'

'What about his father?' Iona asked, realising he'd never mentioned the man.

'He was a rich *pinche gringo*.' Iona had no idea what *pinche* meant but, from Juana's hiss of disapproval, she didn't think it was complimentary. 'Not that any of us know who his father is. No one's allowed to talk about it. *Abuelo* gets mad at anyone who even mentions Zane is half-Anglo—you won't say anything, will you?'

'No, of course not,' Iona murmured, her mind spinning. It wasn't that much of a stretch to guess that Zane might be mixed race, not with those pure blue eyes. But why, when the Montoya family seemed to have embraced multiculturalism—at least half of the guests at the party were 'Anglo' as Juana put it—was his parentage considered such a scandalous secret?

But as she opened her mouth to quiz the girl, Juana hummed with pleasure. 'Oh, look, Maria has cut in on Maricruz. That's so sweet.'

Iona shifted her gaze and her thoughts back to Zane and his dance partner, to see his hands resting on the waist of a statuesque vision in scarlet. All the air rushed out of her lungs.

Sweet wasn't the word she'd use. The woman oozed a stylish and classic sex appeal. Lush dark-chocolate hair tumbled down her back in a cascade of corkscrew curls, her hourglass figure spotlighted in a stunning red dress that hugged impressive curves but somehow managed to look demure rather than revealing.

Maria? Who was she?

But as she watched them together Iona knew exactly who she was. She had to be a past, possibly even a present lover—the familiarity and affection between them apparent in their co-ordinated dance moves, and the way Zane looked at her with none of the chill he reserved for members of his family.

So that was the real reason why he hadn't wanted to come tonight.

As Juana continued to wax lyrical in hushed tones about how sweet they looked together, the sick sensation of betrayal gripped Iona's stomach like a boa constrictor—and her vision dimmed. Why couldn't he have told her that this woman would be here? And why had he insisted on bringing her along?

A red haze began to descend over her eyes.

Was this why he didn't bring dates to family events? Because he knew *she* would be here? And yet he hadn't thought to spare Iona that humiliation.

Okay, maybe they were only a casual fling, and they hadn't mentioned exclusivity, but she'd simply assumed that was a given.

The waltz finished and both Zane and the bombshell turned towards the band and clapped politely. Then Iona watched, the boa in her stomach rising up to constrict around her chest as the woman leaned up on tiptoe, placed a hand on his shoulder and kissed him on the cheek. The love in his gaze was clear and unequivocal even from this distance, the two of them appearing to be in their own private little world as the other guests milled around them. And the boa squirmed and writhed, turning into something more than sickening, more than humiliating.

'Excuse me, Juana,' Iona murmured before threading her way through the crowd at the edges of the dance floor.

She should just go home, forget about him. They had no investment in each other. Just because she'd spent the last three days thinking about him, and the night they'd spent together. This was casual. Less than casual really. And clearly his relationship with Maria was not. She shouldn't care if he had a hundred former girlfriends, a thousand that he cared about more than he cared about her.

But somehow her feet kept moving forward, the boa rising up her throat. And she justified the confrontation she could feel racing towards her.

She couldn't go home. She was stranded here without a car. He'd introduced her to his family as his date. Didn't he know how humiliating this was for her? To have him pawing another woman, while she was expected to stand on the sidelines and watch?

She reached them just as the goddess threw back her head and laughed at something Zane said to her in Spanish.

His eyes met Iona's, the blue depths full of humour and not a trace of guilt or remorse.

No, he didn't know, she realised. Or he simply didn't care. Because her thoughts, her feelings, her pride were of no importance to him.

'Hey, Iona,' he said, but she could hear the tension in his voice.

'Could you take me home, please?' she said. 'Now.'

'Is there a problem?' he replied, the flash of guilt replaced with confusion. Did he really think so little of her that he couldn't guess what the problem was?

'I'd like to go home and I need you to drive me there,' she said through gritted teeth, determined not to raise her voice. 'Or take me to the nearest bus station.'

'Why would I drive you to a bus station?' he said, sounding annoyed now too. 'We've got plans for tonight, remember?'

The red haze went purple. How could he mention that here? In front of his other woman? It insulted them both. 'Not any more we haven't.' Her voice rose despite her best intentions. 'I'm leaving and if you don't want to take me, I'll find someone who does.'

'Think again.' His fingers closed around her upper arm. 'You came with me, which means you're leaving with me.'

She struggled against the iron grip. 'I'll do what I damn well please.'

'Zane, let her go, you're making a scene,' the goddess remarked, her voice calm but her warm chocolate eyes alight with interest.

Zane let her go, but ground out, 'I'm not the one making the scene—she is.'

Iona's chest puffed up with indignation, but before she could give it to him with both barrels the goddess intervened again. 'Iona, it's a pleasure to meet you.'

The snake coiled, but she refused to let it strike. She mustn't lash out at this woman. It wasn't her fault. It was Zane. He was the one who had brought her here under false pretences.

'Look, Maria, I'm sure you're a very nice person.' The venom she didn't want to admit to dripped from her tongue. 'Zane certainly seems to think so. And it's not your fault that he brought me along and then made us both look like fools.' She shot her best squinty-eyed look at Zane to telegraph her anger. 'But I'm not in the market for a threesome.'

The woman's eyebrows launched towards that glorious tumble of curls.

'And I'm sure you're not either,' Iona continued, diligently ignoring Zane's muffled oath and the shocked laugh that choked out of the woman's lips. 'Unfortunately, though, I'm stranded until he gives me a lift. But as soon as I get to the nearest bus station, he's all yours.'

Iona swivelled her head at the hissed exclamation from Zane, whose temper seemed to have dissolved in shock. 'Iona, you've got this all wrong.'

'I don't think so,' she whispered furiously, finally noticing the absence of music, and the sea of watchful faces currently fixed on their little tableau. The sound of muffled laughter rippled through the crowd, making her mortification complete. 'What?' She glared at Zane, who simply thrust a hand through his hair and swore again.

'Actually, Iona, it probably is my fault,' the goddess announced as the laughter finally began to die down. 'As I'm Zane's mother.'

'I beg your pardon?'

She gaped at the goddess. She had to be going deaf, or blind, or both. She simply could not have heard that correctly. This woman looked gorgeous, and glamorous, and not a day over forty. She'd never asked Zane how old he was but he had to be at least thirty? Didn't he?

'Maria Montoya, Iona.' The goddess held out an expertly manicured hand. 'Zane's mother.' She let out another little laugh, her expression friendly and giving, as if she were willing Iona to share the joke. 'And believe me, it really is a pleasure to meet you. My son has always needed a woman with the courage to stand up to him.'

Iona stared at the offered hand, sick waves of nausea hitting the rice and chicken and salsa she'd consumed. 'But that's… That's not possible,' she mumbled, the words barely discernible through the chainsaw buzzing in her eardrums. 'It's not. You're too young.'

'I wish that were true. But I'm flattered you think so.'

The woman's humour and the kindness in her gaze made the churning increase. Iona covered her mouth. What had she done? What had she said? How could she have insulted Zane's mother that way? In front of his whole family? This wasn't humiliating—it was practically certifiable.

'I'm so, so sorry,' she said, then turned and darted through the crowd, who parted before her like the Red Sea—or, rather, like people trying to avoid a certifiable nutjob.

'Iona, wait up!'

She accelerated, staggering past the Red Sea of amused, or astonished or simply stunned faces. These were people he and his mother knew, people who loved and respected him— even if he didn't seem to share the sentiment—and she'd just made that situation even worse.

She raced round the side of the huge house, having to push past those people who hadn't witnessed the freak show she'd put on in the garden, eventually making it to the front lawn and stumbling down the stone steps. The driveway wound through the fields of dark vines plump with grapes, but she headed down it, her panicked mind deciding she would walk all the way back to Pacific Grove rather than ask Zane for a lift again.

She got as far as the last car, when footsteps pounded on the gravel behind her and strong fingers grasped her arm.

'Damn it, where are you going?' he said, hauling her round to face him.

She squeezed her eyes shut, desperate to hold back the tears, but unable to look him in the face. 'I'll be fine. It won't take me long to make it to the road and I can hitch-hike from there.'

'No way are you hitch-hiking anywhere. And it's three miles to the road. And dark.'

'Please, I'll be fine, if you'll just please, please, please, tell your mother how sorry I am.'

He probably hated her now. And who could blame him? She'd made a laughing stock of them both.

'My mother is tickled pink you think she's in her thirties when she hit the big five-oh a couple of months ago.'

'Your mother is fifty!' What was one more shock in so many? 'But how old are…?'

'I'm thirty-four. She was sixteen when she had me.' She could hear the sting in his tone—as if he'd been asked the question a thousand times and was tired of answering it.

'Okay.' Although it wasn't. 'That explains my mistake, but it still doesn't make what I said any less mortifying.'

'Iona, this is dumb. You're overreacting.'

'I said the word *threesome* to your mother!' she yelped. 'It's horrific. Inexcusable. I made a terrible scene in front of your whole family.'

He tucked a knuckle beneath her chin, forced her gaze to his, but the concern she saw made her stomach hurt.

He probably pitied her now. And who wouldn't? Why had she said those things? Why had she even cared that much? Why did she always make such an idiot of herself where men were concerned?

'Iona,' he said, his patience almost as painful as the pity she thought she saw. 'Nuclear war is horrific. The famine in Africa is inexcusable. This is neither one. You made a mistake, that's all. And my family is Latino—and full to bursting with drama queens. As scenes go, this doesn't even register a two-point-five on the Richter scale of family drama.'

She heard the distance in his tone, and while his observation made her feel a little better about the biggest faux pas in human history, she didn't understand it. She'd just humiliated him in front of them. How could he not be mad as hell about that? Did their good opinion really mean so little to him?

CHAPTER NINE

'ZANE, IS IONA okay?'

Iona's stomach revolted at the sight of the goddess—his mother—hurrying towards them down the driveway.

'Yeah,' Zane said bluntly. 'But we're leaving. We've both had about as much as we can take for one night.'

Iona saw his mother flinch a little at the hostile statement and her stomach heaved. He shouldn't talk to his mother like that.

'I'm so sorry,' his mother soothed, looking genuinely apologetic, which only made Iona feel worse. 'I'm frequently mistaken for Zane's sister, but this is the first time I've ever been mistaken for his lover.'

'Please don't apologise to me.' Iona closed her eyes, not sure she could bear this woman's kindness now, after the hideous way she'd behaved. 'You didn't do anything wrong.'

'Of course, if Zane had had the good sense to introduce me to you when you both arrived this would never have happened.' Maria rounded on her son. 'And don't think I didn't see you trying to leave early.'

'I didn't much want to come in the first place,' he protested. 'So don't blame me for this, Maria.'

Iona listened to the conversation in a trance, so mortified she figured the safest option was to keep her mouth shut.

'Zane, isn't it past time for you to let the anger go?' his mother asked, cradling his cheek.

He jerked his head back 'We have to go,' he said, and Iona saw the shadow of hurt in his mother's eyes.

'Zane, please…'

'I'll give you a call during the week sometime.' He cut off her plea, then placed a quick kiss on her cheek, but the gesture was more guarded than giving.

His mother nodded, her sadness and confusion making Iona's chest ache. Why was he being so cruel? It wasn't his mother's fault that she'd made an idiot of herself—and the woman had a point: why hadn't he made any effort to introduce them?

'*Adios,* Iona,' Maria said. 'I will see you again, I hope.'

Iona watched her walk back towards the party, the lingering magnolia of her scent adding a sultry glamour to the earthy perfume of the vines.

'Your mum seems like a really nice person. It must have been great having her around as a kid,' Iona murmured, the wistful observation popping out unguarded. 'You shouldn't have been angry with her. It wasn't her fault.'

'I know that,' he murmured, giving a tired sigh before guiding her to his convertible. 'Come on, let's get out of here.'

His dark hair shined black in the evening light as he opened the passenger door, those spectacular features cast into shadow by the glow of lantern light from the hacienda. But Iona could still see the unhappiness in his face, and felt the sharp stab of compassion. His mother, it seemed, wasn't the only one hurting.

She climbed in, wanting to ask him what had caused the distance between him and his mother, because she had the distinct feeling it had very little to do with her meltdown on the dance floor, but stopped herself. She'd done enough damage for one night.

He settled in the seat beside her, but as he switched on the ignition there was one question she couldn't resist asking.

'Why *didn't* you introduce us when we arrived?'

He slung his arm across her seat as he backed the car down the driveway. Finding a place to turn round, he executed a perfect three-point turn before finally replying. 'No particular reason. I just didn't spot her until she joined me on the dance floor.'

He was lying, she knew it, but was afraid to call him on it. Had he maybe regretted bringing a virtual stranger to the party once they'd arrived?

As they powered down the driveway the rows of vines cast lengthening shadows on the tarmac as full dark fell.

She sank into the car's bucket seat, the leather scent a pleasant accompaniment to the freshening wind, and studied his profile. He really was the most beautiful man she'd ever seen. And so many things about him fascinated her.

Now she'd met his family—and especially his mother—he only fascinated her more. She wondered about him, what it had been like for him growing up. He was clearly close to his mother. When they had been dancing together in the lantern light, it had been obvious how close they were. But where did all the tension come from? Maybe it had something to do with his father? The *pinche gringo* Juana had talked about so disrespectfully. What had this man done that meant that no one in his family was even permitted to talk about him? That couldn't be healthy surely? And was that where the distance between Zane and them came from?

All questions she had no right to ask him. But she simply couldn't resist satisfying a little of her curiosity.

'Why do you call your mum by her given name?'

He didn't answer for a long time, and she wondered if he had heard her, but then he shrugged. 'I used to call her

Mom when I was a little kid. But as I got older, it got easier not to.'

'Why?' she asked, only more intrigued by the non-explanation.

How the hell had they gotten onto this topic?

Zane glanced across the stick shift at the sleepy question. Iona's wide brown eyes blinked owlishly. She looked exhausted.

'I'm not sure I want to tell you,' he said, hoping to stall her until she fell asleep.

'Why not?'

'Because it'll make me sound like a jerk.' Which was exactly what he had been as a teenager. Selfish and volatile and immature. But there was another reason too, which he had no intention of sharing.

'How so?'

He huffed out what he hoped sounded like a relaxed laugh. 'All right, if you really need to know. At high school, she was much younger than the other moms, and well...' he rapped his thumb against the wheel '...built.' He stiffened at the description, and the memory of the wolf whistles and the catcalls she'd endured whenever she'd come into George Wallace Memorial High. 'She got a lot of attention. I'd lose my temper, get into trouble and I couldn't tell her why, because I didn't want her to know what they said about her.'

He pumped his foot on the gas remembering the constant fights, the swollen knuckles and black eyes and split lips, and the endless journeys to the principal's office, where he'd be forced to sit, sometimes for hours, refusing to defend or apologise for his actions. The impotent anger had boiled inside him for years—at the injustices his mother had suffered, simply because she was young and beautiful and had been forced into a life she had never wanted. But deep down there had been another anger, much blacker and more damaging, that seething, pointless self-loathing that he'd been unable to control then and didn't want to acknowledge now.

'Pretty damn dumb when you think about it with the benefit of maturity,' he said. 'If I'd been less proud and less stupid I would have ignored what they said.'

'You were protecting her in the only way you knew how,' Iona said, her voice thick with sleep. 'That's not proud or stupid. It's very gallant.'

Zane shrugged, the pleasure at her support making him feel uneasy—and exposed. 'Not exactly, because then I started calling her by her given name, so the other kids would think she was my older sister instead of my mom.'

Iona sighed gently. He looked across the console as the car eased to a stop at the end of the vineyard's driveway.

'So in answer to your question,' he continued, 'that's how I came to call her Maria, and now I'm a grown man it seems kind of dumb to call her Mom again.'

He couldn't make out Iona's expression in the low light, but she looked straight back at him.

'It's astonishing, isn't it, how cruel other kids can be, if there's something a bit different about your family set-up?' she murmured and he detected a note of wistfulness that made him realise she knew how it felt. 'We're all such horrid little conformists when we're young.'

His shoulders relaxed at the lack of censure. 'Yeah, I guess. But it must have been tougher for you when your mom left?' he asked, keen to steer the conversation away from himself.

'Aye, well, it wasn't great.' He felt the pinch in his chest at the weariness in the words. 'But we got over it.' She snuggled into the seat and yawned. 'I guess the hardest part is the not knowing why. When you're ten you're just egocentric enough to naturally assume it has to be your fault.'

He took his hand off the stick, the need to comfort her surprising, but he went with it. She sounded so hopeless. He squeezed her knee. 'But you know it wasn't, right?'

Was that why she had fallen victim to Demarest so easily? And why she'd jumped to the conclusion this evening that Maria was one of his lovers? Because of some seed planted years ago in her childhood? Being unwanted was a bitch. It could play hell with your self-esteem; he ought to know. He figured he should probably say something reassuring… But then the scent of her, fresh and sultry, drifted across the car, and his gut tightened.

Better not go there. He wanted her and all this serious talk was casting a spell over the evening, making them both reveal more than they probably should.

'I'm sorry I made things so uncomfortable between you and your family,' she said around another jaw-breaking yawn.

Uncomfortable? His heart-rate did a quick skip at the perceptive comment. 'I'm the one who should be sorry,' he said, careful to keep his voice light. 'I had no business dragging you along.'

'I liked your family, especially your mother.'

He heard it then, the slight censure in her tone—and realised that she had noticed more than his uncomfortable relationship with Maria.

He rolled his shoulders, forcing himself to relax, and forget about it. Her observations, her opinion didn't matter, their fling wasn't serious—and she'd never have to meet his family again. He'd make sure of it.

'Do you mind if I have a nap?' she said, her voice groggy with fatigue. 'It's been an eventful night.'

'Sure, go ahead. It'll take about an hour to get back.'

He checked on her a few moments later as they hit Highway One. Curled in the seat, she'd drifted off into a sound sleep.

He'd forgotten to mention that they were headed back to his place and not hers. But he figured she'd find out soon enough. And he'd deal with any fall-out then. He wasn't going to push anything tonight, he could see how tired she was, but he didn't want her out of his sight for too long either. She'd been through the wringer at Maricruz's party. And that was mostly his fault. He should have introduced her to Maria, instead of running scared.

But as the car sped down the coast highway it occurred to him that, however casual their fling was supposed to be, something had changed tonight. Something about Iona pulled at him. Her honesty, her vulnerability, that prickly demeanor she used to hide her insecurities. It reminded him of the kid he'd once been a little too forcefully.

He stretched his neck from side to side as the muscles cramped. He felt protective of Iona—which probably wasn't a good thing. Because whenever he'd got protective in the past, it had generally been a disaster.

He shifted in his seat, the dull ache in his back reminding him of the two wounds that had signalled his exit from the LAPD five years before. He switched on the car's radio, let the pain and confusion from that time in his life slowly drift away on the seductive bass riff of the old soul song.

He was over-thinking. The only reason things had got heavy tonight was because he'd taken her somewhere he didn't feel comfortable.

And while he might feel protective of Iona, he didn't have to feel that way. She was a grown woman, who could take care of herself. She'd certainly proved that tonight. A wry smile lifted his lips at the intoxicating memory of her pale skin flushed crimson with fury as she stalked across the dance floor to confront him while he danced with his mother.

He pressed his foot onto the gas pedal, in a hurry to get home. This was still a casual fling—and he could prove it, because when they got back to his place he wasn't going to pounce on her like a starving man.

'Hey, *precios,* we're here. You want me to carry you in?'

Iona moved her head and caught the strong scent of sea air as the question drifted through the fog of sleep. 'Hmm?'

'Guess I'll carry you, then. Hold on.'

Her lids fluttered open as her stomach became weightless and she found herself being boosted into Zane's arms. The night air closed around them and she held on to his neck to stop herself from falling. The sound of surf and the cry of a nocturnal seagull had her squinting at the huge wood and glass structure that rose up out of a sand dune. 'Where are we?'

'My place. Figured it would be easier to stay here tonight.'

'But I…' she began, knowing she should probably object, but it felt good to be held.

'But nothing,' he said. 'You were exhausted. My place was closer.'

He shifted her in his arms to key a code into the door panel, then shoved open the front door and carried her through the darkened house.

'Relax, Iona,' he said, giving her a soft kiss on the forehead. 'This place has five bedrooms. I'm not planning on jumping you tonight.'

'Oh, okay.' Well, heck, she hadn't intended to object quite that much.

They passed the door to a vast open-plan kitchen, the low lighters illuminating dark marble surfaces and blonde wood cabinets, then entered a double-height living room that had a glass wall leading onto a wide terraced deck. A lighted pathway led off the terrace and out into the darkness.

'You live by the sea?' she said.

'Yeah, beach's just down there.'

The place was enormous and a little eerie, until the sound of claws scratching on wood broke the silence and a couple of excited yips were followed by the arrival of a big bundle of dirty-blonde fur that barrelled across the room towards them.

'Hey, C.D.,' Zane said by way of introduction as he stood Iona on her feet. 'Meet Iona—she's sleeping over.'

The delighted dog's tail wagged so hard its whole body vibrated. Careering to a stop in front of them, it plunked its butt down on the floor, and panted with delight. With a ragged ear, one squinted eye, and a misshapen head that made it look like an unfortunate cross between a lab and a bulldog, it had to be one of the ugliest mutts Iona had ever seen. But as it continued to vibrate with ecstasy, its tongue hanging out of its mouth in a doggie grin, she found herself completely charmed.

'Hello, Cookie Dough, it's nice to meet you,' she said, kneeling down to stroke the dog's head. It immediately flopped onto its back, and offered its tummy for a rub, surprising a laugh out of her.

'Great guard dog you are,' Zane said ruefully.

'You're gorgeous, aren't you, girl?' Iona purred, already in love and undeniably touched by the fact that Zane had chosen to rescue a mongrel pup that most other people would have rejected on sight. 'Pay no attention to him—you're just being friendly,' she cooed. The dog answered with a low growl of contentment as its tail thumped rhythmically on the floor.

'All right, that's enough, you little suck-up.' Zane snapped his fingers. The dog rolled back onto its legs, still shaking with excitement. 'Go on back to bed, Cooks. We'll see you in the morning.'

Iona gave C.D. one last pat and rub, before the dog sauntered off, back to its bed in the corner of the room.

'So that's the infamous Cookie Dough.' Iona chuckled. 'Eater of shoes and drinker of toilet water. She seems very polite to me.'

'Uh-huh, we'll see how that works for you when she leaps onto your bed at dawn.' Taking Iona's hand, he led her across the room, to a wide metal staircase that curved up to the landing above. 'Let's find you a room. You and Cookie can get better acquainted tomorrow.'

Iona followed, her hand clasped in his, and tried not to let her disappointment show. If he wasn't that bothered, neither was she. She struggled to keep that thought front and centre when he pushed open a door on the first landing.

He flicked on the light switch, illuminating acres of thick blue carpeting, a king-size bed made up with luxury linen and the dark deck beyond.

'There's a spare toothbrush in the bathroom, which is through there.' He pointed to a door on the far wall. 'There should be towels too and anything else you need.'

She stared at the empty bed, the pillows piled high against the headboard, and heat flushed through her. She could smell him, that tantalising scent of spicy aftershave and sea air that was uniquely his—and more than anything she wanted him to climb in with her.

'Do you need anything else?' he asked casually.

He leaned against the doorway, his forearm propped against the frame, the cotton of his shirt stretched across that impressive chest. And she got a vision of that beautiful body naked.

Yes, you.

Her mind screamed, making the heat pound into her sex. 'No, that's great,' she heard herself say. 'I'll see you in the morning.'

His gaze lingered on her lips for the longest time. 'C.D. usually wakes me up at dawn to take her for a run, so if I'm not here, I'll be on the beach.'

The words sounded polite, distant, but the husky tone of his voice reverberated inside her.

How could he be so calm, so controlled? 'Right.'

He drummed his fingers against the doorframe, then straightened and let his arm drop.

She stood, unable to relinquish eye contact, her breath catching. Lifting one hand, he skimmed a knuckle down the side of her face. She tilted her head, leaning into his touch. Then his hand clasped the back of her neck and he hauled her against him.

'Just one more thing.'

She opened her mouth as his lips slanted across hers. Heat and awareness shot through her as his tongue delved. Firm, sure, wet and hot. The hunger built as she kissed him back, her knees shaking as if an aftershock had hit the San Andreas Fault. She flattened her palms against his waist, gripping his shirt.

A low moan issued from her lips as he pulled away.

'Get a good night's sleep, Iona,' he said, the rough demand matching the dark dilated pupils. 'I intend to keep you real busy tomorrow.'

Then he walked away, leaving her staring at his retreating back, her body battered by the need coursing through every pulse point.

'You have got to be kidding me?' she whispered as the sound of his footsteps disappeared down the hallway.

There wasn't a chance in hell she was going to sleep a wink now.

Zane slammed the bedroom door and leaned against it. He stared out at the night sky, and waited for the blood to stop pounding southwards.

Whose dumb idea was it to bring her here? And then not sleep with her?

Tugging the shirt off over his head, he wadded it up as he marched into the bathroom, and hurled it into the corner of the room.

Oh, yeah, his dumb idea.

Twisting the shower control, he guided the temperature down to frigid.

When was the last time he'd had a woman in his house, and not his bed? Never, that was when. He kicked off his shoes, dropped his pants and stepped under the spray. Then bit off the yelp as the cold water splattered his chest and hit the erection. Bracing his hand against the cubicle wall, he waited for the inferno to subside under the freezing deluge—it took a while, thanks to the succulent taste of her that lingered on his lips, and the soft sob of arousal that still echoed in his ears.

The woman was tying him in knots—tying them both in knots. She could have tonight, damn it. Because he'd promised himself this was going to be casual, and it didn't feel that casual after the night they'd spent with his family.

But tomorrow all bets were off. He wasn't holding back a moment longer.

He'd never been a pushy guy. Probably because he'd never had to be. But come tomorrow, that was all gonna change. She wanted him. He wanted her. End of story. She'd got back on the horse, now it was way past time for them both to enjoy the ride.

CHAPTER TEN

THE BLAST OF sunlight made Iona squirm as she opened her eyes and curled into the pillows. Yawning, she eased herself into a sitting position—and took a moment to orientate herself.

The glass wall on one side of the lavish bedroom framed a stunning view of rocks and sand and ocean as the events of the night before came tumbling back in a series of disjointed sights and sounds and scents.

The blank shock on Zane's face as she confronted him on the dance floor. The hurt in his mother's eyes as they left. The sense of connection that had made her chest hurt when he'd spoken about his high-school experiences, his knuckles whitening on the steering wheel—and the hot, firm press of his lips that had sent her into a frenzy of longing.

Iona let a slow breath out, and sucked another one in through her teeth. No doubt about it, it had been one heck of a night.

Flinging back the quilt, she climbed out of the bed and crossed the room. Placing her hand against the sun-warmed glass, she peered out. She could see the manicured lawns of a golf course in the distance, but Zane's house stood apart—its elegant modernism in direct counterpoint to the wilder, angrier edge of the bay. The sun hovered above the horizon.

Seemed she'd managed a bit more than a wink despite the distractions of that goodnight kiss.

Working the kinks out of her shoulders, she made a bee-line for the bathroom.

As she treated herself to a scalding hot shower she smiled, thinking of the sunny Sunday morning—and all the hot sex they had to catch up on from the night before.

But once she'd dressed and gone downstairs, she found no sign of him, or his dog, and realised he'd probably gone to take C.D. for a walk. She stepped out onto the deck, dismissing the odd little jump in her belly at the thought of how normal, how comfortable it felt being in his home and looking forward to a lazy Sunday together.

Despite a cloudless sky and the blaze of mid-morning sunshine, a brisk ocean breeze meant she was grateful for the denim jacket. She headed down the narrow stone steps that traversed a rocky outcropping to arrive at a secluded beach framed by gnarly Monterey Cypresses that separated the lot from the one next door.

Her heart bobbed into her throat as she spotted a tall figure jogging down the beach and the bounding hound next to him. She lifted her hand to wave, took several calming breaths to still the frantic thump of her pulse as they approached.

Zane's short hair spiked in the wind, the pair of jogging shorts speckled with water from the pounding surf. A gust of wind flattened the sleeveless sweatshirt he wore against his chest.

C.D. raced ahead to deliver an ecstatic greeting that involved launching herself at Iona, planting two huge sandy paws onto her tummy and nearly toppling her backwards onto her butt.

'Down, Cookie.' Zane's succinct command had the dog plopping heavily onto her backside. Iona grinned at the over-grown puppy and its expression of goofy enthusiasm, glad to be distracted from the silly swell of emotion at seeing Zane again.

'Sorry about that,' Zane said, picking up a piece of driftwood. 'We're still working on polite introductions.'

'That's okay. No harm done,' Iona said, wiping the last of the wet sand off her dress. Was it her imagination or did he sound a little tense too?

Zane lobbed the driftwood towards the tumbling surf. 'Go fetch, Cooks.'

C.D. gave an excited howl, before racing after the stick, arrowing her body into the shallows.

Iona pushed out a laugh. 'That's brave. It must be freezing.'

'More dumb than brave. Even I've got to admit, she's not the smartest dog in the universe.'

They watched the dog barking manically at the waves as it tried to retrieve the stick. 'No, maybe not,' Iona said.

'You sleep okay?'

Her chest compressed as she met the fierce blue gaze.

'Like a baby.' His gaze dipped to her lips and colour fired into her cheeks. 'I hope Cookie didn't wake you up too early,' she added.

'Early enough.' A smile lurked around the corners of his mouth. 'You hungry?' he said. 'I figured we could have waffles for breakfast.'

Her stomach contracted, but it wasn't hunger for food that gripped her. But how exactly did you go about jumping a guy at ten o'clock in the morning on a beach? Was there an etiquette to this sort of thing? Because if there was she had no idea what it was.

The dog came bounding back, pausing to shake out her wet fur and spraying them both with water. Iona leapt back, but this time neither of them laughed.

Zane wrestled the driftwood out of C.D.'s mouth, gave her a hearty rub and then flung the stick back into the surf.

He watched as the dog headed out after it. 'Breakfast it is,' he murmured.

But neither of them made a move. She shoved her fists into the pockets of the jean jacket, the breeze making her shiver. She studied Zane's face in profile and felt the pull of connection and the tingle on her lips where he had devoured her the night before.

He swung round and caught her watching him. Then his gaze narrowed, the blue of his irises even more intense than usual. 'Unless there's something you'd rather do?'

The words came out on a gruff murmur, so quiet she almost didn't hear them over the rushing wind and the crashing surf.

Knuckles rough with sand brushed her cheek and then his open palm settled on the heated skin of her nape.

The shudder of awareness bristled down her spine. 'Well, actually, there might be something…'

It was all the encouragement he needed before his mouth swooped down, cutting off her protest.

He held her cheeks in cool palms and plundered, holding her still for the sure, hot sweep of his tongue, the hungry possession that promised so much more.

She couldn't resist, couldn't control the instinctive response, her body quaking with desire.

He lifted his head first, their ragged breaths mingling in the salty air. His pupils had dilated to black, his voice strained. 'You're sure about this?'

'Yes,' she said, knowing perfectly well there was no point in denying it.

His hands dropped to her waist, hauled her against him and she felt the solid ridge. Her centre melted, the need a wild thing burning inside her. But then he pulled away from her, his expression tense.

'You do understand, Iona, this isn't going to lead to anything else, right?'

She braced her palms against his chest, puzzled by the

concern in his voice. Hadn't they already established this? 'Yes, of course I do.'

Emotion clutched at her chest, making her feel a lot less bold. Had he tired of her already? Was that why he'd left her in the guest room last night—because he was already bored? It should have annoyed her. The arrogance of the man. But somehow all it did was make her feel desperately insecure.

The dog returned and flopped onto her tummy, exhausted after all her sea-wrestling activities. Zane crouched down to greet her, and picked up the driftwood she'd dropped obediently at his feet. C.D.'s tail wagged like a metronome; the dog clearly oblivious to the tension that crackled in the air between them.

He took his time, rubbing the dog's head, praising her prowess, but his body language remained stiff and unyielding.

Iona's heart began to beat in double time when he stood to face her.

'If you're not interested any more, Zane, all you have to do is say so.'

She turned to go, but he grasped her arm. 'Hey, don't…' He tugged an impatient hand through his hair. 'It's not that at all. I just didn't want to be putting pressure on you. Giving you the wrong idea about what this is.'

His eyes remained fixed on hers, his hand absently stroking the dog's neck. He looked more frustrated than contrite, but the admission had her pulse rate slowing.

'I'm absolutely fine with it, as I've already told you, so what's the problem?'

'The problem is I shouldn't have kissed you last night, because I've been up half the night with a hard-on the size of Guadalajara, and it's made me cranky.'

She giggled, his frustrated response washing away her insecurity. 'Guadalajara, eh? That sounds impressive?'

'More painful than impressive.' His lips quirked in response. 'Especially when a two-ton hound leaps on top of you at dawn.'

She covered her mouth with one hand. The giddy rush of relief making it hard to suppress another giggle.

'Oh, you think that's funny, huh?'

Catching her round the waist, he bent over and hoisted her onto his shoulder.

'What the heck!' She rode the solid shelf, kicking and struggling, as he hefted her back towards the house. 'Put me down!'

'No way. We've got unfinished business.'

'And whose fault is that?' she yelped, trying to wriggle free as he hefted her up the steps and across the deck.

The dog leapt and barked playfully beside them, happy to join in the game.

Iona bucked trying to escape. But not trying very hard. Stepping through the sliding glass door into the living room, Zane shut the dancing dog out on the deck and dumped her unceremoniously onto her feet. She tried to dart off, but he caught her round the waist, then trapped her against the wall, his hands above her head, his body pressed into hers.

His lips covered hers, capturing the gasp of surprise. Their tongues tangled, and the relief was replaced by the hot shot of passion. His hands skimmed under the denim jacket, then pushed it off her shoulders, trapping her arms behind her back and drawing her close.

She moaned, her head dropping back, as his lips fastened on the pulse point in her neck.

'You taste so damn good, Iona,' he murmured, his breath hot against the sensitive skin.

She drew a much-needed breath, opened her eyes to find him watching her.

'I aim to please.'

'That's good.' The supremely confident grin coaxed another laugh to the surface—along with the rush of something she didn't quite want to identify. Zane Montoya made her feel good, he made her feel needed, but only in a purely physical sense. 'Because after the night I've had,' he added, 'you owe me one.'

'I don't see why,' she said, faking indignation. 'That good-night kiss was your idea.'

Warm palms snuck up her sides. 'I don't remember you objecting.'

'Well…' She drew out the word, stretching into the caress as his thumbs brushed the underside of her breasts. 'I guess if you put it that way…' she lifted her arms, draped them round his neck and arched against him '…I might consider some payback fair.' He nuzzled her neck, sending the shot of arousal shooting down her abdomen. 'But purely as an act of mercy, you understand.'

It was all the encouragement he needed to grab her hand and head down the corridor.

Zane grabbed the bottle of maple syrup he'd left on the breakfast bar for the waffles as he dragged Iona through the kitchen towards the back staircase.

He had to keep himself from pushing too hard or asking too much. He wanted this to be good, to be fun, to be light and easy, casual, just like he'd promised, but he had a feeling that after the way he'd gotten himself going last night—and this morning—props might be a good way to remind himself of that.

He let the dog in the back door, and Cookie gave them a bark of greeting before settling into her basket.

'What's the syrup for?' Iona asked breathlessly as they mounted the stairs.

'Wait and see,' he said, anticipation making his hands tremble as they walked into his bedroom.

He kicked the door shut, flicked the lock, just in case C.D.

didn't have her customary two-hour nap. As much as he loved his dog, he didn't want company.

He placed the syrup bottle onto the bedside table, the sharp crack reverberating round the room. Then went to the glass wall that looked out onto the beach, and dropped the shade.

He squeezed his fingers into fists, dismayed to feel the clammy sweat on his palms.

Get a grip, Montoya. You're acting like a nervous virgin, instead of a guy who popped his cherry a lifetime ago.

The wayward thought had the rushed, fumbled encounter and the crushing distaste on Mary-Lou Seagrove's face coming back.

'You're so handsome, but I guess you're more Mexican than I thought, because you screw like Speedy Gonzalez.'

He cut off the memory of the casual racism that had sliced him to the core, forced his fingers to release. That first sexual encounter might have been a total disaster, but he'd learned a lot since then—the first being, never pick your sexual partners according to their cheerleading abilities.

Iona stood in the middle of the room, her staggered breathing tightening the fabric on her dress as her breasts rose and fell in quick succession. The slatted blinds cast shadows on her face, but he could still read her mood with remarkable ease, her expression a gratifying mix of nervous and excited.

Forget Mary-Lou. You're not that overeager kid any more.

He sat on the edge of the bed, spread his knees and held Iona's waist. She stepped between his thighs and rested her hands on his shoulders. His pulse leapt as she took the initiative and bent to capture his mouth.

Her kiss tasted sweet and exotic, sugar and spice. He ran his tongue along the seam of her mouth, delved within, lifted the hem of her dress and cupped the firm cheeks of her bottom. Tracing the edge of lace, he slipped his fingers beneath the satin.

She shuddered and rocked against him as he found the slick moist heat, more potent than any aphrodisiac.

'You want to get naked?' he asked, determined to let her set the pace, but not sure he could wait much longer, the hard arousal pulsing painfully back to life in his shorts.

She let out a throaty laugh. 'That would be nice.'

Nice.

The husky burr of her accent made the word sound rich and full this time, instead of insipid and vaguely patronising.

'Great,' he rasped. Finding the zip of her dress, he dragged it down.

She lowered her arms, and stood back to do a wiggle. The simple cotton dress flowed over her curves and drifted down to pool at her feet. The movement was quick, efficient and unbearably arousing.

She straightened, held her shoulders back, bold and determined. The bra was simply made but impossibly erotic in the shifting shadows drawn by the blinds, the dark outline of her nipples clearly visible through the delicate pink lace. He grasped her narrow waist, dragged her back, then, finding the fastening on her bra, he tried to unhook it, but she braced her hands on his shoulders to stop him.

'You'll not have me naked and you fully clothed,' she announced, the brogue much thicker than usual—and a little indignant.

'Point taken,' he said. Standing quickly, he gripped the hem of his sweatshirt, and tugged it off, flung it aside. But when he went to undo his fly, she placed a hand over his.

'Can I do it? Do you mind?'

Did he mind?

He barked out a tense laugh. 'Be my guest.'

Her fingers found the tab and eased it down. He heard her gasp as the straining erection sprang free.

'Oh, my,' she whispered.

He choked out another laugh, stripping off the shorts and

his jockeys. The colour tinted her cheekbones, but she didn't hesitate as she reached out to hold him.

Oh, hell.

His flesh leapt as her fingers curled around him. He sucked in a sharp breath, calling on every reserve he had to stay still, stay focused and submit to the soft touch, the gentle exploration.

'Who says big isn't beautiful?' she said with a joyful laugh, and he thought he might actually die as the last drop of his blood pounded out of his head.

Don't lose it, Montoya, not now, or you'll screw everything up.

He took her shoulders in firm hands, knowing there was a limit to how much of this he could take and he was fast approaching it. He had to take charge, take control. He couldn't let her see how much she affected him.

Her hand dropped away, and her eyes lifted to his face.

'Is everything okay?' she asked, the hint of concern as sweet as the rest of her.

'My turn,' he managed, the words coming out on a croak, his mouth as dry as the Sahara after a fifty-year drought.

He used his hands, to turn her round. Unhooking her bra, he cupped her breasts from behind. The nipples poked into his palms as he nestled the rigid weight of his arousal against her buttocks.

She leaned back against him, arched into his palms as he traced the puckered skin, plucked at the hard tips. He splayed a palm across her stomach, ventured beneath the waistband of her panties. She bucked as he traced the plump lips of her sex, found the slick nub.

Damn, how could he want her this much again? So much he felt clumsy and raw and as if he were touching her for the first time, the only time.

Her hands reached back and gripped his thighs to steady herself, the soft moan almost more than he could bear as he circled and rubbed, beckoning the orgasm forth as he fought to keep the thin thread on his control from snapping. He buried his face in her hair, wrapped his arm round her waist to hold her still as he stroked relentlessly. Her body shook and then bowed back as her ragged sobs signalled her climax.

The scent of seduction surrounded him as she sagged against him. He picked her up, placed her on the bed.

She looked dazed, unfocused, her eyes round with wonder. 'Thank you, you're awfully good at that.'

He basked in the surge of satisfaction—and thanked God that she hadn't noticed his hands trembling.

She glanced at the bedside table, sent him a cheeky smile. 'Are we going to use the syrup now?'

He stared at it blankly. Then reached for it blindly, trying to get his mind to engage. 'Yeah.'

Fun, superficial, relaxed. Keep it light, damn it. Keep it hot. Keep it non-committal.

Twisting the top, he drizzled a drop onto the rigid peak of one breast, watched the areola tighten—then concentrated on adorning the other nipple. The hot blood pounding hard in his groin.

She laughed, shifted, letting the sticky sweetness trickle into the valley between her breasts. 'Watch out. We'll get your sheets all sticky.'

'Like I care.' He forced his lips to lift, then capped the bottle, stuck it back on the table. Gripping her hips, he dragged her beneath him.

He bent to lick off the amber sugar he'd been addicted to since childhood. But as his tongue swirled across the tight peak and she let out a soft sob of stunned pleasure all he could taste was the intoxicating essence of her.

Iona lifted off the bed at the sweep of his tongue over sensitive flesh, her mind still fogged with afterglow. He feasted on her, licking and suckling, until her nipples throbbed, sharp jolts of sensation shooting down to her still-tender sex. She lifted her hips, felt the head of his erection brush her inner thigh.

Holding his cheeks, she lifted his face. 'Please, Zane, I need you inside me.'

Power shimmered through her veins along with the passion as his eyes darkened.

Lifting up, he reached into a drawer on the bedside table, brought out a condom and sheathed himself.

Holding her hips, he bent her knees, positioning her so she was open to him and then surged inside in one devastating thrust. The fullness shocked her, so much more than before. She held on to broad shoulders, her fingers slipping on sweat-slicked skin. But then he started to move and the pressure built and intensified, turning to blinding, burning, all-consuming pleasure.

Her lids fluttered shut as the firestorm blazed through her, seizing her chest, rushing over her skin, making her breath hitch, her mind float, her centre throb.

'Look at me, don't close your eyes.' The words were harsh, demanding, but just beneath was the hint of desperation.

Her eyes flew open and she saw something wild and intense in the brilliant blue. He thrust harder, thrust deeper, stroking that secret place deep inside. Then reached down, expert fingers stroking her core.

'Come for me again, damn it.' The words ground out low and demanding as the wave of orgasm rushed towards her. Hard, fast and unstoppable.

Sensation exploded as her body broke apart, the waves of pleasure battering her. She sobbed, the cry of shock and exultation drowned out by his shout of release as he collapsed on top of her.

Iona drifted back to consciousness, his weight heavy on her, which had to explain the pressure on her chest. She could hear his tortured breathing and felt the hitch in her heartbeat.

Don't get carried away. Good sex. No, great sex. Is all about physical gratification. And nothing whatsoever to do with emotion.

But even knowing that, she couldn't resist the heavy beat of contentment as she stroked her hands over the long muscles of his back. Maybe this was only short-term, but however long it lasted, while it lasted, he would be all hers. The thought made her a little giddy.

She trailed her fingers over the bumps of his spine, smiled at his soft grunt of acknowledgement. And felt a little smug at the knowledge that she had exhausted him.

She stopped, her brows bunching, as her fingertips encountered two puckered scars high on his hip. 'What's this?' she asked.

He lifted up, rolled off her, dislodging her hands. Propping himself up on one elbow, he leaned over her. 'That was really something,' he murmured, dropping a proprietary kiss on her nose. 'For an amateur, you're awfully good at that,' he said, echoing her earlier compliment.

Her heartbeat kicked up a notch at the approval in his eyes and she forced herself not to care that he hadn't answered her question. She could always ask him again.

After all, they couldn't spend all their time together making love. If what had just happened was anything to go by, they'd end up killing each other. Funny to think, though, that she was just as excited about the time they would spend together out of bed as well as in it.

He placed one heavy palm on her midriff, traced the edge of her belly button with his fingertip. She felt the surprising jolt of arousal at her core, and wiggled out from under him. 'Now don't start that again,' she said, bending over to scoop her dress off the floor.

'Why not?'

She sent him a wry look over her shoulder. 'I need a quick shower, if that's okay? And then I need breakfast.' Her lips hitched. He looked so impossibly tempting with that puzzled frown etched on his brow. 'A girl can't live on great sex alone, you know.'

'This is true.' He got out of bed on the other side. She watched him locate his boxer shorts, admired the tight orbs of his backside flexing as he bent to pick them up.

No wonder he was so comfortable naked. Why would anyone so staggeringly good-looking ever have a reason to be self-conscious? But somehow the thought of his looks didn't feel intimidating any more. Maybe because of the memory of his face, harsh with desire and demand, as he'd climaxed.

He pulled the boxers up his legs, and the strips of sunlight rippled over the scars she'd felt on his back. And suddenly she knew exactly what had caused them. 'Who shot you?'

He twisted round. Glanced back. 'Huh?'

She pointed to the circular, puckered scars. 'There on your back—those are bullet wounds, aren't they?'

'Yeah.' He sounded nonchalant, but didn't offer an explanation.

'What happened?' she pressed—the distressing thought of him being shot and in pain making the happy glow from their lovemaking dim considerably.

He shrugged. 'I messed up.'

'How?'

He glanced at her. 'You really want to know?'

'Yes, I really want to know,' she pressed some more, ignoring the shuttered expression.

He heaved a sigh, but to her surprise began to talk. 'We were on a stake-out. A low-level meth head. But we had intell he was in contact with the area's main dealer. When he turned up he had a girl with him. She was strung-out, looked no more than thirteen or fourteen and he...' Zane paused, shrugged, the movement so stiff it made Iona's breath get trapped in her throat. 'I broke cover, against orders and got shot for my trouble, and we didn't pick up the dealer.'

'You protected her,' she murmured, her chest tight.

He looked up, his gaze blank with memory. 'She was a kid. I couldn't sit by and do nothing.'

No, she thought, someone like him with such a strong streak of integrity wouldn't. No wonder she felt so safe with him. 'You did the right thing,' she murmured, impossibly touched by another tiny insight into his past and what it revealed about him.

He gave a harsh laugh. 'My commander didn't think so. He said the kid was collateral damage. I got suspended from duty and quit two months later.'

'You still did the right thing.' Did he doubt it?

He hitched a shoulder, his gaze sharp and intent. 'Maybe.'

He strolled round to her side of the bed, took her hand and hauled her up. 'Let's go grab a shower.' His hands strayed down to her naked behind, squeezed.

She wriggled out of his arms, her emotions suddenly too full to risk that kind of intimacy. 'I don't think so,' she said, keeping her voice light and flirtatious. 'If we shower together we'll get distracted. And it'll be midday before we have breakfast.'

'I've never known a woman to eat like you do.'

'Do you have a problem with that?' she said coquettishly, knowing from his admiring gaze that he didn't.

'Not at all. One of the things I love about you is your appetite,' he said, but she wasn't convinced he was still talking about food.

He grinned as the blush fired up her neck, but didn't offer any objections when she pulled her dress over her head. He might not be self-conscious about his nakedness, but suddenly she was.

Getting off the bed, he sighed. 'Okay, I'll shower in the guest bath,' he said. 'You can take this one. Then I promise to feed you.' He crossed his fingers over his chest. 'But in return I'm gonna expect lots of really dirty sexual favours.'

She scooped up the maple-syrup bottle on the nightstand, inspired by the mischievous look in his eyes and grateful that the rush of emotion had been replaced by the surge of lust. 'Watch it, Montoya, I am now in charge of the syrup bottle.'

He gave a low groan as she swirled her tongue around the neck of the bottle, then lapped at the drops of syrup that had dripped down from the lid. 'And I'm more than prepared to use it,' she finished before shooting off to the bathroom—with his pained shout of frustration echoing in her ears.

She closed the door, her heartbeat thumping with exhilaration and something she refused to address.

This affair wasn't a big deal. But why shouldn't she take pleasure in getting a peek behind that mask of devil-may-care charm he wore so easily—to discover the fascinating and complex man beneath? A man she would have the time to discover fully in the weeks ahead.

And if she had to use really dirty sexual favours to do it?

She laughed, the throaty chuckle filled with a sexual confidence she'd never felt before in her life.

Well goodness, it was a tough job, but someone had to do it.

CHAPTER ELEVEN

'DON'T WORRY, GIRL, not long now.' Iona smiled at C.D., who gave her tail a lazy flap on the deck, keeping up her patient vigil for Zane.

Funny to think she and Zane had been having their casual sex-fling for nearly a month now. The time had passed in a blur of hard work, lazy dates and seriously hot sex—which had only got hotter when she'd moved into his place a week ago.

She'd had her misgivings at first, more than a little concerned about taking him up on his offer of a place to stay when his friend had got a vacation renter for the cottage. She knew she needed to be careful about coming to depend on him too much. But she'd been spending so much time at his place anyway in the weeks before that, he'd managed to make her objections seem like a childish overreaction. They were both adults, both completely clear about what this was and what it wasn't, and why should she go hunting up a new place when he was perfectly happy to have her stay here?

In the end she'd agreed, putting her mind at rest about the intensity of their affair by promising herself as soon as she had the required funds, she would book her return flight to Scotland.

She dabbed the ochre watercolour onto the pet portrait she'd been commissioned to do by one of Zane's clients—

and ignored the flicker of dismay because she hadn't quite got round to booking the flight, yet.

It was simply because she was having such a good time here. Carefree and fun—and she'd also found a surprisingly fulfilling and lucrative outlet for her art.

Never having managed to find any seasonal work in Monterey, she'd been helped out of a financial hole when her neighbour in Pacific Grove, Mrs Mendoza, had asked her to paint a portrait of her Jack Russell, Zapata. Mr Spencer's cat Figaro was her tenth commission, the new cottage industry providing her with another practical reason to stay at Zane's. With all its natural light, his beach house was the perfect place to paint. She choked out a little laugh—and then of course there were the other, more exhilarating benefits of living here to consider.

Zane had looked so surprised when she'd joined him in his shower this morning, he'd dropped the soap. And risen to full attention so fast she'd been a little worried he might collapse from the loss of blood to his head.

For someone whose sex life prior to Zane had been spectacularly bad, the way he reacted to her never failed to thrill her. Hearing his heartfelt groan when she'd sunk to her knees and swirled her tongue over the head of that beautiful erection had been yet more proof that she now had the ability to make men weak at the knees. Or at least this man.

She loved the way he responded so readily to her teasing and her playfulness. Finding Zane's buttons, and pushing them, discovering his limits and then charging right through them had become as addictive as the man himself, and all the things he could do to her.

Iona dropped her brush into the turpentine, and stretched her spine, casting a critical eye on the portrait of the slightly moth-eaten but wise-eyed rescue cat.

She felt pleasantly fatigued and a little achy from standing in the same position while C.D. dozed beside her. She felt the answering ache tug her abdomen at the thought of Zane's imminent return, and grinned.

She rinsed the paintbrushes and packed them up ready for tomorrow. Drawing the easel up, she carried it and the half-finished painting into the house and stowed them in the alcove where Zane had suggested she keep her supplies. The dog's claws skidded on the wooden flooring as Iona slid the screen door closed and headed for the kitchen with C.D. at her heels.

As the weather was a little cooler than it had been the last two days, she'd put together a lasagne. She enjoyed cooking, had learned how as a young girl when she and her father had had to survive on their own. But she'd forgotten how much she enjoyed cooking for others. And now she could use Zane's state-of-the-art kitchen—instead of the tiny kitchenette at the cottage—it had become a real pleasure again. Of course, he'd moaned at first about her paying for all the grocery shopping, but she'd finally convinced him that if he wouldn't accept any rent he'd have to let her at least do this much to pay her way.

After ladling out C.D.'s chow and getting the dog a fresh bowl of water, she began searching for the salad ingredients in the fridge. Funny how after only a week in Zane's house, they'd settled so easily into a routine.

She glanced at the clock on the kitchen wall. Six o'clock. He'd be home in about an hour—and they'd be able to have a leisurely walk with C.D. before they had dinner. Or maybe they'd opt for sex first and dinner later.

The grin widened.

Quite apart from the empowering sex, she'd also got a surprising insight into the man in the last week. He still generally avoided talking about himself much, but their routine had allowed him to relax more and so she'd managed to weasel a few more details out of him, especially about his work.

It was so strange now, she thought as she sliced tomato and shredded lettuce, to think that when she'd first met him she'd been so critical, and more than a little suspicious about what he did for a living. Now she knew about the huge diversity of work his firm provided and how closely he supervised and controlled every aspect of it, she could see why keeping a similar rein on every other aspect of his personal life might be natural for him.

Zane exhibited a real dedication to duty in everything he did, which had made him not only a staggeringly successful entrepreneur, but also any woman's dream lover. But it was when she managed to shake that precious control that she enjoyed their time together the most.

C.D. sent up a series of exited yips, nearly making Iona slice off her thumb, before her less-sensitive hearing picked up the hum of a car engine in the driveway.

She was drying her hands on a dishcloth when the bell chimed. Excitement tickled her skin as she headed down the hallway. Was Zane home early?

Tonight might well be an evening for sex first, dinner later. Her lips twitched. In fact, she might have to insist upon it.

The excitement fizzled, though, when she spotted the silhouette through the glass bricks that framed the front door. That wasn't Zane. And then a white envelope popped through the letter slot.

She picked up her pace and opened the door, grabbing hold of C.D.'s collar to stop the dog barrelling after the woman already strolling back to a shiny red Beemer—with a baby perched on her hip.

'Hello, can I help you?' Iona called after her visitor, her disappointment turning to curiosity as she lifted the heavy envelope from the mat and spotted Zane's name in ornate lettering.

The woman swung round in a circle, making the baby giggle. 'Oh, hi,' she said. 'I thought there was no one in.'

She walked back and Iona felt the prickle of envy at the woman's tall, lithe figure. She exuded the slim, poised confidence of a supermodel with her short, classically cut blonde bob, which accentuated her amazing bone structure and a pair of stunning emerald eyes. The simple cotton summer dress that flowed around long legs and a cropped jean jacket only added to her funky glamour. The baby, who Iona would have guessed was about a year old, had soft curls of dark hair that framed a round face—and appeared to be blessed with the same easy smile and flawless petal-soft skin as his mother.

'I'm so sorry to bother you. Are you Zane's housekeeper?' the woman said, still smiling politely.

A panicked little flutter set up under Iona's breastbone. Okay, this was a little awkward.

The baby clutched a hand of his mother's hair in one fat little fist, and stared owlishly at Iona. As his mother laughed and extricated herself Iona got a much better look at the child. And the panicked flutter became a blast of astonishment.

The child had the same striking, translucent blue eyes as Zane, even down to the unusual dark rim around the irises.

Good Lord. Did Zane have a child he hadn't mentioned to her? She knew he was tight-lipped but that would be ridiculous, surely?

'Um, no, not exactly,' Iona stuttered. Not quite sure what the etiquette was in this situation. 'My name's Iona MacCabe,' she said, deciding that honesty was probably the best policy. 'I'm sort of living here, at the moment.'

The woman looked disconcerted, but gathered herself quickly, the curious smile staying in place. If she was Zane's babymama she seemed remarkably nonchalant about the new arrangements.

'You're Scottish,' she remarked.

'And you're English,' Iona replied, having been so preoccupied with the baby's eyes she had only just recognised the crisp cut-off vowels of her neighbouring countryman.

'How lovely,' the woman said, apparently sincere, and held out her hand. 'Hi, I'm Tess Tremaine. Oh, bugger...' she said, clapping her hand to her forehead as her smile became sheepish. 'Sorry, Tess Graystone. Would you believe it? We've been married for months and I can never remember to use his name.'

She shook Iona's hand with surprising vigour while the baby continued to stare, its fist now stuffed in its mouth.

'Nate thinks it's a Freudian slip because I'm secretly planning to run off with our estate manager, Manolito.' She rolled her eyes charmingly. 'As if! The poor man's seventy if he's a day…'

The husky chuckle at her own joke made Iona smile, liking the woman. And Nate had to be her husband, so maybe she was mistaken about the baby.

'I think I owe your husband a debt of gratitude,' Iona said. 'I was staying in his cottage in Pacific Grove up until about a week ago.'

'That was you?' The woman's eyes lit now with a mixture of both excitement and curiosity. 'And now you're *sort of* living with Zane?'

Iona nodded, not sure why she was getting such an enthusiastic reception, but willing to go with it. 'Yes, that would be me.'

'How intriguing.' The woman jiggled the baby on her hip, making him giggle. 'I'm afraid I'm now going to have to invite myself in for a cup of tea and quiz you mercilessly. Because I've only ever met a couple of Zane's girlfriends and I've got to tell you—' Tess's gaze flickered over Iona, making her hopelessly self-conscious about her paint-flecked T-shirt, faded cut-offs and bare feet '—they were both boringly predictable in comparison to you.'

Iona huffed out a laugh, relieved at the woman's cheeky smile and her apparent candour, and desperately curious herself. 'You're more than welcome to come in for a cuppa,' Iona offered. But as she stepped back to let Tess into the house she got another good look at the toddler who stared at her with Zane's eyes and had to add, 'As long as you don't mind me quizzing you about Zane right back.'

'That seems only fair,' Tess said easily, bouncing the baby on her hip as they walked down the hallway towards the kitchen. 'Although I can't imagine I'm going to be much use. Even though Zane and Nate have been friends for ever, I'm afraid to say, ever since Brandon here was born, he's been a bit of a stranger. That's why I'm here, actually.' She nodded at the invite still clutched in Iona's fingers. 'To make sure he shows for the christening. I'm a little tired of us all pussy-footing around the issue of Zane's relationship to Brandon. So I was going to try to guilt him into making an appearance.'

Iona placed the invitation carefully on the countertop and filled the kettle. *Zane's relationship to Brandon?* So he was the baby's father?

The odd clutch in the pit of Iona's stomach made no sense, so she ignored it. She was just a casual fling—and Tess was the mother of his child. She had no call to feel possessive or resentful—or hurt. But as she pulled two mugs out of the cabinet she did feel she had a reason to be annoyed with Zane. Why hadn't he told her about the boy? The cup clattered onto the countertop as her fingers shook. Surely even a casual fling deserved that much information?

'Is something wrong?' Tess asked, touching Iona's arm. 'You look rather pale.'

'Yes, I…' Iona began, righting the cup and turning to Tess, whose inquisitiveness was now tempered with concern. Iona sighed, deciding it was probably best to just spill it. She'd never had much time for pussy-footing about either. 'You're being ludicrously reasonable about all this, Tess. And I don't know what the circumstances are surrounding the wee lad's birth.' For all she knew Zane might have donated sperm for his friend Nate. 'Zane didn't tell me about Brandon,' she continued, picking up the invite. 'Or this… But I guarantee you, I'm not the one stopping him from visiting his son.'

Tess's perfectly plucked eyebrows launched up her forehead, and then she let out a delighted laugh. 'You have no idea how priceless that is.'

'Why?' Iona asked, starting to feel as if she'd entered an alternative reality.

Tess gave her son a kiss on the nose. 'Brandon's not Zane's son. He's my husband's son. He's Nate's son.'

Iona stared at the boy again. And Zane's eyes stared straight back at her. 'But then how comes he has the same—?'

'Because that sky-blue colour and the dark ring around is a genetic anomaly,' Tess interrupted, clearly knowing exactly what Iona was referring to. 'An anomaly that runs very strongly through the male line in the Graystone family,' Tess added, her tone patient. 'Zane is Nate's brother. Or rather his half-brother. They have the same father.' The woman's smile faded. 'Not that anyone's allowed to mention it. Because as it happens, pig-headedness also runs very strongly through the male line in the Graystone family.'

Iona stared, having been given more information about Zane's father in a single sentence than she'd managed to prise out of him in a month. The one time she'd asked about his father, his reaction had been so cold and dismissive she'd never made the mistake of mentioning it again.

'Doggie,' the baby chortled and gestured wildly at C.D., cutting through Iona's thoughts.

'Why don't you go and give Cookie Dough a hug?' Tess said, letting the baby down and holding his hand as he toddled over to the dog's basket.

Iona's curiosity levels shot straight to fever pitch as she watched C.D. accept the baby's attentions with a patient thump of her tail.

So the *pinche gringo* was his best friend Nate's father too. And Tess seemed like a very nice, and very talkative woman, who was more than willing to be quizzed on the subject.

Iona depressed the switch on the kettle. 'How much time

have you got, Tess?' she asked. 'I have a feeling this is going to take more than one cup of tea.'

Tess laughed and checked her watch. 'I'm at your disposal, for at least another half hour.'

Iona prepared the teapot, hunted up some chocolate cookies she'd made two days ago, and dismissed the twinge of guilt at talking about something behind Zane's back that he'd gone to great lengths to keep private.

The man had shoe-horned pretty much every detail of her personal life previous to the moment she'd met him out of her during their long walks on the beach and over dinner every evening, and ante'd up very little in return, despite Iona's concerted efforts in that direction—really dirty sexual favours included. Frankly, she was obliged to take Tess up on her offer—so she didn't expire from curiosity like the proverbial cat.

And anyway, this was what happened when you dated a detective. You were forced to get sneaky back.

'But that's ridiculous,' Iona remarked, dunking her second cookie into the now tepid cup of tea. 'How can they be best friends, know that they're also brothers and yet never talk about it? Or even acknowledge it?'

'It's beyond ridiculous.' Tess hugged her son, who sat on her lap busy gumming his cookie into a soggy mess. 'Especially now we have Brandon. Zane's his uncle and yet we're not allowed to say so.' She hitched her shoulders in an exaggerated shrug. 'All I know is that they did talk about it when they were kids. And as a result of what happened, Nate refuses to bring it up again, until Zane says something first. And Zane never has. In fact, I have a suspicion that's why he's made himself scarce ever since Brandon was born. So now we're at this ridiculous impasse. You see what I mean about the pig-headedness.'

'What happened when they talked about it as kids?'

'To be honest, Nate doesn't talk about it much, because it still hurts, I suspect. He totally idolised Zane as a boy when he first went to live with his grandfather at San Revelle,' she said, mentioning the fanciful castle that Nate's great-grandfather had built near Half-Moon Bay and where Tess and her family now lived. 'Maria worked as his grandfather's housekeeper and she and Zane lived on the estate, so Nate spent all his free time at their cottage. Nate only found out years later that she'd gone to work there after Nate's parents had kicked her out.'

For getting pregnant by Nate's father, Iona thought, still disgusted by what Tess had already told her of Maria's past and the behaviour of a man who had seduced a teenager in his employ and then discarded her like so much rubbish as soon as her pregnancy started to show. Seemed Juana's assessment of Harrison Graystone was correct.

The Gallivanting Graystones, as the society press had dubbed Nate's parents, had both died in a light aircraft crash over a decade ago, en route to a party in Martha's Vineyard, but had left few people to grieve their parting, least of all their son Nate, who had been estranged from them both for years.

Iona thought it desperately sad, though, that the bad seeds Harrison Graystone had sown could end up destroying the friendship between his two sons. Why couldn't Nate and Zane be brothers, even if their father had disowned one and never acknowledged the other? Especially as they had bonded so young—and had remained friends despite everything.

Tess sighed as she wiped Brandon's mouth with a tissue. 'All I know is that when Nate discovered the truth about Zane's parentage he was overjoyed. He'd always wanted a proper family and he already thought of Maria as a surrogate mother. So naturally, he raced down to the cottage to tell Zane without thinking about Zane's reaction…' Tess's voice trailed off, as if even she couldn't bear to recall what she'd been told. 'He was only twelve, for Pete's sake.'

'What happened?' Iona prompted.

'Zane went berserk,' Tess said softly. 'He punched Nate and kept on punching him until Maria pulled them apart.'

Iona gasped, her stomach hurting now, not only at the thought of what Nate had endured, but also at how angry and confused Zane must have been to react in that way.

He'd once told her he'd been wild as a teenager, but Iona couldn't imagine him being violent. It simply didn't jibe with the man she had come to know—because beneath Zane's lazy, devilishly sexy charm was a man who always strived to keep his emotions on lockdown. It was what made seducing him such a delicious challenge. But now she was beginning to wonder if his control wasn't a symptom of something painful and much more deep-seated than simply a desire to be in charge in bed.

'Do you think Zane might have been in shock?' Iona asked. 'And that's why he lashed out?'

'No, it's more complicated than that.' Tess shook her head. 'Nate's convinced he already knew who his father was. Which is why Nate refuses to mention it to Zane again. Zane rejected their connection once, in the most graphic way possible—so Nate reverted to the Guy Code to salvage their friendship.'

'The Guy Code?'

'Avoidance as the better part of valour.' Tess got up from the stool to bounce Brandon on her hip, who had become a little fussy now his second cookie had been demolished. 'They pretend it never happened.' Tess scoffed. 'Which is patently counterproductive, but Nate refuses to budge.' She pulled a multicoloured rattle out of her purse, and waved it in front of Brandon—who grabbed it and wedged it into his mouth.

'So you thought you might be able to persuade Zane to talk about it instead?' Iona said as realisation dawned. 'By making sure he comes to the christening?'

'Yes, Brandon's even named after him—Zane's his middle name—so I thought if he came he might...' Tess plopped back on her stool, her son now drooling contentedly over the chew-toy. 'It's a stupid idea, isn't it?' she said, resigned. 'Zane makes Nate look like an amateur when it comes to avoidance.' She pushed out a breath. 'But seriously, I'm desperate. I feel like there's this big elephant in the room every time we see him, and, while the two of them are busy avoiding it, I keep tripping over it. I want to know why they can't be brothers as well as friends. And I think Nate does too, although of course he won't say so. But it's worse than that. A week ago Nate asked Zane to be Bran's godfather and he point-blank refused—I think they had a bit of a row about it, in fact, but of course Nate won't talk about that either now.'

'When is the christening?' Iona asked, knowing she shouldn't be interfering, but not quite able to stop herself.

She liked Tess. Had warmed to her instantly, in fact, even when she had believed she might be the mother of Zane's son. And could totally sympathise with Tess's frustration— because she'd been on the receiving end of Zane's stone-walling too.

But more importantly than that, her heart ached for Zane. Why was he so determined to isolate himself, not just from Nate and his nephew, but also from his mother's family too?

Hearing Tess talk about his reaction to Nate's news had re-minded her of the tense, distant way he had handled Maria's family at the *quinceañera*. The more people reached out to him, it seemed, the more he tried to pull away. What was it that made it so hard for him to let people get close?

Iona didn't think for a second that she had any special in-sight into the answer. But she knew it wasn't a good thing. Zane needed that in his life, she knew he did, because during their lovemaking, on those rare occasions when Zane's guard was down, she got a tiny glimpse of all those needs that he was busy pretending didn't exist.

Maybe it was foolish of her, but she wanted to help him in whatever small way she could. Surely that was the least she could do, after the many ways in which he had helped her?

'The christening's next Thursday, the twenty-fifth,' Tess said.

'Right,' Iona replied, trying to think of how she could bring it up with Zane.

'Do you think you could get him to come?' Tess asked, her eyes lighting with enthusiasm. 'I know it's a big ask—and I shouldn't really involve you in all this—but I'm all out of ideas.'

'I'll give him the invite.' She picked the envelope up. 'And make sure he reads it. I'm afraid that's all I can promise.' She didn't hold out much hope of persuading Zane to do anything, especially as she was only a casual fling. But surely it couldn't hurt to at least try.

'That's brilliant, Iona, and so sweet of you.'

'Do you want to give me your phone number, and I'll let you know if I have any luck?'

'Yes, of course.' Tess whipped out her mobile phone and they exchanged numbers. 'So now you need to tell me more about you and Zane.'

'Oh, there's really nothing much to tell. We're just a casual thing...' she said, the words oddly leaden on her tongue all of a sudden... 'It's no serious. Which is why I wouldn't get your hopes up too high about me being able to persuade Zane to come to the christening.'

She tried to shrug off the melancholy thought. She needed to keep a good firm grip on the fact that, however much she might want to help Tess, Zane's family wasn't her family.

'But that's...' Tess's mouth pursed into a thin line. 'That's silly. How can you possibly be a casual thing when you're living in his house?'

'It's not really significant,' Iona said, prevaricating deliberately. Even though she knew Zane and her weren't serious, had never been serious, she didn't want to tell Tess exactly how not serious they were.

'But you're sleeping together? Aren't you?'

'Aye, but only because…' God, why did their arrangement suddenly sound a little sordid? 'Well, it's fun and convenient.' And casual… Remember casual.

Tess blinked. 'Iona, now this is just me being nosey, and obviously I've only just met you. But did Zane ever mention his Golden Rules to you?'

'Golden Rules? No.'

Tess let Brandon wriggle down off her lap, and watched him crawl over to C.D., before turning her attention back to Iona. 'Okay, this is second-hand, because Zane told these to Nate and then I managed to shoehorn them out of Nate when I said how odd I thought it was that Zane had never been snared by some lucky woman. You know, because he's so available and so confident with women and so handsome and so ridiculously sexy—I mean, the man's practically got a sign on him that says "I can make you come till you pass out."'

Iona laughed, while at the same time feeling her cheeks heat.

Tess pointed. 'Bloody hell, I knew he would be phenomenal in bed. He is, isn't he?'

Iona coughed out a laugh as embarrassment warred with smugness. 'Well, I'm no a great judge, because my sex life sucked before I met him—but I will say that, for once, the advertising doesn't lie.'

'Stop right there, before I have to slap you.' Tess held up her hand in mock indignation. 'Do you have any idea how much a toddler mucks up your sex life? These days me and Nate have to make an appointment to have an orgasm. And foreplay? Forget it.'

Iona laughed. 'So what are Zane's Golden Rules?' This should be interesting.

'Okay, let me see if I can remember these correctly. First off, he never sleeps with anyone on a first date, because he doesn't like to appear too pushy.'

'Oh.' Iona felt her colour rising again.

'Ah-ha, I'm getting the impression from that lovely shade of pink that he broke that rule.'

'Well, I…'

'How about this one, then? Another of Zane's Golden Rules is that he always gives his dates The Speech.' Tess did air quotes. 'Before he sleeps with them.'

'What Speech?'

'You haven't even had The Speech? About how this is strictly short-term and lightweight and not to get too attached.'

'Ah, well, yes, he did sort of give me that.' Hadn't he said something along those lines the first morning they'd spent here?

'Only sort of?' Tess gave a considering hum. 'That still sounds like a fairly significant departure from Zane Montoya's Golden Rules of Non-Engagement.' She did a quick check on Brandon, who was busy tugging on the ever-patient C.D.'s one good ear. 'Especially as we already know the last two are already toast.'

'What are they?'

Tess lifted her fingers to count them off. 'He doesn't let dates meet his family—and you went to his cousin's party, right? He even invited you specially.'

'But I think he only did that under duress,' Iona qualified, starting to feel very uneasy.

'Fine, but it's still breaking the rules, and, most important of all, he never lets women move in with him. Period.'

'What? Never?'

Tess shook her head. 'I think he had some live-in girlfriends back when he was a cop and he told Nate they would freak out when he did overtime or nightshifts and didn't mention it. In other words, they had the audacity to make demands on him like any normal person would. So these days anything beyond the occasional sleepover is too heavy for Zane. And yet here you are, living in his house.' Tess sniffed the air. 'Cooking him delicious dinners. Working on your art.

Bonding with his beloved dog.' Tess's grin widened. 'You may think this is casual, but all the evidence suggests it's anything but for Zane.'

Iona felt the pit of her stomach swoop down to her toes.

'Which brings me to my next question.' Tess leaned forward, skewering Iona with a determined frown. 'What exactly makes you think this isn't a serious relationship, with serious potential?'

Iona opened her mouth, to say all the platitudes that had come so easily a month ago. Because her real life was in Scotland and she was buying a ticket home, soon. Because her arrangement with Zane was never meant to be anything but temporary. Because they'd always agreed that this was casual—and not serious.

But not one of them would come out of her mouth, because not one of them sounded true. Or at least not the whole truth. Not any more.

'Th-there are a lot of reasons,' Iona stammered, and heard how lame that sounded.

Tess's eyebrow arched. 'I'm sure there are, but aren't there also some reasons to think this might be a lot more than the casual relationship you say it is? Like Zane's a fascinating, complex, intriguing and gorgeous guy—and you seem to be the only woman who's ever got under his guard?' Tess rocked back on the stool. 'Of course, if one of those reasons is you're not enjoying being with him—'

'But I am,' Iona interrupted, only to realise she'd given herself away big time when Tess's smile became a little conniving.

There was a heavy clatter and both women turned to see Brandon sitting on his butt on the marble floor, his face screwed up in a horrified grimace.

Tess jumped off the stool and scooped him up before the wail let loose. 'Bran, baby, it didn't hurt that much.' She settled the baby on her hip, apparently unfazed by the decibel level as her son howled as if he'd been stabbed in the eye with a hot poker.

'I better go,' she said, cooing at him. 'He only had a twenty-minute nap this afternoon so this is merely the start of the meltdown.' Gathering up her purse from the countertop, Tess leaned in to give Iona a kiss on the cheek. 'It was wonderful to meet you, Iona. And I really, really hope this isn't the last time I see you.'

'I'll do my best to get Zane to Brandon's christening,' she said as Tess's long-legged stride took her down the hallway ahead of her.

Tess paused on the doorstep, Brandon's howls subsiding to choking sobs. 'If you can at least get him to consider coming, I'd be eternally grateful.' She took Iona's hand in hers and gave it a quick reassuring squeeze. 'But could you do me an even bigger favour?'

'What's that?'

'Don't run off back to Scotland too soon. Zane's an amazing guy for all his pig-headedness, and I think he deserves someone special who can shake up his life—and get past all that industrial-strength charm to the man beneath.'

The shot of adrenaline returned, accompanied by the kick of panic.

'But how do you know I'm that someone?' Iona asked, the panic starting to choke her.

Tess shrugged. 'I don't, but then neither do you. And if you leave without giving this relationship a sporting chance, you never will.' She bounced the baby on her hip, her voice sobering. 'I guess it boils down to whether you want to find out for sure?'

With those disturbing parting words, Tess headed off down the driveway. After loading the now hiccoughing Brandon into his car seat, she sent Iona a jaunty wave goodbye.

Iona stood on the doorstep, watching the shiny Beemer

turn into Seventeen Mile Drive and disappear from view. Her heart galloped into her throat.

She pressed her hand to her shaky tummy…feeling a little nauseous.

She checked her watch. Zane would be back soon. And for once she wished he'd take his time. What if Tess were right? She already knew this wasn't as casual for her as it should be, or she would have bought her ticket home by now. But what if it wasn't casual for Zane either? And did she have the guts to find out for sure? To risk having him reject her?

And how the heck was she going to eat the lasagne she'd spent an hour preparing earlier, when her tummy was doing cartwheels?

CHAPTER TWELVE

'THAT'S GREAT. LET'S schedule a conference call tomorrow with your contact in Ocean Beach, then we can turn over the evidence to the San Diego PD.' Zane pushed a hand through his hair and ended the call to his detective.

They were within days of catching the scammer who'd been selling non-existent luxury cars on an Internet auction site, but the sweet rush that usually accompanied closing any big investigation was conspicuous by its absence. Probably because his mind had been less and less on work lately and more and more on what he was missing while he spent the long hours his business demanded away from Iona.

Iona. With her bright, teasing smile, her warm golden-brown eyes, her funny, forthright conversation and that lush full mouth that could drive him wild and scare the hell out of him at one and the same time.

In the last week, ever since she'd moved in with him, it had become a major struggle to leave her every morning, and harder still to stay tied to his desk until he could return each evening. And he knew why. Because every moment he was away from her he could feel the time they had left together slipping through his fingers. The last month had shot past in a haze of spectacular sex and scintillating conversation and easy companionship and he could already see the day when she would get on a plane and return home to Scotland racing towards them at breakneck speed.

Rising from his desk, he opened his briefcase to stuff in the papers he was supposed to be reviewing this evening, but knew he was unlikely even to look at.

It was plain dumb and illogical to be worrying about her leaving so much, when that had always been the plan. But the more time he spent with Iona, the more dumb and illogical he seemed to get.

He grabbed his suit jacket from the hook behind the door and headed down the corridor.

He'd had spectacular sex before and scintillating conversation, but it was the quiet times when he knew he didn't have to talk, didn't have to charm, didn't have to make her feel good because she was already there that he had become really addicted to.

This urgency, this need to have her, would eventually pass. But when? They were a month in and it was showing no signs of waning, yet. He rolled his shoulders, the muscles contracting at the thought of the fifteen-minute drive home before he could see her.

The last couple of evenings, he'd had to put in a titanic effort not to fall on her like a starving man as soon as he got home. He rubbed the back of his neck as he strode through the building. Hell, yesterday evening, when they'd been on the beach, C.D. barking at the surf, she'd laughed and the husky, smoky sound had arrowed right through him—and all of a sudden, he'd been hard as an iron spike.

He gave Jim an absent wave as he passed his office. His mind already focused on putting a stranglehold on the growing warmth in his crotch. How many times in the last few weeks had he driven home with a hard-on? It was a damn miracle he hadn't totalled the mustang on Highway One.

As he walked into the parking lot, the buzz of his cell phone cut the evening quiet. Pulling it out, he spotted his mother's name on the display. Unlocking the mustang, he dumped his briefcase on the passenger seat, and tossed the cell on top, ignoring the prickle of guilt as he waited for the call to go to voicemail.

He'd hardly spoken to his mother since the *quinceañera* a month ago, because when he had it hadn't gone well. For years his mother had tried to get him to talk about his father. And for years he'd never had too much of a problem deflecting her.

But in the last week, ever since he'd turned down his friend Nate's request to become his son Bran's godfather, he'd found it harder and harder to deal with his mother.

Zane's shoulders cramped as the cell stopped ringing. He'd have to call her soon, he knew that, but not tonight. Not when his addiction to Iona was already tying his brain in knots.

Avoidance *was* the answer and it always had been when it came to the question of his relationship with his father, and Nate, and his son Bran, because the alternative was unthinkable. And he couldn't risk going there again.

He flexed his fingers, his knuckles throbbing at the sudden memory of that morning when he'd been fourteen years old and he'd hit his best friend and kept on hitting him. Connecting with bone, feeling Nate's flesh tear, seeing the sticky blood splatter Nate's favourite Spiderman T-shirt, hearing the startled whimpers of pain, the thud of the blows as they landed—and feeling nothing, not even the smarting skin on his knuckles, until his mother's screams had cut through the rage.

The jolt of shame hit harder as he recalled the look on Nate's face last week when his friend had asked him to be Bran's godfather, and he'd come up with some lie about not being all that into kids.

Nate had been shocked and saddened but had remained silent. And Zane hadn't had the guts to tell him the real reason he couldn't be Bran's godfather.

He was into kids, especially Nate's kid; Bran fascinated

him. He could still recall the staggering feeling, tinged with awe, when he'd arrived at the maternity hospital last April and this tiny perfect bundle of humanity had been cradled in Nate's arms. But as Bran had grown, seeing him had brought back echoes of the quiet all-consuming rage that had dogged his every step as a teenager and been kept so carefully contained as an adult.

Brandon was another child with Harrison Graystone's eyes. And that meant Zane couldn't bear to spend too much time with the boy.

He straightened, his shoulders screaming with tension. The sun beating down on him through the car window did nothing to melt the fury and disgust settling in his gut like a block of ice.

His mother didn't know, would never know, how much he already knew about his father, Harrison Graystone. And he would never let her know, because she'd already suffered enough. So until he found a better strategy for avoiding the conversation she seemed determined to have with him about Nate, and Bran and his father, he was forced to avoid her calls instead.

He turned on the transmission and cranked up the AC. But as the clammy sweat dried on his brow he pressed his foot on the gas, speeding back to his house on the bay. Because he knew only one thing would chase away the chill.

Iona.

Sinking into her hot, wet flesh, hearing her broken sobs as she fisted around him would make it all go away—for another day.

C.D.'s sudden barks from the hallway had Iona juggling the lasagne. Her heart rate jumped as she heard the low murmur of Zane's voice and the front door slamming.

And then her heart stopped completely as he walked into the kitchen. How could she not have noticed how seeing his face still took her breath away even now? But then she noticed the creases at the corners of his eyes as he slung his briefcase onto the countertop and the deep grooves around his mouth. He looked shattered.

'Hey, honey, I'm home,' he said with a grim smile.

The dog jumped to prop her paws on his waist, but instead of making a fuss of her, as he usually did, he gave her an impatient shove. 'C.D., will you quit that now?'

C.D. returned to her basket, her tail drooping almost comically. But Iona wasn't laughing. Seemed she wasn't the only one who'd had a disturbing day.

'What's wrong?' she asked.

Strong fingers curled around her wrist and he hauled her towards him. 'Nothing you can't fix.'

He wrapped his arms around her in a hard hug, buried his face in her hair and took a deep breath. But tension vibrated through him as his palms cupped her bottom.

The rush of lust stemmed the panic as she felt the familiar weight of his erection. She hugged him back, absorbed the delicious spicy scent.

Sex was easy. Simple. And it would make her forget her cartwheeling tummy.

The long firm muscles of his back rippled through his shirt as she ran her hands down his spine and felt the steady punch of his heartbeat against her ear.

'Supper smells terrific,' he murmured, framing her face in rough palms. 'But I don't want food right now. I want you.'

'Then we're in luck,' she said as she let all her worries about how attached she was getting be consumed by the insistent arousal. 'Because I know how to reheat it.'

The rumble of his laughter made her heart leap painfully and then his lips covered hers. Making her forget everything but the touch, the taste, the scent of him.

He plunged his tongue into her mouth, his fingers moulding her buttocks, then fumbling with the button on her shorts.

He swore and the button released. Searching fingers cupped her sex through her panties, making her swell against his hand.

'Zane, wait.' She pressed her hand over his to still the exploration, more than a little shaky. Sex was simple, so why did this suddenly feel like anything but?

'Why?' he demanded. 'You're soaking wet.'

'I know, it's…' She glanced over her shoulder, looking for a way to slow him down until she'd got the foolish vulnerability under control. And saw the dog watching their actions with big soulful eyes.

'We should take this upstairs,' she said. 'C.D.'s over there.'

'She's a dog, not a child,' he said, the tone sharp, but he dragged his hand out of her shorts.

Kicking the door open, he clicked his fingers. 'C.D. out.'

The dog slunk out, giving them a disconsolate look.

Zane slammed the door shut. 'Okay?'

'Yes, but…'

Before she could raise any more objections, his mouth swooped down. He grasped her waist and lifted her onto the counter. Dragging her shorts and panties down, he flung them away. Her naked bottom felt cold against the marble. She braced her hands behind her, shocked when he hooked her legs over his shoulders, forcing her to lean back and open for him completely.

He bent to flick his tongue over the swollen flesh. And then concentrated on driving her wild. The hot, rough strokes had her sobbing with staggered pleasure—the last of her defences crashing down as he set his mouth on her clitoris and suckled.

She tried to hold on, to hold back, to stop the rush of sensation devouring her but the ferocious orgasm slammed into her. The glorious wave crashing as she cried out her release.

He raised his head, those sapphire eyes dark with arousal as he released himself from his trousers. She clung to his neck, tasted herself on his lips, as he held her thighs apart, and plunged deep.

The raw shock of penetration—so full, so stretched—was nothing to the visceral shock of renewed arousal as he began to thrust—hard and fast. Digging his fingers into her hips, he held her powerless to resist the depth and intensity of his thrusts, the onslaught sending her back over the edge with alarming speed.

The endless orgasm crested, retreated and crested again. Until at last she shattered, her ragged sobs echoing off the cold hard surfaces.

He shouted as his own climax hit, his forehead slick with sweat as he buried his head against her neck and emptied himself into her.

Iona's hands trembled violently as she clasped the damp hair on Zane's nape, her body caught in the aftershock of the climax, her heart beating so hard she could feel it hitting her ribs.

What had just happened? She felt as if she'd survived a war—just barely survived it.

She groaned, the large erection still firm as he shifted then withdrew. Readjusting his trousers, he cursed and walked away, leaving her limp and trembling and shaken on the countertop.

She could feel the sticky residue of his semen as she climbed down, her legs like wet noodles as she picked up her knickers and cut-offs and put them on.

He stood by the kitchen's picture window, his shoulders and back rigid, his hands braced on the sink and his head bowed. The tail of his shirt hung outside his trousers.

'I'm sorry,' he whispered, the tone raw with an emotion she didn't understand.

His head lifted as she approached but he didn't look at her. The shadows of twilight cast his profile into harsh relief—the lines of exhaustion on his face more pronounced.

'I'm no better than he is.' The words came out on a barely audible murmur as if he were talking to himself.

'What are you apologising for?' she asked.

He dragged his hand through his hair as he turned to face her. 'I behaved like an animal. I didn't even take the time to suit up.'

'I could have asked you to stop if I'd wanted you to,' she replied, confused by the shame in his voice. 'I didn't.'

'What makes you think I would have stopped?'

'Because I know you,' she said, stunned by the question. 'And I know you would never do something like that.'

He shook his head. 'Which proves you don't know me at all.'

She placed her hand on his back, felt the bunched muscles through the creased cotton. 'Zane, what are you talking about? We had rough sex. Rough, consensual sex, which we both enjoyed.' She stroked trying to soothe the tremble of reaction. 'You have nothing to apologise for. I had more than one orgasm. And I happen to enjoy it more when you don't hold back.'

He huffed out a weary laugh, but the muscles remained rigid underneath her palm.

'Who were you talking about?' she asked, although she was sure she already knew. 'When you said you're no better than he is?'

His eyes met hers, the expression in them so sad, so confused she felt her heart constrict.

'My father. He raped my mother.' He straightened, and shoved bunched fists into his pockets. 'That's how I was conceived.'

Shock came first, swiftly followed by sadness at the controlled contempt in his voice. Was that why he strived so hard for control? Always struggled to hold back a part of himself? Because he thought he was responsible for that?

'How do you know? Did your mother tell you that?'

He stared at her blankly for a moment, then frowned. 'Of course not. I've never spoken to her about him,' he said in a broken voice. 'Why would I? When it would only hurt her more?'

She doubted that. The Maria Montoya she had met was a woman who loved her son. Iona couldn't imagine Maria wanting to see Zane suffer like this, any more than she did. 'But then how do you know it was rape?'

'Because I saw them together at the house where we lived, on his father's estate, when I was twelve years old.' The bitterness had returned, tenfold. 'When he tried to do it again.'

'Oh, God.' Iona touched shaking fingers to her mouth, so horrified at what both he and his mother had endured she was momentarily speechless. Had he seen his father assaulting his mother? It was too hideous to even contemplate. 'Zane.' She stroked his arm, trying to offer what little comfort she could. 'I'm so sorry.'

'It's okay—I said he tried. He didn't get away with it a second time. I saw him pawing her through the cottage window.' He shrugged. 'I thought they were kissing. I'd never seen my mother kiss a man before that.' His eyes met hers, the pain in them so naked, she felt her heart tearing in her chest. 'But as I watched through the window, I saw she wasn't kissing him back, she was struggling. I wanted to help her, to stop him, but I couldn't move.'

'Zane, you were probably in shock—it's not surprising.' He sounded so guilty, so disgusted with himself.

'Don't you get it? I didn't do anything.'

'Did he hurt her?' she asked, praying that he hadn't.

'No. She slapped him really hard. And he howled something about what was she getting so pissy about, she'd enjoyed it before. And then I heard her say "I didn't enjoy it, you raped me—and you know it. Don't ever come near me again, or I will kill you." And then he said, "If it was that bad, why did you have the kid?" And then I turned and ran. And I hid.

I heard his car leave a few minutes later and when I finally got up the guts to return, she was there, making lunch. Pretending nothing had happened. But I could see her fingers shaking. I wanted to say something. To apologise. To make it better. But what could I say when I was a part of the man that had done that to her?'

'That's ridiculous, Zane,' she whispered. 'Is that why you won't acknowledge your brother Nate or his son?' she asked, understanding it all now, and her heart aching for Zane and his misguided guilt and stupid gallantry. Had the disgust he felt for his father—and for himself—been the trigger for that too? 'Because you're trying to protect your mother?'

Couldn't he see how foolish that was? And how unnecessary? She refused to believe Maria would have asked that of him. So why did he ask it of himself?

He looked stunned for a second, then his brows slashed down in a furious frown. 'How the hell do you know about Nate and me? You've never even met the guy.'

She didn't flinch at the hoarse accusation.

'Tess called round this afternoon to bring you this.' She pulled the invitation out of her pocket. 'Because she really wants you to go to Brandon's christening.'

She held out the envelope but he only stared at it, until she lowered it again.

'She had Brandon with her and I…' She paused. 'I mistakenly thought he might be yours. So she explained about you and Nate and we had a cup of tea… And a wee chat.'

He cursed under his breath. 'What's a wee chat? Is that Scottish for "I grilled Tess about something that was none of my damn business"?'

The closed fury on his face made it very obvious she'd stepped way over the line. Her throat thickened, the brittle accusation almost as brutal as the dismissal behind it.

If she'd wanted proof that this had never been more than

casual for him, she had it now. Unfortunately, seeing the desolation in his eyes a moment ago had also forced her to acknowledge the truth—their relationship had never been casual for her.

In the last month, she'd come to depend on him and the way he made her feel: cherished and important and desirable, but worse than that Zane had made her feel needed, in those moments when he'd let his guard down.

But now she understood he hadn't needed her at all, not specifically. Everything he'd done for her, even the spectacular sex, had been a symptom of his need to protect her, just as he had needed to protect his mother, and that young girl being brutalised by a drug dealer, and probably every other woman he'd ever encountered.

'No, it's Scottish for Tess and I had a mature conversation about a man who matters to me,' she said, refusing to let him see how much his dismissal had hurt.

'I matter to you? Then maybe you should butt out of this.'

She flinched but refused to let the uncharacteristic show of temper derail her again. This wasn't about her. She could see that now.

Clearly Brandon's birth and his christening had brought Zane's issues with his father bubbling to the surface in the last year—she'd never been the special someone Tess had talked about; she'd simply been a convenient distraction.

But even so, she didn't intend to be a doormat too.

'They love you, Zane,' she continued. 'Not just Tess and Nate and your mother, but her family too. Don't you see how insane it is for you to shut them out, because of some pigheaded idea that you're responsible for your father's crimes?'

She would be leaving as soon as was feasibly possible. And she could never tell Zane that she loved him—because it would only be a burden to them both—but she wanted to at least try and make him see how wrong he was about himself.

* * *

His damn head was exploding. He'd taken her on the sideboard—like a damn animal—without an ounce of restraint. So what if she'd had an orgasm? So what if she'd had twenty? He'd used her in the worst way possible, because his need for her had consumed him. He'd proved that he had the same sick flaw as his father, and she was acting as if it didn't matter.

And now she wanted to talk about Nate and Tess and his mother. Was she nuts? Couldn't she see what he was? What he had always been? Didn't she know he could never be Nate's brother, Brandon's uncle, because he didn't deserve to be? He didn't even deserve to be his mother's son. Any more than he deserved Iona.

She watched him now, those almond eyes wide with conviction. And the realisation that keeping her meant risking doing that to her again—made him want to punch his fist through a wall.

He thrust a hand through his hair, his fingers trembling, and heard the plaintive whine of the dog from outside the door.

He had to get out of here. 'I should take C.D. for her run,' he said, keeping his tone neutral, and plunging his hands into his pockets to stop from hauling Iona close and taking her again.

He didn't even have the right to ask her now if they could make this relationship more, not after what he'd done, the way he'd treated her. He had to find a way to make that up to her. To show her he could control himself. That she could trust him to be careful.

But with his nerves shot and his stomach raw, he couldn't think straight. He needed time to cool down, to figure a way to work this out.

'I won't be long,' he added, making it clear he didn't want company. Not this time.

He saw the shadow of hurt in her eyes, and felt the answering tug in his chest, but thanked God when she nodded. 'Okay.'

He opened the door and the dog bounded in. 'Hey, Cooks,' he said, trying to sound pleased to see the dog as she jumped onto him.

Iona gave the dog's head a rub. C.D. lapped up the attention, as always, but then Iona stepped back, and he saw the single tear slip down her cheek. It pierced his heart as she swiped it away.

'I won't be long,' he said, pretending not to notice her distress. He couldn't deal with this now.

Damn, he might even have gotten her pregnant, he thought, the panic returning. What the hell did he do about that?

She nodded, the wobble in her bottom lip crucifying him. 'All right.'

He placed a gentle kiss on her lips, felt the tiny tremor and hated himself even more.

He'd make it up to her. Tonight. And he'd fix this. Because he had to. Whatever he was, whatever he deserved, he couldn't let her go too.

He returned half an hour later, his suit pants ruined from walking in the surf, but with a course of action figured out that just might work. He'd never had to beg before. But this time, he figured it was the only option.

The house was eerily silent as he followed C.D. into the kitchen. The dog whimpered, as if something was wrong. And then he saw the lasagne dish standing on the sideboard and the note propped against it written in Iona's neat, precise script—and realised what it was.

You're a good man, Zane. Go ask your mum, she'll tell you. And don't forget to take care of yourself and that silly dog.
Iona x

The devastation came first, but the anger soon followed. How could she have left him, without even giving him a chance to make amends?

CHAPTER THIRTEEN

'OPEN THE DAMN door!' Zane rammed his fist against the hardwood door of the pretty little colonial, having already rung the doorbell twice.

Iona had to be here; this was his last hope. He'd driven to Pacific Grove first to check in with Mrs Mendoza and her other neighbours. Then he'd called Nate. Maybe Iona and Tess had only just met, but Tess had always been a meddler, so it was possible she'd offered Iona a place to stay.

But he'd drawn a blank there too. Nate had been adamant. 'There's no one staying with us, I swear. But who is she? Is there a problem, cos you sound kind of weird, man.'

He'd made some dumb excuse and ended the call. There wasn't a problem. Or there wouldn't be as soon as he'd tracked Iona down.

He rang the bell again and the hall light came on.

'Hold your horses.'

The locks clicked and his mother appeared in the doorway. Her usually perfect hair was pinned up in tight curls as she wrapped her robe around her waist. He felt the shimmer of guilt at having got her out of bed.

'Zane, what on earth's the matter? Why are you beating down my door in the middle of the night?'

'It's important.' He strode past her into the house, deciding it was too late for guilt. 'Is Iona here?'

'Iona?' She blinked sleepily following him into the small kitchen that always smelled of fresh herbs and home baking, and switched on the overhead light. 'You mean the pretty Scottish girl you brought to Maricruz's *quinceañera?*'

'Don't act dumb with me.' He shouted at his mother, as all the frustration and panic of the last few hours—while he'd driven around trying to figure out where she might go, and prayed frantically that she hadn't already caught a flight home—made his chest feel tight. 'You know damn well who Iona is.'

The sharp slap cracked out, stunning him into silence and making his left cheek sting like a son-of-a-bitch.

'Don't you dare talk to me like that.' His mother propped her hands on her hips and glared at him. 'You ignore my calls for weeks and now you turn up in the middle of the night and use profanity in my house.'

His temper cooled rapidly as he cradled his cheek—which was on fire.

'That hurt—' He bit off a curse, before he ended up with two sore cheeks.

'That's because it was meant to,' she returned, not looking remotely apologetic. She gave a huge yawn, making the guilt return. 'Now sit down and tell me what's going on and what Iona has to do with it.' She indicated the kitchen table, the moment of temper gone as quickly as it had come.

He hesitated. He didn't want to stay and talk. He had to keep searching. But as the anger and desperation drained away, it was replaced with hurt and confusion. If Iona wasn't here, where was she? Watching his mother placing homemade cookies onto a plate, he suddenly had the overwhelming urge to take the comfort she offered. He slumped into one of the dainty kitchen chairs, absently rubbing his flaming cheek.

His hand dropped to the table, the pain from the slap nothing to the tearing pain in his chest as exhaustion and hopelessness overwhelmed him.

He couldn't keep looking, because there was nowhere else to look.

He waited for his mother to finish the tea-making ritual. Placing the freshly baked chocolate-chip cookies in front of him, she poured some tea into a china teacup and pushed it towards him. 'Now what's all this about?'

Steepling her fingers, she observed him with the firm but compassionate expression he remembered so well from his childhood and something broke open inside him.

He gazed at the cup of tea, the scent of fresh mint making his stomach leap into his throat and then become a huge brick that he couldn't swallow down.

If only she could fix this, as she had when he was little. Back in the days when she'd been able to make nightmares go away. But that had all stopped when he was twelve and he'd first found out the truth about his father.

Her warm hand covered the one he had fisted on the table and she squeezed. 'Talk to me, Zane. Don't shut me out any more.'

He raised his eyes and Iona's note came back to him: *You're a good man, Zane. Go ask your mum, she'll tell you.*

'I did something unforgivable.' The words tumbled out. 'And she left me. And I can't find her.'

His mother nodded. 'Is this Iona we're talking about?'

'Yes,' he said, humiliated when his voice cracked.

'So you've fallen in love with her.'

He stared blankly at her hand where it held his, noticed the solid gold wedding band Terry had put on her finger a decade ago, when Zane had given her away—and the abject panic he might have expected at her suggestion didn't come. Instead it all felt a little unreal. 'Maybe.' He shrugged. 'I don't know.'

'What did you do to her that was so unforgivable?'

He shook his head, tried to swallow past the brick in his throat. He couldn't tell her that, because then she'd know that despite all her efforts he was no better than the man who had sired him.

But then she cupped his chin in cool fingers and raised his face.

'Does this have something to do with your father?'

He jerked his head out of her grasp, so stunned he forgot to mask the emotion. She'd always been intuitive—but now was she a damn mind-reader?

'I don't want to talk about him.'

'I know you don't.' She sighed. 'But don't you think it's past time we did?'

'No. I can't.'

'Why can't you?'

He dragged his hands out from under hers, and blurted out the truth. 'Because damn it, I know he raped you. And I can't stand it. To know he hurt you. And that I'm the result.'

'What…?' Her face went white, with shock or pain, or quite possibly both. 'How do you know that?'

'I saw the two of you together when I was a kid. When he came to the cottage that time. I saw him try to hurt you again. And I heard everything he said.'

'Oh, Zane.' She took his hands in both of hers, clutched them hard. 'I had no idea you were there—if I had I would have explained it to you. Why didn't you tell me?'

'I couldn't. I couldn't tell you.' He pulled his hands away, all the anger and bitterness and self-loathing he'd kept hidden for so long threatening to choke him. Until finally he had to ask the question that had been lurking inside him for so long. 'How can you not hate me?'

'Stop that.' She stood up, and pulled him into her arms. The magnolia scent enveloped him as she held his head to her breast, ran her fingers through his hair. 'Now you listen to me.'

His whole body shook, but the quiver of emotion calmed as her sure steady voice drifted through him.

'Yes, he raped me, but it wasn't as black and white as you probably think. I was young and foolish and he was handsome and sophisticated and married and I had a crush on him. I knew he liked me and I flirted with him, encouraged him. It was only when he came to my room that I panicked. I asked him to stop and he wouldn't.'

She drew back, cupped his cheeks in gentle hands. 'I'm not saying what happened was my fault, because it wasn't. He was a ruthless, selfish and ultimately cruel man who took advantage of my naivety. But even though I hated him at the time, and for years afterward, I managed to find forgiveness for him. And do you know why?'

Zane shook his head, not sure he could bear to hear it.

'Because out of that horror, out of that cruelty and self-ishness, I got you.'

He covered her hands with his, drew them away from his face. 'You don't have to say that. I'm not a kid any more. And I know having me ruined your life.'

'Zane!' Her gaze became shadowed with hurt, and it cut into his heart. 'Don't say that. Don't ever say that. You didn't ruin my life.' She placed her hands on his shoulders. 'You are and will always be the best part of my life.' Her voice strengthened. 'I thought that after twenty-four excruciating hours of labour. I thought it when you were eight and broke a tooth in a fist fight that cost me three hundred dollars to fix.' She gave him a little shake as if trying to force the words into him. 'I thought it when you insisted on losing your virginity to that dreadful girl Mary-Lou who thought it was funny to call you a "wetback."'

'You *knew* about that?' he croaked as mortification engulfed him.

She waved her hand dismissively. 'And I even thought it when you beat up Nate, for no other reason than he wanted to be your brother.' A lone tear trickled down her cheek, and he ducked his head, humbled as all the shame and anger that he had held inside for so long was beaten into submission by his mother's love.

'Why on earth would I stop thinking it now?' she whispered. 'When you've become this big, strong, beautiful man who always tries so hard to do the right thing—even when he doesn't know how?'

She cradled his cheek. 'You may have come from a horrific act. But you're not responsible for it. Any more than I was. And just because he fathered you, it doesn't mean you're like him, any more than Nate is like him. Or Brandon. Think about it, Zane. Because if you're tainted by his blood then so are they and any child you might have. Surely you can see how foolish that is?'

He let out a heavy sigh.

Iona was right. He should have talked about this with his mother a long time ago. It would have saved them both so much heartache.

'That's some speech,' he said, at last.

'If I had known that you knew what you did, I would have given it to you twenty years ago,' she said, giving his cheek a gentle pat and returning to her seat.

He smiled weakly. 'I should have told you.'

'Yes, you should have, but you're a man, so it's not all that surprising you didn't.' She laughed, but then her gaze sharpened. 'Now, tell me all about Iona.'

His smile faltered.

'I knew there was something going on there,' his mother added. 'You seemed taken with her.'

He shrugged, more than a little uncomfortable talking about exactly how taken he had become with Iona. 'There's not a lot to tell.' Or not a whole lot he could tell his mother. 'We've been dating for a while. She's been living at my place this past week...'

What did he say? That he'd fallen in love with her? How

was he supposed to know that? He wasn't even sure what the hell it meant?

'And...? What?' his mother prompted.

'And it's been good. Better than good.' That much he knew was true.

He'd never been so desperate to get home every evening, and so torn when he had to leave every morning. And it wasn't just the sex. He missed her bright aimless chatter. Her enthusiasm for home cooking and the little flecks of paint on all her clothing. Her kindness and her compassion and the easy no-nonsense way she handled C.D. The way she blushed like a blueberry whenever he teased her and then the smart, sexy way she teased him right back. He missed every bit of their time together and not just the time they spent in bed. In fact, better than good was probably an understatement.

'But then...' he began. Then he spotted the sparkle of interest in his mother's eyes and stopped again.

Okay, no way was he telling his mother about the kitchen-counter sex, or the fact that he'd failed to wear a condom. One whack across the face was enough for tonight.

'And then she ran out on me.'

'Hmm.' His mother lifted a cookie and bit into it, sending him a considering look. 'And you want her back?'

'Yeah. I do.' That much he was sure of. And after what his mother had told him, he also wanted an explanation as to why she'd run off, because it seemed he might have overreacted about his part in that.

His mother slung the cookie down. 'Then what are you doing sitting around my kitchen eating cookies?' She got up and hauled him out of his chair.

'Hey!'

'Zane, you've never spoken about any woman like this before. You need to go find that girl.'

'I know that,' he said, feeling exasperated himself when

she shoved him down the hallway. 'But I don't have a clue where she is.'

His mother cocked an eyebrow as she swung the door open. 'Then go get a clue,' she said as he stepped out into the night. 'You're a detective, remember.'

CHAPTER FOURTEEN

IONA RINSED OUT the last of her underwear in the motel's tiny washbasin and began hanging them on the rail.

The dull pain at the memory of Zane's face as he'd left to take C.D. for a walk had her leaning heavily on the sink. She bit into her lip to stop the stupid flood of tears returning.

She'd cried far too much in the last week. And all it did was give her a headache. She needed to get over this now. It had been a fling, pure and simple. A fling that she'd taken a mite too seriously.

And if she had woken up an hour ago and stupidly remembered it was Brandon's christening today and spent the morning moping about hoping that Zane had gone to it, that only proved how delusional she'd become.

The knock at the door had her dumping the last of the wet underwear in the sink. Please don't let that be the piggy-eyed guy on Reception, who kept 'checking up' on how she was doing.

She gasped as she checked the peephole—her knees going to jelly—and opened the door on autopilot.

'Zane, what are you doing here?'

Am I hallucinating?

'What am *I* doing here?' he said. 'Shouldn't that be, what the heck are *you* doing here? Do you have any idea how many favours I had to beg, steal and borrow from my buddies on the force to find you?'

He strode into the room as her hand went slack on the door. Okay, she definitely wasn't hallucinating. The guy in the debonair linen suit making the small grotty room look smaller and grottier was certainly Zane; she'd recognise that devastating face and that lean, muscular build a hundred years from now.

He swung round, his brows drawing down. 'Most of which were borderline illegal.' He checked the time again. 'Do you have something fancy to wear?'

She stared dully at the knickers and camisole she had on to survive the heat—because the air conditioner hadn't worked since day one. 'Why do I need something fancy?'

'For Brandon's christening.' He checked the time again. 'It starts in an hour. So you better get moving.'

She shook her head, worried she might be hallucinating again, but determined not to start bawling. 'I can't go.'

Zane looked disconcerted, but then warm strong fingers wrapped around her forearm. 'No way are you skipping out on this. I spoke to Nate last night, after I finally found out you were here. And somehow got roped into being Bran's godfather.' The puzzled frown deepened.

'That's wonderful, Zane.' Her heart lifted at the news. 'I'm so happy, for you and your family.' But as pleased as she was for him, she couldn't get drawn in too deep again. Or she'd never survive.

'Yeah, it is kind of cool,' he said. 'And you're coming with me.'

'I can't come with you.'

'Why the hell not?' There was that edge again, so unlike the charming, charismatic man who had first seduced her, but so like the guarded, vulnerable man she had come to know and love. She sighed, the tears threatening again. And who didn't love her.

'Because I have no place there.'

She tugged her arm out of his grasp. It wasn't fair that he should come back and make her feel this way again. She'd been stupid and naive and had fallen for a man who wasn't interested, but he hadn't done a whole lot to stop her making that mistake.

He'd pursued her, right from the start. He'd made her feel special and important and safe, given her mind-blowing sex, and some tantalising glimpses of the man behind the facade. And given how well he knew women, he must have known how irresistible that would be, especially to her, a woman who had a few self-esteem issues of her own.

She'd never even got The Speech. Not properly. He could at least have given her that much, so she could have had some chance of protecting her heart.

After all the tears in the last week, the rare spark of temper felt good.

'Tess invited you, didn't she?' he said.

'That's beside the point. Don't be ridiculous.'

'I'm ridiculous!' he shouted. 'You run out on me without a damn explanation and hole up here for nearly a week without a word and I'm the one being ridiculous. When were you planning to tell me where you were?'

'I wasn't,' she declared.

'Why not?' he said, grasping both her arms this time and dragging her to him. 'What did I do that was so unforgivable?'

'Nothing, I just…' She braced her palms against his chest, not wanting to be this close, her limbs shaking and the inevitable heat building. She couldn't tell him, and have her last scrap of pride torn away.

'You could be pregnant and you didn't even give me a forwarding address.'

Pain and disappointment made her throat hurt. So that was the real reason he was here, the invitation to Brandon's christening nothing more than a ruse to finesse the truth out of her. Because Zane always had to finesse women, charm them. He could never ask anything directly, because that would give them the power, she thought, forcing her temper back to the fore to work through the hurt.

'I'm not pregnant. I had my period.'

'You're not pregnant? For sure?' She'd expected him to look relieved, but strangely he didn't, he almost looked disappointed.

'No, I'm definitely not pregnant.'

'Okay, then I want a damn good reason why you can't come home.'

'Home?' she said, the anger faltering.

'Yeah, home. I want you to come back to Seventeen Mile Drive. I want you to give me another chance.'

'I canny do that...' She shook her head, trying to pull away from him now. The tears welling in her eyes, closing her throat. 'Don't ask that of me—it isn't fair.'

'Why not?' he asked, his voice thick too. 'If this has to do with your father, we can go visit him...'

'That's not it. It's because I've fallen in love with you,' she whispered, her throat raw. She hadn't wanted to tell him this, and now he'd forced it out of her.

To her astonishment, he laughed. 'Is that all?'

She struggled out of his arms, the tears falling now. 'Don't you dare laugh at me. My feelings are important.' She rapped her fist on her chest, believing it completely for the first time in her life. 'My feelings matter.' The sob burst out without warning. 'I'm not going to prolong our fling just so I can feel even worse when I have to leave.'

'Hey, hey, hey.' He folded her into his embrace, smothering her struggles. 'Iona, don't cry. I know your feelings matter.' He stroked a hand down her hair, cradled her cheeks, the sapphire-blue of his irises warm and unguarded. 'Because there's nothing more important to me.'

'That's not true,' she replied, shaking now. 'You told me I

had no business talking to Tess. No business knowing about you and Nate. You never let me in, not really.'

'Because I was a jerk. And terrified of you finding out something I'd believed about myself for years and wasn't even true.'

'Your father?' she murmured.

'Yeah, my father.' He walked to the bed, sat down on it, the creak of the springs audible. 'You know what's ironic, when I was a little kid, I had this dumb idea he was a great guy. Back then, it was my mother who didn't want to talk about him. But I knew who he was. Because I'd seen the photos at San Revelle and it didn't take much to make the connection. Why my mom had gotten the job. Why the old guy who owned the place came by to ask how I was getting along from time to time.'

'You mean your grandfather?'

He nodded stiffly. 'But that day, before...' He swallowed. 'Before I saw him with her. I met him. It was hot and my mom had told me to stay away from the big house, because they had guests coming in a couple of hours for a weekend party and I shouldn't get in the way. But he arrived early and parked right next to where I was playing on my skateboard.' He shrugged, the movement defensive. 'He looked me over and grinned, and said, "You're Maria's kid, right?" I nodded and everything inside me stopped. I figured this was the moment I'd been waiting for. That he'd tell me he was my father and maybe he'd take me for a ride in his car.' He gave a sad smile. 'He had a really hot cherry-red Ferrari with white wall tyres.'

She sat next to him on the bed, and placed a hand on his thigh, her heart aching for that little boy. 'You had a passion for cars even then?'

He put his hand over hers, and nodded. 'You want to know the only other words my father said to me?'

She wasn't sure she did, but whispered, 'Yes.'

He gave a brittle laugh. 'He threw me the keys to his car and said, "Tell Mano to get this cleaned before I leave tomorrow."'

'Zane...' She placed her hand on his jaw and kissed his cheek, trying to transmit all the love she had. Not just for the man, but for the boy. 'He was a hideous human being, but that doesn't mean you're...'

He turned and touched his finger to her lips. 'I know. I took your advice and finally spoke to my mother about him.' He threaded his fingers through hers, and held on. 'I told her what I'd seen and...' He paused to stare at the ceiling. 'And you were right—it didn't matter.'

'But, Zane, I don't understand—how could you have ever believed it did?'

'I was angry and hurt and scared, I guess. And when I began to have sex myself, I had this burning hunger.' He dropped his head back, let out a rueful sigh. 'Which I told myself I had to control or else I'd be no better than him.' His firm lips tilted into a sexy smile. 'Then you came along and changed everything, because I couldn't control it any more.'

She wanted to believe him, to bask in the approval she saw in his eyes. But she knew the truth. 'I didn't change anything. I'm just another of your damsels in distress.'

'You're... What?' He chuckled, looking bemused. 'Iona, what the hell is that supposed to mean?'

She pulled away from him, annoyed by the easy smile that sent the dimple into his cheek. And made him look even more adorable and even further out of her reach. 'Isn't it obvious, Zane? Why you were attracted to me? Why you seduced me? Why you were so determined to keep me safe? Why you asked me to move in with you?'

'No, it isn't, not to me.'

She wrapped her arms round her waist, feeling naked under that steady gaze. 'You rescue women, Zane. It's what you do. Ever since that day you couldn't rescue your mother.' She tightened her arms, the blank look on his face making her stomach hurt. 'I was just another one of your rescue projects. That's all.'

He shook his head, the puzzled frown becoming more pronounced, and it was like losing him all over again. Then he said, 'That has got to be the dumbest thing I've ever heard.'

'It is not!' she said. 'It makes complete sense if you look at the facts.'

'The hell it does.' Grabbing her wrist, he hauled her towards him, then tumbled her onto the bed.

'Get off me,' she cried, trying to buck him off. But he simply straddled her hips, and held her captive with her hands above her head.

'Calm down,' he said firmly, ignoring her struggles. 'Because now it's my turn to talk and your turn to listen.' The sharp edge of frustration shocked her into stillness. 'You're right about one thing. I respect women, I want to protect them, and yeah, maybe because of what happened to my mother, I get so mad when I see a woman hurt—whether she's some sweet old lady who's been mugged by a gang member or a teenage hooker who's been beaten up by her pimp—that I have a hard time controlling it. But that doesn't have a damn thing to do with us.'

Bracketing her wrists, he pressed them into the mattress, the cold steel in his voice flatly contradicted by the warmth in his eyes as his gaze roamed over her face. 'Because that's not a tenth of what I feel for you.' The steel softened and her heart throbbed into her throat. He leaned close, the tender touch of his lips on hers bringing tears to her eyes. 'Now tell me you believe me.'

She nodded, her throat too tight with emotion to form words.

Letting go of her hands, he framed her face in rough palms. 'Now kiss me again, *querida*—and show me you mean it.'

His tongue tangled with hers and she strained upwards,

flinging her arms around his neck to give him the proof he needed—the leap of joy in her heart as intoxicating as the hunger coiling low in her belly.

When he raised his head, she could feel the satisfying weight of his erection against the bare skin of her thigh, hear the ragged sound of her own breathing and see so much more than hunger in his eyes.

'So are you gonna stop messing around now and come home to me and C.D.?' he asked.

'I suppose so.' She grinned, the smile suffusing her whole face. 'If you insist.'

The quick grin sent a dimple into that chiselled cheek and took her breath away again. 'Damn straight I do.'

* * * * *

LET'S TALK

Romance

For exclusive extracts, competitions
and special offers, find us online:

- f facebook.com/millsandboon
- 📷 @millsandboonuk
- 🐦 @millsandboon

Or get in touch on 0844 844 1351*

For all the latest titles coming soon, visit
millsandboon.co.uk/nextmonth